# KEEPERS OF THE ROCK

## THE DEBILIS RISING

### BOOK 1

# KEEPERS OF THE ROCK

## THE DEBILIS RISING

### BOOK 1

# E. K. WISE

GoldOwl LLC
Agoura Hills, CA

Publisher's note: This is a work of fiction. Names, characters, places, and incidents either are the product of the author's imagination or are used fictitiously. Any resemblance to actual events, locales, or persons, living or dead, is entirely coincidental.

Published by

GoldOwl LLC
Agoura Hills, CA
http://www.EKWise.com

Edited by Kristen Corrects, Inc.
Cover art design by Damonza Studio
Typesetting by Journey Bound Publishing

ISBN (Paperback): 979-8-9917633-0-1
ISBN (Ebook): 979-8-9917633-1-8
LCCN: 2024921674

For my husband, Dan, for his unfailing
support throughout the development and
writing of *Keepers of the Rock;* you have been
my staunchest advocate and toughest critic.
Your constant faith in me is so appreciated.
I love you so much.

And to my dad. Thank you for your worldly
setting suggestions and for believing in me.
I miss you so very much.

To my four kiddos, thank you for your
unconditional love and support and help
with dinner preparation. I will eat whatever
you cook, with endless gratitude!

***To those who are coping with a learning
difference or love someone who is, never
give up and get evaluated! It is vital for
the nourishment of your soul.***

***Augie***

## Advancement of Unbiased Global Intellectual Exploration

See the adorable owl above? He's your little knowledge guide, Augie. If you read an interesting scientific or historic fact, the Augie at the page bottom will lead you to the footnote(s), guiding you to further information. We at the College of GeoEvolution challenge you to be curious and expand your awareness of the glorious world around you! Keeper Reese believes Augie's acronym is a bit pretentious, but I think it's clever and has a poetic ring to it. He won't admit it, but I know he wishes he thought of it himself! Anyway, go on—we dare you! There's always room to learn more.

*— Keeper Alegria*

***Keepers of the Rock*** **was written to be a four-dimensional experience for those who want to immerse themselves into the story.**

- Read the novel in a setting where you can relax and focus.

- Listen to the songs when they are mentioned. It will help you actively engage with the characters and atmosphere.

- Use Augie and learn more about what sparks your interest.

- Get cooking! Head to an ethnic grocery store and try something new. Appreciate the aromas and tastes of the delicious cuisines mentioned in the novel from around the world. Make a meal with friends!

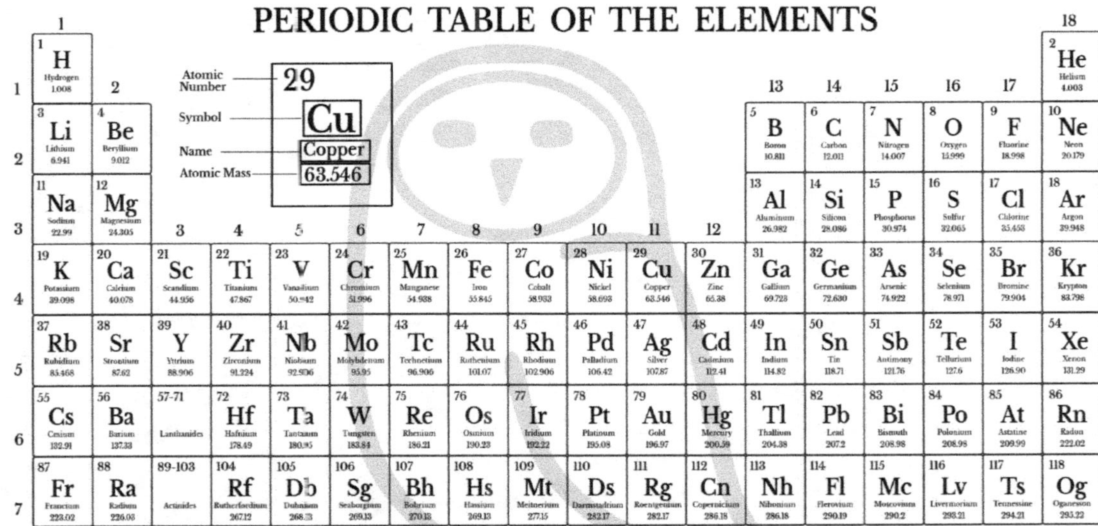

PERIODIC TABLE OF THE ELEMENTS

Atomic Number — 29
Symbol — Cu
Name — Copper
Atomic Mass — 63.546

1 H Hydrogen 1.008
2 He Helium 4.003
3 Li Lithium 6.941
4 Be Beryllium 9.012
5 B Boron 10.811
6 C Carbon 12.011
7 N Nitrogen 14.007
8 O Oxygen 15.999
9 F Fluorine 18.998
10 Ne Neon 20.179
11 Na Sodium 22.99
12 Mg Magnesium 24.305
13 Al Aluminum 26.982
14 Si Silicon 28.086
15 P Phosphorus 30.974
16 S Sulfur 32.065
17 Cl Chlorine 35.453
18 Ar Argon 39.948
19 K Potassium 39.098
20 Ca Calcium 40.078
21 Sc Scandium 44.956
22 Ti Titanium 47.867
23 V Vanadium 50.942
24 Cr Chromium 51.996
25 Mn Manganese 54.938
26 Fe Iron 55.845
27 Co Cobalt 58.933
28 Ni Nickel 58.693
29 Cu Copper 63.546
30 Zn Zinc 65.38
31 Ga Gallium 69.723
32 Ge Germanium 72.630
33 As Arsenic 74.922
34 Se Selenium 78.971
35 Br Bromine 79.904
36 Kr Krypton 83.798
37 Rb Rubidium 85.468
38 Sr Strontium 87.62
39 Y Yttrium 88.906
40 Zr Zirconium 91.224
41 Nb Niobium 92.906
42 Mo Molybdenum 95.95
43 Tc Technetium 96.906
44 Ru Ruthenium 101.07
45 Rh Rhodium 102.906
46 Pd Palladium 106.42
47 Ag Silver 107.87
48 Cd Cadmium 112.41
49 In Indium 114.82
50 Sn Tin 118.71
51 Sb Antimony 121.76
52 Te Tellurium 127.6
53 I Iodine 126.90
54 Xe Xenon 131.29
55 Cs Cesium 132.91
56 Ba Barium 137.33
57-71 Lanthanides
72 Hf Hafnium 178.49
73 Ta Tantalum 180.95
74 W Tungsten 183.84
75 Re Rhenium 186.21
76 Os Osmium 190.23
77 Ir Iridium 192.22
78 Pt Platinum 195.08
79 Au Gold 196.97
80 Hg Mercury 200.59
81 Tl Thallium 204.38
82 Pb Lead 207.2
83 Bi Bismuth 208.98
84 Po Polonium 208.98
85 At Astatine 209.99
86 Rn Radon 222.02
87 Fr Francium 223.02
88 Ra Radium 226.03
89-103 Actinides
104 Rf Rutherfordium 267.12
105 Db Dubnium 268.13
106 Sg Seaborgium 269.13
107 Bh Bohrium 270.13
108 Hs Hassium 269.13
109 Mt Meitnerium 277.15
110 Ds Darmstadtium 282.17
111 Rg Roentgenium 282.17
112 Cn Copernicium 286.18
113 Nh Nihonium 286.18
114 Fl Flerovium 290.19
115 Mc Moscovium 290.2
116 Lv Livermorium 293.21
117 Ts Tennessine 294.21
118 Og Oganesson 295.22

Lanthanides
57 La Lanthanum 138.91
58 Ce Cerium 140.12
59 Pr Praseodymium 140.91
60 Nd Neodymium 144.24
61 Pm Promethium 144.91
62 Sm Samarium 150.36
63 Eu Europium 151.96
64 Gd Gadolinium 157.25
65 Tb Terbium 158.93
66 Dy Dysprosium 162.50
67 Ho Holmium 164.93
68 Er Erbium 167.26
69 Tm Thulium 168.93
70 Yb Ytterbium 173.05
71 Lu Lutetium 174.97

Actinides
89 Ac Actinium 227.03
90 Th Thorium 232.04
91 Pa Protactinium 231.04
92 U Uranium 238.03
93 Np Neptunium 237.05
94 Pu Plutonium 244.06
95 Am Americium 243.06
96 Cm Curium 247.07
97 Bk Berkelium 247.07
98 Cf Californium 251.08
99 Es Einsteinium 252.08
100 Fm Fermium 257.1
101 Md Mendelevium 258.1
102 No Nobelium 259.10
103 Lr Lawrencium 262.12

## CHAPTER 1 – H

SUKHUMVIT, BANGKOK, THAILAND

# EARLY SPRING

Over the years, Rua-Jian Chu[1] had learned that waking up slowly and taking in one's surroundings before acting was best. Who could argue with this habit? He was still alive, after all. He gave his brethren this advice on multiple occasions, if he could call his associates that.

When he opened his eyes this morning, he noticed the plodding movement of the fan above him. The blades were caked with grime and dust, either from neglect or purposeful indifference. A sly smile crept across his face. He could clearly see the fan blades *and* the grime and dust...what a pleasant benefit.

He glanced at the nightstand and eyed the round framed glasses resting on top. He was exceedingly pleased to dispense with that personal flaw. The rest would reveal itself in due time.

Pulling his arms out from under the covers, Rua-Jian frowned as he glanced at his hands. They were a plebeian mess. The broken fingernails were of different lengths; each nail had layers of undetermined filth underneath. A shudder

---

[1]  Pronounced *roo-uh jee-ahn*

swept down his spine and he dared not look at his toenails. While wriggling under the sheets, he felt their threadbare quality—certainly not cotton and probably many years old. He threw them back with purpose, sat up, and looked at the floor. Thankfully, the cheap but new flip-flops he had purchased lay on the sordid carpet, perfectly perpendicular to the bed. Who the hell knew what creatures crawled around this seedy hotel, or if it was ever cleaned.

Dressing quickly in his brown pants and black shirt, Rua-Jian slipped on the temporary shoes and pocketed his few possessions and money. The clothing was not a perfect fit, but that was easily remedied. The itch to get out of this tired hotel in Soi Cowboy, the raunchy area of Sukhumvit,[2] was palpable. He intended to give himself a few days to acclimate at the Sheraton Grande Sukhumvit or the Park Plaza, where he could gather his energy and best prepare in a far more accommodating setting. The promise he made to himself long ago to always live well above his impoverished upbringing remained ever-present in his mind. He pocketed the lightweight glasses and walked to the door.

Regardless of the poor state of his hands, he dared not touch the disgusting doorknob. The greasy layers that accumulated there over time stirred his imagination, but didn't slow his progress. As vile as the hotel room was, the owners committed no crime other than giving the guests exactly what they paid for: paltry conditions at a trivial price.

After a quick, discerning examination, he determined that the knob was composed of a nickel[3] alloy and therefore easily malleable. The process might take longer than normal

---

2   Sukhumvit, a part of Bangkok, Thailand

3   "Nickel." *Wikipedia,* Wikimedia Foundation, en.wikipedia.org/wiki/Nickel.

due to his present condition, but that was to be expected. Rua-Jian's hand hovered inches away from the knob.

Although he wasn't touching the filthy thing, he was close enough to ferret out its flaws and almost invisible fractures; his fingers sensed its smooth and hollow consistency. Energy waves pulsed from his fingertips and he began heating the nickel alloy and manipulating the compounds within. The only resulting sound was a muffled crunch and the clatter of loose pieces as both knobs and latch mechanism compressed and fell to the floor. Placing two fingers in the circular door hole, he exited the room.

When he approached the lobby, he observed the simple dingy room—a small, dark respite from the noises outside. A young man stood behind the lobby counter. Although Rua-Jian was fairly quiet, he hadn't purposefully been so. He expected the young man to notice his movements. The clerk seemed in a daze, however. Upon closer examination, his eyes were red-rimmed and glassy. Probably in some drug-induced haze, knowing this neighborhood. *What a terrible shame and waste.*

Resting on the old Formica desktop were a small cardboard box and a plastic placard, broken at one corner. The placard read, *For complaints, call:* in the native Thai language, Siamese. No phone number was listed. No doubt, he thought, the clerk couldn't handle anything more than the simple exchange of money and room cards. Written on the box in thick black marker were the words *For Lost and Found.*

He reached the counter and finally had the attention of the young clerk who merely stared at him, waiting for him to begin the exchange.

"I am checking out now," Rua-Jian said in Siamese.

The young clerk shrugged. "You paid last night, so you can go."

"I am afraid there was an incident with my doorknob. I'll leave some money for a replacement." He placed his hand in his pocket to remove some cash.

The clerk simply motioned with his hand to the complaint placard on the counter.

Rua-Jian smiled wryly. "Really? I can't leave the manager extra cash?"

"It's not my business," the young man said wearily, as if these types of damages were common.

"I see," he replied. "Regardless, I…" Midsentence, he noticed the clerk lift his head and look off to the side, his gaze focused on something in his periphery. The clerk wrinkled his nose and sneezed violently. A sulfuric odor followed by a trail of pungent yellow gas wafted through the room, followed by an even fainter scent of gingerbread. The clerk looked at him in confusion and sneezed again. Rua-Jian smiled warmly and turned to address the vaporous cloud.

"My friend, we rarely get to arrange a meeting as perfect as this! Your timing is impeccable; I believe it's a sign we will finally succeed."

While speaking, Rua-Jian ignored the clerk's reaction to the disturbance. Instead, he walked to the hotel entrance, locked the door, and flipped the plastic window sign to display NO VACANCY. That accomplished, he went back to the desk and stared into the clerk's face. The young clerk was having difficulty breathing as the toxic odor and smoke swirled around him.

Rua-Jian knew the sulfur[4] and fluoride gas would cause great irritation to the clerk. The clerk's eyes were red and

---

4    "Sulfur," https://www.mindat.org/gm/3826

likely stinging, his nose was running and his throat probably felt raw. Although potential hospitalization was likely, death was not. Rua-Jian didn't yet possess sufficient strength to easily complete the task at hand, but he would manage. He looked at his own hands and examined his filthy nails. *They're not really my hands, not in this poor state,* he considered. *My normal tools are not fully available.*

The clerk continued to struggle for a clean breath. Despite moving around to the back area of the room in pursuit of fresher air, the noxious cloud seemed to follow his every movement. Rua-Jian wandered behind the front desk and nabbed a forgotten hand towel. *At least it's not dusty or covered in snot,* he sneered.

"Such a shame, really," he mused, "to see a young, relatively healthy person destroyed by drug use. I don't think the fates ever planned to be kind to you, poor boy. Living in this area, you hardly had a chance." He went up to the young clerk and placed his hands upon his shoulders. "Let me help end your pain, shall I?"

The clerk nodded vigorously, eager for relief.

"I understand, I really do. It will be over soon." He gently lay the towel around the clerk's windpipe, wrapped his hands around his neck, and squeezed. Despite the clerk's struggles, his strength was minimal, and the commotion soon stopped.

Rua-Jian stood, removed the eyeglasses from his pocket, and placed them into the box provided to be found and repurposed by some future guest. Upon looking inside, he found a pair of large black gloves. "Why, thank you, I believe these will come in handy." He gently placed some baht, the local currency, on the desk.

"To pay for the knob, you know," he said to the circling gas or to no one in particular. "The room is really unusable without it."

He glanced at the gloves now on his hands. They were not a perfect fit, but needs must.

"Can't show these hands at a five-star hotel... Let's get to work now, shall we?"

He looked at the swirling gas as he walked out, his focus now on getting a cab and heading to the wealthiest part of Sukhumvit. Afterward, he needed to see a shopkeeper about a stiletto.

## CHAPTER 2 – He

### CARLSBAD CAVERNS, CARLSBAD, NEW MEXICO, UNITED STATES

# EARLY SPRING

Donald Smithson glanced at his watch again and verified the time. It was precisely five p.m. and all was in place. The seven metal folding chairs were stacked neatly against the sign displayed behind him. The remaining two articles, a box and a folding table, lay adjacent to the chairs. Presently, he waited. The Keepers arrived at their own pace, anytime between now and five fifteen.

He straightened his posture and looked down to examine his United States Park Service uniform. The khaki shirt and forest green pants were clean and freshly pressed, befitting the occasion. Don heaved a sigh when he noticed an offensive splotch. He glanced at the stalactites above, as if they could provide a solution. On his shirt, at the beginning of a protruding stomach, was a quarter-sized green stain—his wife's green tomatillo sauce from the lunchtime enchiladas he'd brought from home. He groaned in embarrassment. How, of all days, did he let this happen? There was no time to change his shirt or try to wash the stain away. And he couldn't abandon his post during a meeting of the Keepers, ever. All there was left to do was stand tall and hope they didn't notice.

Alegria Hinine was the first Keeper to greet Donald and she smiled warmly as she reached his post. He bowed slightly and said, "Keeper Alegria, it's good to have you back."

"Guardian Donald, it is always a great pleasure." She leaned forward and kissed both cheeks, hands on either side of his face; her voluminous curly brown hair tickled his neck. She spoke rapidly in a deep and scratchy voice, the speed of her speech characteristic of her Chilean culture. She stepped back and grabbed both of his lower arms, examining him. "You look well and nourished, Guardian Donald. This is always good to see." Her words were spoken in a complex Spanish accent, with a strong emphasis on the consonants. "What is this?"

To Donald's horror, Alegria looked at the stain on his shirt, took a deep swipe with a bejeweled finger, and placed the finger into her mouth. She closed her eyes and tasted the nuanced flavors of the sample.

"Mmm, yes! This is your wife's green tomatillo sauce, just as I suspected! Thank you for the recipe, again. I tried it, you know, but it did not taste as delicious as this. I think it was missing some of the passion!" She eyed him mischievously with green eyes.

"Thank you, Keeper Alegria," Donald wheezed, clearly mortified. "I'll be sure to tell my wife that my colleague at the caverns enjoyed it."

"I see I have embarrassed you, Guardian Donald. This was not my intention." She spoke fervently with hands clasped to her chest. "You must wear that sauce on your shirt proudly! It is a sign of your wife's deep love for you. To cook so passionately for the man she loves, to keep him satisfied!

You ate it quickly and with relish, which demonstrates your avid appreciation!"

Alegria kissed both his cheeks again and placed her hands over her heart, her eyes reflecting warmth. Finished with her elaborate greeting, she let Donald know she was ready.

"Okay, Guardian Donald. Now we get down to business."

Alegria reached into her pocket and handed him two items. One was a carving of a small animal made from turquoise[5]; it was a moose with shiny obsidian[6] eyes. The other object was a piece of clear quartz[7], shaped into a distinct triangle. Both could easily fit into the palm of his hand. Donald took each item gingerly and turned to the table behind him. He lifted the lid of the ornately carved box and placed each inside, separated by a compartment. The triangle quartz fit into a felt impression inside the box made for the stone. There were six more exact impressions in the felt and together they formed a circle. At the point of each felt indentation was an elaborate gilded initial. Alegria's quartz lay snug behind the A.

When this ritual was complete, Alegria smiled at Donald and caressed his shoulder as she went past. She stopped behind him to grab one of the metal folding chairs and took it with her, heading toward the center of the Big Room.

Donald was a fifty-seven-year-old Caucasian man from New Mexico with a sterling record as a federal Park Service employee and unremarkable in appearance. To all who knew him, he was a kind, responsible, and effective employee. Unbeknownst to almost all, including his wife, children, and the Park Service, he was also a Guardian. Should the occasion

---

5    "Turquoise," http://mindat.org/gm/4060

6    "Obsidian," http://mindat.org/gm/8519

7    "Quartz," http://mindat.org/gm/3337

arise, this kind, responsible man would fight tooth and nail and even die in defense of those he presently guarded. It was his sworn oath and most sacred responsibility, above all others. One day, when he died, the Keepers would mourn him, but no uninitiated person would ever know of Donald's constant, silent vigils.

Donald took a deep breath and cleared his throat, recovering from the whirlwind that was the charming Keeper Alegria. Whenever he saw her, she was in an ebullient mood, as if she were the cruise director for the other Keepers. She seemed to improve the mood of everyone with whom she spoke.

No sooner had he completed this thought when he saw a bright white kufi hat, seemingly floating in air. Seconds later, the tall form of Dumisani Vead came into view. His skin was the color of rich earth, with undertones of purple.

Dumisani Vead began his biannual stroll into the caverns amidst children's cries of "Eww. It smells in here! This is gross!" He smiled and never tired of the youthful exclamations. The Keepers preferred the Natural Entrance partially for this very reason. The smell of bat guano is a double assault on the senses; the ammonium oxalate opens the sinuses and makes eyes water. The onslaught instantly clears the mind and reminds each Keeper to focus on the meeting and gather their thoughts. The limestone cavern was a magnificent gift from the natural world but most importantly, it was a secure place to meet.

Before entering the cave entrance, Dumisani surreptitiously glanced into the thick curtain of shrubs surrounding the cave entrance. After verifying no tourists were around, he quietly addressed his small, equally subtle companion, perched on a strategic branch from which to begin her vigil.

"My dear Salima,[8] I need you to remain outside the cave and keep watch. Remember my friend, you must leave the Cave Swallows alone. They are just as entitled to be here as you."

A few minutes earlier, Dumisani had caressed Salima's neck and discretely fed her a morsel of meat to pacify her until his return. His constant companion, Salima, was a female Moroccan peregrine falcon, who weighed less than two pounds. She was instrumental in alerting the Keeper to danger and was quick, smart, and loyal to her master. Despite this, Salima made it clear that her attachment was by choice and not decree. Her breast was soft and white, mottled with black marks that upon closer inspection revealed a subtle blue hue. She symbolized the marvel of natural perfection: a strong, vibrant, and proud bird, encased in a compact and lightweight body.

Dumisani held out two hands as he approached Guardian Donald.

"Guardian Donald, it is with great pleasure that I lay my eyes upon you this day. I trust you and your wife are in good health and that those you love are in good care?"

He took Donald's hands in his as he spoke. His voice resonated a deep bass and the pronunciation of each letter was emphasized and distinct; he gave slow reverence to each vowel and consonant. His accent, to Donald's ear, seemed otherworldly. He knew Keeper Dumisani hailed from Morocco in Africa, but Donald had never traveled so far away himself.

"Yes, Keeper Dumisani, I thank you for thinking of me—of us," he stammered. "It's good to see you as well. All is prepared as expected. Tourists are cleared from the Natural Entrance and the Big Room. Visitors remain upstairs, but

---

8    Salima—Arabic name meaning whole or to be safe

will complete their tours shortly. The first Keeper preceded you just a moment ago."

"Thank you, Guardian Donald. We can always count on you, I know. You will notice a distinct change in one of our Keepers, Keeper Sahila. You've seen this from time to time, so do not be alarmed, but verify her identity in the traditional manner. Also, I believe Keeper Reese has brought a token for you and your wife, a thank you of sorts from us."

"Thank you, Keeper Dumisani. There is never a need for reward; it is my pleasure and sworn duty to serve."

"Guardian Donald, we deeply value your loyalty and reward your service; it is our tradition and tenet to acknowledge your dedication." Dumisani bent his head again and drew back. He reached into both pockets and handed over two objects, similar to those of Alegria. His carved turquoise animal was a mountain lion with eyes made of red jasper[9]. The triangular quartz was identical.

Donald turned around and placed both items in their respective places in the box, the quartz fitting snuggly into the D indentation.

When he turned back, Dumisani had vanished and one less chair remained. Donald squinted into the passage leading into the Big Room. How had he not noticed his departure? Dumisani was a tall, imposing figure, yet somehow, he removed himself with nary a sound. He was unwavering in his faith in humanity's innate goodness, despite having seen the worst it can deliver. He was the elder statesman of the Keepers and their leader.

Donald faced front again, prepared for the next Keeper, and he didn't have long to wait. Keeper Reese Rolding came swaggering in next, wearing a weathered blue chambray

---

[9]  "Jasper," http://mindat.org/gm/2082

shirt and wrinkled chino pants. On his feet were hiking boots, both comfortable and serviceable. Upon his head was his ever-present hat, this one of straw, perfect for the New Mexico sun.

"G'day, Guardian Donald! It's good to get out of the blue smoke[10] and great to see an old friend! How's it out here in the seeming never never?[11] Glad I dressed right for the weather." He grasped Donald's hand in a firm handshake. "You and the missus are faring well?"

Donald nodded that they were.

"You're up a gumtree,[12] however, if you don't have extra lunch. I don't fancy Keeper Jürgen is goin' to miss the tucker[13] on your shirt there! No embarrassment necessary, mate. Just fair warnin'."

"Yes, I had my wife pack extra for a co-worker—I came prepared. You're certainly a long way from home. You travel all right?"

"It's always a pleasure to visit the rest of the world," Reese commented while he shuffled his feet in the cave dust, unable to stay still for long. He reached into a shirt pocket first and withdrew his triangular quartz crystal, which he handed to Donald.

"Here's that bit…" He rummaged into his pants pocket for his animal carving. "And here's this one. I'm rather fond of it, actually." He handed Donald his stone carving, an opossum with blue topaz[14] eyes. "Looks a bit like me, huh?"

---

[10]   Blue smoke – Australian slang for the city

[11]   Never never – Australian slang for the Australian Outback or in this case, the desert

[12]   Up a gumtree – Australian slang for in trouble or in a pickle

[13]   Tucker – Australian slang for food

[14]   "Topaz," http://mindat.org/gm/3996

Donald looked perplexed.

"Not really, thank goodness! But he's good company. Now, for the last bit." Reese pulled off his hat, revealing dirty blond hair that flopped over his forehead, and pulled out an object wrapped in a cloth pouch. "I found this out on fossick[15] and thought of you and your wife." He handed Donald the pouch. Inside was a rough-cut sapphire[16] about five carats and a business card. The stone was of stunning quality and looked expensive to Donald's untrained eye.

"Keeper Reese," Donald glanced at him, incredulous, "I can't possibly accept this!"

"Guardian Donald, I can assure you that it's well deserved and belongs with no one else." Reese's crooked smile crinkled his vivid blue eyes. "Investing and saving are important. We don't offer you a substantial salary with this duty and only a small retirement when you're done. You guess correctly that it's worth a fair bob,[17] so put it in a safe after you've insured it. If you're hankering to make some jewelry for the missus, there's the name of a good jeweler whom I trust near you. He'll treat you fair. Should you ever need cash, the same man can take care of that for you too. The stone's not been stolen, I can assure you, so no one's looking for it. Think of it as added retirement security for you and the family."

---

[15] On fossick – Australian slang for searching or mining for gems, gold, etc.

[16] "Sapphire," http://mindat.org/gm/3529

[17] Fair bob – Australian slang for a significant amount of money

Reese reached out and shook Donald's free hand. "Till we meet again, mate. When ya see Keepa Jürgen, give him curry![18] It's only fair if you're feeding him, the whinger!"[19]

Donald watched the imposing Keeper grab his chair, fling it over his shoulder, and whistle as he sauntered toward the Big Room. Although Reese gave the impression of openness and ease, Donald felt he kept much to himself. He never doubted his loyalty and dedication to the Keepers. Still, he was a bit of a wild card. A large part of Reese's job was to be aware of the movements and plans of some of the world's more nefarious characters skulking around his domain. Donald wasn't sure how one accomplished that without somehow being affected. He shrugged and unconsciously smoothed his uniform shirt as the next member approached.

Keeper Evren Zin walked toward Donald with his hands in his pockets. He was deliberate in each step, trying not to kick up any cave dust on his pressed clothes. He stopped in front of Donald and bowed almost imperceptibly.

"Guardian Donald, iyi akşamlar."[20]

Stepping closer, Keeper Evren grasped Donald's shoulders firmly. The gesture didn't even wrinkle Evren's expensive white cotton dress shirt, complete with a handkerchief in his breast pocket. He leaned in and placed his right cheek briefly against Donald's. He stepped back and faced Donald again, now out of his personal space.

Donald tried not to appear uncomfortable. He was still not used to the Eastern European male greeting; a handshake was fine by him. He knew a kiss on each cheek was their

---

[18]  Give him curry – Australian slang for giving someone a hard time

[19]  Whinger – Australian slang for someone who complains

[20]  Iyi akşamlar – Turkish for good evening

traditional way to greet a friend, male or female. Donald sensed that Evren modified that for his comfort; behavior characteristic of a man who was a consummate diplomat.

"It is a pleasure to see a good friend today, Guardian Donald. I presume we have a few others already here?"

"Yes, Keeper Evren. There are a few." According to the rules, Donald was forbidden to give any meaningful information to any Keeper until they were verified.

"Good, it's been a while. I hope that you and your family are well and thriving?"

"Yes, Keeper Evren, they are, thank you."

While Evren reached back into his pockets, Donald took note of his shoes, which were expensive-looking brown loafers, probably Italian or Turkish. Even in the casual Carlsbad Caverns, Evren was well dressed. His clothing accurately conveyed what he was: a sophisticated and learned Turk from Istanbul, one of the most cultured and ancient cities in Eastern Europe.

Evren was a skilled diplomat and played that role in the Society as well as among the Keepers. At times, when opinions varied and discussions became heated, Evren could unruffle feathers and find common ground. Donald had lost track of how many languages he spoke fluently, but he knew they included English, Turkish, French, Italian, Arabic, Hebrew, and some Armenian; he thought there might be more.

Evren pulled out of his pockets the quartz rock and his stone animal carving, this one a beaver with amazonite[21] eyes. Amazonite was a veined rock that came in varying shades of aqua and turquoise and thus the beaver's eyes were almost indistinguishable from its body. Donald received the pieces and placed them in their proper places. "So how are

---

[21] "Amazonite." http://mindat.org/gm/184

your grandchildren doing? Did little Emily recover from her scraped knee in good time?"

"Yes, Keeper Evren. Thank you for remembering. She loved the rosewater-scented handkerchief and said it made her feel better. My wife thanks you again."

"Children are one of life's greatest blessings and I think it good policy to always carry a second handkerchief. You never know when it will be needed." Evren bent slightly in Donald's direction, smiled, and said, "Sağlikli kal,[22] Keeper Donald." He deftly grabbed his chair and walked away.

Donald respected all of the Keepers. He sensed that despite his relaxed and peaceful countenance, Evren bore the weight of the world on his shoulders. Finding a happy medium for disparate peoples was rough going; few could successfully navigate those waters and even fewer actually thrived in that environment. Donald cleared his mind and prepared for the next in the party.

He had not long to wait. A stunningly beautiful woman came gliding into view dressed in vibrant emerald green: a short-sleeved fitted silk top and matching capri pants that complemented her bronze skin. Donald noticed the dark burgundy-painted toenails peeking out from brown sandals. He realized, as she drew closer, that her eyes matched her outfit, an equally vibrant moss green. Although he didn't recognize her as one of the Keepers, she had a familiarity about her, one he couldn't quite place.

She stopped at the proper distance from Donald.

"I take it," she said in a clear, but soft tone, "that I am well within the timeframe?" The multicolored comb holding back some of her straight jet-black hair glittered.

---

22  Sağlikli kal – Turkish for stay healthy

Donald looked her in the eye and crossed his arms in front of his chest, choosing a protective and slightly aggressive posture.

"Ma'am, I'm afraid this entrance to the caverns has closed for the evening. The Visitor's Center remains open for a while yet. I'll escort you to the elevator on your right and get you into the visitor's area."

Donald tried to place her voice. It sounded as if she was from India; it was just a guess, however. He was aware he wasn't worldly enough to discern a particular country or region. Her speech was lyrical and she gently rolled over the vowels.

"I admire your fortitude and dedication, Guardian Donald. We are so lucky to have you."

"Ma'am, as I clearly said, this entrance is closed for the day. You have to leave now."

Despite his speech, Donald stayed rooted and made no motion to escort the beautiful lady to the elevator doors. This situation was a rare enough occurrence, but not unheard of. He was well-trained for it and would see how the scene played out—for a scarce couple of minutes; she had two more before he acted.

"I completely understand. Might I please take two items out of my pockets to give you?"

Her hands were small and delicate, with long tapered fingers. A bracelet of some sort was on her left wrist, but he couldn't make out the details. She raised her hands, palms facing Donald in a defensive posture.

"You have one-minute, young lady, before I escort you upstairs." Donald surreptitiously placed one hand behind his back, where his taser rested in his pocket. Using the taser would be unfortunate, not to mention dangerous and illegal. He'd never had to use it before, but he knew never to discount the possibility.

The woman placed each hand inside a pocket and slowly brought out two items; she held them out clearly for Donald to see: a small quartz crystal and a carved turquoise animal that he knew was a porcupine.

"Donald, it is me—Keeper Sahila Yold! I know I am a bit altered in appearance, but I assure you, it *is* me; I was forced due to unforeseen circumstances to have some changes made to my appearance. I may even sound different, but I promise you, I am the same woman you've always known." She wiggled her eyebrows. "Maybe the changes are for the better?" She spun around and smiled brightly.

Donald gave her a critical stare, conveying that he wasn't convinced.

"Okay. Time is running out quickly. What else do you need from me?" she stated.

Donald assessed his options. He was told to expect this possibility—and she *did* have the proper items, especially her distinct talisman. He quickly glanced at her and made a decision. He would be able to know for sure if she was Keeper Sahila by her stone carving.

"May I please see your pocket items, ma'am?"

When she reached over and placed them in his hands, he looked carefully at the stone porcupine and ran his thumb and fingers over it; it was warm in his palm and it felt *right*. The fact that even his logical and practical nature was attuned to this sensation still struck him; he felt a sense of peace and security overcome him when he held the stone.

It was a positive, benevolent energy that harbored no negativity or evil. In truth, the carving slightly pulsed in his hands. A stranger off the street would likely never notice the minute vibrations. It was unusual for a person with Donald's personality to have this awareness, to even think that this stone carving was at peace with its owner, but he could sense that; he remembered why his training was so very important.

The eyes in the carving were made of fluorite[23], a stone that comes in many vibrant colors. In Sahila's porcupine, they were a kaleidoscope of vibrant purple, blue, and green hues all in one stone. Over the years, Donald was given many opportunities to look at length upon those unusual eyes set within the turquoise carving.

He glanced up at Sahila and smiled. "Keeper Sahila, it's good to see you. I know you understand the protocol, however?"

"Of course, Guardian Donald. I understand fully." She opened her arms wide and walked closer. She glanced at his eyes, waiting for him to indicate permission, and, once granted, gave him a gentle hug, conscious of his discomfort with demonstrative displays of affection. She backed away and smiled again. "I need to go ahead now and I am sorry we have no time to catch up. I wish your family well."

She went to grab her chair and grasped it in two hands, lifting it away from her outfit to avoid any potential dust. She walked away rapidly and with purpose.

Donald placed both items in their proper places. He thought of Sahila's changed appearance as he placed her quartz crystal in the proper cushioned spot near the S. It was not for him to speculate about the Keepers; he realized there was a great deal he didn't know. He needed to be ready for the last two Keepers and both were a handful, to say the least. This musing was laced with affection rather than annoyance. He was looking forward to their entrance, truth be told.

---

23 "Fluorite," http://mindat.org/gm/1576

The presence of Jürgen Tilver was first sensed rather than seen. For a decade, such was Jürgen's unfortunate calling card. It wasn't that his odor was pungently offensive and cleansing like the ammonia smell of the bat guano at the entrance to the cave. It was more one of surprise and irritation, until it dissipated. Donald caught a whiff of the two-day-old fish odor in the drafty cave a full two minutes before the Keeper came into view. His eyes watered and he blinked to clear them before Jürgen approached. Everywhere Jürgen went, sweat glands ill-suited to his regular diet preceded him.

"Gud aftrnoon, Guardian Donald, how are ye doin'?" garbled the large man facing Donald.

It took a few seconds for Donald to process the greeting; it was embarrassing to him that he never became faster at processing Jürgen's speech. Another second passed before he adjusted to the faint piscatorial essence. Jürgen had a strong Scottish brogue and lived almost half the year in the Navarino Islands, off the coast of Chile. The Chilean influence on his speech didn't help. Every word came out a rich growl; intense concentration was required to comprehend Jürgen and stand next to him, to be honest. He was a large man with wiry red hair and a ruddy complexion.

"I'm fine, Keeper Jürgen. It's good to see you again. How is it on the other side of the world?" Donald was referring to his home on the Navarino Islands. He noticed that unlike Evren's tailored dress, Jürgen dressed casually, with little regard for details such as ironing and coordination. Nondescript khaki pants, sturdy boots, and an untucked checkered flannel shirt completed his ensemble.

"Cold as always, m' frind. Come visit with your wife when I'm there; it's very beautiful and cold'r than a three-week-old froz'n mink! I could use her cook'n! I mean, your wife's cook'n, not the froz'n mink's, you know. I alwys look frward to a samplin' when I see ye. I got hungry just walkin' this path for the meetin'." He leaned over and raised his bushy red eyebrows toward Donald. His brown eyes looked pitiful. "You wouldn't happn' to have a wee morsel for me, by chance, would ye?"

Donald smiled. He would never disappoint Jürgen. Jürgen was a peaceful man for the most part, but huge—and known to have a temper.

Jürgen grabbed his equally red beard, full but meticulously groomed, and gave himself a contemplative, therapeutic scratch. The facial hair was needed for warmth and it also represented his only bit of vanity. Jürgen also had a passion for food and an appetite to match, so the careful trimming served a practical purpose.

"Fish and crab. I eat a lot of fish and crab when I'm on island, you know. My cook, you see, she does what she can, but there's no chicken or fowl there…" He rocked on his heels while his hand still massaged his chin. "I do get lovely beef brought down from Argentina, but mostly there's…" He sighed to himself. "Mostly there's fish and crab." He pulled his hand out of his beard, caressed his mustache, and held them up defensively toward Donald. "I don' mind fish, mostly…nothin' against them, see. I just get tir'd of it."

"Well, my wife gave me a second generous helping of her chicken enchiladas with tomatillo sauce; I told her I was eating lunch with a friend. I'll give it to you at the end of your meeting."

"Ahh, Guardian Donald!" Jürgen placed a large paw of a hand on Donald's shoulder and gave what Donald thought was meant to be a gentle shake.

"I so appreciat' that. A chicken! That's fantast'c! Okay! Time for business!"

Jürgen placed his hands in both pants pockets and brought out his two items, this time the crystal and a carved turquoise wolf with eyes of malachite[24], an opaque green stone. Donald took them gently and placed the crystal in one of the two remaining indentations.

"Okay, than' you agen' Guardian Donald. It's always good to see ye." He clapped Donald on the back, grabbed the last two chairs in a careless manner, as if they weighed nothing, and shuffled away like a sleepy bear to greet the others.

Donald rolled his neck and blinked to clear his eyes. After a few moments, a figure emerged along the walkway. It was a woman. Although she walked slowly, she moved with purposeful strides and made no motion to quicken her gait when she saw Donald. She was a relatively short, middle-aged woman with a strong and robust body. Her loose-fitting tangerine-colored linen tunic swayed over her white cotton pants as she walked. Brown, practical Teva sandals peeked out from under the pants.

"Welcome back, Keeper Nalin."

"It's been a long while, Guardian Donald. Let me see your hands." Nalin Fink's guileless black eyes conveyed geniality and respect upon seeing Donald and were complemented by a chestnut complexion on a wide face.

Donald, used to this practice, held out his hands, palms up. Nalin grasped them strongly between her own and stared at the palms, searching for what only she could divine. Her voice was deep, but somehow soft. She spoke melodiously, in a pattern familiar to those who have spent time talking

---

24 "Malachite," http://mindat.org/gm/2550

to someone with an indigenous American accent from the Southwest.

"I'm gratified to see that you look healthy."

She looked into his eyes and encouraged him to keep contact with her assessing stare. It was almost as if he couldn't look away, even if he wanted to.

"You're taking good care of yourself. But you must exercise more, Guardian Donald; keep up your strength." Her smoky quartz[25] and turquoise necklace, each stone cut into unique shapes, sparkled on her neck. She narrowed her eyes and added, "You are needed, you know. You are valued."

"Thank you, Keeper Nalin. I appreciate your concern. I have everything you need on the table. He indicated with his hand without breaking the eye contact. "Oh, and thank you for that nice crystal bracelet; my wife loves it."

Keeper Nalin glanced at the table and released Donald's gaze, giving him the break in eye contact she knew he needed. She appreciated his discomfort, although she almost never felt it herself. Nalin held out her hand again. "Let me see yours first, Guardian Donald. I don't want the energies of the others to crowd yours; they are noisy and demanding in comparison."

Donald reached into his pocket and pulled out a small stone dog with blue tourmaline[26] eyes. Nalin told him years ago, when she first placed the figure into his hand, that the dog symbolized loyalty and friendship. Over time he had forgotten about the significance of the tourmaline and was too embarrassed to ask and reveal that he couldn't recall a symbol she considered important. She cradled the small stone

---

25 "Smoky Quartz," http://mindat.org/gm/3689

26 "Tourmaline," http://mindat.org/gm/4003

carving and looked at him with what he'd call a Mona Lisa smile, slight and vague.

"This little carving is a Zuni fetish or talisman. My people in New Mexico began making them thousands of years ago. It offers you protection and good luck. It also embodies the wisdom of the ancients and is in harmony with natural forces. I leave it for you to decide if you are attuned to those forces. Such a big responsibility for a little stone carving, hmm? I notice that he is warm from your pocket and his eyes remain bright and clear. Do you see?"

She brought the little dog talisman close for Donald to see.

"He tells me that you are internally healthy in mind and spirit and that this slight fellow is doing his job properly. Always keep him close to you and he will help protect you. Your wife's bracelet is her talisman—not that she needs one," she reassured. "Next time, bring it in and I will look it over. Oh, and again, I suggest more exercise, Guardian Donald. Take your little dog on a walk, okay?" Keeper Nalin ran her hand down her ebony hair, styled in a complex braid.

"Thank you again, Keeper Nalin. I appreciate the advice, more walks for sure." He'd been meaning to do that anyway, he acknowledged. He would make sure she noticed a difference the next time.

"Okay. I'll take a look at the other items now, Guardian Donald."

"Of course, Keeper Nalin. But may I see your items first, please?"

"Certainly, Guardian Donald." She pulled out of her pocket the crystal and stone carving. Hers was in the shape of a turtle with clear quartz[27] crystal eyes. Nalin glanced at him and smiled. He nodded and kept both items in his

---

[27] "Quartz," https://www.mindat.org/gm/6128

palm; he knew from past experience that he could keep them together in one hand.

He watched while she walked over to the table and looked at the crystals and other talismans that lay within the box. Donald noticed a faint sensation in his palm. It wasn't quite a vibration, but in a way it was. He could only describe it as such. It almost felt as if the items were alive and in imperceptible motion.

He opened his palm and looked at the little turtle with the crystal quartz eyes and the triangular-shaped crystal. True to form, there they lay, motionless. He couldn't parse it out, but quickly scolded himself. It wasn't for him to question the sensation.

Nalin spoke rhetorically. "I have my job cut out for me, for sure. Keeper Reese, you continue to push your luck. What am I to do with you?" she muttered to herself.

She walked the box to Donald, took the objects from his palm, and placed them where they belonged. Her crystal fit into the last impression, this one next to an N. After shutting the lid, she latched the box and carried it by the handle to Donald. She placed a hand on one of his cheeks.

"Thank you, Guardian Donald. We are very honored. I wish good health and security for you and your family."

She grabbed the folded table and the box and ambled away toward the meeting. Donald would stay in place until the Keepers took the same journey in reverse, back to the mouth of the cave, leaving him with the chairs, the table, the empty box, and an empty food container, courtesy of Keeper Jürgen.

He'd see them again in six months. His regular Park Service duties resumed tomorrow morning. When they were here, he never heard more than whispers and the occasional outburst from Reese, Jürgen, or Alegria. The words were always muffled, so even a shout wasn't clear. He was certainly curious to know more, but Donald wasn't invited to listen and that was probably for the best. He stretched his arms above his head and shuffled his legs. Donald stood careful watch and wondered what his wife was making for dinner.

## CHAPTER 3 – Li

### BANGKOK, THAILAND

# SPRING

Rua-Jian gazed at the storefront window display, relatively pleased by what he saw. *I can't really complain,* he mused, *since I haven't visited this location in years.* He had left explicit instructions for the store's maintenance, but gave great latitude in its displays and overall ambiance.

Theoretically, the stores were operating well; they served their specific purpose and surprisingly made a tidy profit. It was ideal, really. His international accounting team saw that the minimal staff in each location were paid their salaries and ran the stores legitimately. Modest bonuses were paid annually to those who performed well and adhered to strict orderly standards.

All stores were located in sophisticated locales and their reputations were spotless. The accountants paid all formal taxes and some informal ones in locations where such practices were expected—"the ends justified the means" and all that blather. His accountants were above reproach and trustworthy. Managing twenty-eight stores for a largely absent owner necessitated such stewardship.

He looked at the store sign above the nondescript door. The sidewalk upon which he stood was spotless and lined with other unique and trendy retail and spa establishments. Although he stayed generally busy with other work, he was involved in choosing each store location. It was vital each one be ideally situated.

A black-lacquered framed sign read XIAN: ARMAMENTS OF THE WORLD in bold scarlet lettering. The window displayed a myriad of replica swords and daggers for the serious collector. All locations sold replica weaponry for those interested in ninjas, the Korean Knights of Silla, European Landsknechts and Medieval knights, Middle Eastern swords of sultans, swords from China, and his favorite, samurai from Japan. He particularly favored the katana, elegance and ingenuity personified.

The location in Los Angeles, California, had made sizeable profits for many years, its reputation solid. At one time, well over half of the weapons used in films made in the United States and photographed for print media were purchased from that store. He enjoyed having blades and knives custom made for exacting directors and petulant actors. Although he kept his prices reasonable, he refused to slash them for a particular cost-conscious studio executive several years ago. *I stand by my decision,* he reflected. *I won't lower my standards to remain partnered with that fickle industry.* As a result, the executive bought elsewhere, and when one studio pivoted, the others followed suit. In all honesty, he didn't care. So long as the stores complied with his overall concept, he remained satisfied.

Although Rua-Jian peevishly wanted to add ESTABLISHED IN 1000 A.D. to the sign, he didn't. It would draw attention to the business in a way he deemed unnecessary and careless.

*And I certainly don't need prying tourists or zealous reenactors delving into Xian's unique history—the less scrutiny, the better.*

In truth, the first Xian location did open for business around 1000 A.D.; the precise date was lost to the ages. Xian was not a retail business at its inception; at that time, it made armaments for real warriors, lethal weapons fit for an emperor. The swords made by Xian craftsmen were legendary. Its owner and his devoted band of loyal artisans made the very best for those who could pay.

There was a time when Xian made weapons for armies too. Xian blades, morning stars, and battle axes, among other lethal aids, helped generals win many a battle. The Xian master blade makers traveled to serve the highest bidder, collecting and carrying with them their arcane knowledge about steel[28] and other alloys used to make their superior weapons. The travels of its tradesmen took them out of ancient China to Japan, the Middle East, and eventually to Europe. Rulers and other craftsmen coveted their trade secrets. Xian eventually acquired its own special security force to prevent the kidnapping of its artisans.

It was a glorious time, lasting until humanity shifted to using more efficient and cheaper methods to exact murder and mayhem on a larger scale in modern warfare, using bullets and gas instead. Once that transition began, Xian needed to adapt to survive. One would think, with such an illustrious history, that the Xian name would exist in history books. Yet Xian business leaders purposely kept only minimal paper records. With opaqueness came mystery, intrigue, and fear.

---

[28] Steel is made by combining iron and a certain percentage of carbon; other elements can be added to create different strengths and types of steel, depending on its function.

This air of the supernatural only heightened its reputation; Xian artisans were respected and considered above reproach.

Despite its reputation, even the great Xian company couldn't escape the vagaries of modernization. The company needed to change with the times, so change it did. With its reputation still solid, the business opened select brick and mortar locations around the world and made real weapons for egocentric rulers and wealthy nobles who fancied themselves brilliant fighters. *Their commissioned portraits hopefully led onlookers to believe such tripe, at least,* Rua-Jian surmised. Once that business waned, it was left with making beautiful replicas from bygone eras, largely harmless facsimiles made for collectors who appreciated the beautiful but deadly weaponry.

Contemplating the storefront, Rua-Jian was satisfied with how his business had evolved. And never one for waste, the retail space offered him dual purpose. He walked into the store wearing a friendly, nondescript smile.

"Good afternoon," he said in English.

The clerk greeted him in kind. "Are you looking for something in particular, Sir?"

The subsequent dialogue always gave him an electric zing that never ceased to thrill.

"Why, yes. I am searching for a Ninja Himogatana stiletto. Might you have one?"

The clerk's eyes seemed to pop out of his head. Obviously, he had been briefed about this rare possibility.

"Excuse me, sir. That's a special-order model. I'll locate my manager immediately. May I offer you some water or tea while you briefly wait?"

"An herbal tea would be lovely, if you have it. Thank you." Rua-Jian smirked. *I know you have it—it's one of the essential details I insist upon.* He didn't drink caffeinated beverages anymore, hot, cold, or carbonated; he preferred to be in complete control of his body and emotions.

A striking, ebony-haired woman appeared before him dressed in a stylish, yet professional manner. *Excellent!* Similar to the other locations, he found the management here to be highly sophisticated.

"Sir, I understand you are looking for a certain item? I hope we can be of service."

"Yes. In fact, I am looking for a particular Ninja Himogatana stiletto."

"Ah, I see. I do in fact have just one available at the moment. I can show it to you, if you'll follow me."

She gestured to him, inviting him to follow. She walked purposely to a corner sheltered from view by a display shelf. She selected a key from her delicate pewter wrist keychain.

*The pewter chain is a nice touch, if I say so myself.* Rua-Jian had them commissioned by an artisan. He believed that the ubiquitous coiled wrist keychains worn by thousands of retail employees were tacky.

The manager inserted the key into the lock of a thin, wide, wooden drawer that extended almost three feet. It matched a set of fifteen similar drawers stacked inside a wall frame. This was unusual, as most of the blades sold were openly displayed in lit cabinets or shelves, shown to their best advantage. She reached into the satin-lined drawer and selected a rather small weapon with a steel hilt adorned with a basket-weave pattern.

"Is this what you were looking for, sir?"

Rua-Jian held out his hands to grasp the stiletto and examine it properly. He looked into her eyes and stated clearly, "Yes. This is precisely what I am seeking."

He ran his hands carefully along the hilt and found the hidden section where the weave was slightly wider than the rest of the pattern. He pushed against it with just the right amount of pressure. The end of the hilt popped open mechanically with a soft *snick*. He upended the stiletto and caught the small keys as they fell into his palm.

Although she maintained her decorum, he still heard her slight intake of breath. He smiled smugly. *You've never had the privilege of meeting me before and probably thought I was an urban legend of Xian lore. Let's see if you remember the name you were given.*

"Mr. Chu?"

"Yes. And you are…?"

"My name is Ms. Srisati, Ms. Chinda Srisati."

Rua-Jian placed both keys and the stiletto in his left hand before he accepted her handshake and bowed slightly. Despite his distaste for germs, he could still be the consummate gentleman.

"It's a pleasure, Ms. Srisati."

"I can't believe it's really you," she whispered in awe, her hands knotting together near her waist. "I was trained to be prepared for you, as was our former staff; they never got the chance to meet you, however. Can I get you anything, sir?"

"The herbal tea would be well appreciated—and a proper case and bag for the Himogatana, please. In the meantime, I have some matters to attend to." He gestured to the larger part of the store. "Please attend to any other customers; I can find my way."

"Oh, of course, Mr. Chu." She turned and quickly departed.

*Oh, you are so curious, aren't you—but not enough to risk your job. I appreciate a smart employee.* Rua-Jian walked farther into the corner section and through the staff door. He knew he wouldn't be followed. Upon the event of his arrival, all staff knew to give him privacy.

He looked at the beautifully crafted stiletto. This one was no replica, but a real Himogatana. *It's always good to have a small weapon at the ready, should one need to resort to conventional methods to get their point across.* Rua-Jian laughed at his own pun. And he was told he had no sense of humor! This particular stiletto, lovingly maintained over its four-hundred-year existence, had seen many a skirmish and ambush. Historically, it was used by ninjas for a surprise attack when in close proximity to one's enemy.

Walking directly into the staff room, Rua-Jian stopped at a small gray box built into the wall. It was designed to be mistaken for a fuse box or other equally mundane technician panel. He noticed the battleship gray paint was scratched in multiple places. Most likely, the culprit was discarded store placards or temporary shelving leaned against it over the years.

He felt a small kinship for the cold metal box. *Isn't this how I've lived much of my life? Hiding in plain sight?* If the box were a person, it would be rewarded for a job well done. Rua-Jian wiggled his fingers in anticipation. *Since I'm the brilliant mind behind your construction, I'll reward myself instead.* He inserted one of the keys he'd retrieved from the stiletto and turned. He flipped on the light switch next to the box to help illuminate its contents.

Just before he could open the inner compartment, he heard a tentative knock at the door.

"Mr. Chu? It's Chinda Srisati."

He quirked an eyebrow. *It's officially Rua-Jian Chu.* Rua-Jian walked quickly over to the staff door and opened it, confident that Ms. Srisati could not see his activity from her vantage point. She held out a black lacquered tray, identical to the shop's outside sign. Upon it was a cup of fragrant tea and an upscale bag embossed with the store's name.

"Here is the tea and the bag you requested, Mr. Chu. Is there any other way I can be of service?" she inquired.

He took the tray and bent forward in a second slight bow. *How I wish I had the time for a mindless encounter; I've no doubt you are willing, lovely Ms. Srisati.* Alas, it was not to be. "Thank you, Ms. Srisati. I will let you know if I require any additional service."

She dutifully left and he placed the tray and bag on the nearby staff table. He returned to the box and opened it.

"Hello, my valuable friends," Rua-Jian purred, taking a moment to refamiliarize himself with his cache. The light in the staff room penetrated enough inside the box to reveal his treasures. One shelf divided the box. The top held velvet gem pouches, several tweezers, and elastic bands. The shelf below displayed a kaleidoscope of color organized on a partitioned felt tray. Handfuls of brilliant clear diamonds[29], blue sapphires, and green emeralds[30] lay there.

Further inside sat fist-sized nuggets of gold and stacks of paper money. He only kept about one hundred thousand in physical currency: American dollars, Chinese renminbi, and Euros. World economies were fickle, ebbing and flowing with time. It was more prudent to rely on shiny rocks, tangible and infinitely more beautiful! Although his expertise lay in an entirely different arena, he no less appreciated the value and beauty of these remarkable gems. Rua-Jian looked into the farthest part of the felt tray and gingerly brought forth one of his most valued treasures.

---

[29]  "Diamond," http://mindat.org/gm/1282

[30]  "Emerald," http://mindat.org/gm/1375

"Hello, my beautiful girl, you are as flirtatious as ever." He beheld the stunning yellow Florentine diamond. The base color was a lemon yellow, but it contained a faint green overtone. It was 137.27 carats of flawless beauty, and worth millions.

Initially, the diamond belonged to France's Duke of Burgundy, Charles the Bold. He died in 1476 at the Battle of Nancy against the Swiss and Lorrainers (from a region in northeast France). A fellow soldier took the diamond and sold it, without realizing its worth. After changing several hands, including a lengthy residence with the infamous Medici family, it wound up traveling with Charles I of Austria when he was exiled during World War I. Shortly after that, it was somehow stolen and never again seen in public, the thief never caught.

Rua-Jian held the jewel up to the light. He had no intention of selling this illustrious beauty anytime soon. The diamond was also called the Tuscan, the Grand Duke of Tuscany, the Austrian Diamond, and a bevy of other names, none of which did the gem justice.

He imagined for a moment the cacophony that would ensue if the diamond resurfaced. *It would almost be worth watching. Thankfully, I need never sell you.* Should the need arise, he really only had two choices. *I can sell you to a pompous individual with more wealth than sense.* That part was easy. *Those people can only imagine the titillating secret of owning a valued stolen prize they could never reveal.* Once they died, however, their families invariably squabbled, often to be caught in a nightmarish web of police and insurance investigators, explaining how their relative came to own the property of a king.

*The second choice does produce some pangs of sadness, I admit.* He knew a select few trusted jewelers who would fracture the diamond along its facets and break it down to form smaller individual stones, easily sold off. He wasn't a fan of this option and if necessary, he would choose the former.

*Whatever trouble the next owner encounters is their problem.* For now, the diamond belonged to him. Rua-Jian replaced the Florentine and picked up a gem pouch. He used the tweezers to fill it with fifteen two- and three-carat diamonds. He also rolled two wads of dollars and Euros and secured them with an elastic band.

Rua-Jian was unconcerned by the loose stones, as they were unmarked. Today, most diamonds were certified and had a minute serial number etched into the girdle of the gemstone. Although not impossible, it was more onerous selling a stolen diamond marked with GemScribe or a similar technology.

He took one last look at the box, shut and locked it. When he left Thailand, if he wound up needing more financial resources, he had twenty-seven other worldwide locations available to him. Each store had a similar staff room with the exact same safe. Gem bag, cash, and stiletto went into the small Xian shopping bag. Rua-Jian took a deep breath. *This time, I will prevail.* He felt it. *I will not fail again.*

He walked over to the staff table and sat down to his tea for a well-deserved moment of relaxation and reflection. From the corner of his eye, he spied what appeared to be a fossilized vermillion noodle stuck to the table, presumably left from a staff member's lunch. *Ick! It looks like a piece of a tapeworm!*

Disgusted, he dismissively dropped the teacup onto the tray, an action that broke its handle and spilled its fragrant contents. He stood up, no longer enthralled with little Ms. Srisati. Despite that small dishwashers were installed in all staffrooms, this travesty! *I can't be certain this teacup is actually clean.*

Rua-Jian walked over to the door and examined the knob. *This is probably filthy!* He placed his hand a few inches away. His fingers shook as the knob took on a fiery orange glow. The color spread until the entire knob and keyhole pulsated with waves of heat. He grabbed the knob, certain it was now sterilized, then turned and pushed the door open.

Ms. Srisati approached him quickly. "Did you find everything to your liking, Mr. Chu?"

"I most certainly did not!" He glared. "Your break room table is vile; I expect far better from my management. See that it's taken care of or your annual bonus will *mirror* your attention to detail!"

Ms. Srisati's hands flew to her mouth in horror as Rua-Jian strode out the store, bag in hand. At the store entrance, he heard her scream in agony; he surmised she grabbed the staff room doorknob en route to examine the table. *Good—she learned her lesson, the worthless tart.* He could still hear her wails halfway down the street. *On to better activities,* he thought, as he cleared his mind.

Now that he was again financially stable, he could buy some new clothes. It was definitely the right time for His Majesty's leadership and eventually, his.

*Soon, I'll be strong enough to finally take the helm, with or without my monarch's blessing. Humanity is still clearly incapable of managing the Earth and its resources, as usual. I alone know best how to deplete her of her riches without her awareness.* She needed to be hoodwinked, like a distracted mother with unconditional love for her child. *You hug her with one arm and rob her with the other.*

Humanity seemed bent on manhandling the earth and mismanaging her resources with no finesse. He never enjoyed watching movies where the antagonist was determined to destroy the world. *Unless they planned to cultivate a lifeless void, the plot is utterly pointless.*

He intended to continue living on Earth and expected both Earth and humanity to accommodate that desire. Quite simply, the world was overpopulated and idiot leaders were destroying it. *Now is the time to cull the herd and start anew.* It was his destiny and the reason for his very existence. *Of that I am certain.*

## CHAPTER 4 – Be

### CARLSBAD CAVERNS, CARLSBAD, NEW MEXICO, UNITED STATES

# EARLY SPRING

EVERY BIANNUAL MEETING of the Keepers began with greetings and ribbing. Dumisani made it his job to intercept each Keeper as they entered the caverns' Big Room. Alegria gave him a passionate hug and a kiss on both cheeks, true to her personality. Dumisani was a compassionate father figure to her, always empathetic and full of practical advice. She knew he was best suited to guiding their unruly family—his patience was legendary. Crises occurred on a regular basis and a lesser Keeper would have faltered long ago. Each time she saw him at a meeting, a weight lifted from her shoulders. So long as Dumisani was at the helm, she knew they could cope with any situation.

On Alegria's heels, Reese sauntered into the room and smiled at the duo. "I'm happy as Larry[31] to see you two!" He approached Dumisani and was greeted with a firm, gentle grasp on each shoulder. Dumisani met his eyes with a penetrating gaze.

"I take it you are well? Are you recovered?"

---

[31]  Happy as Larry – Australian slang for happy

"I'm no whinger…" He put his hands up in defeat as Dumisani's eyebrow rose, questioning Reese's honesty.

"I'm fine, really. You should have seen the other guys. It's all right. It was a sticky situation, but I managed." He shot Alegria a cocky grin. "I always do, don't I?"

"You're arrogant and immature, I'll give you that," she retorted as she approached, enveloping him in a tight hug. "You worry us, you know. But that's how it is with family; we forgive you even as you irritate us with unnecessary bravado!"

"It's almost always necessary, darlin'! And if there is a pretty lady in distress, it's practically a requirement!"

Alegria opened her mouth to reply and was met with a finger wagging in her face.

"Don't you quote any Neruda or even the sainted Bard at me right now, Jillaroo![32] It's too early in the day for that!"

Alegria pursed her lips in faux mild irritation and quickly turned away, engulfing Reese's face in a cloud of curly brown hair.

He swatted at the mass and gruffly barked out, "You don't always get the last word, Alegria!" before sneezing.

She inclined her head coyly and sang out in a sultry voice, "Yet somehow I always do, don't I?"

Keeper Evren stepped into the room just in time to witness the exchange. He smiled and embraced Dumisani and added a swift kiss to each cheek, a little distracted.

"Umarim sağliğin iyidir.[33] Are you already playing the referee with your brood?" he asked with a smile.

---

[32]  Jillaroo – Australian slang for cowgirl

[33]  Umarim sağliğin iyidir – Turkish for I hope you are
in good health

"Umarim sağliğin iyidir. I love all my charges equally as you know, Evren. Alegria, like a sister, can't ignore his taunts. They'll work it out of their system soon enough."

Dumisani also knew that Reese's joking with Alegria and the others was his way of showing trust. To safely give his opinion, without peril, was healing. Subconsciously, he routinely needed these exchanges with those he could rely on to maintain a measure of peace.

"A very reasonable approach," Evren whispered conspiratorially. "It's my nature to play the peacemaker, however, so I'm going to throw myself into the melee and see what happens." Evren offered Reese a cloth handkerchief to deal with the sneezing, but Reese brushed it off, having just used his sleeve.

"Thanks anyway. One day I'm gonna render her speechless, mate. And her hair should be considered a deadly weapon," Reese interjected. "It's overwhelming and it smells like roasted peaches. I really *hate* peaches."

Evren's left eyebrow rose in response and he greeted Reese with a hearty smack on the back. "Well, it's certainly admirable to have long-term goals. I will really enjoy that moment—if it ever arrives. How are you doing, by the way? I heard it was a rough time."

Reese used his other sleeve to clear his watery eyes, the last remnant of his sneezing fit. He leaned closer to Evren and spoke in sotto voce, "Sometimes I still get the feeling that I'm not entirely trusted. That I'm gonna run back to the other side. It's disconcerting." He looked at Evren and said succinctly, "I would never do that. I am *never* going back to that."

"I can promise you that *no one* thinks that, Reese," Evren interjected. "You have to understand, however. You take large risks and we can never trust our enemies, as you are well aware. You're known to gamble with your life in pursuit of your goal and make yourself vulnerable. Naturally, everyone worries; we don't want to lose anyone else."

Reese shifted on his feet, restless. "I get it. I'm *fine* and I know precisely what I'm doin'. I go at full throttle and always have. It's just my nature. I wouldn't be effective if I went about it a different way."

"Just be more careful, if only for the ladies," Evren gestured to Alegria.

Reese snorted. "If you see any, let me know. That one's dangerous and mean."

Evren threw up his hands and laughed. "I'm staying well away from that topic." They headed toward Dumisani and Alegria, who had taken their seats and were waiting for the others.

While walking over, Keeper Sahila Yold stepped into the room. She greeted the four with a jaunty twirl, her arms outstretched like a windmill. "What a sight for rejuvenated eyes!"

Silent stares greeted her in response. The absence of conversation emphasized the beautifully lit canyon room and highlighted the gentle *plop* of a stalactite dripping calcitic[34] water into a pool below.

Dumisani spoke first. "I know you all were made aware of Sahila's altered appearance before the meeting. If she's made it into this sacred space, you know Guardian Donald did his job thoroughly. It is indeed our Sahila."

Alegria jumped out of her seat and ran toward Sahila, grabbing her hands and lifting them up to better observe her new look.

---

[34] Calcitic water is formed from calcite ($CaCO_3$) and is made of calcium carbonite

"You look beautiful! So rejuvenated! It will be fun to go shopping again and have a spa day. I've missed that, you know," she said only for Sahila's ears. "You have no idea how much." The women gave each other a long embrace.

"I have the perfect poem for you on this occasion," Alegria stated. "But…" She looked in Reese's direction and fabricated a wounded look. "I'll share that with you after the meeting, so it isn't spoiled by uneducated cretins. Some can't appreciate the beauty of poetry, you know."

Reese sidled up and lifted his hat to Sahila. "There's a time and place for poetry. And I actually agree wit' Alegria in this instance. We need to hear one about unparalleled beauty and wisdom wit' a dash of innocence and freshness, I think." He grabbed her chin and kissed her cheek. "I can see your soul through your eyes; I knew it was you immediately."

Sahila smiled teary eyed and held Reese's cheek. "Take better care of yourself, please. Will we get the details today?"

"I'll give you the whole sordid tale if you wan'. But for now, Evren is politely breathing down my neck. I reckon I'm in the way."

Evren looked at Sahila with warmth. "He's right. You're definitely the same Sahila. I take it your new choice in appearance is strategic?"

She laughed and added sarcastically, "But of course! Vanity played no part in my choice *at all*. It's all for our new students. Let's just say I felt a little run down and tired and in need of a makeover." She scrutinized him. "You are certainly looking relaxed. Is that an indication of where we stand? I thought we had weighty issues on the agenda."

"It's more a calm before the storm. We do have a great deal headed our way, but we needed to regroup before digging in; you picked the right time for a makeover."

"Well, it was more a coincidence, really and not entirely my choice, as you are well aware. If it was good timing, I'm glad to sacrifice for the cause." Sahila leaned on the tips of her toes and gave Evren a hug and a kiss on each cheek. She headed toward Dumisani to be enveloped in a comforting hug; being in his presence felt like home. Considering they were all so well-traveled and frequently mobile, it was grounding to have him always there. In addition, hugging fellow Keepers became almost innate, especially after such a transformation. The impulse was a survival instinct; the need for connection and validation was vital.

"Are you doing all right? Ready for our next adventure?" Dumisani questioned.

"Absolutely. I feel refreshed and prepared." She held out her arms, displaying her attire for his perusal. "I thought this look would appeal to our new wards."

"It's a very fetching choice; you look lovely." He led her over to the other members. Meanwhile, Evren subtly removed one of his handkerchiefs, this one spritzed with lemon oil, and placed it near his nose. Reese wrinkled his own, sensing something unpleasant, and whispered toward Evren.

"Hey, pass me one of those after all, mate, and be quick!"

Evren slyly handed one to Reese while Alegria cocked an eyebrow and glared. A wide smile spread across her face as she faced the passageway.

Keeper Jürgen lumbered into the room and looked around at the group. "What a happy day to see m' family! I've been waitin' for this, see! How grand!"

He approached Dumisani, whose nostrils subtly flared. Overcoming the onslaught, he greeted Jürgen with a warm but brief hug. "Jürgen, what a great pleasure. It's been so long since I've seen you. You've been too long in the Navarino Islands."

Reese clapped him on the back and while hugging him, took a deep breath from the handkerchief. Since it was spritzed with lemon oil, it temporarily overpowered the odor of fish. *Evren be praised for both his practicality and gentility,* he thought.

"Reese, you're a sight for sore eyes. Ya managed to not git yourself kilt agin'?"

"Nah, Jürgen. I'm made of stronger stuff than that. I can handle being up a gumtree. Kinda like it up there, actually! You sick of eating fish?"

Alegria scowled at Reese and released a frustrated sigh. Half the time she wanted to grab him by the hair and yank for all she was worth. She loved him so much, but he frequently irritated the hell out of her.

Jürgen swiped his hand in front of Reese, as if shooing a fly. "Ah, knock it off, you Aussie fool! You know I got a glandul'r conditin'! It wer' the luck of the draw! Turned out for th' best, tho'," he said, glancing at Alegria.

Reese rolled his eyes. "I'm jus' yankin' your chain, man! It's good to see you. Just lay off some of the fish at school, eh?"

"It's good fur the body, ya know. Lots of vitamins! You should try it!" Jürgen retorted.

"I think you're eating enough for both of us."

"Jürgen," Evren interrupted, effectively ending the banter, "I'm looking forward to catching up with you. Are you ready for new term?"

"Absolutl'y." Jürgen greeted him with a hearty handshake and hug. "I can't wait ta mold new minds! I've heard we've got an interestin' group."

"Whenever a new group of students is ready, I'm enthusiastic to begin," Evren reflected. "And by the time we've graduated a class, I'm ready for a hiatus. That make sense?"

"I feel th' same, Evren, th' same indeed." Jürgen sounded distracted as he glanced at Sahila. Evren retreated, freeing Jürgen to wander over.

"Well Sahila, you clean up okay, don't ya? My goodness, you've gone fash'nable!" Jürgen slapped his forehead. "Sorry, that came out wrong. I mean no disrespect! I jus' meant that you look real good… It's nice, ya see."

"Jürgen, you've no need to apologize. I understand you perfectly." She reached up to give his cheek a kiss and offered a warm hug… "I look forward to being at the school with you. It's been a while."

"Yes, it has," he responded as he noticed Alegria waiting patiently.

Alegria wiggled her arms and called out to Jürgen. "Come over to me now. I've been waiting very nicely, have I not?"

Jürgen approached and stood before her. He whispered, "I always save my favorite for last, my dear heart."

The other Keepers subtly looked away, giving the two a modicum of privacy.

Alegria placed her hands on either side of his face and touched her nose to his. "Mi alma gemela.[35] How I have longed for you!"

Jürgen kissed her forehead and gave her a lingering embrace. "Someday, it will be the right time for us again, my Alegria. In the meantime, we must go forward an' persevere. We're on the right side, after all."

"You well know that patience is not always my strong suit, but for you, I will make it so. Now, go to the chairs on

---

[35] Mi alma gemela – Spanish for my soulmate

the other side." She shooed him away. "My eyes are watering at your dreadful smell!"

Alegria wiped her teary eyes. Whether her tears were from the olfactory assault, her sadness, or a little of both was impossible to tell. Although the scent had decreased dramatically for everyone else, because of her strong connection to Jürgen, the smell for her was overpowering. She could only stand to be in intimate proximity for small periods of time.

The whole group was almost assembled. Their final member was entering the room just as Jürgen reached his seat.

"Hello to you all. I am sorry if I have delayed us; I was just acquiring your familiars from Guardian Donald." Nalin held up the box by the handle. "I tried to get him to relax, but I believe I just made him more uncomfortable. We overwhelm him; the man really needs to learn to meditate."

She placed the table in the middle of their chair circle and set the box on top of it. Task completed, Nalin turned in a slow circle to take stock of the others. She started with Dumisani and made her way around the room, greeting everyone with a quick embrace. When she reached Sahila, she looked her up and down, assessing her new appearance.

"The change suits you, Sahila. You will be very effective with our new students." She gestured to the box on the table. "We have our work cut out for us, today." She headed over to the empty chair and took a moment to get comfortable.

Nalin knew, as did they all, that Sahila's transformation was indeed timely. The recruitment and stewardship of the younger generation was vital for their order's success and continued existence.

Younger generations had a keener awareness of both the regional and global changes in social norms. They were more sensitive to the daily concerns, frustrations, and joys of younger Commoner[36] society at large.

They also had a more fluid understanding of modern technologies. It was hubris for older Keepers to believe their storied life experiences made them omniscient. Thankfully, this perspective had slowly dwindled over time.

All Keepers knew that although their collective experiences were indispensable, it was perilous to ignore the elemental need to recruit and prepare their younger brethren. Strategically, Sahila's fresh look hopefully made herself more relatable to their new students.

Dumisani stood up and clapped his hands together gently to minimize echoing in the caverns. He took a quick glance around the space. "I am always grateful when we are all safely together. That said, we have quite a bit to impart and discuss. First and foremost, let's hear a report on what's happening around the world…as *we* know it. We'll start with our most remote perspective, at the bottom of the world." Dumisani gestured for Jürgen to take the lead.

"Well, I spent another couple of months, as usual, visitin' several stations in the Antarctic. A fabulous bunch of people, ya know, who work there. It's a hard place to live in for any length of time. I finished up there in May, as winter was settlin' in, and as usual I stayed a few days at the Villa Las Estrellas on King George Island.[37] You all know that's run by the Chilean government?" Jürgen raised his eyebrows, looking for agreement from the group. When he saw collective heads nodding, he continued.

---

[36]  Commoner – Regular human beings who don't have Keeper abilities

[37]  Migration, J. "Welcome to SCAR." https://www.scar.org/

"Then I journeyed to the Amundsen–Scott South Pole Station[38] and that became home away from home." Jürgen pulled on his beard while he collected his thoughts. "I'm very comf'rt'ble that everyone who knows me there still believes my cov'r: that I'm a scientific representative for the Sco'ish government who only wants to study penguins in the Antarctic—an eccentric from a wealthy family my government humors, since I pay my own way."

"The eccentric part sure is accurate," muttered Reese.

"Shut your gob, you dunderhead. I'm tryin' to give my report!" Jürgen retorted mirthfully. He could never be *too* annoyed with Reese; they had too much fun poking at each other. Jürgen looked above at the stalactites, pulled his beard again, and murmured, "Now where was I? Oh, yes. It's easy for my story to hold, as you know, 'cause no one stays on Antarctica more than a year and a half. Also, our Guardian within the Energy and Climate Change Directorate in the Sco'ish government confirms my story, if anyone's curious to go poking around.

"Anyway, once I'm at Amundsen, I start asking an' searching around. Ya know, thirty countries have base stations in Antarctica, and there are presently a total of sixty-eight stations. In summer, it's hoppin' with over four thousand people at all of them stations and at the Villa. But in winter, only forty-three are open and only about a thousand people remain in total. So, it's nearly impossible to monitor what's really happenin' there. I use my snowcat and go from base to base to look around. Since my family 'pays' that generous

---

[38] National Science Foundation. "National Science Foundation – Where Discoveries Begin." https://www.nsf.gov/geo/opp/support/southp.jsp

storage fee, they don' mind keepin' my clothes, gear, and non-perishable food while I'm away."

"I'm sorry to interject, Jürgen," replied Sahila with laughter in her eyes, "but I am trying to recollect. When there, you are studying penguin poop, correct?"

"Okay, poke yur fun at me now an' let me know when you're done! You know I'm not studyin' the jobbie[39] of penguins. The real study that looked at penguin poop, dead penguin remains, and predator bones was studyin' past penguin populations and noticed that rare earths can help determine population history. And rare earths is what *I* am interested in, as are all of you!"

"I am so sorry, dear man. I stand corrected," Sahila replied. "I promise to be quiet from now on."

"I'm givin' you a pass Sahila, since we've missed ya. *Anyway,* as you are all aware, the Madrid Protocol,[40] which passed in 1991, prohibits all minin' in Antarctica until 2041. Every country knows that law and abides by it. However, there is no law against *storing* rare earths *on* Antarctica, and tha' is what I am still seeing." Jürgen let the group absorb this bit of news before he continued.

"Jürgen, are you seeing a significant increase in rare earth storage since you last went?" queried Evren.

"Aye, that's what I'm sayin'. The stockpile is mainly in the West Antarctic, near the Amundsen Sea. It's very remote and there are no stations there, you know. When I head over there to take a look I almost always run into a blizzard or cyclonic activity…funny tha'. You can't see more than three feet in front of you when tha' happens.

---

[39]  Jobbie – Scottish for poop

[40]  ATS. "The Protocol on Environmental Protection to the Antarctic Treaty." https://www.ats.aq/e/protocol.html

"But, aye, I sense much stronger amounts of rare earths than before. Someone is storin' a mounting cache of samarium[41], gadolinium[42], lanthanum[43], neodymium[44], dysprosium[45], and cerium[46]. I don' believe that anyone at any station is aware of the fact—and I think, at present, that's for the best. If we alert them, we also alert the persons or group storin' them. We need to figure out who is behind it. I do know that it's Debilis activity. Whoever's responsible is trying to hide it from us specifically, not Commoner scientists. I can just barely smell the decayin' rot lingering on everythin' they touch since it's so cold there." He raised his eyebrows in question to the group.

"I sense that this is part of a much larger picture," Nalin said. "Even for one of us, such an undertaking would be extremely time-consuming. There must be a distinct purpose for such a project, I think?"

Dumisani once again took the lead. "Jürgen, thank you for the information. I think Nalin is correct in her observation. Coupled with other interesting changes, this is part of a comprehensive strategy and something that we have not seen—in a very long time. All of us have noticed of late some hints of potential Debilis activity. We need to put ourselves on high alert as we head into the new school term. Alegria, please enlighten us next."

---

[41] "Samarium," http://mindat.org/element/Samarium

[42] "Gadolinium," http://mindat.org/element/Gadolinium

[43] "Lanthanum," http://mindat.org/element/Lanthanum

[44] "Neodymium," http://mindat.org/element/Neodymium

[45] "Dysprosium," https://mindat.org/element/Dysprosium

[46] *Cerium,* Wikimedia Foundation, 11 Feb. 2024, https://en.wikipedia.org/wiki/Cerium

"Thank you, Dumisani. The fiery eruption from a volcano is one of Earth's most fascinating wonders and continually enthralls humanity; children all over the world are captivated by their dinosaur and volcano displays. Lava is a rare visual glimpse into the mystery of Earth's internal workings.

"This year, as is typical, we have already seen dozens of incidents of volcanic activity throughout the world and we will doubtless witness dozens more. There are still over 1,500 active volcanoes in the world which can erupt at any time. Thankfully these events cause few human casualties. We must never rest easy, however. Even when largely dormant, we respect the destruction these awesome landforms can render. Despite that, it is heartening in these modern times that volcanic early warning systems are vastly improved. Both NVEWS[47] and WOVOdat[48] have made great progress toward alerting people about possible eruptions. Guardian and Keeper colleagues who are fortunate to work with these organizations relay that they are improving these systems every year. I am dissatisfied, however. I won't rest until the warning systems of today match the innate awareness of impending volcanic activity that I and my Keeper brethren possess. In that regard, unfortunately, we seem to be a decade away.

"In addition, we must pair these warning systems with more effective evacuation procedures. In some crowded and dense communities, fleeing can quickly become a survival nightmare. In some regions, Commoners are even afraid to

---

47 United States Geologic Survey. "National Volcano Early Warning System – Monitoring volcanoes according to their threat." https://www.usgs.gov/programs/VHP/national-volcano-early-warning-system-monitoring-volcanoes-according-their-threat

48 The World Organization of Volcano Observatories. https://www.wovodat.org/

leave their homes, because they fear for their livestock and crops, which is their livelihood. So, we have much work to do to become better prepared worldwide.

"Our colleagues are up to the task and work well with our appointed Guardian within the World Organization of Volcano Observatories." She paused. "And since it is impossible for *any* creature on this Earth to harness a significant amount of energy from a volcano, much less use it to their advantage, there is no concern on that score.

"This doesn't stop the Debilis from disrupting the early warning scientific endeavors in communities experiencing more active volcanic activity, however. They sow distrust and fear about the detection devices placed near and on volcanoes. They create false stories about how these devices cause harm to local families. It is all in an effort to control and manipulate the resources in those areas.

"But not to worry—my Keeper and Guardian colleagues have prevented many of these ridiculous attempts and we will continue to do so. And that is all I have, my friends," she finished with a flourish.

"Thank you, Alegria, for the important update. I think we will now hear from Evren," Dumisani said.

Evren looked down at his shoes, ordering his thoughts. "Well, it's been an interesting several months, I'll just say that first." He ruffled the back of his hair while he glanced at Reese. "The United States leads the way in earthquake early warning detection with its ShakeAlert program, and there are constant updates as new technology becomes available.

"Of course, as always, it all comes down to money and who will pay for it. Regardless of its effectiveness, however, my band of Keepers and I can predict an earthquake worldwide fifteen minutes faster than the latest computers."

"The Compressional waves or 'p' waves are the ones the system tracks and gives nearby residents a matter of seconds or up to a few minutes to prepare. Our Keepers within the U.S. Geological Survey[49] continue to work with our Guardian scientists there to shorten this timeframe, but it isn't easy, as you know, to translate *our* awareness into a tangible, measurable format. Even with all of today's modern technology, this eludes us. All my team can do right now is alert our well-placed Guardians around the world as soon as we sense an impending earthquake. They, in turn, need documented proof before an alert is announced, so they watch the targeted data closely and, when they spot the altered pattern, they act. We still lose that precious time to save lives, however." He threw up his hands in frustration.

"You know we are doing all that we can," Sahila gently reminded Evren. "Even if we could sound the alarm ourselves, who would believe us? And those who did would rightfully question *how* we knew it. You know where that path leads, my dear friend; we all do, and we have an entire room at the school dedicated to those we have lost who tried to find another way. We can never risk exposure. That would damage the earth and humanity permanently in a way far worse than earthquakes and volcanic eruptions can, I'm afraid."

Reese threw out his arms. "Look at how upset Commoners become the worl' over when professional athletes get caught dopin' to enhance their performance? If it became known that certain humans have natural heightened abilities and that some are evil and dangerous? It would cause endless fear, anger, and distrust!"

---

49  U.S. Department of the Interior. "ShakeAlert®." https://earthquake.usgs.gov/data/shakealert/

Sahila rubbed Reese's arm in support and in a contemplative voice added, "Don't forget manipulation of our kind, genetic and otherwise; it doesn't matter that it wouldn't work."

"This is precisely why we are embedded deeply within major scientific endeavors," Dumisani added. "We assist humanity by steering them in the right direction, nudging them to our own level of awareness through scientific innovation; it takes far more time that we all would like, but it is how we must operate." Dumisani held up a hand in supplication. "I know I don't need to emphasize this point with you all, but I feel compelled every six months to do so. Call it the prerogative of a hovering parent." He glanced at Evren to urge him to continue.

"On to other matters," Evren continued. "In defense of Reese, I did use my entire arsenal of diplomatic skills to smooth matters with INTERPOL,[50] but we still lack a highly placed Keeper in Lyon, France, where Interpol is headquartered. We're working on it, but it's been difficult finding someone as capable as Alexandre, may he rest in peace."

In unison, all the Keepers, hands at their sides, looked up at the stalactites and said, "From whence you came, return fulfilled and rest in peace."

Evren continued a moment after the others composed themselves. "We'll find someone, but in the meantime, it can be tricky. And it wasn't Reese's fault at all. We were not dealing with the most imaginative of agents." Evren raised an eyebrow in Reese's direction.

Alegria wiped away a stray tear. She'd shed enough for poor Alexandre and needed to look forward, but it took time

---

[50] Interpol (International Criminal Police Organization). "What is INTERPOL?" https://www.interpol.int/en/Who-we-are/ What-is-INTERPOL

to process losing such an appreciated friend and comrade. She still held out hope that he wasn't truly gone forever. She plastered on a bright smile. "So, we now begin the most intriguing part of this meeting!"

"What form of crap did ya step in this time, Reese?" queried Jürgen. "I can' wait to hear this!"

Reese scowled in Jürgen's direction. "Thanks for the positive affirmation! I guess it's my turn for the rough end of the pineapple."[51] Reese knew he didn't need to explain to the group that Keepers at their level of expertise can sense when a Debilis is nearby; they feel their presence—like a prickling sensation of awareness. They can sense a Debilis in another building or even another city, especially when one or more of them are motivated toward action.

"We all have our own abilities and you know mine involves sensin' residual energy born from intense greed, desire, or anger within gems, coins, and minerals." He smiled slyly. "It's one of the reasons you keep me around.

"Anyway, back in March I got wind of a possible large heist planned at a small, but well-endowed bank in Zurich, Switzerland. This particular group of Debilis—five of them to be precise—were arrogant and excited, so they were careless. One of them worked at the bank, with the long-term goal of makin' a big score. He was a trusted employee in a middle management position and he listened keenly while keepin' his nose to the ground. This particular bank catered to the ultra-wealthy, so there was bound to be an opportunity eventually. Once they began their planning, this idiot Debilis couldn't be in the bank without obsessing about their planned score!

---

[51] The rough end of the pineapple—Australian slang for being in trouble or a difficult situation

"The bank's vault is home to over $200 million in loose diamonds alone, and the stones absorbed and amplified that heightened vibrational energy, which magnified his greed an' excitement. I flew there from Paris as soon as I could, just to make the sensation stop! The bastard was giving me a headache! If I'd been in Brisbane, it would have been far less intense…just my luck to be nearby." He stopped and glanced over at Dumisani. "Dumisani, mus' I really give the full version of the facts? Can I just skip to the bottom line?"

"Reese," Dumisani spoke as if talking to a recalcitrant child, "we keep nothing from each other, you know that."

"All right, but don't say that I didn't warn you." Reese took on a pained, almost constipated look and scratched his hair under his hat. "So, there is this wealthy businessman, a Mr. Peter Salavar. He and his wife wanted children and couldn't have 'em, so they decide to fosta' a baby girl through a church not far from their home in Einsiedeln, Switzerland. They wound up adoptin' her and according to dear ol' dad, she's a diamond in the rough." He bent fingers on both hands gesturing quotation marks. "Anyway, in appreciation of his daughta, he decided to donate $20 million worth of his diamonds to various charities that support needy children."

Reese didn't get any further. There was now a collective and, in Reese's opinion, rather nauseating display of emotion. Alegria and Sahila had their hands on their hearts exclaiming the virtues of Peter Salavar. For all they knew, maybe he picked his nose or littered in the streets. Nalin professed that he was an "incredible, generous man" and obviously had an "altruistic soul."

Evren leaned over and stated, "Such praise. *We* should be so lucky."

"They still don' know that I could have *died*…I go' shot! Had Mr. Bloody Salavar donated a check instead of diamonds, like a *normal* person, this would neva have happened!"

"If everyone is ready to settle down again," Evren offered gently, "I believe Reese needs to finish the account."

"Thank you, Evren. Yes, Mr. Assh— I mean, Salavar is a model of humanity and the sun shines out his—"

"Reese! Come, man!" Jürgen shot back.

"Yes, all right!" Reese shouted as he threw his hands up in the air. "But I am so tired of this contrived and fabricated attitude toward diamonds! People are so completely fooled by emotion'l marketin', including Mr. Wonderful Salavar. A pox upon the defunct M.W. Ayer advertising agency! If you wan' to collect a beautiful and rare gemstone, go for tanzanite[52], black opal[53], red beryl[54], or even benitoite[55]. Any one of those will set you back thousands of quid and will hold their value, honestly!

"Humanity, literally the whole world, is obsessed about a nondescript clear crystal stone. Well, they all deserve each other." He released a pent-up breath to continue. "Anyway, so, I arrived a couple days before the planned heist. The group was easy to fin' and I got win' of the details through my standard sleuthing; I won't bore you with the details.

"I notified the proper Swiss authorities an' fed them a fraudulent story abou' hearing a discussion regarding an impending heist at a bar. I opened an account and deposited our standard approved amount to make my presence in the bank legitimate, of course, and then stayed near the area.

---

52  "Tanzanite," http://mindat.org/gm/3885

53  "Black Opal," http://mindat.org/gm/7998

54  "Red Beryl," http://mindat.org/gm/690

55  "Benitoite," http://mindat.org/gm/624

"I sensed the day of the heist because the Debilis was unable to control his excitement an' anxiety; it was more intense than *eva* before. The waves and vibrations from the diamonds were unreal—off the charts, really. I knew this Debilis was somewhat skilled, but dangerous, since he was clearly young and couldn' control his abilities. He was like a baby rattlesnake, more dangerous than a full adult 'cause it can't regulate its venom release, you know?

"Anyway, it started when two of the Debilis's posse wandered into the bank dressed in suits and asked to open a safety deposit box. The others loitered outside a nearby café close to the armored truck. When the security and the Debilis employee got outside with the bags of gems, the Debilis's co-conspirators blocked the bank doors to preven' assistance and brandished guns! They weren't loaded, of course, but the customers and personnel weren't aware of that! Then all hell broke loose.

"Another two Debilis grunts temporarily blinded the driver and the other security using inferior crystal lasers. The Debilis bank employee was slowly harnessin' the stones, but lacked skill. That was the bes' time for me to intervene. It was pathetically easy, I have to say. Those stones were so agitated at that point, I barely had to move a finga. I lifted the three bags using their harnessed kinetic energy and had fun flingin' them at Debilis skulls and knocked 'em out. It was entertaining, actually.

"I can't vouch for the present quality of the diamonds— Mr. Salavar will need spit and polish to get 'em right, but they're not stolen! Anyway, a no-hoper[56] Swiss policeman finally shows up *after* the commotion, and interrogated me! I point out the criminals and then the Debilis employee

---

56  No-hoper – Australian slang for worthless or unhelpful

wakes up and runs off. I go after him and the policeman *shoots* me—twice, mind you—in the back of the shoulder, when I'm doing 'is job for him!"

"Reese," Evren said gently. "Had you gone with the Swiss police, you know we would have gotten you out within hours; you didn't have to resist."

"I respect our code, I surely do. But I am *never*, I repeat, *never* going back into a jail or a station eva again! I don't risk my life and soul for that!"

"Anyway," Evren added, "Interpol is involved because of Reese's shooting and subsequent flight. The Debilis bank employee ran off and fled to France, it appears."

"Evren," Nalin added gently, "*after dark, all cats are leopards*.[57] I suggest more empathy toward Reese. His past will certainly influence his actions in the future, and who can blame him? At least we count him as one of ours."

Evren bowed in Nalin's direction. "Point taken."

"At least we'll get a chance to interrogate the other thieves," Alegria said. "Has the first contact been orchestrated?"

"Yes," Evren stated. "Once they can receive visitors, we'll begin the process. One can hope that rehabilitation is possible. If they prove to be a threat to the other inmates, we'll transfer them to our nearest facility."

"You know," Sahila quietly pointed out, "sometimes it's easy to forget the collateral damage caused by these skirmishes. One could say: Who cares if a rich man's diamonds are stolen? The bank has insurance and the Mr. Salavars of the world can surely afford to lose a few million. It's easy to overlook those who are scarred and left by the wayside."

---

[57] After dark, all cats are leopards – Zuni Native American proverb

Dumisani arched an eyebrow. "Very true, Sahila. Correct me if I am wrong, Evren, but the individual who unknowingly hired the Debilis at the bank was fired, right?"

"Yes, unfortunate, that. She was fired without a reference and will have to find another job. All attempts to reason with the board at the bank failed; she's a single mother with two kids. In addition, the head of bank security was also let go. It's a relief civilians weren't killed this time. We're not always that lucky."

"We have to try harder to ferret these creatures out sooner; we must admit that a fractured soul can elude us at times," Sahila whispered, almost to herself.

"Anyway, good job, Reese. We're glad the damage wasn't worse. Ya could've been shot in the arse." Jürgen winked.

"I got several kisses of gratitude from some lovely lasses from the bank before I got shot," quipped Reese. "That was payment enough."

"And on that note, Sahila," Dumisani said, "would you please enlighten us about our new students?"

Sahila smiled as she stood up in front of the group. "I believe we have a promising group of fresh and energetic young men and women. It's a larger group this term, which is surprising. Our sources have found a total of eight potential students. Having eight students in one term is unique. I want to briefly touch on that.

"My thought is that due to recent worldwide malevolent activity, we are seeing a possible surge from Debilis forces. We have never in our history been able to understand *why* we suddenly locate more young people with our abilities. Yet, time and time again, when we see more trouble brewing, we seem to find more students. Why is that? I know we have examined this from every angle." Sahila lifted a hand and counted off on each finger. "We have researched changes in the worldwide economy, climate alterations, dramatic industrial and technological advancements. We even explored celestial and lunar phases, oceanic alterations, and weather patterns."

She threw her hands up. "We've had our very brightest Guardians and Keepers look into this for centuries and nothing definitive was found. I choose to believe that somehow Mother Nature, some natural force, something intangible to our awareness, understands or senses this upsurge in evil. Somehow, it knows that we need more help to balance the dark energy in the world."

Sahila ran a hand through her hair. "Anyway, I digress. As for our potential new charges, we have, surprisingly enough, an even distribution between young men and women. I'll start with the young men. Receiving our invitation to attend our extraordinary university for free, we have a young man from the countryside in England, another one from the Chinese province of Guangdong, an American from one of the islands of Hawaii, and a young man from Riga in Latvia.

"Among the young ladies, we've located a potential student from Singapore, one from just outside Paris, an American from Ohio, and a student from Panama. All of them are between seventeen and eighteen and are university bound."

"Now we just need to convince them that they want to attend *our* university," interjected Evren.

"We don' often have too much trouble there," Jürgen added. "It's difficult to turn down a free Bachelor's degree in Science from the College of William and Mary[58] and a Master's from The University of Cambridge."[59]

"It's very difficult to pass that up, as well as the stipend paid to the parents," Alegria stated. "If their children study so far away from home and can't bring in any supplemental income from a part-time job, it can be impossible for some families. By the way, Sahila, I agree with you. I don't know why we have these cycles in student population any more than you, but I do sense something—we all do. Reese certainly does."

Alegria looked at him directly. "Something very dangerous is brewing and we need to determine the source. This foreboding seems different to me this time around. Almost as if it's approaching from multiple locations…like a hydra, with a single purpose."

Dumisani directed the conversation again. "It sounds like we have an interesting and rounded group of students."

"Hmm," Jürgen pondered aloud. "International night should be tasty. I wonder wha' types of food this lot likes to eat. I love when cooks do tha' for us. Wha' do they eat in Ohio?"

Evren laughed. "Slow down, Jürgen. We have to convince them to attend first. However, I believe your answer is typically what Americans call a 'meat and potato diet'… I'm being stereotypical, you understand."

---

[58]  The College of Willam and Mary is in Williamsburg, Virginia and was founded in 1693. It is the second oldest University in the Unites States.

[59]  The University of Cambridge is in Cambridge, England and was founded in 1209.

Nalin slapped her forehead. "Oh, this ancient cave will collapse and bury us alive the day you actually insult someone, Evren. You can relax in those chinos a bit, honey."

"On that culinary note…" Dumisani calmly redirected the conversation again. "Let's turn our attention to our schools." He looked to the group. "Evren?"

"Thank you, Dumisani." Evren slipped his hands into his pockets and addressed the group. "You all know that I just returned from my most recent visit to our little university. By all accounts, we are ready to begin a new term. Our current students are beginning their advanced studies in Cambridge and will focus on their specialties. All five students performed well during their summer training, as you all are aware, and are eager to begin this fall; they are spending the remaining time with their families and friends.

"Our standard teaching protocol applies, as usual; we will all alternate between Williamsburg, Virginia, and Cambridge, England, according to your student instruction rotation. This cohort of students all speak and read English fluently, an occurrence we are seeing more frequently, so we won't need to employ a Guardian language teacher and translator. On a separate topic, our self-defense instructor is back and reported that most of the new workout regimens she saw were 'idiotic, frivolous, and designed by blindfolded one-armed baboons.' She holds that most of our old school methods are far more effective. Let's see…what else." Evren looked toward the stalactites while gathering his thoughts. "Headmistress has managed to make all interior repairs caused by our last class. And she reports that the fields had some sort of grub issue earlier on, but despite that, we'll have a bumper crop of fresh vegetables this fall. Oh, and that our chefs are very excited that they perfected their haggis[60] recipe, finally, they think."

All eyes drifted surreptitiously toward Jürgen.

"I see ye all lookin' my way!" Jürgen said, exasperated. "You're all bampots![61] Ye kno' me real well. Chefs kno' me real well. I *hate* haggis! I never liked haggis! I never *eat* the haggis! It's stereotyping, that is! Shame on you all."

"Jürgen," Evren said with a laugh, "I think chefs make it because *someone* always secretly eats it."

Jürgen took on a wounded look.

"You have been known to wander into the kitchen after meals to forage for a snack, Jürgen," Nalin supplied. "I do appreciate our chefs' desire to use almost all of the mutton, however."

"Just not enough to eat the stuff yourself," interjected Reese.

"Come now, Reese," Alegria implored. "There's no accounting for taste. But, in the interest of disclosure, it's certainly not me."

"All right," Nalin said. "Sahila and I have a bit of work to do." She lifted the box gingerly by the handle and turned to Sahila. "Let's go over to that area where the light is best." She gestured with an elbow. "Can you grab the table?"

When in position, Nalin opened the box and sighed over the contents. She spoke quietly, "Reese is struggling a bit more than he lets on."

"It's going to take a great deal of time, Nalin. He has years of damage to overcome."

---

60  Haggis – A traditional Scottish dish consisting of various meat organs of a sheep or other animal mixed with spices and oatmeal. The mixture is stuffed into an animal casing and boiled.

61  Bampot – Scottish slang for a moron or foolish person

"I know. But he must strengthen his ability to trust. His crystal is clouded and stressed. Look at his poor opossum."

Sahila rubbed Nalin's shoulder in comfort. In sotto voce, she added, "We've seen much worse, you know."

Nalin smiled in agreement. "Okay," she sighed, "let's get started." She reached into the box and removed a crystal at random. Sahila lightly ran her index finger over each talisman and after a minute of perusal, selected Dumisani's mountain lion.

Nalin palmed the crystal between both hands and blew onto it, fogging it temporarily. She bent her head and studied it closely, watching as the fog slowly lifted. When it cleared, she turned in the direction of the cave entrance and clasped both hands together, cradling the crystal, and felt her hands begin to warm.

She closed her eyes and took deep, cleansing breaths, exhaling with her mouth slightly open. Heat gathered from her chest and radiated down her limbs, through her fingers. Her exhaled breath took on a colored hue, a whispery vaporous trail of mottled purple, brown, and green, similar to the changing colors of a bruise.

A few moments later, the heat stopped and she was filled with a cool, relieving wave that felt like swimming in a refreshing brook. She opened her eyes, smiled brightly at Sahila and unfurled her palms. The crystal shone clear, as if newly polished.

"Evren seemed to have a fairly uneventful six months, he's ready to go another six." She placed the crystal back into the box and selected another at random and repeated the process.

Sahila examined the mountain lion charm and paid particular attention to its eyes. The red jasper stones were slightly dull, but the turquoise felt cool to the touch. "Reliable and steady, as always," Sahila marveled. "He's had tremendous experience cultivating that peace."

She massaged the turquoise talisman and found a visual focal point just ahead, a long, dripping stalactite. In her head, she began her guided thoughts, never ceasing her light touch on the figure, which began to almost imperceptibly pulsate.

"Wisdom and guidance…strong leadership that never wavers…unbiased empathy." Sahila repeated the mantra five times, only breaking her visual focus to blink. She opened her palm and looked at the mountain lion. The turquoise and jasper had a bright sheen from the warmth and natural oils of Sahila's fingers. It seemed alive, ready to launch itself from her fingers and journey into a new adventure. "All right, he's good for another… Hmm, I'd say three thousand miles." She showed the lion to Nalin.

"You took good care of him, as always. I know I can entrust their little souls to you."

All the talismans were created by Nalin. She learned the craft from the local Zuni tribe in Arizona.

For Sahila, the process remained similar for every Keeper, yet the words for each were distinct. Evren's beaver talisman centered on building relationships and achieving trust. For Alegria's moose, the talisman's shielding reinforced a belief in herself and confidence in her destined purpose. Sometimes tough choices are required and Alegria must be able to act decisively.

Reese's opossum bolstered his skills in strategy and helped render him invulnerable from oppositional forces. The porcupine, Sahila's charm, strengthened her ability to gain the faith and trust of others; it also protected her, so she remained unwavering in the presence of great evil. The fox talisman, belonging to Nalin, represented stealth and an ability to blend in with one's surroundings, becoming a part of the landscape, like crystalline energy. Nalin's fox devoted itself to keeping her invulnerable to invading energy forces. Working in conjunction with her crystal, her fox radiated Nalin's natural energy signature. When bombarded with maligning crystalline energy, they partnered to keep her intrinsic energy unaffected. Lastly, Jürgen had a squirrel talisman. The squirrel excels in gathering and saving for the future. Jürgen's talisman helped him ferret out information and elements alike. His judgment and senses had to remain clear.

Nalin and Sahila continued their tasks, marveling at the good or less than stellar condition of each item.

When Nalin was cleaning the toxins from Reese's crystal, she coughed on the vapors. Thicker, dark-hued colors emanated from her lungs, almost choking her. Sahila rubbed her back and spoke to her soothingly and Nalin finished the task.

"I *never* get used to that. It's like getting a yearly root canal…one dreads it, but must persevere."

Sahila raised her brows. "You've had a root canal?"

"One time, yes. A procedure I plan never to repeat."

"Hmm. I'll take your word for it." Once all was completed, the items were replaced in their respective locations and the two returned to the group.

"All is restored," Nalin announced. "You can reclaim your friends." Collective replies of thanks came from all Keepers as they pocketed their charms and soon the circle was complete again.

Evren began, "I think we are almost ready to adjourn this meeting. We will meet again at school at the end of August. I think we all agree that we must be vigilant to changes on the horizon. Before we go, back by popular demand, we are going to play 'Are They Ready?' This is our, what, fourth or fifth consecutive year?" He held out a hand and counted on his fingers.

"They better be fab this year…honestly!" moaned Reese. "Several from last year really stank!"

"Thank you, Reese; we will expect the best one to be yours, of course," Evren said sardonically. "Just to refresh everyone's memory, the question needing an answer is: 'Are our new students ready…'"

"…to learn what really goes bump in the night," Alegria blurted out.

"to '…tell us, pray, what devil This melancholy is, which can transform Men into Monsters,'" espoused Jürgen.

"That's very intense, Jürgen," Nalin stated. "I can tell you put a lot of thought into that one. Who said that?"

"The dramatis' John Ford. I thought it very apropos. I would replace *melancholy* with *Debilis,* however."

"I give you full marks for the attempt, Jürgen," quipped Reese.

"I've got a lot o' time to read. I bought me'self a copy of the *Oxford Dictionary of Quotations*…I figured it would come in handy."

Nalin added, "to learn that '…in this world, the unseen has power.' That's a Blackfoot Indian proverb."

"Are our students ready to venture into the proverbial rabbit hole?"

"Sahila, that's cheating! Alegria used that last year!"

"Actually, Reese, that's the fruitcake of phrases," Evren laughed. "Someone uses it each year and it doesn't get any better with the telling. Remember class, there's extra points and respect for originality."

"Does the best entry come wi' food?"

"Jürgen, whatever you choose, you always get food from Guardian Donald," Nain reminded him, laughing.

"Admit it, Sahila. You forgot this year," someone added.

"I will never admit to that. I've decided that fruitcake phrase or no, it has a nice ring to it and strikes at the truth, really."

"All right," Reese interjected. "Moving on. Are our new students ready to embrace their exceptional destiny?"

"A bag o' crisps for Reese," Jürgen quipped. "Well done, my man! You didn' even need me quotations book!"

"Well, I try. Even a couple of bullets in the shoulder won't stunt my creative juices." Reese blew on his fingers and brushed his shoulders.

"I think that Reese beat me to it, but I'll share mine anyway. Are our new students ready for the realization that they have the ability and the *obligation* to protect the Earth and dedicate their lives toward that end?"

"We can always count on you, Dumisani, for a dignified, yet sober response," Evren teased.

Dumisani bowed slightly and smiled. "I'm glad I don't disappoint. I feel an *obligation,* if you will, to keep us ever mindful; it's written in the job description. Carry on."

"Okay, that leaves me as the last one this time around. Are our new students ready for Lovelle Drachman's musing, 'blessed are the curious, for they shall have adventures'?"

"Thank you, Evren." Dumisani took back the reins of the meeting. "That's a fitting final contribution. I think we are up to date on recent activities. We all agree that an ill wind is beginning to brew, and we don't yet know why. We must all be on alert and stay in close contact.

"Determining the central source of this vague threat is ongoing, as you all know. Any insights, however incidental or unlikely, should be expressed. We never know who might be reemerging. I will see you all at the start of the new term. Travel safe. I, myself, head to Cambridge to see how well we are preparing for fall term. We are adjourned."

The group of Keepers hugged and kissed, wishing each other well. In small groups of twos and threes they made their way back to Guardian Donald. En masse, he thought they were actually easier to take. It felt like being in a crowded theater. You were part of a sea of humanity and there was nothing to be done but follow the flow of the crowd and tolerate the close body contact. He appreciated their well wishes and pats on the back. In his own mind, he wished them safety and success.

Only this exclusive group, including him, knew of their great importance to the world. Each had an incredible responsibility to keep the Earth safe, so every Commoner, in any country, could go about their day without the awareness of the opposing evil constantly hovering and foraging, eager to gain control. Nothing less than complete global chaos and destruction would occur if humanity became aware of the truth about the world in which they lived, and who shared it with them. He appreciated being on the right side.

Jürgen finally drew up beside him, with a satisfied grin on his face and a pristine beard.

"Oh, Guardian Donald. What a treat that was, a real treat! I so appreciate it. Might I have the recipe to pass on to my cook, when I see you next?" He held out a hand in supplication. "Unless it's a secret family recipe, mind you. I don' want to disrespect the pride o' the cook!" He handed back the plastic container with fork inside to Donald and thumped him on the back. I'll see you again in abou' six months. Take care o' the missus, you know. She's worth a large tanzanite, that one!" Donald smiled and assured Jürgen he would share the recipe when they next met.

Jürgen lumbered back toward the cave entrance. Donald was not concerned about their exit. Few pedestrians ever saw the exodus. And if they did, they usually drew the same conclusion: a corporation or organization had paid for a private tour. If anyone queried beyond that, Donald had his answer ready—a misguided group or latecomers hoping to get in under the wire. It almost never came to that, however. It never ceased to amaze him, the effectiveness and the power of hiding within plain sight. People saw what they wanted to see and largely, they wanted rational explanations.

Dumisani emerged from the cave entrance as quietly as he went in. He perused his surroundings and most everything was peaceful. He noticed a small bunch of loose feathers beneath a large shrub and raised an eyebrow toward Salima. In response, she gave one high-pitched indignant screech. Chastised, Dumisani continued his perusal and found the head of a Trans-Pecos rat snake peeking out from beneath a different shrub. Further examination revealed a satisfied snake, with a small bulge in his or her midsection. Dumisani raised his head again to Salima.

"Pardon me, my friend, for my judgment lapse; I should not have questioned your integrity."

Salima shook her head, ruffled her feathers, and stretched her wings. She flew down to his shoulder to perch, rubbed her head against his neck, and bit his ear gently in punishment; a small bead of blood emerged.

"I deserved that; I know. Here is a treat, a peace offering, and a thank you for keeping watch. He raised his arm and indicated for Salima to travel down to his forearm. We will be getting on a plane in the morning. Why don't you hunt down a meal while I walk to the car?"

Dumisani threw his arm up and sent Salima soaring into the air. He sifted through many thoughts as he walked to his car, some recent and some old, like a dissipating vapor; a tendril anchored in his memory, rarely accessed, but never forgotten.

# CHAPTER 5 – B

## BANGKOK, THAILAND

# EARLY SUMMER

RUA-JIAN CHU SAT at a table in Sala, the outdoor restaurant at the Sheraton Grande Sukhimvit. He enjoyed this little faux oasis. Looking up, he could see the towering commercial buildings that surrounded the hotel. Unwilling to spoil the illusion, the small task of ignoring his extraneous surroundings was relatively easy. Always in the back of his mind, however, he knew the truth: He could never be fooled into believing what wasn't real. This was one more characteristic that set him apart from the lemming masses.

He stirred his herbed iced tea and stretched as he soaked in the balmy weather. It was about twenty-six degrees Celsius in June and the rainy season was not yet in full swing. Rua-Jian was meeting his friend in a few moments. He was not accustomed to waiting for people, yet he needed to have a few reflective minutes alone.

Rua-Jian looked at his fingernails and admired them. Yesterday was another day of rejuvenation and badly needed pampering. Gone were the ragged cuticles and uneven nails; he never went for shiny clear polish, but did desire symmetry and cleanliness. He shuddered to think what bacteria potentially lurked under a dirty nail. He became lost in a distant memory.

*I remember waking up buried in a morass of muddy filth, dirt soaked with the blood of my countrymen. That day, my nails were badly torn or ripped away altogether and the ones that remained were embedded with shards of bone and bodily fluids. I was left for dead, and like the others, forgotten and expected to rot where I lay before burial in a nondescript pit weeks later.*

His compatriot's approach shook him from his reverie. *Joyous memories,* he thought acidly. The memory reinforced his determination. *I will never suffer such indignities again.* He didn't need a psychologist to point out his compulsion for cleanliness or its origin. It wasn't a problem, but a standard to be met. Now, those who didn't meet that standard in his orbit… Well, they *did* have a problem.

His companion reached the table and waited for an invitation to sit.

"Come join me," Rua-Jian offered. "I trust that you are well rested and clear-headed?"

"Yes, sir. Thank you so much. It's a wonder what a few good nights' sleep can do for a body."

"Quite. Rejuvenation and toxicity release takes time. It's absolutely essential to be familiar with your body." Rua-Jian paused to squeeze a fresh lime into his tea. "We are checking out of the hotel today and need to head back. I have ideas of how we should proceed, but they need to be endorsed." *At least for now.* "So, we'll head home and get situated."

He watched the condensation run down the outside of his tea glass. "How much do you know about the caring and feeding of new Keepers, their selection, and their formal education?"

His companion eyed him quizzically, clearly bewildered by the question. "I don't know much about that process at all; they go to great lengths to shield the school and their students."

Rua-Jian scowled. "That much is obvious." This surprises you?"

His ally stammered, clearly aware he disappointed his mentor. "I...I know the general location of the school, it's somewhere in Williamsburg, Virginia. And I know that several attempts to communicate with students over the years all met with failure."

"All true. In the past, it was easier to hide and protect the students. In this century, however, it should prove more difficult to do so. Spotting an anomaly will be less arduous since Keeper faculty stick to their old ways. I'm betting it's a challenge to remain anonymous when surrounded by so much modernity."

"Yes, sir. I see what you mean. If we destroy the school, our work would be easier."

Rua-Jian threw back his head in shock. "No! What put that insane and equally inane thought into your head?"

He, of course, would ultimately love to destroy the school and all activities related to Keepers. *At present, I'm unprepared to attempt such a mission, an issue I won't admit to others. I've been given another chance for a reason and I won't squander it.* "I don't want to destroy anything. I want to *infiltrate* their sanctuary."

Watching his compatriot's face, he saw the need to provide further clarification.

"I want to acquire a student and cultivate him. Learn about their educational process, their strengths and weaknesses. After that, we will return him to their midst to become a fly on the wall. That will be possible because the Keepers are loyal to a fault; this is one weakness of which I am certain. Do you now comprehend? One cannot destroy what one doesn't understand. We will figure out a way…and this time, we won't fail." He watched the awareness finally dawn on his comrade's face.

"Now, let's pack up. We leave for Macao this afternoon."

CHAPTER 6 – C

COLLEGE OF GEOEVOLUTION (SCHOOL FOR
FUTURE KEEPERS)
WILLIAMSBURG, VIRGINIA, UNITED STATES

# EARLY OCTOBER

Reese stood and tossed his pen lazily onto the table. He arched his back and stretched his arms above his head. Glancing at Alegria, he grimaced.

"I didn't know this job was hazardous! My hand hurts from all of that writing! I'm toey[62] and could go for some tucker."[63] He scratched at his chin. "I wasn't the best choice for this job. Why did I draw the small straw again?"

Alegria smirked at Reese and wiggled her fingers, hoping to prevent any writing cramps. "You got shot, as I recall. Dumisani decided you needed to recover."

Reese rolled his eyes.

"Regarding food, we're at the mercy of Chef. Since we're on hiatus here until fall term, we get whatever he is in the mood to prepare for a small staff."

---

62   Toey – Australian slang for restless

63   Tucker – Australian slang for food

"I never get used to these periodic student vacancies," he remarked. "How is it possible we located *no* students last year?! I'm not sure I'll ever understand it."

"It's one of Mother Nature's many mysteries, I believe. If there were future young Keepers, we would have found them—you know that as well as anyone else. Consider it a lucky break, Reese. We get to repair the school and grounds and have a moment to think and reflect!" Alegria looked out one of the few windows in the main office. Absentmindedly, she remarked, "She doesn't often give us more than we can handle."

Reese arched an eyebrow and stared at her. "True enough, but when she does, it's a crap storm. Makes ya wonder what's coming down the pike. The calm before the storm and all that."

She paled, her eyes matching his concern. "Well, let's use this time wisely. Since you *somehow* manage to frequently escape this part of the process, our next step is to let Dumisani know that these acceptance letters are ready to go out in December. After that, we divide up the parent and student regional information sessions. You've done that portion before, so you know we go out in pairs for these and select our staff to ensure maximum student acceptance." She blew some stray hairs from her face, slightly agitated.

"You don't relish that part of the job, I know. It's more up my alley."

"I know it's a necessity—that for the sake of the Earth, we need these students. But I don't like the manipulation involved. I don't like the subterfuge."

Reese rubbed his hands together enthusiastically. "Good that I have no problem with it; I love manipulation and subterfuge." He winked. "As you said, it's for the greater good, lovey. We might as well embrace the task."

She wearily pushed a few curls behind her ear and sighed. "It's our differences that make us stronger, isn't that the saying? Anyway, after that staff pairing is complete, we walk the grounds and make sure everything in disrepair gets fixed. It seems as if we have a great deal of time before next August when we get our new students, but we really don't. There's a lot to be done."

Reese glanced at the handwritten acceptance letters on the table once more; he understood the pretentious tone had a purpose. He still didn't have to like it, however. He motioned for Alegria to follow him to the dining room. They exited the building and breathed in the cool air, musky from the smell of fallen leaves, freshly harvested pumpkins, and fall crops. Alegria turned around and gave the main building of their Virginia school a quick glance.

How many years had she spent teaching and walking into and around this building? She gave the edifice an initial scrutiny, beginning the process of assessing its needs. It seemed to be in fine shape, but weak nooks and crannies always needed reinforcement. It looked vaguely similar to the Wren building, the oldest building at the College of William and Mary. It was also built between 1695 and 1700, but was finished months earlier than the Wren.

The Wren was thought to be the oldest building in continuous use in the United States. In reality, the main building for the College of Geological Evolution (affectionately shortened to the College of GeoEvolution), was slightly older. This fact was little known and appropriately lost to the annals of history. It was widely believed that both buildings were designed by the notable British architect, mathematician, and scientist, Sir Christopher Wren.

Both edifices resembled each other in architectural style, yet the College of GeoEvolution had far fewer windows and none existed to illuminate the sub-ground floor.

The red clay bricks used for both buildings were similar in color and shape. A great number of the bricks used for the College of GeoEvolution, however, were enhanced; they contained certain necessary elements and additives that were expensive and time-consuming to curate and develop.

The final distinction between the two can be blamed on fire; the Wren building caught fire three times throughout its history and needed significant repairs each time.[64] The College of GeoEvolution, however, remained in its true and original form. This condition served to distance the College of GeoEvolution from its parent institution, a happenstance no Keeper had any intention of rectifying[65]

"Look, don't get me wrong," Reese stated around a mouthful of food, "this is bonzer[66] soup, but it could use a snag[67] or some chicken, ya know? It's fall! I'm hankering for a heartier meal."

---

[64]  It caught fire in 1705, 1859, and 1862

[65]  Although architects tried to honor the original design of the Wren building after each fire, cultural design influences played a hand in every subsequent repair; this accounts for the only vague resemblance between the two buildings

[66]  Bonzer – Australian slang for excellent

[67]  Snag – Australian slang for sausage

"Reese, you better watch what you say! You're lucky to get such a lovely meal. It warms our insides and is nourishing. Plus, get used to it," Alegria whispered, sotto voice. "There *is* a limit to what's on offer when we don't have students. Most of what we produce gets sold at the farmer's market or donated since there's barely anyone here to eat it."

Reese spooned another mouthful of soup. "Yum, yum…I am *so* grateful!"

The door to the kitchen opened with a forced *smack*. "Do I hear complaining?" yelled Ngai, the head chef. Brandishing a hand towel, he glowered at Reese.

Alegria had the sense to look contrite and Reese noticed. *What a suck-up.*

"You are a Neanderthal, Reese! This recipe comes from my friend, head Chef Patrick O'Connell, from the Inn at Little Washington, one of the premier restaurants in the country! Would you rather I feed you the three-year-old frozen haggis that fell behind the shelf no one has bothered to retrieve?"

Reese opened his mouth to reply and was halted by Ngai's wife Hattie, who joined the fray.

"Ngai, dear," she implored, speaking in her native Swedish tongue, "Kom tillbaka till köket."[68] She hesitated before adding in his native language, Vietnamese, "He needs your compassion; he has little class and no taste, after all. Give him time."

Ngai knotted his towel, clearly struggling with his wife's request. He gave a curt bow and left, adding, "Enjoy the rest of your day." When he reentered the kitchen, Alegria and Reese clearly heard, "That was the best I could do!"

"He needs to loosen up! It was just a cup of soup."

---

68    Kom tillbaka till köket – Swedish for come back to the kitchen

"He takes pride in his work, Reese. Also, he's sensitive. I'd suggest you don't criticize the menu in the future…unless you want to ensure I never eat off your plate again."

Reese looked aghast. "Point taken."

After lunch, they continued to wander the school grounds, taking notes on what needed to be reinforced or repaired. Out of the corner of her eye, Alegria spotted a figure bearing down upon them. "Ahh. I wondered when she would make her appearance. Gird your loins, Reese!"

"Reese and Alegria! Might I have a moment, please! I must speak with you," the woman trilled.

Xandra Topper approached the twosome and grinned. She radiated and projected her enthusiasm in a formal upper-class British accent. Xandra was Headmistress of the College of GeoEvolution and was responsible for the students and staff. She was also a conundrum for both as well… Xandra's prominent characteristic was her choice of dress, which perennially reflected her mercurial mood. Today she was wearing a midnight blue Victorian dress with black lace, complete with a flounce bustle.

"My word, Xandra, does that come complete with a corset?" Reese blurted.

Xandra looked heavenward and turned her attention to Alegria. "Is he still quite…"

"…a work in progress? Yes. We only take him out in public on Tuesdays and Sundays; he already insulted Ngai."

"Oh dear. And Ngai is a culinary diva. I wouldn't share Reese's plate in the near future if I were you. I'll smooth Ngai's feathers later and have a word with Hattie. Really, my dear boy," she added, eyeing Reese, "you are a handsome devil, but control your tongue. Learn not to speak every nattering thought you have in your head. And, no, I am not wearing a corset," she tutted. "The very notion!"

"So how do things look here for next term, Xandra?" Alegria interjected.

"Thankfully, we don't have too many repairs. And we have sold or donated record amounts of fresh vegetables and fruits, since we have no students. So far, we do not appear to be attracting attention from that. All items leave under our farm name, so that helps. Alesky and I found more fissures in the brick than we would like. We are repairing them, of course, and doubling up on the sensors.

"I cannot help feeling…unsettled and restless, however. Perhaps it is because of this off-term; we teasingly complain about the need for an occasional off-term. And when we get it, I regret my folly and crave normalcy. How is that for gratitude? Mayhap it is because off-terms are never planned; they just occur. It is in the hands of Mother Nature and other powers that be," she mused. Xandra made air quotes with both hands. "'All the world's a stage, and we are merely play-ers,' right? I'm paraphrasing our illustrious bard, of course; may that arse rest in peace." She quieted, seemingly lost in thought. "Anyway!" she suddenly continued, "on a positive note, I have decided the students will act *The Taming of the Shrew* this next term, with a more equitable ending. We have a far more equal ratio of boys to girls, I hear, so it will work perfectly! We haven't done that one in *ages!* Don't look so horrified, Reese, lest I recruit you as well!"

In addition to all of her responsibilities, which Xandra performed with style and acuity, she insisted on forcing all students to perform a Shakespeare play during spring term. Although many of the students were apprehensive, or at least less than enthusiastic with her militant rehearsals, a play both years was required for graduation.

After hearing complaints ad nauseam from staff and students alike, Dumisani once respectfully questioned the necessity of the rule. He was met with such an incensed and horrified Xandra, that he excused himself for a detoxing cup of green tea with honey and cleansing time with his talisman and crystal.

Xandra had informed him, in no uncertain terms, that she was shocked by his lack of sophistication if he didn't see the grave importance for acting classes and the play. In her expert opinion, all students needed the elocution, ability to portray a convincing character, and confidence that acting lessons provided. It was, quite simply, a matter of life and death—and why did he not see that?

Although discomposed by the messenger, Dumisani respected the message. Subsequently, Xandra was free to run her acting studio in perpetuity as she saw fit, eccentricities and all. The faculty at the College of GeoEvolution were intelligent folk and never questioned her method or her madness; students generally fell in line sooner or for some, unfortunately, later.

Reese quickly recovered from the multiple insults. Xandra's barbs never wounded him; she was sharp as a tack and ever capable. But in his opinion, she was definitely as nutty as a fruitcake.

Others shared his belief, but she was afforded every dignity and commanded respect from those circling her orbit. Since Reese was not amongst them, he didn't understand her or know her story. For the most part, her past was her secret, known to a select few.

That this bothered Reese was an understatement. It was in his very nature to ferret out the weaknesses and strengths of everyone he knew or pursued; truthfully, it was one of his greatest skills and what kept him alive. Reese figured that he'd understand her in time, as much as anyone could understand the eccentric woman.

"Xandra," Alegria queried, "is there anything you need us to check or fix? We'll all return before term begins, of course, but this is a good time to shore up."

"I haven't had time to clean and sort the room of electronic antiquities or the humanities classroom. I refuse to expose myself to the dust, detritus, and lingering sweat of adolescent frustration; I swear it oozes from the walls; it's absolutely pernicious!"

Suddenly, a loud commotion distracted them. Hattie's sous chef[69] came running toward them at top speed. "Come!" she wheezed, nearly breathless. "We been breached!"

"What happened?" Reese demanded.

"Alesky caught a Debilis near the gem room!" she panted. "We think it attached itself to the undercarriage of our market truck when it returned from donating the vegetables. It's the only way we think it could have entered." The clearly shaken sous chef leaned on Xandra as she caught her breath. "Alesky is fending it off."

"Stay with her, Xandra! There's safety in numbers." Alegria ordered. "We'll go."

Reese and Alegria ran toward the gem vault. "This couldn't have happened if we had students," Alegria panted. "There'd be too many people on campus."

---

[69]  Sous chef – French for under chief, the senior cook that serves under the head chef and manages supporting staff

"We're always more vulnerable when school isn't in session," Reese responded. "But this is different. We're prepared for the brief summer hiatus; this is more than a year with a skeletal staff. Bugger!"[70]

They reached the entrance of the main building nearest the gem vault. Alesky Petarov Todorov, the Bulgarian grounds manager, was trying to take away the intruder's knife, whose back was to the door. Caught unaware, he was only equipped with his whip chain. Although it was an effective tool, Alesky was clearly compromised. A red and yellow substance had been thrown into his eyes, hampering his vision.

Alegria eyed her angle of attack, braced her legs, and splayed her hands toward the ground. She pushed her inherent energy into the earth, directing it toward the interloper. The ground shook violently near him, throwing both the Debilis and Alesky off balance. Reese took advantage of the chaos and approached from behind. A sharp kick to the back of a knee sent the intruder to the ground. He pressed his foot into its neck, drew his whip cord, and tossed it to Alegria. "Tie his wrists, would you, love? That will be faster than channeling my Resogem[71] skill."

Alegria pulled back the creature's wrists and secured them with the cord. Being in its proximity, she was now certain it wasn't completely human anymore; she could smell its sulfuric aroma.

---

[70]  Bugger – Australian swear word

[71]  Resogem – Someone who is highly attuned to the negative energy stored in rocks, crystals, and certain elements of the periodic table. Those with this ability are skilled in harnessing this negative energy to disarm those who intend harm to others

Reese inspected Alesky's eyes. "Excellen' work, Alesky. But you need to head to the Wellness Center, mate. You got hit with a SS bomb."[72]

The sous chef and Xandra had caught up and approached Alesky, each offering an arm. "I shall fetch the Keeper authorities to dispense with the ruffian forthwith! The very nerve, trespassing onto *my* campus!" Xandra sniffed.

While Alegria sat on the creature, Reese bent down to confront him. To a Commoner, he looked like a normal human being, perhaps a little rough around the edges. A Keeper knew the difference, however. The sulfur stench, mostly undetectable to Commoners, was powerful to Keepers. Commoners would simply be embarrassed for the person or laugh, thinking the individual was passing gas and needed to visit a restroom. In addition, his face was gaunt and his eyes bloodshot—to the uninitiated, maybe a sleepless night or too much partying?

Upon Reese's approach, the thing hissed and sneered, revealing sharp canine teeth from irritated and receding gums, the telltale sign of a Debilis. "You've been mucking

---

[72]  SS bomb – An otherworldly dangerous concoction containing powdered selenium and sulfur, among other trace elements. Both cause intense eye and inhalation irritation. Large concentrations of selenium can cause the eyes to water and burn, alongside dizziness, fatigue, and potential bronchitis. Overexposure to sulfur can cause burning of the eyes and gut and potentially, diarrhea

around with Cinnabar,[73] haven't you? And frolicking through vaporous clouds of mercury[74], perhaps?"

He spat, "I don't answer to you, Keeper serf!"

Reese's grin was malevolent. "Oh, but you will, dero."[75] He pulled a gold coin from a thin lead[76] case kept hidden in a pocket facing his chest. Reese rolled the coin back and forth over his fingers effortlessly. A fun parlor trick, it almost never failed to entrance a creature, already compromised by element and mineral saturation. In a melodic voice, he asked, "Why did you invade our property?"

The creature shook his head. "It was the perfect opportunity," it answered, enthralled. "You have minimal staff, so I seized the opportunity. I have buyers desperate for the enhanced gems. I can make a fortune from even one of them. They are wonderful manipulation tools."

"Did you have support? Anyone else arrive with you?"

"Maaayyybeee," it hedged.

Alegria pressed her heel deeply into a scapula.[77]

The creature screeched. "One. Just one!"

"Did it make it onto the property?"

"I don't know."

Alegria sensed their surroundings, now keenly paying attention. "I don't believe it breached our perimeter."

---

73  Cinnabar-a reddish mineral often found near volcanic activity or hot springs. It contains oxidized mercury and becomes toxic under certain conditions/ "Cinnabar," http://mindat.org/gm/1052

74  "Mercury," https://www.mindat.org/gm/2647

75  Dero – Australian slang for a derelict

76  "Lead," https://www.mindat.org/gm/2358

77  Scapula – Shoulder blade

Xandra returned with two Keeper security guards. "Thank you both, I can take it from here; we'll follow standard criminal protocols. Reese, despite my misgivings, you did a magnificent job. I spoke to Ngai and he appreciates your efforts. He granted you a reprieve. Reese casually saluted Xandra before he and Alegria deliberately stepped over the creature as they left to pursue the other Debilis invader.

They quickly headed to a large vine covered wooden shed with a moss-covered roof. Alegria loved the whimsical sheds littered across campus. Although they were surrounded by nature, it was not always a symbiotic relationship. Weeds needed to be yanked and creeping ivy, although romantic, was a hazard to old, even hardy, brick.

Students learned to accept the occasional creepy-crawly walking around the historic hallways, but easing their entry via climbing vine was going too far. With the sheds, however, a happy medium existed. As long as the interior stayed dry, nature was allowed to encroach on their exterior frames. She gently opened the shed and they stepped inside. In this shed were several rows of various bikes, most vintage, but all in impeccable order.

"Fabek Sobalt isn't a bludger,[78] is he? He seems to have his hand in everythin' here, doesn't he?"

"Fabek would give his life for this place; this school is his salvation." Alegria narrowed her eyes and expounded sarcastically, "since you typically seem to be conveniently absent during this process, you do remember he's in charge of all the crops and maintains the property grounds, right? And Alesky manages the upkeep of all the buildings. He, Fabek, and Xandra are quite the team."

---

[78] Bludger – Australian slang for a lazy person

Reese graced her with a sour expression. He resisted the urge to quip that the word "team" had no 'i' in it, but he knew Xandra believed she was complete mistress of her domain.

Alegria continued. "We'll bike to the fields, touch base with Fabek and stay alert for any lingering interlopers, if our prisoner is telling the truth."

They grabbed bikes without fanfare and sped from the main campus toward the fields. Three-quarters of the property was covered with sustainable, organic farmland. The student and staff diet reflected what was seasonably fresh and available.

Behind the school and satellite buildings were manicured grounds and orchards, full of mature hazelnut, apple, and peach trees. Toward the edge of the property was a sentry of stately walnut trees, where the soil was drier; they were isolated by choice, for their strong roots crowded out nearly any other vegetation trying to take hold.

It took great effort for the sun's rays to penetrate the dense gnarled fabric of tree branches. The area was usually avoided by students until October and November, when it enjoyed two months of attention and spooky speculation.

The scent of unharvested vegetable crops was the first indication they were approaching the fields. There was a strong, but not repulsive smell of manure, mixed with trace notes of a metallic odor, that of iron and perhaps copper. When the multihued green fields appeared before them, they could see a horse, a dog, and a tall, thin man wearing a wide-brimmed straw hat in the distance.

"Ahh. Per usual, he has Phin and Blue Peter with him," Alegria chirped as they leaned the bikes against a nearby cherry tree and walked briskly toward the vegetable rows.

"They keep him company as he wanders around, eh? I don't often get out this way in the fields."

"I noticed. Your frequent absence during harvest time is well documented—always have something more pressing, right? If Fabek's in the field, he usually has both Blue Peter and Phin with him. Blue Peter helps with the sowing, crop hauling, and weed eating, although he's more of a companion, really. And Phin follows him everywhere, except when Fabek meets with Xandra…then he makes himself scarce. She thinks he stinks."

"Phin's a discriminating dog, with good judgement."

Alegria and Reese quickly selected a row of spinach to speed alongside as they headed toward Fabek. The veritable sea of spinach, cauliflower, broccoli, lettuce, squash, and sweet potato before them seemed endless. The soon-to-be-harvested vegetables would largely be sold or donated this season. When they drew closer, a faint, deep, and melodic voice drifted toward them on a passing breeze.

*"As I was going to Charring Cross, I saw a bad man upon*
*a black horse*
*'Twas Charles the First, in his finery, of course,*
*From there his life got very much worse,*
*His severed head 'n form left in a hearse."*

Reese snickered. "I see Fabek's musical repertoire hasn't expanded much." He sniffed the air with caution. "Do you think it's the fertilizer, by chance? Standing in animal crap almost every day can't be ideal. It's on the nose[79] out here."

Fabek noticed them and headed in their direction. He walked slowly and erect, conservative in his movements. Dark

---

[79]  On the nose – Australian slang for an awful smell

brown hair, visible under his hat brim, was loosely curled. His shirt and jeans were comfortably worn and faded, their colors nondescript.

"Alegria and Reese. You've come to my corner of the world." He spoke with a soft Polish accent, faded from years living away from his homeland. Alegria approached him with her characteristic enthusiastic embrace. He accepted it, but kept his hands by his sides. Although rooted to the ground like a tree, he could sway in a breeze, always flexible and prepared for unpredicted weather.

Alegria took in Fabek's steady, calming presence and smiled at the irony. His outward demeanor belied the turbulent thoughts Fabek battled inside. The school and his job were a refuge and both animal and plant thrived under his diligent care.

"Reese and I are helping out to make sure we're ready for next term. We wanted your perspective on where we stood," Alegria offered.

"The great lady always knows how to prepare." He raised his hands and referenced the surrounding fields. "You smell the iron and copper, can you not? We have bountiful crops; the soil is richer in minerals this year than in a very long time. They are all present in ideal quantities: the non-metals, metals, and boron, the metalloid."

Reese sensed that although his tone stayed constant, Fabek was either agitated or excited. He couldn't determine which emotion was present; the feeling was so imperceptible. Fabek continued. "I sift my hands through the soil and can sense the nitrogen, potassium,[80] and the chloride." He

---

[80]  "Potassium," https://www.mindat.org/element/Potassium

crouched and grabbed a fistful of dirt. "The manganese[81], molybdenum[82], calcium[83], phosphorus[84], and zinc[85] are all here in perfect harmonious increments."

Alegria also picked up on the small affectation. "What do you think it means, Fabek?"

"An apple a day is good and hay, but won't keep Josef Mengele[86] away," Fabek muttered, distracted.

Alegria laid a gentle hand on one of Fabek's arms and softly squeezed, her eyes telegraphing empathy. "Fabek?"

"The great lady always knows how to prepare," he repeated. He squinted at Reese and Alegria. "She is foretelling a distant storm; I don't yet have a sense of when; I will let you know when I do. Eat plenty of fruits and vegetables and reserve your strength."

A breeze changed direction and Fabek's head rose, suddenly alert. "Something is here."

Alegria and Reese also sensed the change in atmosphere, just as Phin began barking aggressively. Blue Peter, a noble chocolate Old Type Morgan, nickered and pawed the soil, clearly agitated.

---


[81]  "Manganese." *Wikipedia*, Wikimedia Foundation, 14 Mar. 2024, en.wikipedia.org/wiki/Manganese.

[82]  "Molybdenum." *Wikipedia*, Wikimedia Foundation, 13 Mar. 2024, en.wikipedia.org/wiki/Molybdenum,

[83]  "Calcium," https://mindat.org/element/Calcium

[84]  "Phosphorus." *Wikipedia*, Wikimedia Foundation, en.wikipedia. org/wiki/Phosphorus.

[85]  "Zinc," https://www.mindat.org/gm/4405

[86]  Josef Mengele – Called the "Angel of Death," Mengele was one of Hitler's chief research doctors at Auschwitz and conducted vile and sadistic experiments on Holocaust concentration camp victims

Reese turned in a circle. "Okay, that's not manure I smell—it's sulfur."

Reese began racing down the spinach field, following the odor. "You take another row, Alegria!"

About to follow suit, Alegria noticed Fabek placing his hands over his ears as he moaned. "Don't want to go back, won't go back. I'm safe, I'm safe." He repeated the mantra over and over as he swayed back and forth. Phin pressed against his side, bolstering him as he whimpered.

"You *are* safe, Fabek. Take Phin and Blue Peter back to the stable. We'll take care of this, I promise. We won't let them harm you or your fields." She felt guilty as she spoke the words. She hoped she could keep the promise. "When you get to the stable, send help, okay? We might need transportation."

Fabek nodded curtly and silently headed to the barn, focused on his task.

Alegria chose another row and moved quickly but methodically, constantly looking between rows for anything slithering among the fields. She acknowledged it was a clever place to hide. Although the telltale smell was obvious, it was masked by the overwhelming scent of vegetables and minerals. To a Commoner, the scent of minerals was subtle, but to a Keeper or Debilis, it was a cornucopia of aroma. The unpleasant odor of sulfur might be lost in the noisy bouquet.

Reese wildly gesticulated. "Alegria, over here!"

Alegria bolstered her satchel and ran. Glimpsing Reese's discovery, she admired his calm demeanor when she reached his side. One look had her whipping her head to the side, trying to avoid the visual and nasal assault. "I almost feel sorry for it."

The creature hardly resembled a human being anymore. It lay wriggling on the other side of the fence, its teeth gnashing on a metal fence rung. Blood oozed from its mouth and several teeth lay nearby. Its outstretched fist, wrapped around an open container, was inside the campus grounds.

Reese clicked his tongue. "The copper alloy fence did it in; it didn't have a chance. This Debilis clearly over-cycled."

The border around the campus was an amalgam of several metals, designed to be both strong and cleansing. Copper has many uses. It bolsters immunity, assists with digestion, is used in purifying drinking water, and decreases inflammation.

"Like a toddler, the Debilis used the fence for teething! Gnawing on it gave it relief, but also sealed its fate," Alegria mused.

"Yeah. The copper drew out the inflammation but also took its mineral and element accumulation. That's intertwined with its very life energy."

"It literally drained itself, like a battery. Could it have been on purpose, I wonder?"

"Look at the bugger, it was done for either way. It'll need to be euthanized and recycled since it's beyond our care. The Wellness Center can manage it."

"And the most humane thing, at any rate." Alegria inspected the open container in the creature's fist and fumed. "Never mind. Torch the thing! Before it began pacifying, it was attempting to poison the fields." Rivulets of mercury blended with a silvery white powder slowly seeped into the field soil, mixing with nearby plants. "That's an arsenic[87] and mercury amalgam. How do we tell Fabek? This whole area needs to be purified."

---

[87] "Arsenic," https://www.mindat.org/gm/357

"Thank goodness we caught it early! Will Fabek be all right?"

"He will after a rest. He's dealing with severe PTSD; that's why he's here. It's the only place where he can retain his sanity; you see how vulnerable he is."

"Yeah, and he's certainly eccentric, but I'd never discount him," Reese said quietly.

They headed back toward their bikes. "Fabek is almost always right. He's a veritable barometer for fair or fouling wind."

"We've got our work cut out for us. In less than a year, our new kids arrive."

Alegria, wearing a fierce expression, stated with confidence, "we grow stronger with every new generation. They bring their unique world perspective, enthusiasm, and curiosity with them. That youthful energy is vital—and in truth, we learn from them as well. The day we discount their contribution is the day we begin to fail the earth, and cede ground to pernicious evil."

"All right, fearsome lass. Our day isn't yet finished. We still have work to do."

Needing a palate cleanser after capturing all of the Debilis interlopers, they meandered to a door in the central building labeled with a lacquered wooden plaque when back on the main campus. The words LIBRARY OF INNOVATION was engraved in black. Below that, a rough wooden sign crudely nailed to the door read, GRAVEYARD OF LOST HOPES AND TECH in black sharpie. Reese rolled his eyes and snickered. "Gotta love our students' sense of humor."

"Shall we see in what state our former pupils left this room last term?" Alegria affected a terrified posture. "I really can't blame Xandra, you know. You can *feel* the despondency and incredulity; we'll have to cleanse it for sure."

"It's a bit perverse, but I love watchin' our sad brood come in here and get frustrated; it amuses me to no end."

Alegria turned and placed both hands on either side of his face. She leaned in and lightly kissed his forehead. "I *know* there is an empathetic soul somewhere in there, wee Reese. I'll see it someday soon, I hope."

Reese offered a crooked smile as he opened the door before them. "Hey, I *said* it was perverse. I get brownie points for that, right? The first step in healing is recognizing there's a problem, yeah?"

"Reese, love, you're such a child." She flicked on the room light. "Ahh—*what* did I tell you!"

All basement-level rooms at the school were windowless for security reasons. Some light came from a few well-placed electric wall sconces. The rest of the lights hung from the ceiling. A simple but elegant Tiffany bowl-style shade surrounded each light. In this room, each bowl shade was created from alternating translucent shavings of blue lace agate[88] and amber[89]. The blue lace agate was a striated stone, with alternating patterns of cornflower and sky blues and similar subtle hues in between.

The amber used in the lamp was either a translucent light caramel or a rich honey color. Although actually a fossilized tree resin and not a stone, amber contained powerful healing properties and was used around the world in many capacities. In one particular shade, upon closer inspection, three amber

---

[88]  "Blue Lace Agate," http://mindat.org/gm/699

[89]  "Amber," https://mindat.org/gm/188

panels entombed the bodies of four small insects, long-ago visitors ignorant of the hardening resin. No doubt, this was an Easter egg the craftsman found amusing. The room radiated a warm and calming glow that belied the total chaos littering every surface available.

The room was a haphazard tribute to the history of computer innovation. Long wooden tables set in a U formation held the original shells of various computers, from the earliest models to the most recent.[90] A large clear quartz bowl held dozens of cell phones. Littered among the desktop dinosaurs were motherboards of every size and style and various pieces of rare earths, as well as smaller bowls holding pieces of copper[91], silver[92], gold[93], platinum[94], palladium[95], and other elements.

The Smithsonian's National Museum of American History in nearby Washington, DC had a permanent exhibit dedicated to computer innovation. Their staff would never come calling, however, because each machine had been roughly opened, haphazardly pried apart, or even occasionally thrown, if the many dents in the walls were any indication.

---

[90] The tables contained a Tandy Color Computer 3, an Amstrad CPC 464, and a Sinclair ZX80. There were several Acorn Atoms, Commodore PETs, Apple IIs, and a few Radio Shack TRS 80s. On another table rested an Atari 800 XL and some Commodore 64s, as well as some Acer, Apple, and Microsoft laptops

[91] "Copper," http://mindat.org/gm/1209

[92] "Silver," http://mindat.org/gm/3664

[93] "Gold," http://mindat.org/gm/1720

[94] "Platinum," http://mindat.org/gm/3236

[95] "Palladium," www.mindat.org/gm/3067

When the machines first began arriving with students back in the late 1970s, every pupil expected they would operate as intended. They soon learned, however, that each device was most useful as either a paperweight or in a science experiment testing Newton's Laws of Motion. Faculty opened the machines to discuss the many uses of elements and natural materials in modern technology. More importantly, they always ceased to work when brought onto the school's grounds.[96]

Teachers offered tired explanations and exhausting clarifications, but some students were determined to be the first to create a working model of any kind. In over four decades, the success rate was zero and all was currently covered in a light layer of dust.

Alegria sneezed as Reese turned on a battered boom box complete with a CD player. Since it used simpler mechanisms than those installed in computers and cell phones, it appeared to work. Pushing play emitted a loud Sir Mix-a-Lot singing "Baby Got Back."

He shut it off after a few lines. "Ahh. The *Mack Daddy* album. I remember that one. I think I know the two stooges responsible for this." He ejected and held up the CD.

"No doubt. Are they enjoying their time in Cambridge?"

"As far as I hear. As long as it includes torturing each other and their professors."

"Hmm. Better there than here," Alegria mused. "Okay, let's get to work, shall we?" From her bag, she produced two large air pressure canisters.

"Yes! I get the fun job!" Reese swaggered as he grabbed both canisters, blew on each, and pretended to holster

---

[96] A few frustrated students occasionally took intact devices off campus to try to make them work, but this was always futile.

them. He began blowing the dust off the computers and cell phones. Alegria produced two palm-sized felt pouches from her satchel. One contained two large handfuls of rough-cut diamonds and the other, jet stones[97]. She warmed the diamonds between her palms for a few minutes, and placed them on the quartz tray located under a small fan. After switching it on, she turned her attention to the jet stones. These were gently laid inside small wells hidden inside each ceiling lamp.

"Reese, I know you can tell me the origin story of each of these gems and rocks and can sense if any contain traumatic energy." She smiled slyly. "With a glance, no doubt you also know the current legal and black-market value of each. However, can you tell me why they are utilized in this room?"

Reese wandered over to the Tiffany lamp and gently tapped on a piece of blue lace agate. "I sensed when we met this morning that your hidden bags of jet and diamonds were conflict free... albeit a little stressed, and contain trauma-free healing energy. Let's not bother with street value. Considering their age and provenance, I'm fairly certain they are priceless; those gems could tell both a lifetime of stories and stories of lifetimes."

"That was beautifully put, Reese, and correct. Each of Sahila's gems, minerals, and stones are like children...she's connected to each one and is aware of their individual temperaments, so to speak. Our Tiffany-style lamps were not actually created by Tiffany Studios. Before they were made, however, our lighting designer *did* meet with Clara Driscoll herself. Although she only worked with glass—quartz sand, if you will—she did advise our craftsman on how to best create the lamps. In our library, we still have the actual letters

---

97  "Jet," http://mindat.org/gm/9355

between our designer and Ms. Driscoll, should you care to take a look." She raised an eyebrow when Reese looked at her askance.

Alegria sighed. "To each their own. The blue lace agate helps relieve stress and depression among other troubling emotions. Amber helps filter out all of these feelings from the body. You can imagine the frustration of our students as they work in this room. To have a clear understanding of the properties of a technology and how it fits in the world and then realizing that it doesn't work for you can be vexing. The diamonds, in this capacity, help with respiration. You can see how dusty it is in here. They will also help clear and purify the air. Jet soaks up the depression and angst Xandra referred to."

"So, the room will be ready for business next fall?"

"Sahila will return to inspect my work and see if it passes muster. I don't have her ability, but we are just performing maintenance and I'm qualified to do that."

While Alegria completed the air purification, Reese dusted the floor, but yowled about it like a disgruntled tom cat. He was mollified only when Alegria promised to secure three or four of Chef's famous brownies. Reese's smile was back in place as he visualized the delicious dark chocolate gooeyness as they walked toward the humanities classroom. In this room, the students learned history, the great works of literature, geography, and psychology.

Alegria put her hand reverently on a door in front of her. "This is one of my favorite rooms; although I often teach science, I love leading the literature classes."

"Ahh…'the unpleasant, acrid smell of burned poetry,'" Reese quoted dryly.

Alegria rolled her eyes. "I'm pleased, at least, that you are somewhat learned. Do you enjoy P.G. Woodhouse?"

Reese shrugged. "You know how some bits tend to stick with you; it was a long time ago," he stated cryptically.

They entered the room labeled HUMANITIES AND PSYCHOLOGY and Alegria took a leisurely turn about the room. Waist-high wooden bookshelves bordered three-quarters of the room, except at the front, where the teacher and their desk resided. This room was two floors above the basement and had thin rectangular windows along one side.

The clear, almost cerulean sky brightened the room and highlighted its main feature. Along three of the walls hung a line of oil portraits of great writers of literature and historical figures in dignified poses. A cavernous fireplace complete with wood logs and the requisite family of house spiders sat at the back of the room.

Traditional wooden desks with attached chairs sat in rows facing the front. They were of rich mahogany and polished to a fine patina from both use and abuse. Inside each desk, either carved or written in pen, was a "gift" or two left by previous inhabitants: advice for future students to help them excel, camaraderie unaffected by time or fraternity. *This is a safe distance from Jürgen,* read one. *Memorize some Neruda and get an "A" from Alegria,* was another.

The room had a warm and safe presence, partly due to the Tiffany-style ceiling lamps. The inverted bowls were covered with thin pieces of grass green aventurine stone[98]. Aventurine boosted confidence in social groups, encouraging students to speak their opinions freely. Connected to the bottom of every aventurine panel was a row of small platinum rings linked to one another around the lamp shade... Each one

---

[98] "Aventurine," http://mindat.org/gm/436

contained variant hues of peacock or sea-blue azurite[99] which stimulated clear thinking.

Reese and Alegria perused the lifelike renditions of Edgar Allen Poe, C.S. Lewis, Maya Angelou, Mark Twain, Jane Austen, Mary Shelley, Pablo Neruda, Oscar Wilde, F. Scott Fitzgerald, and others. Alegria halted along the back wall. She gesticulated toward one portrait. "Not again! Seriously, who thinks this is amusing?"

Reese saw a yellow sticky note attached to the frame of Christopher Marlowe. His framed neighbor to the left was William Shakespeare. The sticky note displayed an arrow pointing to Shakespeare and the phrase, *I'm with half-wit.*

Alegria spoke in rapid-fire Spanish as she dragged over a desk and stood on it to remove the note. Although he couldn't completely follow, Reese got the gist about not respecting one of humanity's greatest linguistic heroes.

"Think our new students will be ready to learn the truth about William Shakespeare?"

"Probably not. I imagine it will be a surprise; but he was a great man and a dear friend to us Keepers; he deserves better. ¡Dios Mio!" She blew hair from her face. "This was done to irritate me and it always works. Some pushed buttons cannot be ignored."

Once the room was put to rights the two rewarded themselves with the aforementioned brownies and ate them outside.

Reese glanced at the sky and mused, "I wonder what our future students are doin' right now? They exist on the same earth an' are just mindin' their own business, clueless about how their life will completely change—if we can convince them to join us, that is."

---

[99] "Azurite," http://mindat.org/gm/447

He turned to Alegria. "Hey, let's grab tucker in town. I need updates from our Guardian retailers and see if any new perverse elements have taken root since last term."

Chapter 7 – N

Kailua-Kona, Hawaii, United States

# EARLY OCTOBER

The four football players jogged along the campus pathway toward the high school locker room and field. Yet again, their math teacher dismissed them slightly later than expected. This was her one small act of rebellion against the athletic department, and she was clever: She excused the students only one minute late, never late enough to draw attention to herself and thus be exposed to blame and ridicule. In her mind, the coach would perennially conclude the young men were dragging their feet, distracted by something or other—they *were* high school boys, after all. Math was the far more important pursuit and that extra minute she exacted from her students was time well spent. She went to all the games and cheered like all of the other teachers. She took comfort, however, in knowing that *her* students were better prepared for the real world, one that, statistically speaking, would not include playing professional sports.

"Why does Ms. McKee always delay us, every time? You'd think Coach would believe us when we tell him what time she lets us go!"

"Nah, it's all about politics, Nate! My bet is that he does know and he ignores it, 'cause bad grades means no playing ball; he needs her on his good side… 'Sides, we get there on time almost every day."

"I'm tired of getting my regular clothes sweaty from running to the field; my mom makes me do my own laundry now. Hey, Kame, what the hell are you doin' man?"

"I'm just grabbing a cool rock I spotted. I'll be quick!"

"Kame, we're gonna be late, man! Coach will give us extra laps. Can't you grab it on the way back?"

KameKona Johnson, known by his friends as Kame, ran off the sidewalk into the nearby lava field, disrupting a gaggle of Nene geese resting a few yards away. They honked in great displeasure, as if to say, *Sweaty human boy, don't you know we're the rarest geese in the world? Get off our lava patch and leave us alone—unless you have food, of course. Then we're cool!*

The students knew feeding the Nene was illegal; that didn't always stop the occasional soft-hearted student, however. At present, the smell of adolescent male sweat was a deterrent.

Lava rock was plentiful on the Big Island, also called the Island of Hawaii, and was created over time by the eruptions of multiple volcanoes. KameKona loved rocks; he had as long as he could remember. For whatever reason, probably because he lived in the state of Hawaii, he loved volcanic rock the most.

Across the eight major Hawaiian islands were multiple types of volcanic rock and KameKona had samples of nearly all of them. He bent down to pick up a particular sample of 'A'a lava[100] he'd spotted from the sidewalk; he was drawn to it somehow.

---

[100] A'h lava – Pronounced *ah ah.*

He couldn't explain why this particular rock sample mattered. KameKona was used to occurrences like this—it was as if the rock spoke to him, which he knew was ridiculous. He was relieved his friends accepted his particular hobby and rarely teased him about it. He did feel a tinge of guilt grabbing the sample now; after practice he could find that specific piece unerringly, since it had caught his attention. He shouldn't risk all of them being late to football; that was a crappy thing to do.

He turned back and ran to his teammates. In truth, he'd only delayed them by another few seconds. "All right, I got it. Sorry! I'll take the heat from Coach if we're late."

KameKona looked down at the sample. His fingers grazed over the prickly pumice texture of the rock. It was sharp and could easily lacerate human flesh if not handled carefully. To him, however, it was a comfortable presence, sitting in the palm of his hand. If he squeezed hard enough, he knew the rock would feel like it was melting and becoming viscous, almost like holding loose chocolate chips for too long.

He smiled and his teeth were bright white against his smooth mocha complexion. KameKona was half native Hawaiian. His father, a black US Navy officer, had been stationed at Naval Base Pearl Harbor years ago. After injuring himself at work, he wound up falling in love with his civilian nurse, a native Hawaiian from the Big Island. They eventually married and made Hawaii their home after he was medically relieved and continued his job as a civilian contractor. KameKona and his two younger sisters were lucky to have spent the majority of their upbringing on Oahu.

"What's so big a deal about this rock, Kame, that it's worth risking Coach's wrath?" questioned Nate.

"Plus," joked Alex, their other teammate, "It's illegal to take that stuff home, you know. School staff might get mad or worse, Lady Pele[101] may come after you, man! She'd be worse than any pissed off school administrator!"

"Nah. I never take my samples off the islands, dude. They're all at home."

While still jogging along, Jake held out his hand. "Toss it over, Kame."

KameKona wiped the sweat off his face and smoothed back his shoulder-length hair, gathered in a small ponytail today. Although he would never admit it if pressed, the solid, almost six-foot tall football player with large, soulful brown eyes let his little sisters routinely mess with his hair. While they were frequently annoying, he could deny them almost nothing—he partly kept it long for them, truth told. KameKona lobbed the rock in Jake's direction, knowing that as the team's main receiver, Jake would catch it with ease.

Jake did catch it—and screamed. He stopped running, dropped the sample, and clutched his hand to his chest, confused. "Crap! That rock cut my hand! Dude, it really frickin' hurts!"

Nate and the others raced over to him.

"Jake, man. Let me see it. Coach is going to be pissed! How can you play this Friday with an injured hand?" Nate queried.

Jake outstretched his palm for his friends to examine.

"Jake…Jake, your hand isn't cut, dude. It's burned! You have a second-degree burn! What the hell?"

All eyes shifted to KameKona. He held out his own palms and looked at them, perplexed. He wasn't burned from holding the rock! They felt pleasantly warm when he picked

---

101  Pele – The Hawaiian goddess of fire and volcanoes

up an outdoor sample and the warming sensation increased only slightly after the rock sat in hand for a few minutes.

"Nate," he whispered. "Man, I am so sorry! I don't know what happened. We have to get you to a doctor immediately!"

Cradling his hand again, Jake grimaced at KameKona. "It must be your Hawaiian blood, KameKona Johnson," he quipped, putting on a brave face, despite the intense pain. "You probably have lava in your blood. Do me a favor and let Coach know what happened, will ya? Second stringer's up for Friday's game, I guess."

The group turned around and raced back to school. Before KameKona broke out in a full run, he glanced back at his friends and at his palms. He had no idea what had just happened and it freaked him out. And then he ran, knowing he owed it to Jake to explain to Coach. The 'A'a sample lay on the sidewalk, forgotten, to be scrutinized only by the Nene. Unbeknownst to KameKona, heat waves rose from the rock and drifted into the mild breeze.

## Sen Signet Hotel, Outram, Singapore

Lydia Rieman always admired the jewelry box when at Ming's home. She never tired of its intricate woodcarving decorations, size, and endless cubbyholes, nooks, and crannies. She snickered; it seemed like she was describing an English muffin, not a massive five-foot freestanding home for jewelry.

Her cell phone buzzed with yet another text message, no doubt intended for her best friend and the owner of the box and the jewelry within it. No matter how new the model was, Ming's cell phone was never reliable.

Lydia wiggled her phone in the air, disheartened. "Are you going to answer any of these, Ming? Don't you find it annoying? Are you flattered or do you feel…I don't know…used?"

Ming shrugged. "I don't mind all that much, since I have friends I can trust. If not for you, Jen, and Lina, I imagine I'd get irritated."

"What is with these students? Can't they just go to a school dance and worry about their outfit, shoes, and dating, like normal hormone-crazed teenagers?" Lydia felt justified in her censorious comments. She was the editor-in-chief of their school newspaper and remained unimpressed with the superficial columns most students favored.

Ming remained neutral, however, and was therefore better liked. And when she did experience justified anger for a slight against a friend or an unreasonable grade, she was just as quick to be empathetic and reconsider. Maybe Lydia shouldn't be so quick to judge? She was willing to listen and reason. Lydia appreciated that this was an admirable trait. It also made Ming a frequent target for being taken advantage of and used by other classmates. This evening was no exception.

Lydia cocked an eyebrow. "Want to see who's texting you?"

"Sure, go ahead and read them. I doubt I'll know three-quarters of those students."

"I'm sure you won't. Okay, here's one from Petcha. Isn't she the girl with the black hair and the 'barely there' skirts, from New York? The one who gets sent home twice a month for questionable wardrobe choices? I won't ask her to contribute to the style column, believe me."

Lydia snorted. "She writes: 'Hey Ming, excited to see you at the dance tonight. I'm trying to get John Lee's attention, but he doesn't seem to know I exist. Is there something I can borrow that might help me? I promise to take care of it and return it tonight.' *What a peach!*

"Ah, here's one from Addie Smith," Lydia continued. "She's that shy freshman. You know, the one who tried out for the school musical and choked. Poor kid, I felt for her. She wrote: 'Dear Ming, I'm sorry to bother you. I'm uncomfortable even texting you, but I definitely didn't want to call and disturb you. I want to try to go to this dance, but I'm terrified. My parents are forcing me to go and say I need to start socializing more. I'd rather stay at home with some friends. I'm sorry to ask, but if you can spare it and I'm really careful, do you have something I can borrow that can help make me braver tonight?' Man, I sorta feel like you're a fairy godmother and the granter of wishes. I know how she feels—I was terrified to go to our freshman dance."

Ming gave Lydia a dubious glance. "Have you really ever felt the way Addie does? You're the most self-assured person I know."

"Then I guess my fake bravado is really effective! I practice it for my future in New York or LA; I'm going to need it if I plan to be a senior magazine editor someday."

The girls looked over a couple more texts and found that other than the one from sweet Addie, all the others had to do with looking hot, not getting sweaty feet, or trying to get the attention and interest of someone else.

"Ming, I was sick for the last dance. Did you get these text messages as well?"

"Pretty much. Most of the time I honestly don't take the time to look at them, since my phone is often wonky. And bonus, I can truthfully say that I didn't get a chance to read them before I left for the dance."

Ming knew her mercurial popularity had less to do with her and more to do with the contents of her jewelry box. Although she enjoyed the occasional bangle and bauble, her interest was not really in jewelry itself, but in the precious and semi-precious stones. Ever since she could remember, she loved their colors and the individual faint vibrations they emanated; it almost seemed as if each one was speaking to her and telling her their individual story. She loved the feel of them: first cool and after she held them, comfortably warm and giving.

She also loved the way they made her feel. Ming always wore a necklace or a bracelet with a single gemstone or a few carefully selected stones. If she was feeling sad, tired, anxious, or out of sorts, she always felt better while wearing one or several of her gemstones; she couldn't fully describe the sensation. Ming felt grounded and content; she felt safe.

Ming was fortunate to have a wealthy and indulgent father. He certainly tried his best, especially after her mother had died when she was young. Her dad appreciated her hobby and gave her a healthy allowance to add stones to her collection.

Ming never abused her father's trust and was very selective; she knew that few daughters were encouraged to cultivate expensive hobbies such as hers. He never had to worry, however, for when she went to auctions or gemstone curators, all researching and purchasing was under the watchful eye of Ming's maternal grandmother, an astute businesswoman.

Her jewelry box contained single stones, most of a modest size. Each stone was subtly cut, keeping to the natural shape as much as possible, and was attached to a small "o" ring at both ends made of either silver, gold, or platinum. This way, Ming could select her chain length and attach whichever stones she wanted to wear on the chain, bracelet, or necklace. She could create any number of combinations and designs.

Once dressed, Lydia looked out the window to the city far below. She had to admit that living on the penthouse floor of a five-star hotel had many advantages; she always had fun spending time with Ming at her "house."

She turned to find Ming selecting a stone from her collection. She put the dark orange gem on a gold chain. Crimson red veining ran all along the surface of the gem, like a fertilized bird egg about to crack.

Ming smiled. "Let's give this to Addie to wear tonight, okay? Can you text her and tell her to meet us in front of the school in forty-five minutes? I guess *technically,* I didn't see the other texts myself, right?"

"Yes, I will text Addie and absolutely, you did *not* see the other texts; that's the total truth. What is that stone? It's beautiful!"

"It's carnelian.[102] It comes in various shades, from almost black to orange. The ancient Romans used it in jewelry for signet rings, and as a seal on documents—the stone doesn't stick to wax, you see. Other ancient cultures used it as well. But most importantly, many believe it helps strengthen confidence and courage."

A gentle knock-on Ming's bedroom door interrupted further conversation.

"Come in," Ming projected over her shoulder.

The door slowly opened, revealing a small and fragile-looking elderly woman. Her rheumy eyes had a weary look to them. She smiled at the two young ladies. "Good evening, Lydia. We're pleased that you can attend the dance with Ming tonight. I'm sorry to interrupt, Ming, but I require a moment of your time."

---

[102] "Carnelian," https://www.mindat.org/gm/9333

Lydia pointed a thumb toward the door. "Ming, I'll wait for you downstairs in the main hall, okay?" She briefly kissed Meihui Sen's[103] cheek as she left. "Hello, Ms. Sen. It's always great to see you."

"Ming, my dear. I'm sorry to trouble you at this time; I know that you are ready to leave now to see your friends."

"Grandmother, you never delay me. What do you want to talk about?"

Ming's grandmother sighed. "I'm bothered that I need your assistance sooner than I expected. I'm finding that I'm more tired than usual and I ache in my joints. Your father still needs my guidance as much as ever. I think one of his senior executives is making mischief, more so than normal; I told your father that I don't trust him, but he is naïve and wants to believe the best of his colleagues. I must guide him to hire better senior leaders and it frustrates me that my advanced age makes this work challenging." She shuffled in her slippers to a chaise lounge in Ming's room.

"Let me look, Grandmother."

Ming reached down toward her grandmother's neck and gently pulled on the necklace she always wore. Tugging on the chain revealed three small platinum rings. Attached to the end of each was a gemstone in the shape of an elongated teardrop; the stones were warm, almost hot to the touch, and were shades paler in color than their natural vibrant hues. One was red jasper, a deep, blood red stone shot with small brown patches of various minerals; the second was green jade[104] in a gentle pastel shade; and the third was black tourmaline, a slick and shiny opaque stone.

---

[103] Meihui Sen – Pronounced *Mee-Wee*

[104] "Green jade," https://www.mindat.org/gm/10403

"Grandmother! You should have come to me sooner! No wonder you feel tired! These poor stones are working overtime and have lost most of their energy!" She picked up the red jasper first, cupped it between her palms, and gently rubbed it. She felt the stone lightly pulse, fainter than its normal resonance and began to concentrate.

Ming took a deep breath and calmed her mind. She deliberately thought about events and objects that relaxed her, gave her peace, and made her feel safe. She brought forth images of her gem shopping outings with her grandmother, amusing times with her good friends, and as always, birds. She loved watching birds soar and lift on an invisible breeze; she could watch them for hours. Ming began to visibly relax.

The power of red jasper was harnessed for several uses. The pervading wisdom, for thousands of years, was that it was excellent for aiding in relaxation and healing, among other properties. It was for this purpose that Ming's grandmother wore it now.

While Ming worked, Meihui sighed and took a deep breath. "I love that visual of the birds, Ming. I'd have picked a Pacific golden plover—they are so graceful when they fly."

When the Jaspar began to pulse more strongly, Ming opened her palm and gave it a glance. The stone was three times as vibrant and had regained its former luster.

Ming got up, went to her bedside nightstand, and picked up the bottle of water she kept there. She walked back to her grandmother and took a long, quenching sip. Cool water in her mouth, she grasped the jade teardrop in both hands and slowly allowed the water to slip down her throat. She closed her eyes and focused on the trail of water as it flowed through her system. She traced its path toward her stomach and imagined it flowing into her kidneys and beyond. She thought of the marvel of the human body and what a beautiful machine it was. For thousands of years, many societies believed that jade helped in the healing of the kidneys and the immune system.

When she opened her eyes, she blew gently on the jade, giving it the protection of slight condensation. It had regained a shine and was now only lightly warm, matching her grandmother's internal temperature.

Ming rested the last stone inside her left palm and caressed it between the first joint of her index and middle fingers. She placed her right hand on top of the stone, matching the fit with the left.

She rolled the stone up and down the fingers from first knuckle to second, ending at the tips of the fingers and back down again. In sequence, she visualized opening jars with her hands, palming and throwing a basketball, turning knobs on doors, and walking up stairs.

Meihui groaned. "I ache all over. Getting old is not my choice, Ming. Thank you, my child; it's starting to ease."

Black Tourmaline[105] was thought to help repair inflammation and arthritis. When the stone felt cooler, she stopped and glanced at it. She took a deep calming breath and blew out the exhalation three times and stood up.

"All right, Grandmother. You should feel more energetic and the pain should dissipate in a few minutes. Don't wait so long the next time, okay?"

Her grandmother swiveled on the chaise lounge and stood. The rheumy look in her eyes had disappeared and she felt cleaner and almost youthful. She kissed Ming on the forehead. "You need not worry about me, dear granddaughter. Go have a good time at your party. Your dress complements

---

[105] https://www.mindat.org/photo-194631.html

your expressive black eyes and ebony hair." She walked over to the front door and at the last minute, turned back to face Ming again. She spoke in Tamil, a language spoken in Singapore that Ming did not really understand. *"If not for you, I would have died ten years ago."*

"Grandmother, you know I don't speak Tamil. What did you say?"

"Oh, merely that you are a blessing to me and to your father."

Ming smiled as she left. She was very close to her grandmother and loved this special time with her, especially since she lost her mom at the tender age of five in an unusual traffic accident. Although she was now eighty-five, Meihui Sen was still the family's quiet matriarch. She often recommended to Ming which stones to purchase, while simultaneously offering sage business advice to her son-in-law.

Ming's mother was born and raised in Singapore and had met Ming's father, a successful British businessman, when he went to Singapore to pursue the expansion of his growing hotel chain. He was now the owner of the Sen Signet hotels, a luxury worldwide hotel chain, named after his wife's maiden name.

Ming grabbed her sweater, picked up the necklace meant for Addie, and met Lydia near the front door of the penthouse.

Lydia looked at the necklace in Ming's palm. "Do you think that will really work, Ming?"

Ming reflected as she held the stone in her palm, warming it and looked up at Lydia. "I don't know why, but I really believe that it will. But only if Addie believes in it herself."

## Bradford, West Yorkshire, England

From the living room, they had a great view of Aedan Colston mowing the lawn. Every two weeks he stopped by after his homework was finished, as long as it wasn't raining, which happened often. If it rained, he spent hours on the weekend catching up. He was saving for university and worked for several neighbors in the area. Although many thought the work was tedious, Aedan found it rather relaxing and peaceful; he got to be outside, messing around in the dirt and grass, and away from his four younger sisters and brothers. The sun was out today and shone on his blond hair, giving his fair complexion a good dose of Vitamin D.

"Libby, dear. Are you happy with young Colston cutting the lawn for you? I was thinking of asking him round to give it a go, if I can convince Robert, mind you. You know he pulled his back out last month mowing it himself, the foolish man. He said to me, he said, 'Beatrice, I'm retired now. I can't ask that young man to help, I have all the time in the world now to do it me'self.'"

"Don't worry, Bea," Libby's husband Peter chimed in. "I'll talk to him in a few days when the time's right."

Beatrice smiled, grateful. Peter was also retired and a few years older than Robert, so Beatrice figured he had more sense. Surely, he could convince Robert?

Libby continued absently, "Aedan's father works at Morrison's, right? He's in management there? I imagine, even with a corporate job at that grocery chain, the extra money will help pay for university? They've got five children to put through school, if each has the mind."

"Bea, Peter will convince him. Don't give it another thought. Is he enjoying visiting your son in London this week? Oh, look. Aedan stopped working. I imagine he'll use his detector now."

Beatrice peered more closely through the window at him. "Is that a metal detector he's using?"

"Aye. Sure is. I think he fancies himself a budding archaeologist. He uses it to look for Roman artifacts and such; we encourage him, you know. Most of his clients do. If he gets the job done, we don't mind," Peter said absently.

Beatrice looked slightly alarmed. "But what if he finds something valuable? Surely, you'd want whatever he finds?"

"Ha! If he found a silver penny from Eric the Bloodaxe or some other Viking artifact, yes, those are quite valuable. If it's anything Roman, however, he can have it... Good riddance, in fact!"

Beatrice looked unconvinced and slightly horrified at the prospect of giving a valuable cache to a teenage boy.

"Libby, do you remember our trip to *Antiques Roadshow* a few years ago?"

"Ah, as if I could forget!" she laughed. "Peter was mucking about in the yard one day and you found a small grouping of Roman coins, right?" she glanced at Peter for confirmation. "Anyway, he ran into the house as excited as a young boy who discovered buried treasure. He looked online and found that *Antiques Roadshow*, one of our favorites, would be at the Royal Hall in Harrogate. You know the Royal Hall, right, in the north?"

Peter waved his arms enthusiastically. "I was so excited. We booked a hotel and decided to take the train, to make a whole weekend out of it. Convinced myself I had quite the find! Well, the evaluators were very polite, I will admit. But by the time we paid for the hotel, food, and the train, we had spent a bundle and had nothing to show for it. Turned out those coins were worth five quid if they were worth anything! I gave the coins to the grandkids," he laughed. "Young Aedan can take whatever he finds."

Beatrice peered into her tea, as if swishing the remaining leaves would reveal an important sign. "I wonder if Roger and I should get a detector too and look for anything Viking in the lawn? Did you say Eric the Bloody Hat?"

Aedan Colton was oblivious to the conversation inside the nearby house. He moved the defunct metal detector along a perfunctory mental grid. He loved this time to himself; he considered it his reward for finishing the job. He mowed the lawns, because the money would help pay for university and assist his parents, who worked hard enough.

In truth, however, he really did it to gain access to the lawns and practice without interruption. The detector had a pitiful signal. On its best day, it might pick up a discarded aluminum[106] can. He picked it up for five pounds at a garage sale and it had never worked properly from the start. Aedan didn't need it, however. It was only a prop, there to discourage questions and lend credibility.

He gripped the detector in his left hand while his right rested by his side, or so it appeared to any passerby. His right palm was actually parallel to the ground, sensing the earth. He moved along at a calm pace, daydreaming about fishing with his father the next day: a whole day alone with his father, relaxing and talking and doing nothing.

He stopped when he tasted the vague trace of iron in his mouth and his hand felt a magnetic pulsing. He bent to the ground and covered his hand over the small portion of earth where he detected the sensation. He clawed and pulled at the ground gently, and after a few moments, he felt the

---

[106] "Aluminum," https://www.mindat.org/gm/107

hard shape rise through the surface, almost like a water vole pushing its way through the soil. Aedan grinned.

"Aha, got you!"

The object was exposed to the sun—a chunk of iron, just as he thought. It was probably a piece of broken farming equipment.

He stood up to brush the earth from his find and examine the broken piece of forgotten iron. He thought about catching perch with his father while he palmed the iron clump; he remembered the meaningful conversations he and his father had over the years while fishing.

Absently, he handled the iron with both hands. It grew warm and he could naturally sense the weakness in the metal, the fractured corners and sides. Aedan pushed and smoothed, molded and twisted, almost like handling clay. The sample became hotter to the touch as he manipulated the iron, but Aedan barely registered this change.

When he realized his task was finished, the clump of iron radiated intense heat. He sucked in a great gulp of air and blew onto the iron, instantly cooling it, as if he had dunked it in cool water. Coils of steam rose from the now structured object in his hands. He raised an eyebrow, bewildered.

"Why am I surprised you are a fish?" Nestled in his hands was a sculpture of a perch, complete with molded scales. Aedan examined his work more critically. "Really got the tail right this time." He shoved it in his pocket before he moved on; he had one more house to mow.

His mother would add the piece to her collection. He realized that it should probably be the last. She now had quite a menagerie on the shelf in their living room and was developing a theory.

"I want to talk to your history teacher, Aedan. I think we might have discovered something important!" she'd say distractedly before another child commanded her attention. "What if these sculptures are ancient Roman, love? Maybe it's something to do with this region of the country? I think it's more than a coincidence that these beautifully sculpted animals are buried all over the countryside in these parts; how lucky your device keeps finding them! I must ask him next parent tea time."

### DAYTON, OHIO, UNITED STATES

She felt closer to her dad sitting at his workbench. Over the years, they spent countless hours there together, tinkering and creating. She would assist him when something around the house needed fixing and came to his defense when her mom needed convincing that a new tool was essential for the job, even when it wasn't. When she had a school project, her dad would sit beside her and talk her through it if she needed help. The workbench had a smorgasbord of tools, saws, and soldering irons. When her dad's engineering job was eliminated a year ago, he took to consulting; it paid well, but now he traveled for months at a time and flew all over the world.

Tessa Horton missed him fiercely and hadn't seen him in over two months. She tried to channel him now while she worked. In front of her was her brother's valuable watch. She had exposed its interior to see why it was malfunctioning and her suspicions were correct. She wanted to do something exceptional for her older brother. If she was totally honest, she could admit that she'd been a complete pain in the ass the last few months. Guilt was the main impetus for fixing it.

Although confident in her abilities, Tessa was filled with anxiety. She was perfectly capable of replacing the watch's crystal oscillator. But this watch belonged to her brother, Scott, given to him by their dad before he left on his first consulting trip. If something went wrong, her brother would freak out and consider sororicide; she didn't think he could take anymore. It was bad enough that he had taken a leave of absence from college for a year to be closer to home… *because of her.*

Scott constantly reminded her that he was away from his friends and was taking classes at the nearby community college…*because of her.* Their mom was amazing and sup-portive, but she had ultimately requested that Scott come home because her nursing job's unpredictable hours made it difficult to keep tabs…*on her.* It made her angry and ashamed that she brought this kind of stress upon her family. Did they think she wanted to cause trouble at school? She didn't do anything on purpose—not much, anyway. She could behave impulsively and was easily distracted sometimes. It seemed as if she had to work twice as hard as other kids to do well in school, and it wasn't fair.

Sitting at a school desk for hours at a time didn't suit her. No one really understood her, except for her dad. They would video chat and email back and forth, but she never troubled him with her innermost thoughts and feelings; that was always done in front of the workbench, their sanctuary. Tinkering with her hands calmed her and was where she excelled…it was her happy place.

So, the watch was a peace offering for Scott. She put on her headphones to listen to her favorite eclectic mix. The

Dominoes crooned "Sixty Minute Man."[107] She adjusted the light, squinted to hold her jewel's eye lope in her right eye, and wiggled her fingers.

Tessa whispered, "And the crowd immediately stopped talking. They knew the stakes were high. Could Tessa Horton successfully operate without incident?"

"I don't know, Bill, Tessa's in a tough situation here. She correctly identified the problem. The watch's crystal oscillator has malfunctioned. Do you know why that might have happened?"

"I'm not sure, Jill, but word is that Tessa's dad is an engineer. Experts tell me that in his work environment, the watch was exposed to vibrations and electrical pulses, both of which could cause the quartz crystal oscillator to fail. The quartz also might have minute fissures or microscopic pieces missing, which can also cause the oscillator to fail."

"Why that's fascinating, Bill. I thought you only knew about golf."

"I'm a man of many talents, Jill. Now, let's go back to watching Tessa repair this watch."

Tessa snorted at her antics as she removed the old and clearly damaged crystal oscillator and replaced it with the new one. She mumbled, "I don't think you are oriented in quite the best way."

She knew that inside its metal casing, the crystal was sandwiched by what looked like a metal tuning fork. She pinched her thumb and finger together and slowly slid them above the oscillator, as if pulling a needle and thread through fabric.

---

107 "Sixty Minute Man" released in 1951 by Billy Ward and the Dominoes (Federal Records).

Although it was encased, she could sense the sliver of crystal inside pulling away from its tuning fork-like housing. She circled the connected thumb and forefinger until the crystal was better oriented to fit in its home. Backtracking her finger gestures, the crystal slid firmly back in place, secure. The only other way to perform this adjustment was to open the oscillator housing, which would destroy it.

When she sensed that the crystal's best facets were ideally situated, she used the smallest soldering iron she had to secure the new crystal oscillator in place. Into the watch also went a new battery, whose job was to send a current of electricity to a microchip in the timepiece.

She was able to order good quality parts from their favorite appliance store, owned by a retired engineer. The microchip "told" the crystal to vibrate thousands of times a second. Those vibrations were sent back to the microchip and ultimately after several other steps, made the hands on the watch change position in precise movements, which accurately displayed the time for people wearing the watch.

Tessa could design her own crystal oscillator, but it would be similar to what she purchased and she didn't want to risk the extra time. Tessa replaced the cover on the watch and made sure it worked accurately.

"And the crowd is going wild, Jill! They can't believe she did it! And in such a short amount of time too!"

Tessa couldn't believe she actually had sweat running down her forehead. She wiped it off with her sleeve. In retrospect, it made sense. She valued her life and if she messed up the watch, her brother might have ended it.

She took off the earphones, turned around, and screamed. Scott stood behind her, hands on hips, incensed. She could always tell, because his eyebrows practically meet together as he scrunched his forehead. *This process is almost fascinating to watch… when his temper isn't directed at me.*

"What the hell are you doing, Tessa?" he bellowed.

"Hi! I wasn't expecting you. Thought you were in class."

"Are you kidding me right now? Why are *you* home early?"

"We had a half day field trip, remember? We finished early."

"Tessa, don't make me ask again!"

His furrowed eyebrows were almost touching, Tessa observed, kind of like Bert's from *Sesame Street*. Except Scott's showed more expressive anger, if that was possible.

She squeaked, "I was trying to do something nice for you, big brother?" Tessa was now less confident in her choice of good deed.

"Anytime you are down here without Dad, Tessa, I'm *filled* with dread and exhaustion. Nothing good ever seems to come of it! Quit stalling!"

The comment really stung, especially since his statement held little truth. The majority of the time, what she designed was helpful. Literally, there were less than a handful of instances when her tinkering resulted in school suspensions. The idiots she unleashed her creations upon were deserving of her wrath; if someone hurt one of her friends, they felt her justice.

"I fixed Dad's watch for you, so it works again. See?" She held out the watch for him. "The crystal oscillator was broken and I replaced it for you. You can wear it again."

Scott stared at his watch in Tessa's outstretched hand. "I can't believe you had the gall to touch this! How dare you even contemplate touching it, let alone messing with it!" He grabbed the watch from her and looked carefully at it, noticing that it indeed now told the correct time. He sighed heavily. "Tessa, don't you understand? You should have asked me before you went into my room and took Dad's watch. When are you going to get it?"

"Scott, if I asked you to do this, you would have said no; you wouldn't have trusted me to do a good job. It still wouldn't work and it would stay that way! You never have faith in me."

"Tessa, have you given me a reason to trust you? Thanks for the watch fix, but please don't mess with my stuff again. You're lucky your fix worked." He headed back upstairs, heavy footed.

Tessa blew the hair out of her face. To most observers, she looked like Tinker Bell's trouble- making cousin. She was petite and pixie-like, with a short crop of auburn hair, which often hung low over her right eye. She preferred to keep it short and simple to style, with a slight punk look. Her eyes were a keen and intelligent deep green.

"It wasn't luck," she murmured to herself as she turned off the lights and unplugged the soldering iron. When she calmed down, she would bike to Dya's store at the mall. She needed to be where she was appreciated.

SHAOGUAN, GUANGDONG PROVINCE, CHINA

Tú Chen pulled up the lapels of his jacket, so his exposed neck wouldn't be easily accessible to the constant gentle rain. Though it was a bit annoying, he welcomed the raised goose bumps. The cooling air energized him and helped him to focus. It was pointless to be aggravated by the incessant sprinkling anyhow; it was the monsoon season in China's Guangdong Province, after all. He should be grateful it wasn't pouring.

While he trudged along the well-worn path up the familiar hill, he tried to ignore the emotional discomfort he felt whenever he thought of his "big lie." His parents were older when they had him and while both were coping fairly well, their age and his mother's health issues took a toll. They worked at one of the white tea companies in the area.

His parents hung all of their hopes and future dreams on Tú, their miracle boy, born against all odds. They loved and trusted him and thought he was working at a national park after school to earn money for college and to help the family. They were so proud their son had found a job at the Zhangye Danxia National Geological Park—what a fortuitous opportunity for a boy interested in geology! Tú wished he *actually* worked there and probably *could* be hired. His English was excellent and he could easily speak with many of the tourists who visited the park every year.[108]

If he worked there, however, he would never make the amount of money he earned now. This was his big lie. He could never tell his parents what he was really doing, and he was ashamed. Also, his work was technically illegal and potentially dangerous. "But I'm not hurting anyone and it really helps a mā and a bà."[109] They made many sacrifices for him and now it was his turn; they only had him for support and, for that reason, he took the risk.

Tú's job was tailor-made for him. He was a quiet and observant child. He valued stillness and, in that silence, Tú felt and heard the pull of the earth, while those around him remained oblivious. He reached the summit of the hill and placed his hands in his pockets.

---

[108] The Zhangye Danxia National Geographic Park spans more than one province and attracts thousands of visitors a year

[109] A mā and a bà – Cantonese for mom and dad (informal)

Tú shuffled around and kicked loose rocks, behaving like a teenager finished with school, releasing tension on a late afternoon hike. He looked around for other people, but was not surprised to find himself alone. Not many chose to climb this hill at dusk, which was why he chose this location.

He took a deep, cleansing breath and exposed his face to the mist. His hands came free and he closed his eyes to hyper-focus on what he felt—to be exact, the *magnetic force* he felt.

If he had to describe the initial sensation, he would say it was a little like playing that American game Duck, Duck, Goose with your eyes closed; when a person snuck up close to you and you sensed the invasion into your personal space, almost a knowing—like a tingle. A person could get a similar feeling closing their eyes and slowly bringing their hand to their forehead, without touching. When concentrating, sensing the magnetic pull of a particular small rock, an element, felt like that to him.

Tú took off his glasses and put them in a pocket; although nearsighted, he didn't need them for this task. He blinked away the rain from his large black eyes and knew his bangs were now a conduit for rain to drip into his face.

He scanned the summit once again before beginning. His feet were solid on the ground and he opened his mind to the pull of the elements, specifically *rare earths*.

"I know you are here; I feel you." He moved his arms in slight arcs, sensing where the elements were hiding among the earth and rocks. Each rare earth had an individual magnetic signature and he started with Neodymium[110], used in cell phones for the vibrating function and in industrial turbines

---

[110] "Neodymium." *Wikipedia*, Wikimedia Foundation, en.wikipedia.org/wiki/Neodymium.

and drills; it was always a popular one with his buyer. The tiny pieces of gray element rose up from the ground and drifted gently toward Tú. The individual magnetic matter grouped together in small clusters and began to swirl around him. With a looping gesture from his left index finger, he gathered them into a small pile next to him. Although he could make another pass for more, he wanted to focus on getting some erbium[111] and some dysprosium today, different rare earths becoming more in demand around the world.

Tú took a heavy-duty plastic bag from his backpack and directed the neodymium to collect inside. Once there, he closed the bag and stuffed it into his backpack. If caught up on the hill, he wanted the least amount of evidence visible.

Once, after he collected a rare earth into a pile, a young couple had arrived at the top, hoping for a quiet place to talk. Tú had to quickly spread out the pile and say "watch for the big anthill" to the couple, before walking off. He missed out on a good deal of money that day.

With the first element collected, he focused on the second. Erbium was very popular in major Chinese cities and around the world. It was used for making pink glass, assisted with pulses of light in fiber optic cables, dental surgery, and treating the skin.

When he was in the mood and had extra time, for fun, he altered the flow of the element he sought. Today was one of those days. The erbium rare earth bits swirled around in a small tornado pattern and began to cluster together, taking shape. All the pieces landed on the ground and formed a small gray prairie dog. He remembered seeing a video about them when he chose the creature for an essay in middle school about mammals.

---

[111] "Erbium," https://www.mindat.org/element/Erbium

Tú focused and wiggled his fingers to manipulate the grouped elements into making the prairie dog take a few careful steps and stand on its hind legs, tentatively sniffing the air. He felt free of stress and at peace when he had this time to play. Tú laughed to himself as he made the prairie dog zigzag around the ground a few times, as if looking for an alternative hole to its underground labyrinth.

He sighed, remembering his purpose, and motioned for his little friend to jump into a second plastic bag. When inside, he splayed his right palm and the loose pieces of erbium fell into the same bag. He checked his watch to see how long he had been on the hill.

The last rare earth, dysprosium, was used in building electric vehicles, a hot commodity in this day and age. He quickly did a sweep with both arms to seek out his quarry. Once he recognized the magnetic signature he wanted, he pulled it up from the dirt and dumped it into a manageable pile, bagged it, and shoved it in his pack.

Certain that he was finished for the day, he began walking down the hill, ever casual. With little work, he could easily be his employer's largest supplier. Tú was acutely attuned to how the organization functioned, however, and he gave them just enough to keep them interested, but not enough to draw excessive attention to himself. Tú didn't want to transition from appreciated employee to coerced laborer, threatened with dire consequences.

Tú knew his ability wasn't normal, but who could he talk with, who could understand and would not abuse him for his strange quirk? No, he was alone and adrift, as he had felt for most of his life. He once again promised himself that when he was older, when he was stronger, he would come back and try to reduce the rare earth black market. He headed toward home, with a quick stop to drop off his bounty and collect his earnings.

MONTREUIL, SEINE-SAINT-DENIS, PARIS

Madame Monmarte paced before the grass field in front of her, impatient, and pondered her dilemma. The staccato beat of her brand-new Manolo Blahnik shoes on the pavement kept in time with the pace of her thoughts. The exceptional assistant headmistress of an exclusive international college preparatory school was ever flexible…*however,* she was growing rapidly irritated with the ward before her.

The recent phone call from the teen's mother ran in her head like a ticker tape: *"You must ensure that Élise attends every etiquette session! This is very important for her future and for our family and is to be taken very seriously! We have hired the best guidance coaches and expect you and your staff to see that she is prepared!"*

Madame Monmarte wanted to scream back at the calculating Madame Peters-Comtois, "It is your responsibility to force your peevish daughter to become a debutante when she detests the very notion! This is a family issue and not a concern of this school!" She tossed her hair and screeched in French one more time at the young lady wandering ever further away on the wet sports field. "Élise Peters-Comtois! Tu dois venir immédiatement à ta classe de l'étiquette! Tu es déjà cinq minutes de retard!"[112]

Madame Monmarte knew that shouting was a worthless endeavor; Élise began losing her hearing at a young age and was now completely deaf. Yelling helped release some of her

---

[112] French for you must immediately come to your etiquette class! You are already five minutes late!

frustration, however... She tentatively took a step onto the grass and felt her heel sink into the recently watered field. "Merde!" she cursed as she pulled the defiled shoe out of the muck and risked a glance.

This was not worth the destruction of her beautiful and exceedingly expensive shoes. She might not be wealthy, as were most of the families at her school, but she had her pride. Madame Peters-Comtois would just have to take a flying leap! Getting her petulant daughter to her training was not her responsibility. She turned on her heels and marched off to let the pricey tutor know that Élise refused to attend the lesson; she would not take the blame for it.

Farther up the field, Élise felt the departure of the vain Madame Monmarte and smiled. Thank goodness she was gone; another worthless class avoided. Her mother would text her within the hour on her unreliable cell phone and silently yell, threaten, and shame her, but she was not to be deterred.

Her mother insisted she follow in her sister's footsteps and become an international debutante. After secondary school (at the preferred university, of course), Élise was expected to date and marry a suitable gentleman of wealth in order to elevate her family's—correction, her *mother's*—social status.

Her mother was forever chasing her dream to elevate the family name back into the wealthy international aristocracy. It was an age-old story, and so trite it was embarrassing to even contemplate. Her mother had descended from an aristocratic French family that had long since lost its wealth. She managed to marry a successful American international lawyer who indulged her dream to return the family to its rightful status. Her father thought her mother's single-minded purpose was charming and harmless. If successful, the elevation could only help his career …so, why fight it?

Élise breathed in the fresh air and closed her eyes. Her sneakers were dangling from either hand as she dug her feet into the rich earth and felt the vibrations and life within. This is where she felt most at peace. Unbeknownst to Madame Monmarte, Élise could feel the headmistress's every stomp and stride.

Even before she began to grow deaf, she was sensitive to vibrations and motions in the earth; she felt grounded to it, a part of the earth. When she actually lost all hearing, her family, especially her mother, was devastated. Élise was now compromised, they thought. She was disabled and would slowly find her world growing smaller.

To Élise, the reverse actually happened—it was as if her hearing interfered with and disturbed her growing relationship with the earth; it opened itself to her immeasurably. She still didn't understand why, but she believed there was a purpose to her new life and she figured that she would understand it someday.

Her easy acceptance of her situation was the source of another deep-rooted conflict within her family. She was an ideal candidate for a cochlear implant. With a simple procedure and some training, she could greatly benefit from the implant and begin to hear again. Her mother was determined to get Élise the surgery.

Although her mother vehemently denied it, Élise thought it was because she was embarrassed by her affected speech. How could she further her mother's ambitions if she was a walking and talking advertisement of a debutante with a disability? All imperfections must be corrected; Ms. Peters-Comtois bore two children and one of them was broken.

Élise knew she was a constant disappointment to her mother. But she instinctively knew that if she went through with the surgery, something vital would be lost. The constant noise of a busy world was distracting to her and unimportant. If she chose the implants, Élise was afraid she would lose her intimate connection to the Earth among the white noise; she was perfect as she was, even an improved version of herself.

Almost daily, she wandered out onto the fields. This morning, when she woke up, she immediately noticed a subtle shifting in the Earth, a tiny rumbling of a future quake. When she was little and she felt the sensation, she would ask the people around her, "Did you feel that?" Her question was dismissed, and it was thought that whatever she felt was related to her "disability."

She never asked anymore. Élise knew she was different, even beyond the deaf community. It never bothered her, this awareness of the Earth's movements. Over time, as she studied plate tectonics and earthquakes, she understood that she was sensing the shifting of the Earth.

She would feel a movement and search for validation on the European–Mediterranean Seismological Centre[113] website several hours later, or on the site closest to her location if she was traveling. Élise realized that she could predict, with uncanny accuracy, when an earthquake or movement would occur a couple of hours before the latest man-made sensors did.

She grew to believe this ability, this "knowing," was a special bond between her and Mother Nature, almost like a secret. She figured she could someday use it to help people and it gave her life meaning.

---

[113] European–Mediterranean Seismological Centre site (EMSC): https://www.emsc-csem.org/#2

Behind her, she felt a dancing beat of feet, in a rhythm she and her best friend Mellie had created. Élise turned around and smiled, her blue eyes danced with victory; her blond, almost white waist-length hair lifted in the breeze.

Mellie looked at Élise, making sure she could see her face before she spoke. "I just saw Madame Monmarte stomping up to the main building, her face mimicking one of the gargoyles on the roof! She was sooo pissed! You're gonna be the reason she breaks the heel off one of those prized Manolo Blahnik shoes someday and she'll try to send your parents the bill!"

Élise smirked and rolled her eyes after reading Mellie's lips. "Perhaps she'll finally understand. I feel a bit guilty that I've put her between a rock and a hard place. She has to deal with my mother after all; it will be my present to her when I graduate and leave!" Élise both spoke and signed.

"Why are you out here, Élise? We have tennis practice in less than an hour!"

"I know. I just needed to have a break and breathe some fresh air, you know?" *Plus,* she thought, *I had a feeling that a slight earthquake was going to occur near Paris and I got here just in time to feel it.* At Mellie's concerned face, Élise quickly added, "Okay. Let's go. I'm fine!" The quake, she realized, was nothing alarming, just a baby one, probably unnoticeable to most people. She wanted to get back and check the EMSC site to see if she was right.

Mellie raised her right eyebrow. "Neat dance party trick we have there, weirdo. Let's go grab a quick snack—notice I said *quick,* Élise. I don't want to be dragged into your nefarious schemes to piss off your parents further by being late to tennis too!" She grumbled, "I can't get anything lower than a B in that class!"

## Riga, Latvia

Nikolai Ivanova assessed the customer shrewdly as he entered the Bezgalība Jewelry House. He could tell from the customer's apprehensive glances around the store that he was a seller. Perhaps he had fallen on hard times and needed to relieve himself of some family heirlooms. He felt a pang of empathy for these individuals, but it was business, and he didn't know the reason for the family's downfall. He was an upstanding and trusted member of the community and wanted to keep it that way; he steered clear of people who involved themselves in unsavory business.

"Labdien, ser? Kā es varu jums palīdzēt?"[114]

The gentleman reached into his pocket and produced a linen-wrapped bundle and placed it upon the glass counter. "Good afternoon, Mr. …Ivanova?"

"Yes. I am Mr. Ivanova. How may I assist you today?"

"I unfortunately need to sell some of my mother's jewelry. She has passed and I am the beneficiary."

"I see. We are terribly sorry for your loss. We are, however, always interested in acquiring heirlooms and curious pieces. Might I see the jewelry you brought? I can let you know if the pieces are ones we can accept."

"Certainly." He carefully unwrapped the jewelry bundle. Inside were three items: a beautiful emerald and diamond necklace set in silver, a pair of earrings to match, and a gold ring with an oval ruby.[115] Mr. Ivanova immediately saw that they were quality pieces; the stones were clear and cut beautifully with no visible fractures.

---

[114] Labdien, ser? Kā es varu jums palīdzēt? – Latvian for good afternoon, sir? How may I help you?

[115] "Ruby," https://www.mindat.org/gm/3473

He would need his eye lope for a closer examination, obviously, and he would have to verify the gold and silver content as well as the durability of the links. Pending those tests, however, the pieces were worth acquiring and could fetch a nice price.

"Can you give me the history of these pieces, please?" He could see that his question had taken the man by surprise.

"They have been in the family for several generations; they belonged to my mother's mother. I would give them to my wife, but our bills have become too great. My mother had a lengthy illness. My wife understands and she would rather be free from debt, as would I."

"I see. What a tragic story," Mr. Ivanova stated, and he clearly did. To his mind, this was a troublemaker and a thief—and not a very good one at that, considering the unimaginative story and his furtive nature.

Mr. Ivanova craned his neck and called to the back room, "Demyan, can you please come meet our customer?"

"Of course, Uncle Nikolai." Demyan Ivanova entered and faced the customer. He held out his hand in greeting and expected the man would shake his, as was the custom around the world. "I'm Demyan Ivanova. How are you today?"

The man looked with confusion at the tall and gangly brown-haired youth with the impenetrable hazel eyes...

Perceiving the man's discomfort, Mr. Ivanova added, "Forgive me, sir. I am training my nephew in the business. He assists me on weekends; he's coming along quite nicely. Demyan, please take a look at the beautiful pieces this gentleman wishes to sell."

Demyan glanced at the man and knew instantly not to trust him; something about him was disingenuous.

He couldn't put his finger on what it was, but the gems would know.

He picked up the necklace and held it in his hands. He let the weight of the emeralds balance in his palm and settle naturally; he held them, sensing their story. Demyan looked at the piece and felt the negative energy stored in the stones seep into his skin. This necklace had touched violence and death…and it was recent, not ages old, like a carbon-dated archaeological find.

He placed the necklace onto the linen and picked up the ring. He would normally set it in his palm and cover his hands over it for the best sensation, but for show and subterfuge, he examined it closely in between his fingers and turned the ring, so the ruby caught the light.

It was a beautiful stone, clearly over two carats, and flawless—but again, it had touched recent evil. He took a deep, cleansing breath and rubbed the ruby lightly, staring at the man. He saw him visibly squirm under the scrutiny.

"These are lovely pieces, Mr. …?" he began.

"Mr. Illavich. I thank you. Yes, your uncle said the same. Is there a possible value you can give me?" He glanced at the senior Mr. Ivanova.

"Mr. Illavich," Demyan continued, keeping steady eye contact, "how might you account for the recent blood on the emeralds?"

"Blood? What blood? Why would there be blood on the necklace? What are you accusing me of?" He grabbed at the necklace roughly and used both hands to examine the piece.

"The ring has it as well, Mr. Illavich. It's quite obvious, actually." He ceased massaging the ruby and held it in his palm, offering it for examination.

The emerald necklace negligently clutched in his fist, the man snatched the ring and examined it as well, his agitation palpable. He blinked several times, as if suddenly forgetting his train of thought.

In a calm, distracted daze, he looked at Demyan and said, "That cold bitch wouldn't give them to me, so, I killed her." It was only a brief moment of confusion before the man came back to himself, oblivious to his confession.

He grabbed for the cloth, snagging up the earrings within it, and shoving the other jewelry inside. He began shouting at both employees.

"This is outrageous and I refuse to be treated with such disrespect! What kind of fiendish child are you? You show no empathy for a devastated man!" He whirled on his heels and left in a rush.

"Did you get a good photo of his face, Uncle?"

"Indeed, I did, Demyan. I forwarded it to Lieutenant Kuznecova. The tip might even be worth some of those chocolate dumplings we love!" He furrowed his brow. "Demyan, how did you know those jewels were violently stolen?"

Demyan answered cryptically. "Oh, you know, Uncle. It was just a hunch, based on what he told us and how he carried himself. I think he was feeling guilty and couldn't hold back the truth."

"But you said there was blood on the stones! I didn't see any."

"No, Uncle. You are right, there was no blood. Again, I sensed, just as you did, that he got the jewelry in a less than honest way; I baited him on purpose, like Mr. Kuznecova does with criminals."

"Hmm. Good work, Demyan. I'll have to tell your father what you did today, for us and for the poor woman he killed, perhaps even his own mother! I bet your father will be proud—or at least he should be!"

Demyan was appreciative of his uncle's efforts, but he knew his father wouldn't be pleased. Working in his brother's jewelry store, no matter how profitable it was, was a waste of time in his father's mind. Demyan was foolish in his father's opinion; he should be working in the steel industry or construction management, both booming in Riga. The two might never see eye to eye. He sighed and took his lunch break, knowing Lieutenant Kuznecova would arrive soon, ready to take their statements.

## Chapter 8 – O

### Macao Special Administrative Region of the People's Republic of China

# OCTOBER

Rua-Jian Chu entered the penthouse of the luxurious apartment building centrally located in Macau. Although modern in design, it was artfully and harmoniously decorated with furniture and artifacts from different eras in Asian history. It resembled a museum exhibition, but visitors were made to feel welcome and comfortable. The valuable items were priceless, but were practical and meant to be used. Rua-Jian approached the man dressed in chic, yet casual clothing sitting at a dining table set for tea. Rua-Jian bowed before him in respect and waited to be acknowledged.

"Rua-Jian Chu, your appearance suits you. Do you feel restored and rested?"

"Your Majesty, I feel much restored and thank you for the concern."

"Come sit and have some tea. We have many items to discuss."

An unobtrusive staff member dressed plainly in black approached and poured for Rua-Jian.

"Thank you, Your Majesty."

"It's been a while since you've been to my home. Macau has undergone some change, has it not?"

Rua-Jian smiled in agreement. Although the peninsula of Macau belonged to China, it was independent and fell under the "one country, two systems" policy. It relied on Mainland China for military protection, but had its own political, legal, immigration, currency, customs, and security systems. Tourists flocked to Macau to enjoy its many splendors.

"I can monitor all that goes on in this world from here; Macau is very connected. We spoke several years ago about our predictions, where we thought humanity was headed."

Rua-Jian nodded. This topic was not a surprise.

"I am sorry to see that our foresight was correct. Do you agree or do you have a different perspective?"

"You are correct in your beliefs, Your Majesty. I find that humanity is struggling more than ever to properly maintain the Earth."

"I am not impressed by the future of space exploration and colonization. Those who choose to begin again on a foreign planet may do so at will. Earth is where humanity began, however. It needs to be valued and sustained and I do not see this occurring worldwide with any consistency or organization."

His Majesty stood and walked to an antique mahogany apothecary cabinet. It contained over one hundred wooden drawers, each affixed with a platinum handle. He opened a drawer and took out an item in a small glass jar, then placed it on top of the cabinet.

He absently wiggled the fingers of his right hand, passing them in front of the many drawers, as if he had trouble choosing a pastry at a café. He selected another drawer and another, placing the contents next to the first item on top of the cabinet. Although the drawers were not labeled, he seemed to know what each contained. After repeating this task five times, he carried the glass jars over to the table and placed them near Rua-Jian. He sat again and smoothed down his thin black mustache.

"As you know, Rua-Jian, it used to be that people knew where their tools and precious belongings came from. They were cognizant of how they were crafted and were aware of what it *took* to create them. They often designed and assembled these items themselves. People lived this way for thousands and thousands of years.

"Today, however, people often don't know how their belongings are made. There is little or no awareness that ingredients from the Earth itself are inside their object, medicine, and even food. Whatever they buy or collect comes in disposable packaging, also made from our Earth's bounty, and then thrown away with little regard. It is an epidemic of ignorance and apathetic neglect."

He selected a glass jar seemingly at random and opened it. He turned it over and dumped the contents into his waiting palm. The objects were bluish-gray in color, rectangularly shaped, and seemed heavy. His Majesty carefully stacked the little items on the table on top of one another.

"Lead[116] is an element humanity has used for millennia, mostly to its detriment. Today, it's used in batteries and bullets and in the making of glass and ceramics." He pushed the pieces of lead into the table, smashing them into one another and creating a kind of lead paste. He looked at Rua-Jian while he gathered a small amount and began rolling it along the table, like a clay snake.

---

[116] "Lead," https://www.mindat.org/gm/2358

"Queen Elizabeth I, that brilliant and fearless great lady of Britain, contracted smallpox as many did during that era." He continued to work the lead while he spoke. "Embarrassed by her pockmarked face, she began using Venetian Ceruse on her face, also called Spirit of Saturn; it was a popular makeup during that time. She mixed it with either water or egg white and placed it on her face daily to hide her scars. It was made from lead. She was a paranoid monarch, convinced there were constant plots to overthrow her. She was correct, of course. However, throughout her reign, it sadly never occurred to her that she was her own worst enemy; unbeknownst to her, she slowly poisoned herself. She died from blood poisoning from the lead makeup."

He selected a thin, hollow wooden reed from a table decoration and easily slid the lead inside its middle. "Nature has bounty to give, but it must be used properly and respectfully. Lead has important uses, but it can harm as much as it helps when used thoughtlessly."

He handed the reed to Rua-Jian, who raised his brow at the gift. "Yes, it's a pencil, Rua-Jian. I wouldn't lick the tip if I were you, however. Not that it will matter much. It was the lead coating on the outside of the pencil that was dangerous, not so much the lead itself. That coating idiocy ended in the United States in 1978, thank goodness. Graphite is a much better choice for a pencil anyway."

His Majesty took the next glass jar and opened the lid. Tiny white crystals flowed into his palm. He laid the crystals on the table and moved his fingers gently above them. They began slowly swirling around the table and rose slightly into the air.

"Salt, a compound of sodium[117] and chloride, as you know. We have used it since the dawn of early man; it's one of humanity's most essential substances. Nearly all animals, including us, require amounts of it to live, and it transforms our food into gourmet delicacies, often with only a pinch. We also use it in glass and soap manufacturing. Of course, most people are unaware of this.

"A long time ago, it was so valuable a substance that soldiers were even paid with it. Did you know that *sal* is Latin for salt? The French word *solde* means pay or salary. It is how the phrase 'worth his salt' came into being.[118] I love the etymology of words, don't you?" he said absentmindedly. "Anyway, salt has helped people survive since the first early man took a risk and ate it. Over time, we discovered many other benefits from it. Ever eat a pickled vegetable or a cured meat?" The salt crystals ceased their movement and rested on the table in an intricate snowflake pattern. His Majesty looked down at his work. "Ah, one of my best attempts, I do believe."

The next glass jar he selected appeared to be empty. His Majesty reached into his pocket and removed a shiny green item that he placed on the table. Next, he warmed the bottle with his hands, rolling it back and forth.

His Majesty grabbed the green object in one hand and removed the stopper to the vial with the other. He placed the opening of the green object over the vial's head. Rua-Jian watched as the object expanded, revealing itself to be a balloon. It grew quickly in size and when at its capacity, His Majesty grabbed the base of the balloon and handed it to Rua-Jian.

---

[117] "Halite," https://www.mindat.org/gm/1804

[118] Kurlansky, Mark. *Salt: A World History*. Penguin Books, 2002.

"Tie this off, will you," he asked Rua-Jian. Rua-Jian obeyed and felt like a fool, holding a child's toy. "Obviously, it's helium, correct?"

"Of course," Rua-Jian replied.

"It's one of the most plentiful gases in the universe. Here on Earth, we utilize it for balloons, air conditioning, and to cool off magnets in MRI machines, among other uses. Unbeknownst to most people, it is not limitless on Earth. It's a component of natural gas and is a by-product of decaying rocks—people can't make it! And because it is so light, once released, it disappears forever from our reach into the greater atmosphere. The universe has the collection of our helium folly. It's greedily and ignorantly wasted on party balloons. Only when the supply runs low, when it's harder to find on Earth, will humanity take notice and panic." He waved his hands in the air, pantomiming a panicking person. "Such is the nature of humanity, a typical and pathetic response." He took the balloon and let it sail toward the ceiling.

His Majesty grabbed the second to last container with determination. After opening the lid, he dumped the contents onto the table, now littered with the detritus of the other displayed materials. The dark silver nuggets skidded across the table and came to rest haphazardly.

His Majesty stood up and with a repeated flick of a forefinger hovering over the table, brought the nuggets into a collected heap. He grabbed some in both hands, squeezed the pieces, and blew onto them with a steady stream of moist, burning hot air.

"Play with this," he ordered Rua-Jian.

Palms open, Rua-Jian accepted some of the flowing molten metal. While working the other pieces of metal with his hands, His Majesty began again, slightly agitated.

"Aluminum is used everywhere. It's in refrigerators and in cars. Pots and pans and silverware are made with it. People wrap their leftover food in it. Do you think when a person buys aluminum foil they stop to think of how it was produced or where it was mined? Of course not! They think, 'Oh, this brand is on sale at the store, so I can use it for my daughter's Halloween costume *and* cook our corn on the grill with it.' There are even individuals obsessed with alien invasions and conspiracy theorists who believe it will protect their minds from alien control! Unfortunately for these foolish mortals, the Electrical Engineering and Computer Science Department and Media Laboratory at MIT did a study in 2005 that proved these ridiculous contraptions actually *amplified* radio and other frequencies."[119]

He blew into his hands again and placed his created object on the table. The shiny, mottled elephant, complete with long and elegantly formed tusks, stood proudly. Any collector would be thrilled to add it to their menagerie.

Rua-Jian placed his formed aluminum creation alongside that of His Majesty's. A smooth and slick great white shark, menacing with its jaws open, displayed row upon row of perfect and dangerous serrated teeth. For the space of a moment, Rua-Jian thought that this juxtaposition of their impulsive art creations perfectly encapsulated their goals and personalities.

His Majesty, for all his power and authority, had left his passion and aggression on the battlefield years before; his

---

[119] Rahimi, Ali, et al. "On the Effectiveness of Aluminium Foil Helmets: An Empirical Study." Accessed February 17, 2005. https://mozai.com/writing/not_mine/aluminium_helmets_research.pdf

approach was now more philosophical. Rua-Jian ultimately rejected this mindset.

Although calm, he felt the anger coursing through his blood, the necessity for volatile action percolating throughout his system. Rua-Jian comprehended that His Majesty was aware of his nature, but was confident in his First Lieutenant's loyalty and complicity. Rua-Jian saw no reason to dispel His Majesty of this notion anytime soon.

His fealty was constant and had been for years. He would remain dedicated, so long as His Majesty protected and promoted their mission. If he saw any weakness or dilution of their goal, he would act and supersede him. They had come too far and had waited what seemed an eternity for their current opportunity. His life was dedicated to this purpose and no action he took was ever in vain. He vowed to himself years ago never to waste any moment of his life; he would never again be a pawn in someone else's game.

His Majesty looked at Rua-Jian and saw more than he acknowledged. He reached for the last container and, opening the lid, rolled the items into his palm. They glittered and reflected into one another and around the room. Each piece of the clear and lustrous substance was a different shape. His Majesty carefully placed each crystal on the table and lined them up in a row in front of the shark sculpture.

"Quartz is one of the world's most plentiful rocks." He held the last one between two fingers and examined it closely, turning it to capture the best light.

"Few would ever claim it was rare or worth stealing as a valuable jewel, not when it is clear like this. So, few people know that they are a critical material in our watches, cell phones, televisions, landline telephone systems, and radios." He glanced at Rua-Jian. "You well know that they are *piezoelectric,* they vibrate at a constant frequency and produce an electric charge when put under pressure. Man doesn't even need to mine quartz anymore. It can be manufactured in a lab. Even that crystal, however, is made from quartz fragments or silica, which, of course, is glass. So even this modern world is absolutely dependent upon nature. Quartz is also used in water purification and GPS. It is seemingly ubiquitous, yet largely unappreciated by the masses."

His Majesty rubbed his hands together and touched the first quartz crystal in the long line. It began to vibrate and heat waves rose from its core. A second later, a white beam shot out from the first quartz and entered in to the adjacent crystal, creating a domino-like effect. The last quartz released a laser beam and hit the shark square in its middle. The shark wiggled briefly with energy and seemed to swim along the table before it abruptly stopped.

The laser, although slowed in velocity by the shark obstacle, continued on till it hit a leather couch encased in an elaborately carved wooden frame. The smell of cooked cowhide and burning wood emanated from the furniture.

A quick look at the shark revealed a hole the size of a small pea. A path of liquid aluminum leaked from the wound; Rua-Jian wisely observed the events silently.

"Well, that was unfortunate," quipped His Majesty. "I rather appreciated that couch; it's quite comfortable."

With a sweep of his arm, His Majesty sent all the elemental and rock detritus toward the end of the table. The containers shook lightly, but remained in their place.

"Rua-Jian, this little demonstration should convince you of my certainty. We gave humanity more than enough time to change its destructive path. However, continued global warming trends and abuses of power by various world leaders have not abated. Uneven attempts by the few to warm the hearts and minds of the many are failing. We are at a pivotal time in history, Rua-Jian, when we can finally take control. Weaknesses in their defenses are evident, in a way where we can *finally* make our impact!" His Majesty's fist rose with tenacity. "We have not had this much leverage in a long while."

Rua-Jian felt adrenaline course through his system. He had waited so long to hear these sentiments from His Majesty. Perhaps all would be well to stay by his side. "Are we to take over major countries and create a dominating power?"

"Good gracious, Rua-Jian," barked His Majesty. "Have you ever attended a session of Congress or Parliament or any other governing political body? Have you watched the attempts of a dictator to persuade and police his populace?"

Rua-Jian shook his head. "I can assure you; both are exhausting and largely thankless. I have no interest in setting tax rates and fighting over budgets and education requirements and convincing underlings to do our bidding. Even Alexander the Great only reigned twenty-four years! If there are two major lessons we have learned, Rua-Jian, it is to be both efficient and perceptive."

"Your Majesty, I mean no disrespect, but a firmer hand may be what's needed at this point. We must reduce populations worldwide for our other goals to be successful."

His Majesty gingerly picked up the shark and ignored the viscous aluminum as it slowly ran along his wrist and into a shirt cuff. He turned it in the light and showed Rua-Jian its teeth.

"Rua-Jian, I need to be clear. Although a swift mass destruction might satisfy your anger and desire to command again, it is not efficient and creates more problems in the short term." He placed the shark near Rua-Jian. "No, as they say in the British game Whist, we must play the 'long game,' although it will take considerably less time than all other previous efforts took, *combined.*"

That sentence certainly got Rua-Jian's attention.

His Majesty gestured to the elements and rock littering one edge of the table. "Humanity foolishly relies on its technology and continues to become even more enmeshed. So few know how to *make* objects and so many don't even keep paper records anymore. Therefore, Rua-Jian, we begin efficiently—we attack them where we achieve the most impact, where humanity is weakest. Inanely they believe it's where they are actually strongest, a misguided notion…the hubris." After a pause, he asked, "Where do we start, Rua-Jian?"

Rua-Jian raised an eyebrow. "We follow the money."

"Precisely. We begin with the world's financial systems. You've seen what happens during past financial crises and how they trickle to other regions in the world. The plans I have in mind are staggering in proportion. And in time, when the impact of our event is realized, the rest will take care of itself. Nature will react, as she usually does: a result of world financial crises is often a health crisis as well as the general breakdown of society's rules and laws. Major health crises beget…"

"Crime and the spread of major disease."

"Precisely, Rua-Jian. And thanks to the pharmaceutical industry, so many people around the world take antibiotics unnecessarily." His Majesty checked the manicure on one hand. "Will something be found in time that isn't already overused and ineffective? Not our problem, really. We'll leave that to the experts."

Rua-Jian looked at His Majesty. "I am planning on taking one of the new students of the College of GeoEvolution. I think we can create a mole and get an inside view of how they are preparing to counter our efforts."

His Majesty lazily raised a hand in marginal support. "You have an obsession with that goal, Rua-Jian, and have yet to be successful. I wonder why you are so driven, thus." He waved the same hand again. "If you believe it will aid in your larger efforts, then so be it. Don't let this be a distracting enterprise, however. The quieter life is at that school, the better for us. Mark me, Rua-Jian."

His Majesty stood and walked to a small round table, upon which rested a metal mallet and a plate containing a large rose-colored quartz crystal. Embedded into it was a wire, which rose to the ceiling and followed along the edge of one wall. He picked up the mallet and hit the crystal with a decisive blow. "Let's have some refreshment while we hammer out the details, shall we?"

CHAPTER 9 – F

COLLEGE OF GEOLOGICAL EVOLUTION

*March 15*

*Dear [KameKona Johnson],*


*After learning about your myriad accomplishments and abilities, we are pleased to offer you admission to the exclusive College of Geological Evolution. Our College was founded in 1693 in Williamsburg, Virginia and is a premier institution for those interested in pursuing their passion for geology and related earth sciences. You were specially selected to join our elite student body and faculty based on your interests, aptitude, and dedication to Earth's sustainability.*

*Our unique program is available to only a small group of students around the world who possess the passion, intellect, and imagination to earn a degree from our historic university. We are aware that you did not apply to our school; our distinct program operates differently than most higher learning institutions: We independently select the students whom we believe are most qualified to study here.*

*This very unusual program includes free tuition, room, and board. For those students who help support their families financially, a stipend will be paid to your parent(s) until you graduate, should your work consistently meet our standards and you demonstrate studious intent.*

*The course of study will take three years to complete. The first two years will be in Williamsburg, Virginia, at the College of Geological Evolution and one year will be spent at our*

*Cambridge, England, location. Upon your matriculation, you will earn a BS in geology and a master's degree in your specialized field. The College of Geological Evolution is its own school, but has deep founding ties to the College of William and Mary and The University of Cambridge, two of the most prestigious and oldest higher learning institutions in the world. Due to this relationship, your diplomas will reflect this notable affiliation.*

*Soon you shall receive another letter requesting a home visitation from some of our professors to meet you personally, explain the program in detail to you and your family, and answer any questions. On the accompanying page, you may find our frequently asked questions and contact information.*

*We look forward to introducing our school and ourselves to you.*

*Staff of the College of GeoEvolution*
*Williamsburg, VA*

CHAPTER 10 – Ne

COLLEGE OF GEOEVOLUTION

# EARLY MAY

Sahila inhaled the fragrance of chamomile and honey as she held the warm cup. Hattie mixed her own leaves, flowers, and spices and the resulting tea always refreshed; it was comfort in a cup.

She peered at her companion who sat at the other end of the table, at least for a short period. Sahila no longer felt shame over the reactions everyone had toward Jürgen Tilver. The condition was not his fault and was actually protective, at least for he and Alegria.

As for Jürgen, he was no longer self-conscious and was always considerate toward others. At present, she joyfully watched him tuck into a coq au vin[120] with relish. Ngai had a soft spot for Jürgen, no doubt because he was his most appreciative customer.

"Sahila," he huffed as he wiped a drip of broth from his beard. "Ah don' mean to be so rude. Anno I become a

---

[120] Coq au vin – A savory French chicken stew, traditionally containing chicken, bacon, carrots, onions, garlic, red
wine, and thyme

fool in fron' o Ngai's food, ya ken?[121] But this chick'n! It's edible poetry!"

Sahila laughed and relaxed further in her chair. "It's good to be back from my interview tour with Reese. It's always a learning experience for us both when we are paired. I teach him the finer points of the acceptance process—and he introduces me to black-market hellholes he manages to ferret out while searching for pilfered gemstones and ill-gotten coin. It's most illuminating. According to him…" she sighed dramatically, "my knowledge in this arena is sadly lacking." Sahila held up a hand and began counting on each finger. "Let's see. On this last trip, I was cursed by a fraudulent fortune teller, chased down by an indignant cymbal playing capuchin—that was Reese's fault, and given three marriage proposals, if I promised that my gem collection would be my dowry. Overall, I learned a great deal."

Jürgen's shoulders shook and he smacked the table. "You will neva have a borin' day spending time with young Keeper Reese, that's a fact. How'd the visits go?"

Sahila paused and spoke with reverence. "I am forever humbled by the parents or guardians of our future students. Our offer is an uncommon and unique opportunity, coupled with a virtual guarantee of lifetime security and personal growth. Yet, to most, we are a foreign entity and we are asking these parents to entrust us with their most priceless valuable: their child.

"Our school is also thousands of miles away in an unfamiliar location. A place they can't easily travel to, even if given the opportunity. After we assuage their concerns and assure them that their child will be safe and well educated, brave

---

121 Ken – Scottish slang for you understand

parents swallow their fears and acquiesce. And that includes overcoming any reticence from their child; it's humbling...

"We couldn't entice the student from Panama, unfortunately. She decided she wanted to remain closer to home and study seismology there. If we're lucky and she's a good fit, we may convince her to be a Guardian someday.

"Our task is never easy and there is a certain amount of subterfuge involved, to convince them of the merits of our program. Because, unbeknownst to them, their attendance is for the benefit of humanity and the earth. But it never sits well with me and I guess it shouldn't. It's an uncomfortable space in which to exist. I feel it keenly, until the middle of fall term when we see our kids relax and thrive."

Jürgen glanced out the window and pulled on his beard contemplatively. "Sahila, your empathy for humanity is wha' makes you so good at this job, ya ken? I kno' it isn't easy fo' you. Ironic'lly, if you became numb to the process, you'd no' be so good at it anymore, right? It's why we're here tho', you kno'? Why we even exist."

Sahila nodded and proceeded to tell him about her and Reese's visits. Their first stop was the small, but meticulous apartment of Tú Chen in Shaoguan, in the Guangdong Province of China. Although Tú's parents agreed to the impending visit with Sahila and Reese, they opened their door with requisite apprehension. Sahila always played the concern in her head: *Who were these people from a strange school they had never heard of, a school to which their son had certainly not applied? And how did they even know their son?*

Tú was a responsible young man. He respected his parents, followed their rules, and exceeded their academic expectations. The Chens worked hard and rarely traveled outside of Guangdong, let alone their city, due to the compromised health of Tú's mother. Fortunately, they lived in a beautiful area of China with natural and cultural wonders; they had little desire to wander from home.

Before they entered the Chen's home, she and Reese removed their shoes and left them outside. They sat on the floor next to a table and were served Lechang Baimaojian tea.[122] The subtle fragrance gently rose around them as Sahila explained to the Chens in Mandarin how they learned of Tú's aptitude for geology from his grades and related essays.

"We have worldwide regional scouts, whose job is to seek suitable candidates who possess the aptitude, intelligence, and dedication toward Earth's sustainability." At their quizzical expressions, Sahila continued politely. "Did Tú enjoy digging in the dirt and collecting rocks when little?"

Tú's mother smiled and began recalling many instances when their son had spent numerous hours collecting little pieces of rock, even at the risk of missing his piano lesson.

"It never occurred to us that this little childhood hobby could cultivate a viable career," Tú's father added.

While his mother mentioned her recollections, Sahila caressed her necklace. Subtly, without incurring attention, she selected the two stones she wanted: her forest green tourmaline and her carnelian, a chalcedony stone. She pulled both teardrop-shaped stones toward her chest, easily lowered from the main neck chain by tiny, but strong perpendicular chains. Her hands were moist and warm from the ceramic teacup. The stones heated in her hand as she listened.

The green tourmaline began to radiate the thoughts and feelings from Tú parents. In response, Sahila diffused feelings of confidence and the urge to relax one's fears into the

---

[122] Lechang Baimaojian tea – A raw white tea produced in Shaoguan

room. She radiated the belief that new challenges for their son were positive and safe, that there was no need to worry.

Next, Sahila harnessed the carnelian. It was blood orange in color with white stripes, brown and dark orange specks, and natural iron inclusions. Through it, she projected feelings of well-being and diminishing sadness. It was a powerful combination and one that Sahila believed might assist the Chen's in their decision to let Tú attend the College of GeoEvolution.

When Chen's parents finished speaking, Sahila gently smiled. "Each of our students is given a valuable and relevant education; our college is located in a harmonious and safe environment and the cultural values and norms of our students are respected."

"Do you have any questions about the college or its curriculum?" Reese queried.

They discussed classes, class sizes, and the global nationality of its student body and faculty. The Chens were given a brochure containing pictures and descriptions of the campus. Sahila mentioned that Tú was awarded a full scholarship, including a generous monthly stipend for the Chens to offset the loss of income their son provided. His travel to and from the school was also covered and a visit during parents' weekend could be arranged, if so desired, also free of charge.

Jürgen interrupted Sahila's recounting. "Di' either parent or Tú ask what he coul' get a degree in?"

"Mmm," Sahila responded, after a bite of a Madeline.[123] "Tú asked the question. When Reese suavely mentioned the possibility of focusing on a specific area of study, such as rare earths, Tú became very engaged."

---

[123] Madeline – A French shell shaped buttery spongy cookie with hints of lemon or vanilla

"Did'ya give 'im me gift?"

"Of course, Jürgen! I wouldn't forget."

"I gave it to him after we talked about the educational opportunities." Sahila gave Tú the small figure of a lion made from mischmetal.[124] "I asked him if he could make it roar," she giggled. Sahila recalled the look on Tú's face, the quiet recognition and understanding in his eyes, and a brief glimpse of what she thought looked like hope.

"He going to be one of ours, do ya ken?"

"After the look he gave me upon receiving your token, I can confidentially say, yes. He's a very special young man, Jürgen—enormous potential and an engaging and empathetic spirit. I'm fairly certain we'll receive his acceptance letter very soon. Let's now talk about Ming." Sahila began to relate the experience of their next visit, one entirely different from the first.

The signature Sen Signet hotel in Singapore was a pleasant and impressive diversion for Reese. It was opulent, but elegant in an understated manner. The muted, earth tone colors invited guests to relax or conduct business without distractions from garish and frivolous décor. Sen Signet hotels were designed to blend with their natural surroundings and geographical environment, using the latest green technology available.

Reese and Sahila were more relaxed for this visit. Here, they were among friends and trusted advocates. An informational interview with Ming and her family was easier and didn't require subtle manipulations. Unbeknownst to Ming

---

[124] Mischmetal – A soft alloy made up of several rare earth metals, often a combination of cerium, lanthanum, and neodymium

and her father, the Sen family included Guardian members, past and present. Although they were a close-knit family, the sacred bond between Guardian and Keeper was stronger. The Keepers sensed Ming Sen's abilities and interests for themselves, but had also been alerted to her potential when she was just a toddler.

Although unaware, Ming was fortunate to be raised in a family that included a Guardian. Similar to other future students of the College of GeoEvolution, Ming knew, at a tender age, that she was fundamentally different from other children. Yet, unlike those who suffered their uniqueness alone, she was embraced and mentored consistently.

Ming grew confident under her grandmother's watchful eye, able to explore her abilities, yet taught the need to keep them hidden from the larger world. Ming had no knowledge of the Keepers or their large organization, especially one so established and widespread.

So, upon meeting with Reese and Sahila, Ming was curious, but not anxious. She listened with an open mind and felt an instantaneous bond with Sahila; Reese wisely knew that she needed to take the lead. Ming was interested in gemology, a branch of mineralogy, and was excited that she could specialize in this field. Skilled gemologists worked in museums, fine jewelry stores, and in gemstone mining companies.

"Do you own some gemstones already?" Sahila had inquired.

Ming was only too happy to escort Sahila to her collection. Each time Sahila held one of Ming's stones and discussed its name or an occlusion, she placed the gemstone back into Ming's palm.

Ming noticed the sensation each time they shared this exchange. It was unlike anything she had ever experienced before! Each stone she received from Sahila's fingers was warmer than it had felt earlier and had a stronger energy. It was as if each one was *given* a supercharge of its own characteristics, more intense than she had ever created herself. She could *feel* the power and innate trait of each stone. When her grandmother needed to improve her strength or health again, the stones were optimized to their maximum capacity, far greater than her ability allowed. Ming knew instantly that this Sahila was incredibly unique and understood her better than anyone she'd met before; she could learn a great deal from her.

Mr. Sen, Ming's father, was oblivious to this exchange. He was far less enthralled with this strange opportunity; he only had one child and he wanted to keep her closer to home. He was inclined to refuse the offer on Ming's behalf, but was halted by Ming and his mother-in-law, Meihui.

"This opportunity is essential for Ming's education! My daughter would want it."

Ming looked at her father imploringly and he knew he was outnumbered. When it came to Ming, he deferred to Meihui. She dedicated her life to the family, especially after their great loss. Her opinion and insight were valued and always benefitted Ming and his company. Thus, to Ming's delight, the offer was accepted on the spot; he would feel his intense loss in private.

"I'm sure you were pleased wi' the outcom'? Jürgen quipped. "You must be so excited to have a new protégé! Does her jewelry box come with her?"

Sahila mimed a "mind blown" gesture. "And what a collection it is! The stones will follow her, but the box will not. You know an Emogem[125] always works best with stones that are familiar and comfortable. They'll retain Ming's residual energy signature, which makes them respond faster to her touch. Despite that, she'll also work with the non-energy-loaded stones. A gifted Emogem must be able to harness the inherent characteristics of every stone; there are situations we find ourselves in where using our own is impossible, inadvisable, or even perilous."

"Hmm. Righ'. I remember."

"Ready for the last?" She frowned. "I'm almost talked out and the madeleines are gone."

Jürgen gesticulated that he'd get more with little fanfare.

"No." She shook her head. "Let's not bother Chef. I think I've had my share anyway."

Jürgen raised an eyebrow. "What a whopper! I had twice as much and you know it."

Sahila waved him off. "Anyway, our last stop, of course, was Riga, in Latvia."

"Aye. I've frozen my bahooky[126] a time or three there in winter."

Sahila rolled her eyes and took a fragrant sip of her tea. "That sweet Demyan boy. I hope he's coming; honestly, I feel like we're *rescuing* him."

"What's his partiality? Another emo?"

---

[125] Emogem – Someone with an inherent ability to harness the energy and properties of rocks, crystals, and certain elements from the periodic table, primarily used to heal others

[126] Bahookie – Scottish slang for a person's bottom or butt

"Not quite. He's actually closer to Reese. More of a Resogem."[127]

"Hmm. Reese mus' love that!"

"We met Demyan Ivanova at his uncle's jewelry store, with his father, mother, and uncle all there. Demyan was enthusiastic and his parents were naturally wary. The uncle seemed supportive, but reticent to voice that opinion. He later told Reese he was convinced Demyan had found his calling."

Sahila remembered Reese's tactic to appeal to Demyan's father, Hugo Ivanova. He spoke the language of finance and world markets, profits and risk.

"I'm forever impressed by Reese's financial acumen. For all of his sardonic bluster, he's incredibly astute—a master market manipulator, if you will."

"He's involved in preservin' and growin' the Keeper's financial portfolio. He's got a shrewd mind, our Reese."

Sahila held up a palm. "He brought his 'A' game to this interview. Reese flattered Mr. Ivanova about his business success. He offered a convincing argument about the gem and mineral economy and how an expert in this area could add to the Ivanova holdings. Mine ownership is a perennially vibrant business, whether his haul was intended for jewelry, science, or industry. And if young Demyan had an interest, why not invest in his future, starting with a proper and targeted education?"

Sahila knew that Reese never lied; it risked the trust placed in him by his more unsavory business contacts and snitches around the world. Manipulation via ego flattery, however, was perfectly fine.

----

[127] Resogem – Someone who is highly attuned to the negative energy stored in rocks, crystals, and certain elements of the periodic table

Mr. Ivanova and his wife contemplated Reese's perspective. Demyan's mother appreciated he would gain a world-class education in a safe environment, away from the pressure of his two older siblings and a domineering father. She had a soft spot for Demyan since he had a distinct passion, unlike her other two children, who appeased their father.

Mr. Ivanova believed investing in mines and gem purchases was risky and he was unsure if he wanted to venture into that territory. That said, he *could* afford to let Demyan explore this area of study. He had an heir and two spares and two of them were following in his footsteps. He did also appreciate the special bond that his brother had with his youngest boy. Nickolai understood him and thought this school the best course of action.

Demyan was thrilled with the possibility. Ms. Sahila and Mr. Reese seemed to understand him even more than his uncle did. He couldn't put a name to the feeling, but it was there all the same; he sensed a kinship.

When the conversation was over, Reese made eye contact with Demyan, shook his hand, and pressed something into it, warm and almost as large as his palm. When Reese's hand dropped, Demyan's palm contained a heavy coin, predominantly silver with gold accents.

On one side around the top edge were the words *College of GeoEvolution* with a picture of a large rock with a fissure alongside. The rock was topped by an erupting volcano, complete with gold lava streams and smoke rising from its crater. In the center of the rock's craggy surface, almost hidden, were raised images of a pickaxe, sword, and a geode, the last cracked open to reveal its inside cache of gold-colored crystals.

Above the volcano was a golden sun, its rays drawn toward the rock. Along the bottom edge were the words

*Established in 1693.*[128] On the other side of the coin was a rendering of the school's main building. Demyan smiled at Reese and thanked him. The coin filled him with warmth and a sense of calm.

"What can ya tell me about the coin, young Demyan?" Reese asked.

Demyan palmed the coin, glanced at both sides carefully, and felt its weight in his hands. "It's gold plated and is made of nickel—my visual observation, the feel of it in my hands, and the weight tells me that."

"Too right. You got that in one. What else can you tell me?" He whispered quietly, "How does it make you feel when it's in your hand?"

Demyan's eyes widened at Reese, sensing that his answer was important and honesty was essential.

"It feels warm and peaceful in my hands. It was minted with good intentions and has been carried around recently in the pockets of a couple of people..." Demyan paused for feedback.

"Go on, Demyan."

"Of the people who had recent possession, one was very content and trusting. The other one was...less so. Not hateful or angry, however." Demyan was quick to explain with a glance at Reese, "Just more complex and emotionally cloaked. I guess that's the best way to phrase it—emotionally hidden."

Reese barked, "thanks for that, Demyan...I think."

After they left, he grumbled to Sahila. "Dumisani walked around with that coin for a week before I got it. Glad I made such a positive impression," he quipped sarcastically.

---

128 The font is Baskerville Old Face, designed by John Baskerville in 1757 and largely not appreciated until well after his death

Jürgen resettled in his chair. "I wonder how Alegria and Evren's visits went," he mumbled while he wiped his beard and mouth. "All I know is that Alegria tol' me that it was quite illuminatin'!"

## CHAPTER 11 – Na

### AKRON, OHIO

# EARLY MAY

Tessa Horton rode her bike as if chased by malevolent forces—or in her case, drug dealers, if the neighborhood in which she was pedaling was any indication. The balmy late afternoon was at odds with the stormy turmoil she was facing within. *Good ol' Tessa! Looking before I leap again. What an idiot, biking through this crime ridden 'hood.*

The feelings that assaulted her were polarizing and exhausting, cycling between eager anticipation, anxiety, and melancholy. Adding to her misery was apprehension of the unknown. When little, Tessa sensed she lived in a parallel existence, that there was more to the reality that comprised her world.

She was unprepared to have that belief validated all in one morning, however. Tessa managed to keep her cool during the meeting with the College of GeoEvolution staff. And even after the guests had left, when she had to talk further with her mom and later, her brother.

"Well, Tessa, hon, we'll miss you terribly, but this is a great opportunity," her mother said only fifteen minutes after meeting the visitors and looking at the brochures.

"You should totally go, sis. I'll miss ya," her brother said as he walked out the door.

Tessa's mouth hung open, hurt beyond words. "I shouldn't let the door hit me on my way out, right? Umm, shouldn't we talk it over with Dad first?"

"He'll trust my judgment, Tess. He's out of pocket right now."

Tessa frowned. "I'd at least like to hear his opinion!"

*Finally,* Tessa could go to the one person who innately understood her and have a freak out. No one liked to be misunderstood and unappreciated. It was painfully clear that she didn't belong in her family. She was forever the odd one out, the irritating pariah, and they couldn't hide their relief that she had an opportunity to leave.

She continued biking, more wary of her surroundings. "How can you blame them, dummy," she chastised herself out loud. "You can finally get out of their hair." *You do cause them lots of headaches.*

Diamond Lee, "Dya" to her friends, smoothed her Kelly-green silk dress, which flattered her bronze skin and textured dark hair, and began dusting her merchandise with a microfiber wand. It was eleven o'clock on a Saturday and there was a lull in the pedestrian traffic.

She was expecting a busy day, which hopefully produced a healthy sales profit. She was on the second cup of her favorite chamomile tea mixture, enhanced with a drizzle of East Akron honey and a squirt of lime. The calming and gentle scent of the tea put her in a relaxed and centered frame of mind.

She caressed one half of a vibrant amethyst geode resting on a shelf.

"Who will inundate us today, I wonder? Will it be the usual clientele? A mixture of curious teenagers, earnest young adults, and titillated middle-agers, walking in for the first time as if attending a Victorian séance?"

Depending on the day and the month, bets could be taken as to which group would hold sway. "It is May, my sparkly friend, so *love* is in the air," she said, winking with a lilting black eye. She waltzed around the store, making sure everything was to her liking. Dya talked to her rocks and gems. Like plants, she believed they soaked up the positive energy and radiated it outward.

"Customers want to attract love to them; better appreciate the person already in their lives, or become less stressed from an irascible family pet, so they don't boot them out the door! Who am I to judge?" This was the time of year for weddings and proms. Her bets were on a heavy traffic of teenagers, young adults, and a sprinkling of Mother of the Brides today. *Mother Earth, help me if I get a bridezilla!*

Natural Illumination was a retail establishment on the second floor of an upscale Akron mall. Her location was strategic, if not stimulating. Although she'd prefer a stand-alone building with a good view of a park, Dya understood the importance of her setting. When she moved in over ten years ago, she'd immediately insisted that the typical track lighting be removed and replaced with softer, more natural light. Her bread and butter depended on it.

Dya sold only the finest quality gems, minerals, crystals, and rocks and knew the provenance of every object she stocked. She helped those who believed that such items could enhance their lives, health, or homes, but also catered to non-believers who were compelled to own a special stone or gem, *just in case this stuff actually works.*

Those who lingered and behaved themselves were offered chamomile tea in china cups and saucers. She never judged any clientele, but the curious impulse buyer, who wondered if she sold magical or occult-like junk, were encouraged to move along and acquire their moderately priced disposable trinkets elsewhere.

In her periphery, Dya noticed the largest object in her store darken in hue. It was her familiar and protector, the talisman she most relied upon to alert her to potential trouble beyond her own heightened awareness—a towering cathedral smoky quartz geode. Immediately, all of the gems on display reacted, causing a sensational refractive light show throughout the store.

"So, who wanders toward my little paradise in a such tempestuous mood?" Dya queried under her breath. The question was rhetorical, considering the mottled and continually shifting brown shades in the smoky quartz geode. She knew who was approaching. The geode was strongly responsive to anyone emotionally connected to Dya.

Dya watched as Tessa Horton all but raced her way through her store entrance, only to stop the instant she got inside the glass walls and spied her, sagging in relief.

"Great Goddess Gaia, what monster is chasing your tail?"[129] Dya watched as Tessa closed her eyes and took several deep, calming breaths. "For a pint-sized tempest, you can certainly fill a room with your boisterous presence!"

The forlorn tears in Tessa's eyes brought Dya over for a bracing hug. "Oh, honey, I think it's time for a tea break."

---

[129] Gaia – The ancient Greek goddess of the Earth

Dya locked her door and switched the affixed placard to TEA BREAK. VENTURE BACK SOON. She busied herself pouring another cup of tea, the gentle clink of porcelain china the only sound in the store.

Tessa took another slow, cathartic breath. Dya's store was pleasant and calming, a complete juxtaposition to the turmoil Tessa felt within. It always felt this way in Natural Illumination, her favorite place and Tessa's safe harbor. She watched as Dya laid out a few of her favorite Scottish short-bread cookies, made by an ex-pat Scotswoman Dya knew. She only offered them to her most select clients or friends.

"I think a few of these are in order today, Tessabear. What say you?"

"Okay," she whispered and sniffed.

Dya angled her head to the left, gesturing that Tessa follow her to the hidden alcove in the store, blocked from view by a display shelf. A small table and chairs were nestled around smaller shelves filled with office paraphernalia, retail detritus, and cleaning supplies, all very organized. "Join me in the tea cozy."

Tessa dropped her backpack off her shoulder onto the floor and slumped in a chair. Her hands immediately curved around the cup, soaking up its heavenly warmth and subtle fragrance.

"I wasn't expecting you until next weekend, Tessabear. Experiencing more pressure at home or school? Did your brother appreciate the watch repair?"

"Ha. About as much as a fossilized teacher appreciates a student pointing out errors he made on a chapter test."

"Ahh." Dya scrunched her nose in sympathy. "Good ol' Mr. Schedwick strikes again, I see. Did the administration check his pulse or at least find in his coffin the trail of exsanguinated[130] rat skeletons and empty Jujyfruit cartons?"

Tessa snorted and slurped her tea.

"Tessa Horton, do not defile my Royal Crown Derby bone china with your pedestrian manners during my precious tea sojourn."

Tessa sighed dramatically. "Yes ma'am. I had a…a life-altering day."

"I can see something has affected you to your very soul." Dya wondered if Nalin Fink encountered many hurdles when she met Tessa's mother. She made a mental note to contact her and get the details.

"Do you remember when you told me I needed to hold on, that I needed to keep my head down, and just muscle through the rest of the year, because this was just the beginning of my journey?"

"Of course. Everything I say and act upon is deliberate, Tessabear. You know that about me."

Tessa nodded, contemplative. "A woman came by the house this morning from a college. Her name was Nalin Fink and she was dressed…unconventionally."

Dya covertly smiled before she sipped her own tea.

"She's not from anywhere I applied. I've never heard of the place, but it's apparently renowned. It's really old and has an amazing earth science program. And it's historically attached to the College of William and Mary, but is kind of separate."

Tessa conveyed a confused look and shrugged. "*And,* I would earn a master's degree from The University of Cambridge in *England* as well—in three years! *And* it's *paid* for…I would have a full scholarship! Apparently, they look

---

[130] Exsanguinated – When blood is completely drained

for kids, students like me, throughout the world. It's very international. I'm not sure how they do that; it's weird. But if it's real, why would it happen to me?"

In Tessa's mind, to say that the experience was weird was an understatement. It was disconcerting. On one hand, "Big Brother" was watching her, and on the other, it was as if she had an angel on her side, just one who finally realized Tessa was part of their care portfolio after a heavenly audit.

"I can't find out any real information about it online. I just get sent to an official site with a Q&A page. Ms. Nalin told me there are paid internships every summer and that the administration makes sure everyone has a job after graduation! It seems too good to be true. And if it's valid, *why would they want me?*" Tessa glanced at Dya, grabbed a cookie, and brushed it absentmindedly along her bottom lip. "The one perennial characteristic attributed to me is that I am a giant pain in the ass."

Dya quirked her mouth to the side in a sly smile. "Believe it or not, I am actually very familiar with the College of GeoEvolution. I even know some of the professors. You could say that we have an affinity of interests. I can tell you that Nalin Fink is someone you can trust. She will understand you as well as I do and will mentor and protect you. Don't look so shocked!"

Dya swept an arm dramatically. "Look at the world in which I surround myself. Is it so surprising that I might have a connection? In fact, I'll be completely honest and let you know I contacted Nalin about you a few years ago. I wanted her to know about you—and your potential. I had a feeling you and the school would be a good fit and I'm happy to see that my instincts were correct. They usually are."

Tessa stared incredulously and nibbled on her shortbread while she processed the news.

"People are not mice or squirrels, Tessabear. Eat with deliberation."

Tessa shoved the whole cookie into her mouth and chewed with forceful defiant bites, and swiped another from the plate.

"Oh, my, you really showed me didn't you! If you accept the offer, and I strongly believe that you should, you will be a handful," she sighed.

She held up a hand to ward off a knee-jerk reaction from Tessa. "But I don't think that will be a negative issue. You need to be tempered a bit, to have your actions and thoughts refined, and to become more purposeful. And you must learn how to master your impulsivity, which gets you into trouble. You have excellent instincts, Tessa, but lack the education to act on them appropriately. I want you to acquire the skills to harness your frustration and anger and understand their underlying origins. You have great potential and strength within you."

Tessa's eyebrows drew together in frustration. "Why am I the last to know about this possibility? Don't you think it would've been helpful for me to learn about this school earlier? It would have saved me a lot of time and stress; I can tell you that much!" Ruminating about standardized tests, studying for those tests, completing college applications, submitting scholarship applications, and writing endless college essays gave her indigestion.

"The College of GeoEvolution finds you, not the other way around," Dya said calmly. "One doesn't apply to the school, one is invited. It's manner in selecting students is unique and has found great success for well over three hundred years. I trust the process, Tessabear. It's not my place to make their existence known to those students whom I think are qualified."

"My whole family, they are completely prepared to ship me off to this school, knowing nothing about it. They're relieved it's free and that I'll be someone else's discipline concern. I know they love me, but I can palpably feel their relief. Maybe a bit less on my dad's side, but a bit from him too. It feels terrible and lonely, but I probably deserve it."

"There are times in our lives when we face crossroads, my Tessabear. When this experience first happens at a young age, it can be liberating or terrifying or a little of both. Until that point, however, most major choices were made with help from your parents or other significant influences and you had little or no input in that determination. To not have that responsibility can be a relief; it's part of childhood to not be burdened by such weighty life-altering decisions.

"You grasp the importance of this moment, however, and fully comprehend your family's shortcomings regarding your well-being, regardless of how much they love you. You are ready, Tessabear, to make this first momentous decision. But take heart—you are not entirely alone, because after all, the College of GeoEvolution *did* find you, just as they found me, once upon a time long ago."

Tessa looked shocked, her shortbread plopping into her lap, forgotten. With as much sang-froid as she could muster, hiding her hurt, she responded, "I'm guessing that I haven't earned the 'need to know' security clearance?"

"In a way Tessa, that's true. Most times, it doesn't benefit to be introduced to the preternatural aspects of the world before you are ready. Usually, the result is emotionally and psychologically damaging. On the other side of the coin, it's equally harmful to have a nebulous awareness of its existence without validation; that often leads to madness. So, for years, you and I have walked perpendicular paths together toward our major crossroad, and today is the day where we meet and you make your first big decision, but not alone."

Tessa was much like a prickly pear cactus. Similar to that plant's fruit, she was prickly on the outside with a tender, if not exactly sweet interior. On the taste spectrum, she was tart with a vague glimmer of sweetness. At any rate, Tessa was moved by Dya's support and greatly relieved. She hoped they could remain in close contact when she left for school, because she was taking the offer from the College of GeoEvolution.

Just as Dya had mentioned, Tessa had sensed the shadowy existence of *otherness*, a vague understanding that there was more to know and understand about the world than what her family and almost everyone knew. Dya not only sensed it, it was deeply ingrained within her. If there was one thing Tessa now knew, it was that she couldn't live a life in ignorance and frustration; she was meant to be a part of this otherworld and was called to it.

"I've been working on a gift for you and was waiting for the right moment to present it. I think now might be the appropriate time."

Dya collected a velvet-lined tray and a small jeweler's pouch. She gently upended the contents of the pouch onto the tray. Tessa noticed a silver ring band and six stones of various sizes and shapes.

"I chose platinum for the band, because I think it will suit you best. It's far more durable than silver or gold and although it's less scratch resistant than gold, I don't believe that will concern you. The choice of the stone, however, is yours to make. I selected options that I believe suit you, but you will know which of these will work best."

Tessa's smile wobbled, clearly touched. She reached out, but quickly pulled her hand back, hesitant. "Can I touch them?"

"But, of course, how else will you find the right one?"

Tessa lifted the tray at an angle and glanced closer at the stones. She could see they were different rocks, all about a carat and a half.

"You may recognize both diamonds and quartz crystals, all excellent specimens. Obviously, the diamonds are worth far more at market sale than the quartz, but you and I both know that's not what's important or desired for our purpose."

Tessa picked up each stone and looked at it critically. She closed her eyes and touched all of its facets blindly, getting a feel for the stone with her fingers. She returned each one to the velvet box and created a line of stones, sorting them in a different order.

"Tell me about your classification choice, Tessabear."

"Each has a different temperature signature; some became warmer faster than others. Those felt more comfortable, like they belonged with me and were an extension of myself. Does that make sense?"

"You know that it does. Take a look above my head."

For the first time since their tea, Tessa noticed a poster board on the wall above Dya's head. She raised an eyebrow and snorted with mirth. Colored renderings of recognizable nefarious evildoers were pinned on the poster board.

She spotted what looked like Genghis Khan, a club-wielding cyclops, a dark-gray-mottled ghost silhouette with angry eyes, similar to those found in most Scooby Doo cartoons, and a half-decomposed zombie wearing an Ohio

State cheerleading uniform, complete with one pom pom, since her other arm was missing.

"Random much," Tessa spoke, sarcastically as she viewed the images.

"Well, I wanted to offer a *random* sampling, to cover all of your possible cultural references and preferences. What do you ultimately believe you are meant for, Tessabear? What does your subconscious whisper to you when you are listening?"

Tessa stared at the poster board and considered Dya's question. Who was she really meant to be? Who was she becoming? During her quietest and calmest moments, what did she understand to be true about herself?

Honestly, she still didn't know. Wasn't that what furthering her education was all about anyway—to get a chance to determine that? She needed a neutral place, both physical and emotional, where she could block all the other noise around her that came from the adults in her life who felt the need to lecture her or pressure her with their preconceived notions about her future.

"Tessabear, don't overthink it, don't get mired in minutia. What do your instincts tell you?"

Frustrated, Tessa placed her palm over the velvet-lined box and concentrated, sensing the stone that felt the most right, the one that belonged just to her. She grasped the one whose heat and natural vibrating energy was the most comfortable. In a blur of motion, she picked it up, familiarized herself with its facets, and glanced down to corroborate what she felt.

Tessa noticed a pinpoint-sized pyrope garnet[131] inclusion in the diamond she selected. She appreciated that enhancement, and aimed it toward her intended target. Angling

---

[131] "Garnet," https://www.mindat.org/gm/10272. The pyrope garnet has a deep red color, like a claret wine.

herself into the path of natural light, she channeled her internal energy to radiate from her core and travel toward her left hand. When it felt warm and tingly, she merged it with the energy from the stone. Held between thumb and forefinger, she willed the stone to shoot a bright red-colored laser beam, so precise that it only burned the image on the cardboard she wished to destroy. Her eyes widened in surprise. Although Tessa could never see the laser beams she generated, as they are not visible to the human eye, she always sensed when they radiated.

"I think that response was pretty emphatic. Want to explain your decision?"

Mouth open in shock, Tessa glanced between the smoking hole and the rock between her fingers. "Holy crap. That was pretty intense!"

Dya raised an eyebrow. "Well, they didn't accept you for your eloquence!"

Tessa smirked. "Should I continue?"

"By all means, Tessabear."

"I think, in the moment, *protection* is what came to mind. That I had to shield you from the evil monsters. And that I have an ability to protect you from evil. I don't know *how* I can better learn to do that, but that's what seemed most clear and correct.

"And I smoked the ghost, because that seemed the most obvious choice. I sense there is great evil in the world, as well as weird, unexplainable stuff, but it's not obvious to me yet where it is or what it is. That said, I don't think it's a cyclops or a cheerleader with poor judgment in dating partners. And Genghis Khan was merciless, but a brilliant leader. Presumably, one could try to reason with him first, but he's been gone for centuries, so probably not a threat."

"Let's openly address the elephant in the room," Dya interjected. When did you first notice your ability to harness light energy?"

"I realized it when I was very young, around five, I'm pretty sure." Tessa remembered kids on the playground taking little plastic magnifying glasses and burning blades of grass with the heat from the sun. Tessa could do that without the magnification or the sun. She just needed a simple piece of quartz from the dirt. It never occurred to her to tell anyone, because she didn't think it was special.

"When I became older," Tessa continued, "it seemed like a marvel of science and something anyone could do. By then, I was socially…*distinct*, and had few friends to impress anyway. As I took more challenging science classes, however, it slowly began to dawn on me that most people couldn't do what I could. I kinda figured, as difficult as things were at home, that keeping it to myself was the best course of action—or inaction, as it were."

"You picked the diamond with the garnet inclusion."

"I think it picked me. Certain garnets make effective solid-state lasers,[132] because of their crystalline structure and potential rare earth load, among other important factors. Of course, not all garnets work, and most used in lasers are now man-made. Since there are too many variables that need to exist for them to be effective, they are not always used. Anyway, the small garnet inclusion inside this diamond has *just* the right amount of rare earth and proper crystalline structure to enhance the stone's laser potential. I *love* it!"

---

[132] Solid-state laser – Laser that uses a solid medium, like garnet, other rock, or glass to amplify its beam. Uses of a solid-state laser include medical treatments like eye surgery and precise metal cutting; there are many other uses, as well.

"I'm impressed, Tessa. A great deal of thought went into your choice."

Dya was really going to miss Tessa's frequent visits. It would be an adjustment, Tessa moving on.

"I'll have this stone set for you by the end of next week. You'll wear it on your middle finger, so you have maximum flexibility, okay? It will become your familiar, Tessa, your personal touchstone and communicator. It will be an extension of your personality and will reflect your moods and experiences. You need to respect the stone by getting in tune with it, understand? We'll practice several times before you leave and I'll show you how we can keep in touch as well.

"The diamond is an Asscher cut, a less familiar style, octagonal in shape. Its cut isn't flawless, but I'm going to leave it as is—I think it's most effective in this state, all right?" Dya gave Tessa a fierce and lingering hug and a kiss on the crown of her head. "Okay, Tessabear, you've eaten enough of my Scottish shortbread and slurped enough tea; I have to reopen my store and earn money to buy more cookies! Out you go."

Tessa left Dya's store feeling loved and supported, her cup full. How was she going to survive without seeing Dya?

She was focused on this concern when she heard raised voices a few stores down. Three girls from her high school were crowding another classmate, Henrietta. Although she was reserved and Tessa didn't know her well, she always admired her unique fantasy/steampunk clothing style. Tessa heard them fire off questions and comments almost on top of one another.

"Like, that's such an…interesting…look, Heiny. Can I call you Heiny?" one remarked.

"Why are you at the mall anyway? Like, don't you shop at thrift stores? Everything for sale here is new, you know," criticized another.

"Aren't you worried those thrift clothes smell like old BO? You'd probably have more friends if you dressed less weird," the third chastised.

When two of them raised their cell phones to snap picks of Henrietta, presumably to add to their social media feeds, Tessa had seen and heard enough.

*This poor girl, minding her own business, is brave enough to dress in a cool, unconventional style. Her clothing choices are disturbing absolutely no one, except these bored, bullying harpies.*

Reaching into her pants pocket, Tessa removed a specific crystal from her velvet pouch, selecting it by feel alone. Although her back was to Natural Illumination, she was close enough to harness the light from Dya's store. She glanced around her surroundings before subtly angling both herself and the crystal *just right*. She aimed for the harpies' phones and a targeted pinpoint laser shot out and hit both cell phones, one after each other, milliseconds apart.

"Ouch! My phone is burning!"

"Mine too! What happened?"

Tessa dropped the crystal into her pocket and appeared fascinated by a store's window display of prom dresses. Considering that laser beams are not visible to the human eye, she felt safe from the group's scrutiny.

"Noooo! My phone doesn't work! I'm pissed! My mom insisted this case would protect it! She's gonna have to buy me the next model *and* that crystal case I wanted! I'm gonna guilt trip her!"

"Ha! Nice to be you!" the other student snarled. "My parents are going to ground me! I promised I wouldn't drop it. I bet that creepy rock store caused it. The lady who owns it is such a freak!"

"You're only saying that 'cause she kicked you out last month for asking that question about…"

They walked off without a backward glance at the traumatized Henrietta.

"I love thrift store shopping, actually, but I never find items that cool," Tessa said when she approached Henrietta. "Don't mind those morons. It's better to be unique than boring and basic any day." Tessa offered Henrietta her favorite rose quartz[133]. "The woman who owns that rock shop, Diamond Lee? She's sold this to me. She's amazing and is the nicest. Show this to her and tell her Tessa gave it to you. Play your cards right and you'll be eating the best Scottish shortbread in your life."

As Tessa rode home, she was still miffed those idiots disturbed her peaceful vibe. *I'm going to that college. Dya's right—as angry as I feel right now, I need to learn some control. I could really hurt someone.*

Despite that thought, her face showed the grin of vindication. *Their cell phones are permanently fried, but will show no damage. Must have been their butter fingers!*

---

[133] "Rose Quartz," https://www.mindat.org/gm/3456

## CHAPTER 12 – Mg

### BRADFORD, WEST YORKSHIRE, ENGLAND

# EARLY MAY

Alegria and Evren chose first to go to Hawaii to meet KameKona Johnson. They arrived in the early evening to find the entire family home. Alegria spent time introducing the school in the same manner as with their other young prospects, but spent more time discussing the courses relating to volcanoes.

Upon learning about the Master's in Volcanology, KameKona waved his arms toward his room enthusiastically. "Can I show you my collection of lava samples?"

Alegria was thrilled to feel the residual heat signature from KameKona's samples when she approached them. She sensed KameKona had the potential to be a powerful Volco.[134]

"These are impressive! If you attend, I imagine you will be sad to leave them behind. We *do* have a legally approved

---

[134] Volco – An individual who is highly attuned to volcanoes and their activity. A Volco can detect volcanic activity far sooner than expert volcanologists. They have the ability to harness energy from a volcano, and manipulate igneous rock and lava streams. No Volco is strong enough to cause a volcano to erupt or stop a volcano from erupting

path for you to bring them, however, if you like." She winked. "We have special dispensation."

KameKona's eyes widened. He would need to verify this claim. It was both illegal and culturally discouraged to remove lava from any part of the Hawaiian Islands. KameKona proceeded to ask several impressive questions about the program. Although he loved playing football, KameKona's interest in volcanology was a stronger and more economically viable career option. He knew that less than one percent of high school football players made it to the NFL. In addition, if he attended this college without cost, his dad could save his GI bill for his sisters.[135]

Alegria sensed the Johnsons' conflict. Sending their only son far away to school was a daunting prospect, no matter how exciting. When KameKona lobbed a forgotten bright pink satin ribbon in their direction, however, his look of mortification settled the matter. When it appeared as if they were visually out of range, she and Evren heard KameKona's imploring voice.

"Mom, Dad, come on! I love them like crazy, but I need a break!" He conducted his entire interview with one of his sisters' hair bows attached to the back of his head! Alegria found it endearing and liked him all the more.

On the eve of that success, Alegria and Evren traveled to Paris to meet Élise Peters-Comtois. Élise's exacting mother appreciated Evren's flawless French. Alegria also spoke French

---

[135] GI Bill – Allows military personnel to attend college for free or almost free or pass the benefit on to their children or spouse

fluently, but her enthusiasm resulted in a passionate patois, too earthy for the pretentious Mrs. Peters-Comtois.

Élise was thrilled at the prospect of escaping her mother's unpalatable goals and immediately connected with Alegria. Alegria was versatile in ASL and competent in three other sign languages. When around unstable volcanoes and the chaos and destruction that ensues, communicating with hand signals is preferable and often required. It can be difficult or even impossible to have conversations on site, depending on the surrounding noise level.

"You speak very clearly, sign beautifully, and read lips expertly," Alegria complimented Élise. "Despite that, we can provide an ASL interpreter in each class if you desire."

"Thank you, I appreciate the compliment and the offer. I'm very interested in learning more about the geology and seismology classes Mr. Evren spoke about."

"Why don't we get some fresh air in your family's garden and you can ask any questions you have."

Evren took this opportunity to persuade Élise's mother. "Ms. Peters-Comtois, I'd like to remind you that Élise will receive two very prestige degrees that are well regarded and often result in lucrative employment opportunities."

Mr. Peters-Comtois saw his daughter's enthusiasm and it warmed his heart. He gave his wife great latitude regarding the girls, but knew Élise would never fit into the mold his wife expected; it was time to free her and end the constant tension they all perennially experienced. When he approached his wife, Evren excused himself and joined Élise and Alegria outside.

It was a manicured French garden and contained herbs and the requisite foliage of a space not enjoyed, but faithfully maintained. Evren walked the garden's perimeter with Élise and stopped near one particular corner.

He caught Élise's attention. "Can you feel the vibrations underfoot?"

Élise looked shocked. "You can feel the Paris Métro too?[136] It's so many miles from the house!"

When young, she asked her sister, father, and even a few friends if they could sense and feel the rumble of the trains. Naturally, they all thought she was imagining the sensations or joking. She quickly learned to keep her observations to herself.

Evren nodded his head. "You are not alone, Élise Peters-Comtois. There are others who share your understanding of the world; I am but just one of them."

Élise beamed. Kindred spirits, in the form of sophisticated world-traveling professors, were offering her the opportunity to learn in an environment where she was understood and accepted! She felt relief and excitement for the first time in ages.

Alegria and Evren's last visit was to Bradford, West Yorkshire, England, to meet young Aedan Colston and his parents for tea. Aedan's parents lived on the outer edges of town in an older neighborhood. Although the house was roomy enough for a family of seven, the muffled din from Aedan's younger siblings was impossible to completely ignore.

Martha Colston made a double batch of her best scones and supplied a nice variety of Jaffa cakes for tea. Whatever

---

[136] Paris Métro – The Parisian underground rail system

wasn't eaten during the meeting would quickly be scavenged by her other children.

"Evren," Martha said while waving a Jaffa cake, excited, "I'm fascinated that our Aedan can study mining, metal design, or metallurgy. I'm still wrapping my head around how you know his interests. Just as important, however, Aedan must show you both the metal animal sculptures he found all over the area! Perhaps he should also study history or archaeology instead? No one else in our whole neighborhood ever finds these metal animals!"

Aedan flushed beet red. "Mum, they didn't come all this way to hear about that!"

"But really, he might be finding Viking artifacts. Beatrice mentioned an Eric the Bloody Hat who used to roam all around here forever ago, doing God knows what… Beatrice was very adamant about it."

"I believe it was Eric the Bloodaxe, dear," Matthew, Aedan's father, interjected.

Aedan shifted in his seat, his anxiety increasing.

Alegria gracefully stood. "While Evren shows your parents our brochure and further explains the program, why don't we take a walk in the yard?"

"While we're out here for a quiet moment," Alegria mused, standing in the large yard, "can you sometimes sense the presence of those who were here long before us? Can you feel their residual energy?"

"How did you know that?" Aedan said, startled.

"We have a colleague from New Mexico with whom you will study, should you attend our college. She is a member of the Zuni tribe, which has existed in the River Valley in New Mexico for almost four thousand years. When she goes home, she can sense the existing energy of those who came before her, from generations long ago. Here, Romans wandered this area almost two thousand years ago, and your Eric the Bloodaxe about five hundred years later." Alegria reached into her pocket and pulled out a palm-sized piece of shiny obsidian.

Alegria held out the fragment, reflective and sleek in its design, before closing her fist around it. She offered Aedan a radiant smile before briefly closing her eyes to block out external stimuli; she drew on both her own energy and the residual around her.

Focusing on Aedan, she worked the rock in her left hand, squeezing and manipulating it with her thumb. Her eyes shone with eagerness and purpose. Next, she sandwiched the stone between both hands, turning the fragment and molding it in certain places with her fingers. Visible waves of escaped heat rose from her hands as her pressure on the rock intensified.

"Well, what have we here," Alegria teased. She presented her gift. "You might want to keep this little one from Mum's prying eyes. It's *my* primary medium, but even 'Eric the Blood Hat' didn't use obsidian," she quipped with a wink. She placed the black glossy field mouse with its tail curled around itself into Aedan's outstretched hand. "You may want to cool it a bit more."

Aedan looked at the gift and Alegria in awe and recognition. He blew on the little mouse, cooling it instantly.

Evren intercepted their little twosome when they headed back to the house.

"Aedan, from what we know about you, your focus is tied to humanity's need for Earth's resources. Now, the rate at which people are harnessing what nature provides has shifted dramatically and is unbalanced. It's absolutely imperative that we quickly focus on sustainability, for both Earth's sake and for that of humanity. We think you have a keen sense of this balance."

Aedan smiled. "Thank you. I understand. And you arrived at just the right time. My sculpture subterfuge was becoming exhausting!"

## Chapter 13 – A1

### Macau, China

# Early June

R ua-Jian Chu was eager to leave the opulence of Macau and part company from His Majesty. He relished his position as the most trusted confidant and training supervisor for all His Majesty's employees. It was time to be his own master again, however. He longed to return to Bangkok and take care of his personal affairs before they began to enact their plan. Rua-Jian looked up to see one of his trusted assistants enter the luxury condo.

"Thank you for being on time. I need to make some adjustments regarding one of my portfolio managers; you know the importance I place on loyalty and competence. When I can't be at the helm, I hire only the best and they tend to not disappoint. In this circumstance, however, there must be a parting of the ways. Due to his recent mistake, my trust in this individual has ended."

Rua-Jian Chu handed over a piece of paper to his confidant. "I need you to head to this location and make my dissatisfaction known. I want it clean and quiet, with the usual protocols in place; see that there is no waste. I expect a lesson to be taught, not an eradication; his crimes are not so terrible as that. He is a family man, after all, and has obligations and responsibilities; those must always be respected. Do I make myself clear?"

## Chapter 14 – Si

### Long Island Sound, Connecticut, United States

John Myers walked onto the deck outside his waterfront home along the Long Island Sound near Shippan Point, sunglasses in place. He welcomed the cool morning air. The heat of summer had arrived and he enjoyed the breeze coming off the Sound as it dried the sweat from his morning workout. It was before six in the morning, the house was still quiet, and he cherished the silence. Although he loved his wife and raucous four children, he certainly appreciated the moment of calm his exclusive address provided.

He took a deep and cleansing breath, taking in the briny air redolent with the detritus of decaying algae and mussels, a rotten egg-like perfume. He didn't mind the odor; it was part of nature after all, and it reminded him daily how far he had come. Some might find it unpleasant, but it was an expensive bouquet to inhale.

He never took his good fortune for granted. His success was obtained from both a hard-earned college education and an MBA paid for by himself; he hadn't wasted time attending frequent parties, neglecting homework, or skipping classes. After that came long hours of diligent work and painful but fruitful ladder climbing, with dues paid along the way and tough lessons learned.

When time permitted, he and his wife involved themselves with several impactful charities to help those less fortunate. That he could take his family on exotic vacations and enjoy his beautiful home, complete with its occasional sulfur-like smell, was a goal long sought.

Another breath vented his latent anxiety. Stress of one form or another accompanied his chosen career. He was a private wealth manager for clients whose affluence greatly exceeded his own. And as such, he was responsible for the growth of their portfolios. His education and training dictated that he knew, much better than the average Joe, how to grow or preserve a dollar—or in his case, a lot of dollars.

He should be confident riding out the vagaries of world market forces just like his moored boat calmly road the swells of the Sound. John watched the cluster of boats in the distance rise and fall with small ripples in the water. And although he should be impervious to investment undulations, and rarely became apprehensive when an economic storm surged, he wasn't calm today.

Even the talented John Myers made a miscalculation once in a while. It wasn't from neglect or disinterest or even greed; he simply and reasonably expected one of their fund portfolios to rise and it had fallen precipitously instead. And all because the CEO of one of the companies included in that fund found himself in trouble with the law; its stock plummeted as a result.

This was truly not John's fault. His job within his company was to match the funds they designed and managed to his customer's needs. Other brilliant business executives in the company created the funds by choosing which investments to include. He was the face of the company in his clients' eyes—their first port of call, so to speak, and the first person to blame.

Despite having a personal relationship with a leader in every company included in the fund, it was illegal to be made aware of any impending ripple—in this case, the tidal wave that would rock his company. That kind of knowledge was considered insider trading and was a serious ethical violation, which could result in prison time and large fines.

The fund would doubtless regain its value; it was built from a solid group of stocks. But it would take time and some of his clients would be nervous, and doubtless some angry with him as well. He didn't expect his company would fire him, however; the markets were mercurial and even the best took a hit once in a while. He needed to contact all of his clients today to explain his plan. It would be a difficult day, but he hoped not to lose any of those clients; they would weather it together.

John looked again at the row of undulating boats and little dinghies clustered together. He noticed a few new ones and figured they belonged to friends of nearby neighbors. Out of the corner of his eye, he saw movement from a new boat far away from the biggest cluster. He squinted out of curiosity, wondering if someone decided to sleep on their little boat at night. Generally, that was frowned upon by their neighborhood association.

Before he could process the movement, an intense beam of purple[137] light shot from a porthole of the boat. The light reached John instantaneously, leaving him no time to react. The searing pain in both eyes was all consuming, and as John instinctively turned away, he felt the light beam burn a trail along his skin toward his scalp and ear before it stopped.

He ripped off his sunglasses, fell to his knees, and covered his face, screaming, feeling as if his eyes had been removed by a hot poker. As his family ran out, the sunglasses lay

---

[137] Though John perceived the light as purple, it was actually violet. Purple is not on the electromagnetic spectrum.

smoking on the deck with perfect retina-sized holes in each lens. The little boat slowly drifted away, as if it were negligently unmoored.

# CHAPTER 15 – P

## CONNECTICUT, UNITED STATES

Dumisani Vead entered the hospital in Connecticut sporting a bespoke[138] dark gray suit and tie, instead of his traditional professorial garb. After signing in at the front desk, he rode the elevator to the appropriate floor and checked at the nurse's station, a genial smile on his face.

"Good morning. I'm Dr. Dumisani Vead and I'm here at the request of Dr. Pilsen."

"We're expecting you, Dr. Vead. Are you with Health and Human Services?"

Dumisani tilted his head to the side, reflective. "In a matter of speaking. I'm associated with the Agency for Healthcare, Research, and Quality; it's an organization under Health and Human Services."

The nurse leaned over her desk. "Thank goodness you are here," she whispered. "It's such an unusual situation; Dr. Pilsen's been anxious to meet with you."

Dumisani nodded and stepped aside. Although most at home in his kufi hat, he wore many proverbial hats depending on the situation. He *was* actually associated with AHRQ.

In the United States, anytime a hospital or clinic treated a patient with an unusual or mysterious injury or condition, a report needed to be filed with the AHRQ government arm of the Department of Health and Human Services. If staff encountered a dangerous or strange disease, the Centers for Disease Control was contacted instead.

---

138 Bespoke – A British term for custom made

Dumisani sighed internally. He didn't relish this responsibility, as critical as it was. He was here today because a Guardian at AHRQ contacted him, letting him know that a Commoner was likely injured by a Debilis.

Anytime a suspect report came into AHRQ, their Guardian contact, a senior-level AHRQ employee, would let Dumisani know. He or one of his regional Keeper doctors would immediately visit the patient, no matter their location.

If a Debilis inflicted the injury, he and his staff first offered guidance and advice regarding treatment—the most effective and accessible Commoner remedy available. Second, they verified and potentially altered the AHRQ report, creating a Commoner explanation for the injury, as true to the facts as possible. Last, at the hospital or clinic, they reinforced the AHRQ explanation quelling any gossip relating to the mysterious and unusual injury. Depending on the trauma, this step could be easy or exceedingly difficult.

Ethics was one of the classes Dumisani taught. Being Head Keeper, he also lived by a strict moral code and disliked any kind of subterfuge. The need to protect the Keepers of the Rock Society was paramount, but he didn't enjoy crafting lies.

Nalin and Evren reminded Dumisani periodically that this internal conflict demonstrated his moral mettle. Feeling uncomfortable was a good sign; it meant he still cared about humanity and the needs of Commoners. Debilis never felt remorse.

He pasted on a smile as Dr. Pilsen approached. They introduced themselves and she ushered him into an unoccupied patient room.

"Dr. Dumisani, I appreciate your prompt arrival. I've been in practice for over twenty years and never seen this type of ocular injury outside of a workplace setting. Mr. Myers lost his vision completely. It almost seems as if a targeted industrial laser burned through his eyes! We've contacted the police, of course, and they've started an investigation. Can you please take a look and let me know if my treatment protocol is sound? I don't envy Mr. Myers's situation; his whole life has completely changed."

Dumisani listened, a somber expression on his face. "Of course, Dr. Pilsen."

After this visit, a Keeper with expertise in regional law enforcement would closely follow the case and make sure the police conclusions essentially mirrored his own. They were due to discuss the situation tomorrow, to make sure they corroborated each other's findings. Mr. Myers had mentioned a recent fund devaluation disappointment to the police. He would have his compatriot look into a potential link.

While studying the case on the journey to the hospital, Dumisani internally seethed over the likely explanation: a callous act of retaliation on a Commoner by a vindictive Debilis. These cases of cavalier retribution were uncommon, but he'd seen too many over the years.

For now, he needed to listen, recommend, come up with a believable Commoner explanation, and spin. "Steady, man," he whispered to himself. The famous line from Sir Walter Scott's epic poem was ever-present in his mind as he followed Dr. Pilsen: "*Oh, what a tangled web we weave, when first we practice to deceive.*"[139]

---

[139] Scott, Walter. *Marmion; a Tale of Flodden Field.* Cambridge, 1895.

## CHAPTER 16 – S

### COLLEGE OF GEOEVOLUTION

# MID-AUGUST

Xandra Topper waited outside the international passenger arrival area at Newport News/Williamsburg Airport. Little did her new charges know, this was their last major interaction with the general public for a while.

Xandra stood rigid and proper, the model of efficiency and competence. To emphasize the look, she wore her khaki World War II British Auxiliary Territorial Service[140] uniform, complete with Service Dress cap and hair pulled back in a tight black snood.[141]

Although she might appear unapproachable, vast experience taught her that exuding authority and capability was more appreciated at this moment. In addition, traffic was ghastly and she was in no mood to offer hugs and uplifting innocuous drivel. She might have arrived in a better mood if Fabek had allowed her to drive the school's van—heaven

---

[140] National Army Museum. "The War on Glamour." https://www.nam.ac.uk/explore/war-glamour

[141] Snood – A decorative mesh hairnet worn over a bun or gathered hair, usually at the nape of the neck; a very popular look in the 1800s and again in the 1940s

forbid! He was forever slow and meticulous and took this role as seriously as any other. However, since they were good friends, she tolerated his eccentricities.

Xandra was expecting the first of three students momentarily. It would take two trips to retrieve them all. Although this airport was international, it wasn't entirely metropolitan. It was relatively small and received only a few international flights from several main carriers daily.

Her charges would be jet-lagged and uncomfortable, having traveled on multiple flights from far-flung places around the globe. Nothing good sleep and healthy food couldn't fix.

She caressed the broach on her lapel, the one non-regulation item on her uniform, not that it mattered anymore. It was a perfect circle, housing two half-moon-shaped gemstones, a golden-yellow citrine[142] and a clear sea-blue aquamarine[143]. The whole was surrounded by perfectly matched emerald-green tourmaline baguettes.

She activated them again with the heat from her fingers, infusing them with benevolent thoughts of safety and resilience. The citrine helped amplify cheerfulness and clear thought, while the aquamarine served to calm anxiety and nerves. Harnessing energy from both, the green tourmaline soothed frayed nerves and calmed weary travelers.

When the students first met Xandra, the benefits of the pin were sure to counteract any sourness from her. Today, she was set to meet Ming Sen from Singapore, KameKona Johnson from Hawaii, and Tú Chen from China, her Pacific theater contingent. Arranging travel from various worldwide

---

[142] "Citrine," https://www.mindat.org/gm/1054

[143] "Aquamarine," https://www.mindat.org/gm/289

destinations was always a challenge, especially when the goal was to take as few trips to the airport as possible.

Bedraggled travelers began to flow from international customs, so Xandra prominently displayed her SGE sign, attached to a wooden dowel. She knew whom to look for by sight, although they would appear exhausted, and her insight was quickly validated. Tú Chen was first, followed closely by KameKona Johnson. They stopped in front of her, self-conscious and shy.

"Hi. Ms. Topper?" KameKona asked.

Xandra was usually addressed as "Keeper," so the "Ms." title gave her pause. She was not often away from school grounds except for jaunts such as this, so she forgave him his faux pas. Once back on school grounds, their formal education would begin.

"Yes, I am Ms. Topper and I believe you are Scholars KameKona Johnson and Tú Chen?"

Tú nodded and shot a quick curious look at KameKona. "Yes, ma'am, Ms. Topper. I am Tú Chen."

"Marvelous! We are almost a complete happy party for today." She glanced around and gesticulated toward a third newcomer. "Are you rounding out our group today, young lady?"

Ming Sen swept her eyes around the three people in front of her, a small, anxious smile on her face. "I beg your pardon. Are you Ms. Topper from the College of GeoEvolution?"

"I am indeed. Am I to presume that you are Scholar Ming Sen?"

"Y-yes…I am. I am sorry I was delayed. Customs took longer than I thought."

"That is bureaucracy for you. No matter. This is Scholar KameKona Johnson and Scholar Tú Chen. You all are in possession of your traveling bags? I can assure you that your steam trunks, with all matter of familiar bric-a-brac, excess clothing, and whatnot, has already arrived at the school and been delivered to your rooms. Please follow me to the passenger conveyance and our driver and man about school, Keeper Fabek Sobalt. He's been waiting a while, and although he is very patient, as a rule, he doesn't relish ingesting motor vehicle exhaust."

"Oh, no doubt, Ms. Topper. I don't think anyone relishes inhaling car fumes." KameKona stated politely.

"Quite." Xandra turned in a flurry and walked purposely out of the airport terminal.

"Are those the school uniforms? I didn't know we had one. It looks very formal," Ming whispered.

"I don't believe that it is a school uniform," Tú said quietly. "I think it's a woman's World War II British Army uniform."

"Oh, man. I thought that looked familiar. I've seen that in a World War II history museum," KameKona stated, sotto voce. "That's pretty wild."

Before they could talk further, they approached a nondescript van, silver in color. A tall and gangly man sat in front. He nodded briefly to the three newcomers before looking to the road ahead.

"Before we proceed, there is an exchange that needs to take place for our collective safety. Do you remember the protocol?"

Ming and the two others dug into various clothing and jacket pockets and each produced the same enlarged silver and gold coin that Reese handed to Demyan. Although thought to have begun during World War I,[144] the tradition of challenge coins actually had its start during the time of the Romans. It was the Keepers who first adopted the practice during the First World War; Keeper lore suggests that a Guardian appreciated the custom, appropriated it, and it was allowed to become a Commoner tradition as well.

Ming rubbed her coin along its ridged edge and handed it to Xandra, who inspected it critically. When satisfied, she handed Ming a similar-sized coin in return. Each new student's coin was designed personally for them and was made of a nickel and copper alloy, a combination similar to that of the US penny.[145]

Ming's medallion had a bird's eye map of her homeland, Singapore, in the center of one side of the coin, along with her name along the perimeter. On the other side was the same rendering of a split geode with crystals found on the coin she handed Xandra, with *College of GeoEvolution, established in 1693* embossed in the Baskerville Old face font.

Tú had a similar coin, but the personalized side of his displayed a cluster of rare earth rocks transitioning into a uniform square, a symbol of the many devices that depend on rare earths to work. Lastly, KameKona's medallion showed the same erupting volcano displayed on the main coin, but without alternate-colored lava.

---

[144] World War I lore suggests that a downed airman's life was spared upon showing the coin to the French resistance. Both the British and Americans claim it was their service member: Lange, Katie. "The Challenge Coin Tradition: Do You Know How It Started?"

[145] Although not made from valuable and expensive metals, they were designed with practicality and expedience in mind. These coins could be created and produced quickly to individual specifications

After the exchange, Xandra stated, "You may climb aboard and place your bags anywhere you please. There is a short thirty-minute drive to our school, your new home away from home."

The three, worn out and feeling out of sorts, piled inside and sat in separate rows, respecting one another's personal space. Although quiet, it wasn't awkward, since lack of sleep, proper nutrition, hydration, and being in a foreign location was overwhelming.

Xandra addressed the silence. "I contacted Keeper Sahila at school and your families were notified that you arrived safely into my care."

Fabek slowly maneuvered the van into traffic. The muted din of vehicle congestion served as ambient music for the first several minutes until the familiar drive lulled Fabek into a sense of complacency. He began humming from among his favorite repertoire.

> *"Ding Dong Bell*
> *London is in hell*
> *A fire has come to burn it down,*
> *But th' Plague is gone, so that's all well,*
> *Ding Dong Bell."*

Xandra smiled and quipped, "Very nice, Keeper Fabek. But do remember good man Dryden: *'Rhyme is the rock on which thou art to wreck.'*"

"Hmm," Fabek responded and recited something else:

> *"She is older than the rocks among which she sits;*
> *like the vampire, she has been dead many times,*
> *and learned the secrets of the grave…"*

"Oh, you do flatter me, Keeper Fabek. I so appreciate Walter Pater." Sitting up front near Fabek, she turned to the group. "Pater was referring, of course, to Da Vinci's famed *Mona Lisa*[146] painting."

Ming, KameKona, and Tú looked at each other in alarm.

Chanting in a low voice, KameKona sang, "Never trust a man in a big white van." He brushed a hand along the backside of his short dreadlocks, as if hoping to encounter a familiar ribbon.

Tú looked confused by the comment and Ming supplied, "It's a familiar internet trope, about not getting kidnapped by a stranger in a van."

"My sisters used to sing that phrase on the military base and it was totally embarrassing, since most of the vans *were* white and at least half were driven by men. I'm not gonna lie, guys. This seems a little sketch to me."

"We had to exchange tokens to verify both of our identities, though," Tú added, as he palmed a handful of silver-colored magnetic rocks. To relieve anxiety, he absent-mindedly used his hands to create a rendering of a black bird, complete with a large and menacing beak.

Ming and KameKona were mesmerized, grateful for the temporary distraction. The eyes of the bird were piercing and shiny. Suddenly, it turned its head and inspected the van's occupants while it ruffled its feathers. The bird's mouth opened as if to squawk its opinion but thought better of it. It jumped from Tú's palm and perched on the top of the bench seat in front of him, preening at the group.

"Sorry, it's a habit."

---

146 "Mona Lisa." *Wikipedia*, Wikimedia Foundation, en.wikipedia. org/wiki/Mona Lisa.

"Let me guess," Ming surmised. "It's a raven…you know, *Nevermore?* Very *Poetic;* I get the sentiment. This is not how I had imagined our initial welcome meeting would go, to be honest—more than a little creepy."

"Your bird is killer, man," KameKona added.

Xandra clapped her hands and brought everyone's attention toward her. "All right, young pupils. We will be entering the grounds shortly. Please don't forget to bring all of your items with you, although I doubt that you will."

Ming Sen raised her hand and Xandra responded with a cocked eyebrow in anticipation.

"Yes?" Scholar Ming.

Ming held up an iPhone 10. "I found someone's phone between the seats in my row."

"Oh, how useful. You can hand it to me when you depart from the van. We'll leave it in the Graveyard of Lost Hopes and Tech room. There, someone may unleash their frustration or misguided and feeble resuscitation attempts upon it. We always need new fodder in that room to keep it well supplied."

"Oh, someone isn't looking for it?"

"Let me ask you a question in return. Are you pleased with the relationship you have with your technological devices—your cell phones and computers? Do they work properly for you most of the time?"

Three sets of eyes greeted Xandra's statement in recognition.

"Just as I thought. Yes, this will be explained in your classes. Soon, your devices will become dust-collecting paperweights or lovely additions to the Graveyard room. All in good time, all in good time."

Fabek parked the van inside the grounds after they drove through the farmland property of the school. Slowly and with trepidation, the three students gathered their items and Ming handed Xandra the phone. Tú's raven followed him silently, hopping from vinyl booth to booth.

Xandra smiled gleefully at the bird as it approached and lifted her arm, an invitation to perch. "Scholar Tú, he's masterful! I'd like to offer him a home if I may?" At his assenting nod, she added, "I will call him Edgar, on your recommendation, Scholar Ming." Edgar perched on her shoulder and began biting the hair that had dared escape Xandra's snood.

The school was in late summer glory and greeted the three weary travelers with relief. It looked like a stately traditional college should, complete with ivy and old, well-maintained buildings. They were shown into the main student building and to their individual rooms. Since the students would spend the majority of their day together and would follow the same curriculum for the next two years, it was decided, from the school's inception, that individual rooms were best for all, given the constant close proximity. Considering the buildings were still standing and in good condition, the decision had obviously been a good one.

The rooms were generously sized and included a main room for sleeping and dressing and a sitting room; this contained a large desk, two sizeable overstuffed sofa chairs, and a working fireplace. For conservation reasons, the fireplaces were only used occasionally and burned wood collected from fallen trees found on the property. Similar to other colleges and universities, students were encouraged to personalize their space, without poking holes in the walls, of course. That seemed to be a universal stipulation the world over, to the consternation of students everywhere.

Upon their arrival, to minimize stress and anxiety, the students were welcomed to the school and escorted to their rooms only by Keeper Alegria Hinine. She greeted them in a simple peasant skirt and blouse in muted tones of blue and green.

Her turquoise moose was pressed into service and sat at her waist, temporarily acting as a belt buckle ornament. Its obsidian eyes twinkled as she walked and his presence helped foster a soothing and calming atmosphere, as well as serving as an icebreaker.

Once settled into their rooms, they would be escorted to the main dining hall for their first meal. Alegria and Xandra would join them to answer any questions and further calm nerves.

When dinner time approached, Alegria walked Ming, Tú, and KameKona to the main dining hall, where they were greeted by an enthusiastic Ngai and Hattie, eager to meet some of their new diners. To them, food comforted and nourished the body and soul. They started with Tonkotsu ramen[147] and Tom Ka Gai,[148] aromatic soups that warmed the insides with gentle but intense flavors. Ngai also made vegetarian versions, until he and Hattie knew of their students' dietary preferences.

---

[147] Tonkotsu – A traditional pork broth flavored with leeks, scallions, onion, mushrooms, and ginger. It is served with pork belly, ramen noodles, and an optional whole egg—with a soft and creamy yolk, so it mixes perfectly within the broth

[148] Tom Ka Gai – A Thai soup flavored with coconut milk, lemongrass, lime, and mushrooms, traditionally served with chicken or shrimp

In addition, with students hailing from all over the world, heat or spiciness in a dish is very subjective. While one student finds a dish mild, another student thinks a five-alarm fire is burning in their mouth. To accommodate all palates at his table, Ngai served food traditionally made to be spicy in a mild version. For those who preferred their food "to bite them back," as Keeper Reese was fond of saying, Ngai had an impressive collection of hot sauces and spice enhancements to pair with his expert creations. At every meal, a lazy Susan was placed on the table, showcasing the spicy options best suited to the meal served.

In addition to the soups, Ngai offered traditional salad and potstickers.[149] All three students were familiar with Asian cuisine and Ngai wanted to welcome them with a comforting meal. For dessert, Hattie offered sweet profiteroles.[150]

The next day Xandra and Fabek journeyed back to the airport to meet the last four of the new students. They considered this group their "European" contingent, with one exception: Tessa Horton from Ohio.

Xandra once again left Fabek with the van and went inside, this time dressed in a trim midnight blue Edwardian riding habit. The outfit included a full-length skirt with a

---

[149] Potstickers – Asian-style dumplings

[150] Profiteroles – A pastry stuffed with cream or ice cream and served with chocolate sauce; this version was filled with green tea ice cream

fitted jacket worn over a shirtwaist.[151] A riding hat with a plumed feather and a leather crop completed the look.

Although a slave to her particular fashion, Xandra was ever aware of the changing world around her. A riding crop might be considered a weapon by the TSA,[152] so she left that in the van with Fabek.

The first to emerge from international arrivals was Aedan Colston from England. Although visibly tired, his gunmetal blue eyes slightly glassy, he carried a heavy-looking bag over his shoulder with relative ease. He had an easy, quick gait, despite his tall and broad-shouldered frame. He approached Xandra with polite respect and waited for her to speak.

"Scholar Aedan, I gather?"

"Yes, ma'am, I am. Thank you for meeting us here." Further conversation was halted by the arrival of Élise Peters-Comtois. She slowly approached the small party and positioned herself to the side, with Xandra's and Aedan's face visible to her.

Élise pointed to the sign Xandra held. "Excuse me," she signed and spoke, "are you from the College of GeoEvolution?" She spoke slowly, enunciating each word with precision, with her unique patois. Her English was clear with a gentle French accent, although it sounded somewhat monotone to Xandra and Aedan; since Élise could not hear inflection in others' speech, her sounds were a bit subdued.

Aedan smiled at Élise and began signing, "Hi. I'm Aedan. I've arrived as well for the College of GeoEvolution."

---

[151] Shirtwaist – A fitted shirt for women with a collar and cuffs, worn in Edwardian times

[152] TSA – Transportation and Security Administration for the United States, tasked with ensuring that traveling is safe and secure

Élise, visibly surprised, signed back and said, "You speak sign language?"

Aedan laughed. "Only a small amount, I'm afraid. My uncle is deaf, so everyone in my family picked up the basics." Although Aedan learned BSL[153] and Élise knew both ASL and LSF,[154] the languages were similar enough that they could understand each other with relative ease.

"That's fortuitous," Xandra added. "I am glad you are both here, Scholars Aedan Colston and Élise Peters-Comtois. We are awaiting two more in our party. You both looked knackered, but otherwise none the worse for wear. A good meal, some soothing tea, and a decent sleep should revive you."

Élise smiled in gratitude and realized that another person had joined them. He was also tall, had penetrating hazel eyes, and deep sable brown hair cut close to his head in an almost military style. Where Aedan appeared congenial and approachable, this student seemed wary and discerning.

He nodded to Xandra and the group. Nonplussed, Xandra quipped, "Greetings, young man. And you are—?"

"Demyan Ivanova, from Riga."

"Oh excellent. I hope your uncle is faring well." At his assurance she nodded. "Very good. I'm happy you can join us. We are shortly expecting Scholar Tessa Horton and then we can depart."

While everyone got acquainted, Demyan snuck glances at the other two students. Élise was otherworldly—a Viking princess with long, almost white blond hair and light blue eyes, dressed in chic jeans and a fitted top. She was a sharp contrast to Aedan's shaggy dark blond hair, worn jeans, and an untucked shirt. A somewhat comfortable silence

---

153 BSL – British Sign Language

154 LSF – French Sign Language

permeated the group as they quietly assessed their surroundings and each other.

The last one in their party was about to greet them, but Élise seemed to be the only one aware of their impending arrival; she raised her head and turned around, searching the airport for something. Within a minute, the others heard the sound of stomping and dragging. A pair of black worn Doc Martens boots came into view, attached to a tiny pixie with short spiky red hair and green eyes. She looked decidedly cranky.

"Hi. Are you Ms. Topper?"

"Ah, Scholar Tessa, you have arrived."

"If I fly again this side of never, I'll be thrilled! I didn't know layovers could last that *long!* And I came from Oohhiio! I sat next to a heavy breather on one side who played the drums on his tray table the whole time, and let me tell you, his rendition of 'Another One Bites the Dust'[155] left a lot to be desired! And on the other side was a cute six-year-old girl, but she kept leaning over me to look out the window and spilling her Goldfish snacks. If that wasn't bad enough, she proceeded to grab them from my hair and the back of my jacket and eat them! I will never eat another Goldfish snack for probably five years. And they were the cheddar flavor, which was my favorite, so thanks for that!" Tessa finished her diatribe with a breath that blew the hair from her eyes. "What? Am I late? Sorry about that. Not my fault. I mentioned the long layover, right?"

Half of the group stared at her in confusion and the other in wonder.

---

[155] 'Another One Bites the Dust' released in 1980 by Queen on their 'The Game' album (Musicland, Munich).

"Well, that was quite the travel experience, my dear. Hopefully great lessons were learned by all. Every experience provides that if you take the time to pay attention. All right, my chickens, let's move onward."

Xandra led the group out the exit and toward the van. Fabek had circled the terminal multiple times to avoid attracting the attention of airport security. Not liking confined spaces for long periods of time, he was decidedly antsy and bounced a leg on the floor, eager to leave.

"All right, before we board, we must exchange our tokens. Are you all prepared?"

Just as before, everyone reached into various pockets to pull out their coins. Aedan's had the United Kingdom on one side with his name and a picture of a lump of iron and a pickaxe on the other. Élise had a picture of a patch of Earth, cracked into two with an uneven fissure dividing the halves and a map of France on the other. Demyan had a rendering of a gem displayed in a box on one half and a map of Latvia on the other. Finally, Tessa had a crystal pyramid prism on one side with a laser ray shooting out of it on one side and a map of the United States on the other.

As tired as the students were, they seemed relieved when the coins were exchanged and they could board the van. As soon as their bottoms hit the bench seats, the van pulled out with a lurch. Xandra began her explanation about the short drive, their individual rooms, and the restorative meal. In the middle of her speech, a black bird alighted on her shoulder and opened its mouth in silent diatribe, seemingly parroting what Xandra said.

All the students were fascinated by the bird's liveliness. It was so lifelike, yet also mechanical in nature. How did this creature move so fluidly? The appreciation and wonder continued until the bird began to drop little black pieces from its nether regions. Some landed on Xandra's shoulders and tangled in her collar. Others bounced off the floor and magnetized to the metal base of the bench seats.

"Oh, Ms. Topper," Demyan began. "I'm sorry to inform you, but your bird seems to be fouling the van."

"Wow, that's an incredibly proper way to say, 'Heck ya, he's pooping everywhere,'" Tessa added, looking at Aedan.

"Oh, don't mind Edgar," Xandra replied. "His manners are decidedly atrocious. He was gifted to me just yesterday by Scholar Tú and I haven't yet had time to train him." She turned to Edgar and put her face near his beak. "You're a badly behaved birdie, aren't you moppet?" she crooned. Before the others had time to process, a song emanated from the front of the van.

*"Vlad Dracul, Vlad Dracul, what are you going to do?*
*Impale my enemies on pikes and watch them suffer, and you?*
*Vlad Dracul, Vlad Dracul, that's very cruel*
*I don't give a fig and neither should you*
*Lest you find yourself up there too."*

Xandra ignored Fabek's musings to brush away the gifts Edgar lavished upon her. The van had arrived at the school and the newly arrived could escape, slightly worried about the choice they made.

"Scholar Aedan, before you leave, can you please collect Edgar's body parts? They need to be reattached."

"Oh, of course, Ms. Topper."

Aedan climbed out of his bench seat, ready to search for the various pellets Edgar shed. He rubbed his large palms together and blew between them, creating heated friction.

When satisfied they were at the proper temperature, he held out a hand and intensely looked around the van, spying the various bits of loose rare earths. Pieces began flying into his outstretched palm, forming a magnetic ball. The other hand created sweeping arcs, maneuvering the various pieces into the waiting palm, like a maestro conducting a symphony. It was elegant performance art, and for the first time, Aedan felt free and relaxed. He could practice his skill without concern or fear; he was around those who understood and appreciated what he was inherently able to do.

Within less than a minute, all the loose rare earths were amassed and Aedan handed the ball into Xandra's outstretched hand. She looked at the ball, at Edgar, and sighed. She handed the ball back to Aedan.

"Be a dear and give this to Scholar Tú when you introduce yourself. Let him know that Edgar chose to complete his toilette in a vainglorious manner, naughty bird, and that these bits need to be reabsorbed; it's vital he remain whole. Once done, he will be returned to his former glory." Xandra turned away and added to no one in particular, "… but perhaps Edgar sloughed off the rare earths because they were extraneous? If so, what a clever bird!"

Aedan scratched the back of his neck, pocketed the ball of rare earths, and followed the group into the main living quarters to get settled.

Tessa could not believe she had arrived. After all the planning and packing, second guessing, and tearful au revoir to both her family and especially Dya, she was here. She chastised herself for her first impression. *Why do I babble stream of conscious nonsense? As if everyone wants to hear my anxious rambling!* On the other hand, she often spoke her thoughts, so others knew where they stood with her.

She sighed and continued to sort her items. A knock on her door interrupted her musings. It was that blond student, the French one. Élise waved one hand in greeting as she stood in the doorway. Tessa thought she looked like a princess from an old-fashioned fairytale, with her long blond hair and stylish clothes. She mentally kicked herself; she didn't like to form rash opinions about people, but had a bad habit.

Tessa was the furthest thing from a princess. She identified far more with the secondary characters in a fairytale, the misfits or quirky sidekicks. Although she drew laughs from others with her sarcastic humor, she wasn't popular and didn't desire the label anyway. She felt comfortable in her own skin but needed to shed the ever-present chip on her shoulder; it was an old security blanket. Before she left, Dya had told her to work on that.

She well remembered the words: "That will never serve you well, Tessabear. It will make it harder to make solid and trusting friendships, potentially lifesaving relationships." And here she was, falling back into bad habits. *Not this time.*

"Hi," Tessa responded with a bright smile, making sure she was facing Élise. "Are you settled in? I'm sorry I don't know any sign language yet."

"That's okay. I've learned how to read lips pretty well," Élise signed as she spoke. She tentatively began the conversation with this quirky and seemingly awkward fellow student. An expert observer, Élise immediately noticed the expressions playing across Tessa's face. Tessa was deciding how she would interact with Élise and what she initially thought of her. It didn't bother Élise; it was a situation in which she was very familiar. She had long ago learned to emotionally disengage from these initial encounters and to not get wounded. She was a complex, multifaceted person who didn't belong in any one category or box.

"I imagine that it's really challenging to learn to read lips from people with different accents."

Élise laughed. "Yes, it was a struggle when I first lost my hearing, especially when I went to an international boarding school. But, you know, you figure it out when you have to." Élise looked at Tessa's left hand. "That's a beautiful ring."

Tessa glanced at the only ring she wore. She brushed the band with her thumb absently, an innocuous habit. "Thank you. My mentor surprised me and gave it to me before I left; she graduated from this college too."

"You're lucky to have someone care so much about you to give you such a beautiful gift."

Tessa snorted accidentally when she laughed. "And here I was thinking how lucky you are to have that incredible hair and know how to dress like a fashion model."

Élise gently smiled back. "It's about time for dinner. Should we go down and see what's going on? I haven't really had time to meet anyone else yet."

"Sure." To lighten the mood, she gesticulated wildly with her hands. "Will I pick up sign language by osmosis if you keep signing when you speak to us? Oooh, you can teach us some great swearing signs, maybe a language none of the teachers understand?"

Élise rolled her eyes and shook her head. "I don't know. I guess that remains to be seen. Let's go."

## CHAPTER 17 – C1

## COLLEGE OF GEOEVOLUTION

Ngai sighed with contentment—his dining area was filled with life. Hattie and he had no children of their own, but they thoroughly enjoyed spending time with the pupils of the College of GeoEvolution. He loved making meals, even if only for an audience of one, his beloved Hattie.

Nothing, however, compared to serving a full house. He was classically trained in the French fashion, but was versatile in cooking various cuisines and thrived on experimenting with international dishes. He and Hattie considered themselves indispensable cogs in the waterwheel that turned and brought energy to the College of GeoEvolution.

Every employee had an integral role to play toward preparing every student, each a future Keeper, for the vital job they were destined to hold. They were charged with making all students feel at home, and food and drink were essential to that pursuit.

He and Hattie's ability to offer comfort and a familiar cuisine to one so far from home helped ease the monumental transition. They were happiest when they could offer this sustaining support. Once the pair spent more time with their students, they would easily learn their preferences and dietary restrictions. Ngai couldn't wait for the pneumatic tube system that connected the classrooms to his kitchen to resume its familiar sound.

Tonight's meal was a smorgasbord of flavors. When Demyan saw Hattie place ceptas kartupelu pelmeni dumplings on the table, he beamed. "This is amazing! They look so delicious! They are pan-fried potato dumplings filled with bacon and onions. And they even have the sour cream to eat with it. I hope you all love it."

Hattie also added mellenu klimpas, a blueberry dumpling soup, a favorite seasonal dessert in Latvia. She and Ngai knew the light and flavorful Eastern European and Baltic dishes would be familiar and welcoming to Scholar Demyan.

Regardless of what the duo prepared, however, leftovers and less favorable dishes were quickly dispatched into Jürgen's bottomless and appreciative digestive system, for nothing Ngai made ever tasted bad.

The food was appreciated by a mostly quiet group of tired and reticent students. Xandra sat at one end of the table, joined by Sahila and Evren, the most diplomatic and calming among the Keepers. There was no benefit to overwhelming the new pupils with enthusiastic personalities so soon after they arrived. They would be introduced to the rest of the Keeper educators the following day.

The next course was a hearty and filling British pasty that mirrored the recipe of the Cornish Pasty. Similar to France and their Champagne, the pasty couldn't be given the name Cornish Pasty unless actually made in Cornwall, England.[156] Ngai, being a man of the world, respected such European rules and regulations and adhered to them.

---

[156] The dish was given a PGI in 2011, a Protected Geographical Indication, that prevents chefs from using the proper name for the dish unless it was created in the particular region for which it is named

Hattie imparted these gastronomical educational lessons onto her young flock with great enthusiasm. She insisted that their students embrace the international world of food and culture to become sophisticated gourmands. At the very least, she encouraged them to try almost anything once.

Their version of this delight, a nod to traditional fare in England, had a buttery crust filled with cubed beef, onions, turnips, and sliced potato. Ngai also created a delicious savory vegetarian version filled with sliced potato, fresh peas, carrots, and turnip.

While eating, Tú accepted the ball of rare earths from Aedan and slipped it into his pocket, ready to be returned to a reluctant Edgar at some later date. Aedan appreciated Tú's handiwork.

"Can you show me how you do it? I don't usually work with rare earths."

Although both were able to work with magnetic substances, their mediums were different. Tú worked mainly with rare earths, whereas Aedan had the ability to manipulate iron as well as other minerals and rocks.

When talking with Tú, Aedan was reminded of the reluctant parting with his metal detector. He donated it to a secondhand store and quietly purchased a new more sophisticated model, one that actually worked, and gave it to an eager younger sister. The lawn mowing job went to his next oldest sibling, a brother, who was starting secondary school. He missed his family already, although he just left them a day earlier. He knew that it was time, however; he needed a break from his family. Where did he fit in the larger world?

Although he loved his family, Aedan was fundamentally different, the cuckoo in the nest.[157] Keeping his true nature from them was a lie and a half existence. Aedan didn't want to live like that anymore and needed to be around others who understood him. He needed to be able to freely explore the entirety of who he was. Aedan knew he would always be a part of his family; for as much as he craved this new chapter in his life, he didn't want the apron springs fully severed. He figured the physical distance between them would give him time to figure it all out.

"I hope you are all settling in well enough. Please let us know if there is anything you need," Evren began as dinner wound down.

In addition to the pasty, the meal was paired with a simple green salad with tomatoes and fresh cucumbers coated in a delicate olive oil, lemon vinaigrette, and shallot dressing. Dessert was traditional chocolate eclairs and palmier cookies.

Evren began. "Tonight, and over the next few weeks, we want you to become acclimated to this country and to our own particular corner of the world." He smiled as he glanced around the room, empathizing with everyone about the kind of exhaustion that comes from traveling to different time zones. "Most importantly, we want you to become used to being free, to fully being yourself for perhaps the first time in your lives. This is a safe space for you. It was designed from the very beginning with you in mind and for those who came before you, all the way back to our first opening day, in 1693.

"Over the next few weeks, you will get to know each other well. It may be hard to believe that you will soon consider

---

[157] Cuckoo birds are brood parasites. They lay their egg in another bird's nest to be raised by the unsuspecting parents

each other family, since other than your unique connection to the natural world, you hail from very different parts of this Earth and may not have much in common. I can assure you, however, it will happen. It always does."

Sahila picked up the reins of the conversation. "I wish you all a hearty and warm welcome to our beautiful home. In the morning you will receive a full tour of all we have to offer here and will develop a much clearer sense of what and how you will be learning. Tonight, however, we reserve this time to begin to get to know each other. Being a very old college, we have quite a few traditions. As you see"—Sahila waved a hand around the table— "we are an incredibly small institution. This is by natural design and has been this way since the beginning. Ultimately, we don't determine how many students we receive each term, if any; this is in the hands of far more powerful forces." Sahila smiled broadly and chuckled. "*It is far beyond our pay grade,* as the popular phrase goes."

Sahila and Evren looked around the table, weighing the reaction of their new pupils. They knew this information was not entirely a surprise. One didn't possess unique talents such as theirs and not wonder as to the ultimate explanation for their abilities. Over time, they would delve into this more deeply; Rome wasn't built in a day, after all.

"So, let's end this evening with a little introduction from all of you," Evren stated. "We'll go around the table and we'd like to hear about your preferred medium material and what works for you."

Aedan raised his hand reluctantly. He didn't consider himself to be shy, but was indeed reserved and introverted. Away from his large family for the first time, he decided that he needed to step out of his comfort zone more. No time like the present.

"Hi, I'm Aedan Colston, from West Yorkshire, England. I most prefer working with finished iron. I like magnetite the most, as a raw material, but I'm most satisfied when I find an iron object in the ground I can manipulate."

How did Aedan explain this without sharing too much with a group of strangers? He imagined everyone would understand, but he felt vulnerable. How to explain that finding an older fabricated piece of iron made him feel less alone? He sensed a kinship with other metalsmiths, whether the object was made a few years ago or created thousands of years ago by an ancient Roman.

"I think it's really cool to touch a piece of iron history, you know? Getting to work with a piece someone else already rendered is special. If I find it, it has a purpose again. My favorite is an antiquated piece of Roman metal. The filial connection is the strongest. And it makes me sad when a piece like that is abandoned or neglected and lost in the ground. The person who took intense effort to create it was ultimately forgotten." He could see in his mind's eye the metalsmith hammering and firing the iron in his workspace, could hear the hiss as the piece cooled in the water, and almost feel the spray of water on his face and arms as the water vapor reacted to the intense heat of the ore.

Everyone was paying close attention and seemed to accept what he said, so he sighed with relief and was glad his turn was over.

Élise, sitting to Aedan's left, was slightly freaked he volunteered to start. Logically, she was next if they were taking turns. She raised her hand and waved it, signaling her willingness. She wanted to get it over with after her quick burst of bravery.

"If I have to pick a favorite type of earth shift, it would be a reverse fault at a convergent boundary," she said and signed. "At least something amazing can result from it, over time, you know?"

At the other students' blank glances, she demonstrated with her hands sliding along one another. "A reverse fault happens when one plate, an earth plate, slides along and above another one. A convergent boundary is often located where there are mountains. So, the reverse fault can continue the growth of the mountain over time. Sometimes, earthquakes can be so destructive to people and wildlife, but at least this kind of earthquake can create something beautiful."

She paused. "It was a reverse fault at a convergent boundary that I first felt—when I first sensed—an Earth movement, when I was four. So, I have a special affinity for them. Although my mother took me to the doctor thinking my deafness was giving me balance issues." She rolled her eyes. "That was fun. I didn't tell my parents that I could feel the ground shake after that, especially when no one else seemed to sense it but me. It became my little secret with the Earth, my special bond," she trailed off with a distracted smile. "I'm Élise Peters-Comtois, by the way—Paris, France."

Evren smiled gently. "Thank you both for sharing; we know it isn't easy to be so open just after you've arrived."

Tessa raised an eyebrow. "Well, I don't know about that; I'm often the queen of oversharing, or so I've been told. I think my filter is broken, but hey, we all have things to work on, right?" She blew some wayward hair away from her face. "When I was really young, I loved to dig in the dirt, make mud pies, you know? My mom would get so irritated, 'cause I'd be such a mess, usually right before she had to go to work. She's a nurse."

Tessa glanced at Tú and Élise. They sat with perfect postures and looked so put together. She had on her favorite ripped jeans and wore a wrinkled T-shirt that proudly stated, *Beam me up, Scottie, and don't forget the shortbread.* She had it made at the mall one Christmas and gave another one to Dya, who only wore it to sleep in, of course. Tessa distractedly thought that Élise and Tú probably didn't know what a mud pie was.

"When I was about five, I was playing in the dirt and I found a quartz crystal. It was small and fractured, so it wasn't perfectly symmetrical. But I picked it up, fascinated, and cleaned it up. I remember being mesmerized by its simplicity and its facets. I turned it 'round and 'round in my hands, squatting in my mud puddle.

"Then I held it up to the sun and rotated it again, really concentrating on the way the light filtered through and was refracted. I'm assuming a laser beam shot out from the crystal, because light hit my metal shovel, which reflected back toward the right side of my face, and ultimately hit the top of my ear. I was wearing my sunglasses, at least, thank goodness."

Tessa moved her hair off her right ear and displayed the small scar, still visible. "My mom came out when I screamed and I told her I hit my ear with my shovel. It was a burn and she knew it, being a nurse, but she just treated it, and never said a word about it. I was a handful right from the outset." Tessa shrugged.

Demyan sat to Tessa's left. He placed his right hand over Tessa's left one and let it hover. He glanced at her and raised an eyebrow, silently asking her permission to touch her. She nodded subtly, and he laid his fingers gently over hers, particularly touching the ring Dya gave her. "This ring is new to you, correct?"

"Yes. My mentor, Dya, gave it to me shortly before I left to travel here."

"This stone is an Asscher cut, octagonal in shape, and it has a strong history." Demyan's fingers encircled the stone and he felt it radiate heat and energy into his fingers. "It has a strong provenance and was worn before by someone for many, many years, an exceptionally long lifetime. This stone was in a simple and functional setting, not ornamental. It was worn as a ring, like now, and was worn in wartime, but was not utilized to incite violence or cause destruction.

"The person who wore it…" He closed his eyes. "The *woman* who wore it was hopeful; her goal was to preserve life. She was no stranger to dangerous situations. I can sense stress and fear under the hope. She suffered losses, but overall, there is great joy and perseverance. She was a great lady."

Suddenly, Demyan's hand flew off of Tessa's as he noticed light dancing around the stone facets of her ring… The light ceased radiating almost immediately, but not before charring a golf ball-sized mark on the ceiling. Demyan shouted, "Tas sāp!"[158]

Tessa looked in horror and covered her mouth with both hands. "I'm so sorry! I didn't mean to!" She turned to Demyan. "Are you okay?"

Demyan held up his hand and turned it over, back and forth. "I am okay. It doesn't hurt anymore; I was just surprised."

Sahila stood up and walked over to Tessa, whose eyes were bright with unshed tears from both frustration and embarrassment. She leaned down and gave her a gentle squeeze.

---

[158] Tas sāp – Latvian for it burns

"We specialize in those who are considered handfuls. In our experience, these students are misunderstood; their brilliance is not easily recognized by those who lack imagination, creativity, and a little bit of patience." Addressing everyone, she added, "You will all learn to harness that energy properly, and when necessary, to cloak and sometimes separate your emotions from your abilities."

Evren motioned for everyone to follow him out of the dining room. They could continue their share time the following evening. Tomorrow would prove to be a pivotal day.

Sahila walked out with Tessa and casually petted the back of her head. "Dya was right to recommend you to us. She has excellent instincts. You are in the right place, Scholar Tessa. Don't be so hard on yourself, okay?"

Everyone was tired and settling in for the evening after a long day. Since every day was part of a new experience, it wasn't surprising the students were exhausted. Tú was ready to store away the last of his painstakingly folded shirts into a drawer when he forgot he had one more. He turned around to grab the last one. Suddenly, the bureau began to violently shake.

*What's happening?*

He watched, mystified, as the shirts fell en masse onto the floor in an undignified and unfolded heap.

Alarmed, he held on to various bedroom surfaces as he scrambled out of his room. He was relieved to see the others making their way down the residential hallway.

"What's going on?" Aedan shouted.

"I don't know!" Tessa yelled before she fell to the floor and began crawling down the hall.

Evren appeared breathless at the entrance to the hallway. "It's okay! We have it under control. Drop to the floor and crawl to that room on the right!" He pointed the direction he wanted them to go. "Put your backs to the wall once you are there. The building is earthquake safe and that room is safest. You'll be okay!"

They looked like a stream of ants racing into the room. Once there, everyone looked around, frightened. It didn't feel safe. They could hear books toppling to the floor and the occasional glass breaking.

"Can you see anything outside the window?" someone asked.

Tessa impulsively peeked out. KameKona grabbed the back of her shirt and yanked her back forcefully. She smacked her shoulder onto the ground and yelped.

"You're not supposed to be near a window, in case glass breaks!" KameKona yelled.

"It's Élise!" she shrieked. "She's on the front lawn; she's freaking out!"

Several heads went to the window and KameKona smacked his forehead, giving up on keeping anyone safe. They were worse than his sisters, and that was saying a lot!

A floodlight outside illuminated the scene below. Élise stood on the front lawn, her legs spaced wide apart. Her head was thrown back and she was screaming as loud as she could and stomping. The look on her normally welcoming face was murderous.

"I think she's causing the earthquake! Alegria's running out!" Ming announced. Alegria ran in a diagonal pattern to keep from falling as she raced to Élise.

Around Élise, thin sections of grass parted. Rabbits, squirrels, groundhogs, and other furry critters scattered over the lawn, leaving their burrows for safer ground. The buildings around the quad swayed precariously and looked as if they might topple. A small outhouse building crumbled upon itself and what looked like mice and bats scurried out and flew in all directions.

Tessa shivered. "Well, that's just creepy and gross."

Within seconds of Alegria reaching Élise, the shaking stopped.

"Oh, sweet Élise! She's crying! Alegria's hugging her." Ming reported fervently.

"Sister, she's not crying, she's flat out bawling," Tessa remarked.

Aedan looked taken aback. "That's a bit judgmental, isn't it?"

"Oh, no disrespect meant. I know from experience, believe me."

They watched as Alegria led a limp and spent Élise to the residence building. When she and Alegria returned to the residence hall, Élise smiled wanly, clearly embarrassed. "I'm so sorry; there's no excuse for my outburst."

Alegria gave her shoulders a squeeze. "No harm was done; the lawn can be repaired and the animals will return tomorrow. Our buildings were built for this in mind. Do you honestly think we would create a college for teenagers with these kinds of abilities and *not* be prepared for the occasional emotional meltdown? Isn't that in a teen's job description? I certainly had my fair share!"

"Still," Élise said and signed. "I'm really sorry; I've never done that before. I got a call from my mother tonight. It's two in the morning in Paris right now! Who does that? She wanted to make sure I understood that the debutante community in Virginia is vibrant and that I can still participate if I am willing to prepare. I am finished with that nonsense! It's one of the reasons I moved thousands of miles away from her! I just became so furious and I couldn't stand it anymore."

Ming leaned over and gave her a hug. "I would say you've made great progress."

Élise looked at her as if she was crazier than she felt.

"Seriously! For the first time ever, you felt safe enough to release your anger!"

"Totally!" Tessa concurred. You just released it all at once!"

## Chapter 18 – Ar

## College of GeoEvolution

Recovered from the previous night's event, the residents of the College of GeoEvolution awoke with anticipation. The hum of intrigue was palpable—as if every building had a muscle memory, vibrating with residual energy housed in their bricks and mortar. Today was Elucidation Day, the official term for the first day of school since its initial founding. It was the day when the pent-up anxiety, excitement, and residual doubt was openly addressed. New students finally met all of their professors, staff, and the campus itself. Most importantly, each student would validate that they had made the right choice.

Breakfast was a brisk, but filling affair and despite its level of tastiness, no one was paying much attention. Those with nervous stomachs ate little and those who found food to be soothing ate without appreciating. Clearly the day was meant for more important activities.

Dumisani looked around at all seven of his young, wide-eyed charges. This was one of his favorite days to interact with them. They had an innocence and curiosity about them before the realities of their new world were revealed. Moving forward, they would carry the weight of their responsibilities on their shoulders; a burden assigned by destiny.

It wasn't as if Dumisani had little empathy; on the contrary, he exuded it. He continually pondered many weighty issues, so he deeply appreciated this day. Dumisani was a compelling and thoughtful leader, one of Keeper Society's finest.

Humanity at large was unaware that his skilled leadership protected them. He remained unsung, largely unknown, appreciated only by fellow Keepers, Guardians, and students alike. Seeing the hopeful and enthusiastic expressions of future Keeper leaders was inspirational and energizing to him. In quiet moments, he recognized that developing the next generation was his greatest motivation.

Dumisani lifted his arms enthusiastically. "Welcome, eminent scholars, to the College of GeoEvolution! We eagerly prepared for your arrival. I am Dumisani Vead, the dean of the College of GeoEvolution and one of your history and geology professors. Welcome to our day of elucidation. Without further delay, let's begin!"

He led them from the dining hall into the main area of instruction, located anticlimactically, in the basement. For security purposes, the majority of classes was conducted underground. Although the classrooms were mostly windowless, the lighting was designed to brighten each room. And by design, students circumnavigated the whole campus every day, so they could enjoy as much fresh air and natural light as possible.

They were met by Nalin Fink and Sahila Yold when they entered the main academic hallway. Nalin introduced herself and nodded at Tessa, the only student who had already met her. Before reaching the main classrooms, they approached a room emanating a faint buzzing sound, a constant low hum. Sahila approached the door and hovered her hand over the knob and keyhole, made of tarnished copper and intricately designed in a beautiful swirl pattern. She placed the palm of one hand on the knob and put each finger and her thumb around its circumference and waited patiently. Seconds later, the lock disengaged with an audible click.

Élise said and signed hesitantly, "Keeper Yold, may I ask a question?"

Keeper Yold smiled openly and raised an eyebrow in anticipation.

Emboldened, Élise continued, "Why is there a keyhole if you don't need a key to open the door?"

Sahila nodded enthusiastically. "An excellent question, Scholar Élise." Addressing the group, she answered. "You will learn very quickly that all inquiries are welcome and there are no inappropriate questions. The main building was designed with safeguards in place. Our founders believed that if the buildings were infiltrated by Debilis or other unsavory forces, and staff were somehow detained, our *Guardians* should be able to use one of the few keys to lend assistance."

"Debilis?" Tessa repeated. "What are those?"

"I studied a few languages in high school," interjected Ming. "The word comes from Latin, I believe. I think it means 'weak' or 'feeble'?"

"Nicely done, Scholar Ming," Nalin added. "They are weak, soulless humans who lack any form of empathy. We call them 'decayed ones', because they develop a rather pungent odor as they age; like a chemical half-life, their humanity seeps out of them and rot is all that's left. They are evil human-like creatures who cause chaos and devastation —our great antagonists, if you will. You should have little fear of them here, however. As Keeper Sahila said, the building was designed by our founders with safeguards in place. Shall we enter?"

Sahila pushed open the door and allowed everyone to enter the room. "Although most rooms on our campus are available for your use and curiosity, a few require supervision for your protection. This is one of them. In full disclosure, however, we have no secrets from you. We'd rather you know all the proverbial skeletons in the closet than go hunting for them yourselves."

The lighting in this room was muted, unlike in the classrooms and hallways. The room was open in the center with tables and curios lining the walls. Heavy lead glass containers filled with mostly shiny-colored objects rested on the tables. The faint buzzing sound was slightly louder now that they were inside the room. Everyone could hear Ming's audible gasp once she had a good look at the items inside the containers. Demyan sidled next to her and said in a whisper, "I've never been in a room with so many."

Ming nodded in agreement.

"This room is unnamed for obvious reasons. Each item has been painstakingly acquired and sometimes it took years to track down and take possession," Sahila explained. In each display case was a piece of jewelry, a solitary gem, or an uncommon rock, cut to optimize its natural facets and polished to a brilliant shine. While walking among the cases, the students watched the light hit the various facets, creating a kaleidoscope of color that dispersed along the walls and ceiling.

"Since our school's founding, we began collecting these ominous pieces," Nalin added.

Demyan rubbed his temples. "I can feel the ļaunums—I mean evil—radiating from these pieces. Where are they from?"

Sahila noticed Demyan's behavior. "We won't keep you here long, obviously. Some of you will be more sensitive than others. Demyan and Ming, you most likely will know that stones, gems, and rocks don't have emotions originally attached to them. That is to say, their natural radiating energy does not lean toward good *or* evil. These emotional energies are layered upon these stones by damaged human beings or the occasional animal who acquires them."

Sahila gestured to a particular sample. "A piece of jewelry, gem, or stone can exude a positive and healthy vitality if owned by a benevolent person with an empathetic soul. The piece absorbs the positive energy when held or worn for lengthy amounts of time or, in rare cases, when in the presence of an entity imbued with heightened energy. Unfortunately, as with most things in life, there is a balance, a ying and a yang—good and evil, if you will."

With a somber expression, she spun in a slow circle and walked down the center of the room, gesturing to the cases. "The pieces you see here, forty-two at last count, are *extremely* dangerous, as they are enhanced with malevolent energy. These items were used to encourage the harming or killing of others and the destruction of families, businesses, lives, and even the occasional political leader. Commoners and animals do not possess your special abilities and natural protections from them. So, they are susceptible to these objects and are unwittingly manipulated into harming others when in possession of them.

"In other instances, damaged individuals knowingly *choose* to use these stones to render such damage, further loading them with more negative and hateful energy. When a stone, gem, or rock is abused to this extent, this malicious energy remains and becomes embedded into the piece's very atomic structure. It can never be in circulation, for whomever owns it will be influenced by the evil trapped inside."

Sahila crooked her finger, summoning her charges to a particular case. "Take a look and see. You will no doubt recognize some famous items inside the cases. They are each housed separately, because, if placed together, they will influence each other and further amplify their negative energy."

She gently caressed the nearest case.

"Waterford Crystal[159] created all of these lead crystal boxes and curios. The ratio of lead is higher than in their normal crystal ware, used for drink or food. In certain lights, you can see a slight gray hue to the crystal. Thankfully, over the years we were able to amass most of this collection by purchasing the pieces. When the owners couldn't be persuaded to part with their treasures, however, we relied on other measures. Because, ultimately, our goal is to create a safer environment for humanity. When humanity is affected, the Earth is affected."

The students wandered around the room, looking at the beautiful pieces that lay inside equally gorgeous cases. Some were elaborate, comprised of diamonds and stunning gemstones. Others were simple, made of a single stone and a band or chain. Still others were only a gem or stone by itself.

"You have a lock and key mechanism for each box," Tessa noted. "How does that work?"

Nalin explained that a skeleton key worked for all of the boxes. She was met with puzzled glances, no doubt confused about the seeming lack of security for such dangerous items.

Nalin waved a hand dismissively. "Have no concern. Both the key and key cylinder are made of strong platinum. Several copies are kept in particular locations on campus and elsewhere. *And* merely inserting the key and turning the lock will not open the boxes. Inside each lock is a mechanism similar to an early thermostat. Have you ever studied the

---

[159] Crystal made exclusively in Waterford, Ireland

work of the British clockmaker, John Harrison?[160] In 1789, he developed a coil made of two different metals that heated and cooled at different temperatures.

"Harrison designed what was called a marine chronometer. Early thermostats used this technology to help regulate the heating and cooling of homes. So, based on that principle, inside each lock is a coil made of copper and steel thick enough that it must heat above 115 degrees Fahrenheit to become malleable and allow the lock to turn. The platinum key in turn must heat up to at least this temperature to heat the metals inside for this process to occur. Only those with our abilities are able to do that. And only our staff, a select few Guardians, and now you students know this fact."

The group gawked at the case contents. Élise pointed to a particular one that housed a necklace of diamonds shaped into flowers surrounding an emerald heart the size of an apricot. "I've heard of this necklace!" she said and signed. "It was reported stolen and the owner went bankrupt. He lost what had been a very successful multigenerational family business. The Heart of Melania."

Sahila shook her head and sighed. Facing Élise, she remarked, "Ah yes. That story was in the paper for weeks several years ago. That necklace caused mayhem to whomever owned it."

"I don't like being in this room," Ming interrupted. "Even in their cases, I can sense the negativity." Her head snapped up when she heard a delicate *crack*, like ice cubes breaking in a cup. Sahila and Nalin quickly motioned for everyone to head for the exit.

---

[160] Royal Museums Greenwich. "Longitude Found – the Story of Harrison's Clocks." www.rmg.co.uk/stories/topics/harrisons-clocks-longitude-problem

"I'm sorry! I feel like my head is going to explode," Demyan whispered, as he covered his ears. "That buzzing noise is so irritating. I can sense the evil, especially from that case!" He motioned with one elbow to the right corner. Nalin briskly walked down the line of cases, looking for the one Demyan mentioned. She stopped in front of a case with a hairline crack on its crystal lid. Inside was a large opal pendant encased in gold, also displaying a new crack along the face.

When Nalin returned to the students, she looked concerned. "Are you okay?" she asked a visibly calmer Demyan. "We'll work on your repelling ability. It takes time to learn how to become impervious to these forces. That said, you are very strong, Scholar Demyan. The cracking sound was from one of the cases, which now has a shallow surface fracture; I'm very impressed. You also managed to damage the opal that belonged to Vlad Tepes, the ruler of Wallachia, Romania—known as Vlad the Impaler. A good choice, by all accounts. He was an aggressive ruler with a penchant for torturing his enemies and impaling them on spikes."

Demyan tugged at his hair. "I am so sorry! I didn't mean to break anything."

Nalin squeezed his shoulder. "Not to worry, young scholar. All is well. This *is* a school, after all, and you are here to learn and hone your skills."

They rapidly exited the room and continued down the hallway, stopping at a random classroom where they were greeted by Reese.

"Well, good mornin', all! You're not knackered[161] yet, so I can still cram some information into ya."

He motioned for everyone to take a seat. The chairs were in the shape of an inverted U, facing the teacher's desk

---

[161] Knackered – British word for tired

and board. Reese leaned against the teacher desk, arms and ankles crossed.

"I'm Keeper Reese Rolding, everyone's favorite professor; some of you already met me during your home visits." He swept an arm around the room. "This is the regular arrangement for all of our classrooms. Solely designed for us to be certain no one falls asleep! Nah, I'm just joshin' you. We've never taught a boring class here—at least I haven't. Not sure about those two." He pitched his head toward Nalin and Sahila. "Truthfully, we teach this way so we can all participate equally. To facilitate that, we'll have a Guardian ASL language instructor this year to help everyone learn Élise's language. I have no doubt she'll pick up our distinct accents in no time, but we can all benefit from learning a silent language; you never know when that skill will come in handy.

"We have several interesting features in our classrooms. My favorite is by far our pneumatic tubes over there." He gestured with an arm to the front corner of the room. "The best modern innovation our school received in 1900, other than indoor plumbing! These tubes are placed throughout campus, but most of the classroom tubes head directly to the kitchens! When one of you lot answers a particular question correctly or makes a profound statement, we'll let you choose the tucker for the following night's dinna! You can pick anything you want, such as a particular cuisine from home, and Chef will prepare it for everyone. And if it happens to be a chicken dish, Keepa Jürgen will be 'specially thrilled. He's obsessed with chicken, that one."

Tú raised his hand.

"Yes, Scholar Tú?"

"If I may ask, what are those brass[162] tubes hanging behind you?"

Reese turned around and looked up at the "tubes" Tú was referring to. They were long rolls encased in brass that ran the length of the front slate board. There were several, all stacked horizontally, one beneath the other. He grabbed one by its brass handle and pulled it. "You mean these babies?'"

What turned out to be sturdy cloth lengthened past the slate board. It was a flat atlas of the world.

"We use the older maps for our history discussions. This one is for World War II. In the cabinet to the left, we store all the other maps we use throughout the year."

Reese pulled on the map and let it roll back into its brass canister. "Now, Scholars, please turn your attention to what I've written on the board. The following is the list of classes you will take here for the next two years at the College of GeoEvolution; it's the same list of classes we shared with your parents." On the board, written in chalk,[163] was the list of classes already familiar to each of the students:

*Classic Literature*
*Evolutionary Studies*
*Geology*
*History of World Leaders*
*Human Anatomy and Physiology*
*Introduction to Chemistry and Chemistry II*
*Introduction to Economics and Economics II*
*Introduction to Ethics and Ethics II*
*Introduction to Psychology and Psychology II*

---

[162] *Brass*, Wikimedia Foundation, en.wikipedia.org/wiki/Brass.

[163] Chalk – A soft form limestone (sedimentary rock) comprised mainly of calcium carbonate

*Introduction to Physics and Physics II*
*Kinesiology*

"I don't have to remind you that our school and all of you"—he outstretched an arm and swept it across the room— "are gloriously unique. We are not your typical college or university, as I am sure you're aware. You all are gifted with abilities not familiar to the average Joe or Jane Blow Commoner. That's our term for those without our abilities—regular human beings, by the way." Reese raised a hand, halting for emphasis. "Raise your hand if any of this information is news to you or freaks you out."

Everyone looked around the room, at each other, and shifted in their seats, but no one made a sound or raised a hand.

"That's what I thought. All right, Keepers Sahila and Nalin, may I proceed?" Reese glanced behind his shoulder, eyeing the two Keepers resting against the door frame. At their apparent acquiescence, he continued. "You all know that there's more to this world than what you see. Having such abilities must reinforce that feeling, that awareness. Well, you are correct. I'm gonna give you the drum[164] now.

"*You are the few, the proud, and at times, the cursed, to have this understanding.* So, what do you do with this special gift you've been given? Do ya wander through life, pretending to be one of the herd, hoping no one finds out or ignoring what you inherently are? Would that not be a waste or an insult to whomever entrusted this ability to you? Are you worthy of it? What do you do? Well, one would hope that you choose to 'use your powers for good,'" Reese stated, making air quotes. "Incidentally, that's the *last* time you will hear us

---

[164] Drum – Australian slang for information

speak this word in this context. Okay? *You don't have power.* That word suggests you have the right to manipulate or take choice away from others using your inherent advantage. That route only leads to unhappiness and madness. Trust me, I should know. So, we're back to the question, what do you do? Well, since you are all out of the top-drawer sticky beaks, you choose to come here, and that's the first step."

At the collective confused glances Reese received, Nalin explained, "You are all top-quality inquisitive individuals." Nalin clapped slowly, teasing Reese. "Anyway, after that illuminating revelation," Nalin said, eyes sparkling with humor, "we will briefly touch on your actual classes before we continue with the tour. We shared with your families the curriculum you will be studying, as you all saw during your interview. And although these are indeed your classes, we were not entirely forthcoming; we didn't give out the precise details of each class.

"We did this for the simple reason that most of your family members would not understand or be able to cope with the truth. I would like a show of hands—and be honest now—how many of you have a family member who knows about your true selves?"

Ming and Tessa were the only ones to raise their hands.

Ming said, "My grandmother is aware of what I can do; she guided me while she helped raise me. She somehow knew about your existence and she's the only person in my family who knows. I was taught never to talk about it with anyone other than her and only when we were alone."

Tessa waited for her turn, all but sitting on her hands to prevent herself from interrupting. "My mentor actually went to this college and graduated. I only found out a few months ago; I've known her for years and she never revealed anything to me before then."

Nalin offered a nod to Ming and Tessa. "Thank you for sharing, Scholars. So, back to my previous statement: Most of your families and friends don't know about your abilities. We take the concealment of both our existence and the existence of this college very seriously. So, until we are certain that you are going to be a student, sitting right here for Elucidation Day, we do not share the details of our curriculum."

She took a moment to soberly look into the eyes of every student. "We have followed this tradition since our inception and continue it today. Our effectiveness in this world and our ability to help, heal, and protect is dependent upon this secrecy. At times, our very lives and the sacred bonds with those who are aware of us are dependent upon it. We never take these responsibilities lightly. *Today begins our trust in you.* And we are confident, through all of our research and analysis, that it is well placed."

Nalin stepped back and made room for Sahila to take the lead in the classroom. "Again, welcome to our nonpareil[165] home. While Nalin was talking, Reese was writing down the details of each of your actual classes. I imagine that you all realized that your education will be unconventional. Periodically, we will discuss what you may choose to do with your dual degree once you are unleashed upon the world. That's a discussion for another time, however. I'd like to turn your attention back to the slate board."

---

[165] Nonpareil – Without peer or no equal. Also, little decorative balls of sugar, often put on top of round chocolates

## Classic Literature through Multimedia
*The Influence of the Keeper on literature and film and the partnership toward the preservation of the Keeper Society*

## Evolutionary Studies
*The Evolution and Impact of Keepers and their influence on Earth throughout history*

## Geology
*The study of the Earth, rocks, minerals, and elements*

## Heroes and Villains: The History of Keepers and Monsters in the World
*Understanding the existence of Keepers and their purpose*
*The study of human monsters vs. Debilis*
*The effect of evil on Keepers over time and lessons learned*

## Human Anatomy and Physiology
*The biological study of the human Keeper*
*Heightened human biological limits and the impact of physical contact with geological materials on anatomy*

## Introduction to Chemistry *and Chemistry II*
*The Elements of the Periodic Table and the science of Keeper abilities upon geologic chemistry*

## Introduction to Economics *and Economics II*
*The study of Debilis behavior and its influence on world economy*
*Sensing Debilis activity and understanding the business of the geologic black market*

**Introduction to Physics *and Physics II***
*The study of matter and energy and how Keepers manipulate*
*matter in unique ways within the universe*

**The Ethics of the Keeper**
*The essential lessons of right versus wrong*
*How Keepers should interact with Commoners and what*
*impact the Keeper should have on humanity*

**Psychology**
*The in-depth focus on the mental health of the Keeper and*
*the effect of negative influences upon the soul*

**Kinesiology**
*The study of the physical movements of the Keeper and the*
*impact that reactions to geological materials have on Keeper*
*anatomical movement; the healing power in movement*

**Paranormal Studies**
*The study of the supernatural world known to the Keeper and*
*how to handle such forces*

The room was quiet as each student absorbed the information. After several minutes, KameKona raised his hand tentatively. "Keeper Nalin, can you please explain what you mean by the word *monsters?*"

"Ah—yeah," Tessa interjected. "To what exactly are you referring? I thought Dya was joking about that. You don't mean, like, the Creature from the Black Lagoon, do you?'"

Reese rolled his eyes and quipped, "Don't besmirch the Creature from the Black Lagoon! He's actually not a bad bloke." After being met with confused looks, he added, "I'm kiddin', of course. Are there monsters in the world? Yes, indeed, there are. But not in the manner you are thinking. You will not run into a werewolf, zombie, or vampire on this campus or in the larger world. And they will not plague your dreams unless you allow them to do so.

"In our world, we actually have a soft spot for these legendary monsters; they serve an important purpose in our history. In time, you will learn everything you need to know regarding them and we humbly ask that you trust us to enlighten you when the time is right. Now, let's take a break and have a bit of fun!"

Reese removed two black velvet pouches from the inside of his blazer and placed one on the table in front of him. The other one he rested in the center of his right palm. "You each have a dominant hand, I'm guessing, unless you're ambidextrous. We get students with that skill every once in a while. You will learn to favor your preferred hand, since your natural energy is always stronger in the dominant."

He lightly shook the items in the pouch in a circular motion, almost absentmindedly.

"Every element, stone, and gem has its own energy signature—its own heartbeat, if you will—even if each one is of the same material and size. They absorb more energy as time passes, depending on who owns them, where they are located in the world, and whether they are in the atmosphere or below ground.

"Keeper Sahila mentioned earlier that every stone can absorb either positive or negative energy. Even if a rock, by its very nature, has healing properties, it can still absorb malicious energy if it's strong enough." Reese stopped circling the bag and squeezed his hand around the pouch for a moment while every student looked, mesmerized.

Sahila continued the conversation. "Each of you has unique abilities. Subsequently, you will interact differently with whatever Keeper Reese has in his little pouch; each one of you will tap into different aspects of its character and thus will have a different influence upon it."

With a glance and a finger pointed toward Nalin, Reese indicated that he wanted her to distribute the items in the pouch on the table. Nalin went from student to student and placed a small jeweler's loupe on each desktop. Each teen barely noticed her actions, however as they continued to stare at the remaining bag. It was moving, as if it contained little creatures trying to find their way out. The bag looked to be shaking, but was actually vibrating.

"Let's let these little guys free for a while, shall we?"

Reese opened up the pouch and made a scooping motion over the top of the bag. A small clear stone shot out of the bag and headed over to KameKona's desk. He caught it mid-air, surprised. In quick succession, Reese repeated the motion and aimed stones toward every student. Some were quick to catch them, like Ming and Demyan. Tessa got hers caught in her hair and Aedan's sailed through his big hands and pinged off the back wall. Tú almost caught his, but knocked it into his lap instead. Élise just sat there openmouthed, clearly surprised. Her stone bounced off her nose and landed near her foot.

Sahila crinkled her eyebrows and said, sotto voice, "These aren't, by chance, the property of Mr. Peter Salavar, are they, Reese?"

Reese smirked. "They'll make their way back to him shortly. I figured they were a perfect teaching tool; he won't miss them for a while. Besides, he owes me. I got shot rescuing his precious cache and I never got so much as a flower delivery!"

Nalin hid her face and shook her head. "You can lead a horse to water…"

Tessa finally managed to wrangle the stone out of her hair. She took a good look at it. "Wild! This is a loose diamond!"

"What can you each tell me about your diamond? I will reveal that each is one carat, is round in shape—which is known as a brilliant—and has a *VS2* clarity, which means it is very slightly included. What's an inclusion, Scholar Demyan?" Reese asked.

"Oh. An inclusion is a mark inside the gemstone, often called a birthmark; there are many different types of them. When figuring out the value of a gem, especially a diamond, inclusions are used to help grade the diamond. They are not considered a flaw, because real diamonds are made from heat and pressure deep in the ground, so almost all diamonds have some kind of inclusion. A *VS2* means that you can almost easily see an inclusion mark with a ten-times power loupe. So, it's a high-quality diamond."

"Knew I could count on you, Scholar Demyan! The last information I can give you is that the diamonds have an *F* color rating. Scholar Ming, what does this mean?"

"What?" Ming looked up cluelessly, her attention having been on the little shiny gem in her hand.

"I asked you to tell us about diamond color, if you please," Reese repeated.

Ming blushed and looked at her fellow students. "Um, *F* in color means the diamond is on its way to flawless and is almost colorless; it's of great quality. A *D* diamond *is* flawless, which means it has no color at all; these are rare. Diamonds can be one of several colors and many people prefer a colored stone to a colorless one. But on a color scale from *D* to *Z*, *Z* being lightly colored, an *F* diamond is almost without color and therefore considered more valuable."

"Excellent, Scholar Ming. First, please use your loupe and look on the girdle of your stone to see if can detect a serial number; it's the narrow band that separates the top from the bottom. Two of the most trusted companies that provide this number are American Gem Society Laboratories and The Gem Institute of America. If there is no serial number, the diamond might be a blood diamond, but not necessarily.

"I'm guessin' these diamonds all have serial numbers and were purchased through The Kimberley Process, which means several things. They are conflict free and were not found using inhumane labor processes or were illegally traded or bought and the money earned from mining them is not funneled toward buying weapons to fight legitimate governments. A blood diamond can be excavated using any number of these nefarious practices.

"*This concept is incredibly important:* We run into trouble with gems garnered that way. You were just in the vaulted room, no? Don't take this lightly. Since humanity began, people have killed and died harnessing gems similar to that which you are cradling right now. And it will continue to happen, as long as Commoners exist in the world. Just like a crow, many Commoner idiots and Debilis are drawn to the expensive and the shiny."

Each student picked up their loupe and looked at their diamond, turning it in different directions. Shouts of "I found it!" and "It's so tiny!" could be heard throughout the room.

Reese, Sahila, and Nalin watched as their new charges used the loupes to examine their loot. After looking at the serial number on his, KameKona pinched his diamond between his thumb and index finger, holding it securely. He could feel the energy exchange between him and the stone. He glanced over at Aedan and asked, "How warm does yours feel?"

Aedan shrugged and gestured that they switch stones. With a gentle toss between their neighbors, they made the switch and inspected the diamonds they now had. "Yours is hotter, I think," Aedan remarked to KameKona. Aedan placed the diamond he received from KameKona on top of his desk and started to watch the others as they manipulated their stones. He focused on Tessa. He liked her sense of humor, but she was unpredictable. One of his little sister's overused phrases, "She's a hot mess," came to mind. He kept most of his impulsive thoughts to himself.

"Aedan!" Ming shouted. "Your diamond!"

Aedan glanced down at the stone resting on his desktop just as he detected a faint burning wood odor. "Oh, shite!" He scooped the diamond back up into his palm. How had he missed the smoke right in front of him? There was a perfect round scorch mark on the seasoned wood desk. Aedan groaned and looked up at his new professors, chagrined. "I am so sorry!"

KameKona offered, "Nah, man. It's my fault."

Aedan glanced back at KameKona. "No mate, it's on me."

Reese came to stand near Aedan's desk. "Thank you, Scholar Aedan. You've just desecrated a three-hundred-year-old desk. Way to go!"

Aedan looked crestfallen. "Sir, I am really sorry. It was unintentional. I'll do what I can to fix it!"

Sahila rested her hand on Aedan's shoulder. "I can assure you, Scholar Aedan, that Keeper Reese is pulling your leg.

Of all the professors here, Keeper Reese cares the least for our furniture. Please put this boy out of his misery."

"You're no fun, Sahila. Sorry, Scholar Aedan. Just having a bit of a laugh. Rest assured, I've done far worse since I've been here. It's an old desk, mate. I can't wait to see the look on that busybody Keeper Xandra's face, however! I'll take the blame. Pretty sure she thinks I'm a dero anyway."

Regardless, Aedan's face was beet red and he shuffled his feet. Ming left her seat and gently approached him.

"Aedan."

When he looked up at her, she quietly held out her hands, her diamond in the center of one palm.

"Take my hands for a moment."

He looked unsure of himself and she cupped her hands around his.

"Look at my eyes, Aedan, and just focus on the sensation in your hands."

He shyly looked at her and tried to relax. Ming concentrated on Aedan and his embarrassment. She further pushed her energy into the diamond and radiated its natural healing properties into his hands.

She imagined a clear crystal stream, surrounded by emerald-green moss, both being cleansed by the carbon[166] of the diamond. She enhanced the diamond's purity and its ability to cleanse the body of mental dismay and fear. Aedan breathed an audible sigh of relief and hung his head forward, visibly relaxed. Ming smiled demurely and stepped away.

Aedan lifted his head and opened his eyes, amazed. "How do you do that? I feel so much better! Better than I have in a while, in fact!"

---

[166] Diamonds are made entirely of carbon. "Carbon," https://www.mindat.org/element/Carbon

Sahila approached Ming with a smile. "Good work, Scholar Ming. You are farther along than I thought. Do you feel better, Scholar Aedan?" At his assent, she smiled. "I'm glad. And don't worry about Keeper Xandra. Her bark is definitely worse than her bite."

Alegria peeked through the doorway, with Evren trailing behind. "Looks like we've had some excitement here! Everyone having fun? Why don't you return those beautiful diamonds to Keeper Reese and follow Keeper Evren and me on the rest of your tour."

Everyone began to file out. Bringing up the rear, Alegria whispered to Reese, "I suggest you buff out that burn mark before Xandra sees it. She's going lecture you till you turn puce. Fabek can no doubt guide you through a repair."

Reese responded to her exaggerated stink eye by blowing her a kiss.

## CHAPTER 19 – K

## COLLEGE OF GEOEVOLUTION

The students silently followed Alegria and Evren down the hallway, lit with wall sconces resembling old-fashioned torches. Evren pivoted and began to walk backward as he drew attention to the lighting. "Of course, for safety and environmental reasons we no longer burn oil for illumination. The old-fashioned look of this current lighting was designed intentionally, wherever modern technology was instituted. These improvements keep us current, yet we are still grounded in our past. When you stray from your history, you forget why we are here. We may be eccentric, but as the saying goes, there is method to our madness."

Alegria reached the door to the Library of Innovation. The acerbic sign GRAVEYARD OF LOST HOPE AND TECH was still there, reflecting the opinions of previous classes.

She gestured to the door with a wrist flourish. "You will either come to love this room or hate it. From what I've been told, there is no in between. Most importantly, however, it will make a central aspect of your lives clear to you." She opened the door and the curious students filed inside with gasps and exclamations of recognition.

"Most of this tech is super old!" Tessa mentioned.

KameKona barked in laughter. "My grandparents have a few of these models in their attic."

"Why is all of this stuff here?" Demyan added.

"Well, let's analyze that," Evren stated, switching to professor mode. "What do cell phones and computers contain inside them?"

Tú raised an eyebrow. "Rare earths, crystals, and various metals?"

"Correct," Alegria supplied. "Any of you have a difficult time using your sundry technology? I would even hazard a guess that the newer the technology, the more issues you've had."

A light dawned on Élise's face and her mouth dropped open. "You've got to be kidding! Seriously?"

Aedan glanced at her in surprise. "You've had issues too?"

That was followed up with Tessa. "I thought it was just me—it usually is!"

Ming covered her pink cheeks with her hands. "I'm embarrassed to say. My dad buys me a new cell phone each year, because there always seemed to be something wrong with them. At times, I could get various text messages, but it wasn't consistent. Same with my computer. I just kept complaining about the brand that I had, that it was a faulty model or something."

Tessa blew her hair from her face. "That explains so much! I didn't get to upgrade, however. My family just assumed I was mistreating my tech."

"It isn't just you." Alegria smiled apologetically. "It's a bit of a relief, isn't it? Keep your devices if you like, and by all means, try to use them. Sooner or later, however, you will realize that other means of communication are more effective and efficient for you. You are welcome to try to fix any or all of these models. That said, I will warn you, some of our most successful students have tried and failed."

Evren offered the explanation: "Quite simply, your various abilities, especially untrained, fry internal motherboards, melt soldering, and activate installed crystals, making them unable to work as intended. The result, in due time, is a malfunctioning machine, one you can't trust."

He didn't add that this characteristic made these devices potentially dangerous as well. No need to alarm anyone of this issue just yet; they had plenty of time. Heightened digital energies attracted attention and usually the wrong kind.

"Okay," Alegria chirped, "enough of this windowless floor. Let's head outside for a walk in the fresh air for the rest of our tour."

Evren approached the door and placed his hand around the copper knob for a few seconds. After a muffled *click*, he turned the knob and opened the door. "Over time, the doorknobs will recognize your individual heat and energy signature. We train the knobs inside the buildings first. Obviously, if you are inside, you were permitted entry. Once those knobs are familiar with you, training on the outside doorknobs begins. It's standard safety protocol for our campus." Everyone followed him outside.

The group was instantly enveloped by moist humidity. August in Virginia was not for the faint of heart. Traditionally, members of Congress and many residents of nearby Washington, DC, the nation's capital city, ran away from the mosquitoes and the oppressive heat.

Evren and Alegria led the group toward the Wellness Center to introduce them to the resident medical staff. Suddenly, Evren stopped in his tracks.

"Well, that's a new one."

Ahead on the ground was a shiny black bird, hopping along in a disjointed fashion. It appeared to have a leg attached to the top of its head, like a bizarre weathervane. It turned toward them and silently screeched, as if the party was hampering its present migration.

"Ah, Alegria, do you know anything about this?"

KameKona laughed and turned toward Tú. "Dude, your Edgar seems to be in need of an adjustment."

"An Edgar?" Alegria questioned. "What's that?"

Tessa offered an explanation while Tú approached Edgar slowly. "Tú made Edgar for Ms. Topper on the way here from his collection of rare earths; it was a gift to her."

"Ahh," Alegria said. "One of Keeper Xandra's eccentric pets. Yes, she and Keeper Fabek have a tendency to add to their menageries. He's cute."

Tú was gently wrestling with the bird, trying to remove the leg from his head and reattaching it where it belonged.

"He keeps losing parts of himself," Aedan added.

The bird, finally restored to his former glory, hopped away indignant and dropped fresh pieces of rare earth in defiance. Embarrassed, Tú quickly pocketed these bits, presumably for future restoration. "I don't understand," Tú stated as he scratched his head. "My animals never have this much personality. They usually don't move much!"

"Well, for future reference," offered Evren, "when it comes to the incomparable Keeper Xandra, always prepare for the unexpected."

"Oh," Alegria said with enthusiasm. "Did we tell you that she's in charge of our mandatory dramatic arts program? A Shakespeare play every spring!" Alegria didn't wait for reactions as she continued leading the way.

The Wellness Center was gratefully cool, nestled within a forested part of the campus. Strategically placed windows allowed a soothing view of lush and verdant deciduous trees.

Appreciation for the view lasted as long as it took the group to notice various glass jars on a shelf lining a wall. Each one contained various substances that looked like dried grass or mushrooms, roots, and assorted colored powders, presumably for restoring health and vitality.

Further exploration revealed a tank sitting on one counter. What can only be described as black and brown mottled or striated slimy creatures undulated in the tank or crawled along the glass interior. The students gathered around, equally fascinated and horrified.

"Ah, beg your pardon," KameKona started. "Sorry. What are those *things?*"

"Let me educate you, my new friend." Tessa rested her hand on Aedan's shoulder. "We have those in lakes near my home; they are best friends of every kid attending summer camp! I jest, of course. Those are leeches[167]—thirsty little bloodsuckers."

"Um, why does the Wellness Center need leeches?" Ming asked, a grossed-out look on her face.

"Well, hello there!"

A voice with an Irish lilting accent was *heard* before the group noticed the two new adults in the room.

"We were in the treatment rooms takin' inventory for new term. Our new fledglings have arrived, Nurse Hestia!"

The woman approaching them was tall and lithe and had a stunning mass of vibrant curly auburn hair pulled into a ponytail. A pair of tortoiseshell glasses was perched atop her head.

The second woman was much shorter in comparison and could be described as petite. The pair were a stunning juxtaposition of opposites. The tall woman had a creamy

---

[167] *Leech*, Wikimedia Foundation, en.wikipedia.org/wiki/Leech.

freckled complexion and her co-worker, a rich bronzed one which enhanced her green eyes and straight shoulder-length jet-black hair. Both wore matching lab coats over their civilian clothes.

"I'm Dr. Slaine Kelly," the tall woman stated, "and this is my partner in health, Nurse Practitioner Hestia Patel."

"It's nice to meet you all finally," Nurse Patel stated, equally enthusiastic. Her accent was rich and multi-toned, with notes resonant of Eastern India and a British heightened Received Pronunciation—a posh accent. The result was soothing and melodious and the students visibly relaxed.

"Dr. Kelly and I are responsible for your health and well-being, among other duties. Over the next few weeks, you will have an initial health assessment. We will ascertain a baseline of your element blood and skin levels. Over time, while you develop your abilities, those levels will increase. By show of hands, let me see: has anyone had any one of the following ailments: strep throat, the flu, bronchitis, or pneumonia?"

No one raised their hand.

"Just as we thought," Nurse Patel continued. "We'll examine your charts, but I imagine we'll see that you are all quite resistant and resilient to many illnesses. That is in line with both our formal and anecdotal research."

Dr. Kelly offered a warm smile. "Nurse Patel and I partner together to create a holistic health approach toward your care. My training is in modern medicine, and I can assure you that I keep up to date with the latest treatments and techniques, should you need them. The University of Virginia is about two hours away and their medical school is excellent; they keep me well informed regarding important medical advances.

"Modern medicine withstanding, we also firmly believe optimized individual health is achieved when partnered with traditional natural remedies, gathered from many cultures all over the world." She gestured to her colleague. "And that is Nurse Patel's specialty. As much as I like to advocate for the fine medical institutions around the world, you are not representative of the normal population. Far from it, in fact. And as such, your abilities enhance and impact your bodies in ways vastly different from the average Commoner. We are here to support and further understand that marvelous phenomenon: your body."

Nurse Patel continued, "Please take a moment to examine the chart on the wall behind you."

### <u>ELEMENTS OF THE HUMAN BODY</u>

*Only 6 elements in the periodic table*
*comprise over <u>99.9%</u> of the human body mass*

Oxygen
Calcium
Carbon
Hydrogen
Nitrogen
Phosphorus

**Honorable mentions:**
Aluminum, Arsenic, Bromine Chlorine, Cobalt[168], Copper, Fluoride, Iodine, Lithium[169],

---

[168] "Cobalt." *Wikipedia*, Wikimedia Foundation, 22 Mar. 2024, en.wikipedia.org/wiki/Cobalt

[169] "Lithium," https://www.mindat.org/element/Lithium

Magnesium[170], Molybdenum, Nickel, Potassium, Selenium[171], Silicon[172], Sodium, Strontium[173], Sulfur, Vanadium[174], and Zinc.

"At this point in your lives, you have not differentiated much from your Commoner counterparts. Therefore, whenever your blood or other body fluids were tested, every element was within normal range with no unusual levels indicated. Shortly, however, this will begin to change. Between the ages of eighteen and twenty, your bodies will begin to dramatically increase in all of these essential elements, far beyond normal human limits. This occurs to enhance your abilities as well as to protect you."

"Quite simply," Dr. Kelly interjected, "you are each a remarkable natural phenomenon. And not to worry, by the way. Once you graduate from our program, should you ever need to see a doctor or receive a blood test for any reason, we have locations all over the world that will be able to properly assist you, without alerting the rest of the world to your unique biological composition."

"You will learn all about that lifelong benefit later," Nurse Patel added. "For now, let's take you on a quick tour of our facility. You already met our wonderful assistants, Agnetha, Anni-Frid, Björn, Benny, and their friends."

She stopped at the tank of undulating creatures and summoned them with the crook of her finger. At their confusion

---

[170] "Magnesium," https://www.mindat.org/min-45888.html

[171] "Selenium," https://www.mindat.org/gm/3611

[172] "Silicon," https://www.mindat.org/min-3659.html

[173] "Strontium," https://www.mindat.org/element/Strontium

[174] "Vanadium," "Vanadium." *Wikipedia*, Wikimedia Foundation, en.wikipedia.org/wiki/Vanadium.

she added, "Have you not heard of ABBA? Only one of the best musical groups in history. They won the Eurovision Song Contest[175] in 1974. Legendary! Don't worry. They *do* bite and then suck, but it doesn't hurt, I promise!"

Nurse Patel laughed at her own joke. Everyone else had expressions ranging from mild distaste to downright disgust on their face as they watched with fascination.

"We share our high-quality leeches with Colonial Williamsburg. When they have earned a well-deserved retirement, we donate them to the historic living museum, just a few miles away. As gross as these magnificent beasts seem, they are incredibly useful and helpful. Some of the leeches we gave to Colonial Williamsburg helped a gentleman with the reattachment of his ear after he lost it in a car accident.[176] When a leech attaches to another living animal or person, it begins sucking blood; that's its entire life purpose," Nurse Patel explained enthusiastically. "When they suck, they release a chemical called hirudin which prevents blood from clotting. This allows the leech to freely eat without interruption. At the same time, they also release an analgesic, which numbs the bite area, so the victim doesn't feel pain. When the leech is full, it simply drops off—no harm, no foul—usually in about thirty minutes.

"So, you see, when reattaching body parts, they are very effective in creating great blood circulation, as well as reabsorbing excess blood that overwhelms the reattached limb. We, of course, don't expect any of you to ever need

---

175 Eurovision. https://eurovision.tv/

176 Weatherford, Greg. "Colonial Williamsburg Internship Gives Pharmacy Student a Chance 'to Do Something Unusual.'" blogs.vcu.edu/pharmacy/2019/11/colonial-williamsburg-internship-gives-pharm-d-students-chance-to-do-something-unusual/

an appendage reattached. We have the leeches here to help with ingestion of excess elements in the blood, should you somehow absorb too much, such as with hemochromatosis, when there is too high a level of iron in the blood.

"Our leech families have been with our school since the first day and have a noble lineage. They were not randomly pulled from a local murky lake"—Nurse Patel paused to wink at Tessa—"and aren't normal medicinal leeches, either. Most leeches only have the capacity to keep blood from clotting and ingesting ten times their body weight in a short amount of time. Our leech brethren are as uniquely original as you are."

Dr. Kelly motioned with her arm that the group should accompany her toward the back of the room. "Accompany me to our main treatment room."

Everyone followed her toward the back of the clinic and observed the various jars of dried substances and colorful powders as they passed. Suddenly, there was a distinctive *plink* sound, as if someone were throwing pebbles at a window.

Dr. Kelley stopped and turned around, facing her entourage expectantly. "So—we have a magro among us, I gather?"

After glancing at their questioning faces, she walked over and picked up a glass jar filled with smooth and oval-shaped rare earth rocks. They continued to smack against the glass and when she neared the group, the energy of the rocks exacerbated.

"Ahh! Our magro! What's your name, dear?"

Tú gave his name distractedly, while he continued to stare at the jar of agitated rare earths.

"We use these rare earth neodymium magnets to help quickly reduce toxic levels of negative gem and crystal rock energy. You went to our nameless museum of rock horrors, correct?" Considering her question rhetorical, she continued.

"These magnets create a static field that helps to rapidly eliminate that energy for those afflicted; they do not, for obvious reasons, work on magros, however—those with the ability to manipulate rare earths. We have other ways in which to assist you. I am sure you all notice that these neodymium rocks are attracted to the energy flowing through Tú. Quite fascinating, really." She replaced the container. "This way."

She led them to a beautiful dark mahogany door, complete with hinges, a knob, and a lattice view finder in the upper center of the door made of brass. Dr. Kelly opened the door while Nurse Patel instructed them.

"Please take off your shoes before entering the treatment room."

She and Dr. Kelly slid out of their shoes and placed them inside a nearby wooden cubby. Slowly, everyone complied and stored their footwear. Tentatively, Tessa and the others walked inside the cave-like room.

Inside, the space was completely covered with salt. Salt stalactites covered the ceiling and soft salt chunks littered the floor. The walls were covered with salt bricks and the whole room was bathed in a soft light from wall sconces and floor lamps also made out of salt. It was immediately soothing and peacefully quiet, save for the low melodious binaural beat music piped throughout the room. Adjustable chairs, nestled within the salt, were placed in a semi-circle.

Nurse Patel broke the silence and spoke at a low volume, just above the music.

"Take a seat and spend five minutes relaxing. Lean your chairs back and close your eyes, then take slow, deep breaths." She moved her hands in a repeated cyclical motion from her chest to her core. "Fill your lungs with air and then slowly release it, completely emptying your diaphragm of carbon dioxide before taking in more air. You are in our salt cave treatment room. The cave is comprised entirely of salt—sodium chloride, as you all know. It is one of the most fundamental and elemental substances on earth and exists within every human being."

Nurse Patel walked to each chair and repositioned those who appeared tense. "For well over one hundred years, humanity has known about the benefits of salt therapy. It can help eliminate toxins from the lungs and skin. People with bronchitis, allergies, asthma, colds, rosacea, psoriasis, and other conditions can attain many benefits from simply sitting in a salt cave periodically. It has antibacterial and anti-inflammatory properties."

Dr. Kelly placed a sizeable piece of salt near everyone's sternum and gently smiled. "You all will spend an hour every two weeks in here, taking the time to relax and reflect."

Nurse Patel continued. "Feel the sensation of your feet digging into the salt and wiggle them around. Our salt comes from the Dead Sea in Israel and from Poland, some of the most mineral-rich salt found on earth. For all of you, it will help eliminate excess elements through ion exchange and restore you to a natural balance. Salt caves are not mandatory for you throughout your life, but they serve to keep you in optimal health and greatly reduce stress, anxiety, and fatigue. Take a few moments to relax and recharge."

Nurse Patel silently shook with laughter when every student fell asleep within two minutes. They left the room and gave them twenty minutes to rest.

"Happens every time," Dr. Kelly whispered.

"It never fails," Nurse Patel agreed. "It's no wonder. They've ventured down a rabbit hole and are seeing the world from an entirely different perspective. That would exhaust anyone."

They listened to the various breath exhalations, sighs, and the occasional snort as they went over their schedule for the rest of the week. Nurse Patel would discuss training in mindfulness and meditation later in the week, when the new charges were less overwhelmed.

Training in these practices was essential for their health, success in their future field of work, and safety. It was imperative that each future Keeper was attuned to their bodies and how their abilities affected them on a dynamic level. Powerful Debilis who wished them ill could cause damage imperceptibly if self-awareness wasn't constantly maintained.

After twenty minutes, Nurse Patel and Dr. Kelley reentered the room and clapped twice. In a volume meant to reinvigorate her students, Nurse Patel announced, "Please keep your arms and legs in your deck chair until your vehicle has come to a complete stop. Please remember to collect all belongings as you exit the ride."

Demyan surreptitiously wiped the drool from his face, while KameKona stretched fully and fell off his chair.

Tessa blinked her eyes rapidly. "My contacts are stuck to my eyes. Anyone got any saline solution?" As she rose, Dr. Kelly put a bottle of saline drops into her hands.

"You can always look to us for assistance," she announced to the group. "We'll always be here for you. Now gather your shoes and head outside for the last part of your tour… an actual ride!"

The group found Fabek sitting at the front of a quintessential farm wagon, complete with hay bales and loose hay scattered throughout its bed. Sitting with Fabek was Jürgen Tilver. He hadn't met the students yet and appeared imposing—a large heavy-bearded man, as equally peculiar as Fabek.

"Climb aboard, climb aboard." Fabek gestured to his new charges.

Eyeing one another, they climbed into the wagon and were relieved when Alegria and Nalin joined them. It was immediately apparent that the wagon had a vague fish odor; the source of the smell was mysterious.

As Blue Peter and his equally magnificent partner, Petra, another Chocolate Old Type Morgan, pulled the cart, Alegria spoke about the sustainable organic farming on the property.

Whenever possible, the vegetables and herbs used in their meals were grown on the property. She mentioned the orchard and nut trees as well. During harvest time, although Fabek managed a reliable staff, all students were expected to pitch in on particularly busy days; it was considered part of their education. When finished, she added that she wanted to introduce their final professor.

"I'm 'xcited to f'nally meet you all," Jürgen stated as he turned to meet his new students. Expectant and perplexed faces greeted his introduction. "It's a luverly time o' year to begin school, aye?"

Jürgen remained composed and affable; he was well used to not being immediately understood. His unique patois, influenced by both the Chilean coast and Scotland, was unusual, strong, and took time to decipher. Acclimating to his particular "perfume" took time as well. He could see

Alegria try valiantly not to smile at his predicament. Jürgen comprehended that humor was the best way to handle the situation. For now, however, he acted as if he was perfectly understood. It usually took a full class lesson for students to make sense of his unusual brogue.

Although Reese tended to perversely enjoy his pupils' struggle, Jürgen was an empathetic man. He continued to smile although he heard whispers from the huddled protégé: "Do you understand what he's saying?"

The wagon meandered along the main road between the fields; they were headed toward some vegetable sections yet to be harvested. Fabek unconsciously serenaded his audience as he drew closer to the lettuce field:

> *"She is older than the rocks among which she sits;*
> *like the vampire, she has been dead many times,*
> *and learned the secrets of the grave…"*[177]

He chanted the prose somewhat monotone, oblivious to his audience. The smell of healthy soil, abundant with nourishing elements and manure, mixed with the lingering fish smell. A bird cooed nearby, heard, but unseen.

The new students seemed remarkably unfazed by this unfamiliar experience. As a collective, they were quickly desensitizing to the unusual environment at the College of GeoEvolution. This habituation was expected and made sense. When someone was attuned to their own uniqueness, the eccentricities of others were less alarming.

---

[177] Walter Pater (1839–1894), famous British essayist, novelist, and critic

*"Vlad Dracul, Vlad Dracul, what you going to do?*
*Impale my enemies on pikes and watch them suffer, and you?*
*Vlad Dracul, Vlad Dracul, that's very cruel*
*I don't give a fig and neither should you,*
*Lest you find yourself up there too."*

Fabek pulled the cart over and stepped down to wander into the fields. He took a small curved knife, like a miniature scythe, and swiftly cut away a head of spinach. He brought it back to the wagon and climbed back inside. Standing, he eyed Aedan squarely and when certain of his attention, lobbed the spinach toward him.

"Draw out the iron, Scholar Aedan."

Aedan gingerly held the spinach leaves, afraid to damage them. "I'm sorry, sir. What did you need from me?"

Fabek wiped sweat from his forehead. "Draw out the iron in that spinach. Don't think about it, use your instincts."

Aedan looked to the others for direction. This action had Alegria smiling at Nalin. Although it was unlikely the other students knew what to do, Aedan had addressed his fellow students instead of them; the strong bonding process had begun. It still amazed Alegria how quickly that began.

"Do not worry, you can do it," Demyan whispered at the same time KameKona nudged him with an eager shoulder.

"You got this."

Aedan narrowed his gaze and eyed the spinach, sizing it up as he would a dangerous foe. He placed his right hand on the leaves and drew it back, his fingers curved and vibrating with energy.

He repeated the motion again and this time, a few gray wisps of material drew away from the spinach. He continued the process, each time producing more of what became silvery gray sticks, like splinters.

The small amount of iron collected onto itself around his fingers. The spinach head and its leaves began to wilt and lost some of its vibrant green color, clearly vanquished. Aedan exhaled a cooling breath into the sky, releasing the pent-up energy. The whole process took about a minute.

When he looked up, he jolted at the sight of Fabek, Jürgen, and Tú, who sat closest to him. All were lightly covered with spiny silvery shavings. It collected around their faces and fingers and on the pockets of Tú's pants. Tú withdrew a rare earth rock from one and ran it around his face, hands, and pants, collecting the iron shavings. After amassing them into a ball, he passed it to Aedan.

"Those spinach leaves had very little iron. Where did the rest come from?" Aedan inquired.

"Look around you, Scholar Aedan," Fabek responded with the sweep of an arm. "You are in a field filled with iron."

Jürgen laughed heartedly and slapped his knee. "You'll learn t' target your strength," he garbled, finally sounding more comprehensible. "You're like a youn' rattler, injectin' far more poison than needed. You need to gain control o' your abilities. It must come as no surprise that these skills are importan' for a reason. In a crisis, you and your classmates may no' be near leeches or salt caves for healing. And there are those who use similar abilities to render harm. What you can draw out, others can embed, you understan'? Those like you have limits on how much of an element you can tolerate. An' your new friends have differen' abilities. They don't work with iron, so they are more susceptible than you, you ken?"

While each student digested this information, Fabek, who was attending to the horses, turned back to address the group. "Who can tell me which elements make up ninety-nine percent of the human body?"

"Excuse me, Fabek, for jumping in," Alegria interrupted. "Before someone answers the question, Nalin and I want to create more incentive to get the answer correct."

Nalin reached behind a hay bale and brought forth a cage containing the creature responsible for the intermittent cooing. Inside was a pigeon who calmly eyed her audience as she perched. Nalin gently took the pigeon out and cradled her between her hands. "This is Cher Ami Deux and she is a Black Check Cock carrier pigeon and a direct descendent of Cher Ami, the famous World War I carrier pigeon. Does anyone know the story of Cher Ami?"[178]

A collection of head shakes was the response.

"We use carrier pigeons here at the College of GeoEvolution for various reasons that we'll explain in due time. Carrier pigeons were used successfully throughout World Wars I and II. During World War I communication was often spotty, as you can imagine. It was incredibly dangerous to lay new wires for either telephone or telegraph use, especially in battlefield areas. In order for militaries to communicate, they often used carrier pigeons to convey messages.

"They are remarkable creatures. They can fly up to fifty miles per hour and have incredibly sophisticated mental navigation systems. There are several famous carrier pigeons who are credited with saving many people and doing their part to end horrific wars, such as President Wilson and Winkie."

Nalin went on to tell Cher Ami's story. A battalion of American soldiers was trapped behind German lines in the Argonne Forest in France and Allied forces began shelling

---

[178] National Museum of American History. "Cher Ami." https://americanhistory.si.edu/collections/search/object/nmah_425415

the area, unaware the American battalion was there. The only way to alert the Allied forces to the situation was to send a message via carrier pigeon. Several birds were released and were killed in action by German soldiers. Cher Ami, although shot in the breast and leg, valiantly managed to fly home twenty-five miles in sixty-five minutes.

"She sustained more enemy fire, was blinded in one eye, and was soaked in blood. Despite that, she made it safely to her home roost and delivered the message. The shelling stopped, which saved the lives of hundreds of soldiers. The French awarded her the sacred Croix de Guerre with Palms and she retired.

"You can visit Cher Ami at the National History Museum's Price of Freedom: Americans at War exhibit in Washington, DC. You might want to pay your respects someday. Cher Ami Deux is a direct descendent and every bit as intelligent as her predecessor. And she will assist one of you this afternoon with an easy task," Nalin finished as she gently petted the bird's breast.

"Whomever first correctly answers Fabek's question gets to select tomorrow night's dinner; whatever they like!"

Although everyone looked interested, they were still largely impressed by Cher Ami Deux and crowded around her for some gentle touching, an event Cher Ami Deux tolerated with quiet dignity. Her calm demeanor was not lost on Tú, who studied her intently in comparison to Edgar's decidedly undignified antics.

"Any takers?" Alegria prodded.

Several hands shot up and attempts were made with mainly correct results. Tessa raised hers and rattled off all six in the order listed in the classroom.

"Well done, Scholar Tessa," Fabek replied.

Tessa beamed. "I guess it's the engineer in me—I think the periodic table is cool."

"Congratulations on winning the first meal challenge. What meal will Cher Ami Deux inform Chef Ngai to prepare for tomorrow?" Alegria queried.

"Umm. How about lasagna with sausage, but without ricotta?" Her nose wrinkled. "I'm not a ricotta fan; a mixture of cottage cheese and cream cheese is *waay* better. And a vegetarian version, you know, in case anyone here is one. And a salad, I guess. And ice cream sandwiches. I totally miss those."

Nalin finished writing on a long, thin piece of paper. "Sounds delicious." She rolled it up small and placed it inside the tiny steel canister attached to the leg of Cher Ami Deux. Nalin stood up and tossed her into the air. "Make your way home, smart girl."

Fabek searched for something in the wagon. Unsuccessful, he jumped down again and walked purposefully back into the fields. He stood, long and lean, hands-on hips, searching the ground with his head at an angle.

Tessa's hand flew to her mouth and she whispered, "He looks a little like a scarecrow from a horror movie!"

Fabek finally bent down and grabbed a soil filled bucket, hidden in the spinach bed and swung it rhythmically as he walked back, mumbling:

> *"Remember, remember!*
> *The fifth of November,*
> *The Gunpowder treason and plot;*
> *I know of no reason*
> *Why the Gunpowder treason*
> *Should ever be forgot!"*

He climbed back into the wagon and offered the prize to his guests. With long bony fingers, Fabek dug into the bucket and pulled out a handful of earth. He let it sift through his hands and repeated the action. Several fat earthworms wrapped themselves around his fingers before dropping back into the bucket; he was gentle and treated them with reverence.

"Scholar Tessa, your answer was correct. Ninety-nine point nine percent of the human body is made up of those six elements from the periodic table. This soil also contains those elements, including some honorable mentions. They are *elements*, because they are in their purest and simplest form; the basic building blocks of human beings, animals, and even soil, from which our food grows. Almost everything we create and design is made from elements. Never forget that. You all are uncommon, because you are *elementally* tied to the Earth and can uniquely interact with her." Fabek pulled out a handful of dirt, picked out three particularly fat worms, and dropped them into Ming's unsuspecting palms. "Protect my little darlings, please."

Ming swallowed and quickly hid her grimace with a toothy smile.

Élise beamed and said while signing, "She'll guard them with her life, right?"

Ming laughed and held out the palmful of worms. "Want to help worm sit, Élise?"

Fabek ignored their repartee and wiggled the fingers of a hand over the soil. He drew his fingers back, as if manipulating the strings of a marionette, brows drawn in concentration. Wisps of a silvery white substance drew away from the dirt. He blew on it as it gathered near his face, so it drifted away on a breeze.

"Potassium is absolutely essential to human, animal, and plant life. It helps regulate fluid balance in all three. It can reduce high blood pressure in humans and assists in the circulation of carbohydrates and nutrients in plant life."

He swirled his hand over the bucket again and wiggled his fingers away, taking with them a thin trail of silver blue metal-like pieces, the pied piper of zinc.

"Zinc resides in the cells of the human body and assists with maintaining the immune system to help fight off viruses and bacteria. It's so important, it also assists with the manufacture of proteins and DNA in the body. In plants, zinc assists in the development of chlorophyll and helps in the formation of some proteins. It also can assist plants with resisting frost damage."

Fabek dumped the dirt back into the bucket and grabbed the handle. Throughout his lesson, the worms were passed around and divided among willing participants. Hopes of returning them to the bucket were dashed, however.

Fabek brought the bucket to his face and began inhaling through his mouth, as if sucking from a straw. A silver powdery substance stirred in the soil and rose into the air, swirling like a mini tornado. Once formed, Fabek guided the whirlwind with his hand and sent it spinning along the wagon bed among the students. Tiny powdery flecks drew away from the funnel and dropped on eyelashes and eyebrows, like snowflakes.

"Molybdenum helps to keep toxins from building up in the body and breaks down sulfites. In plants, molybdenum is an ingredient in two enzymes that assist with the conversion of nitrate to nitrite and then ammonia; it technically helps with amino acid production, necessary for plants. We really are what we eat, in the truest sense.

"You are here because of your link to the earth and all of its myriad life-giving components. This Earth sustains you and in turn, you must protect it with *your* life, if necessary, and keep her healthy and alive. Many individuals in this world seek to destroy this Earth from willful ignorance, purposeful destruction, or angry negligence."

Fabek nodded to his students before facing the horses. He set Blue Peter and Petra in motion toward the school. Phin, who had been running through the fields chasing mice, jumped into the wagon and proceeded to introduce himself to his new adoring fans, enjoying the pats and snuggles. The three worms were unceremoniously chucked into the nearby field as they rolled past. Nalin and Alegria smiled, but kept quiet confidence, lest Fabek be offended.

## CHAPTER 20 – Ca

## COLLEGE OF GEOEVOLUTION

Xandra huffed in displeasure when she finally located Reese. "Have you been deliberately hiding from me, Reese? I tried contacting you by crystal, yet somehow you failed to notice?"

Reese raised an eyebrow. "Deliberately ignore you, Xandra? And risk your reproach?"

She narrowed her eyes. "I need you to follow me immediately. You have an important visitor."

Disregarding Xandra, Reese perversely continued to inventory the amassed coin collection he used in his classes. "I'm not expecting anyone."

"Reese. You are not a petulant student, yet I am getting the impression that you want me to treat you like one. Should I assume the role of a parent?"

Reese raised his head and glared.

"A representative from the legal council is here to speak with you, no doubt regarding your recent incident."

Reese tossed down a coin bag. "Xandra, for schist's[179] sake! I've already talked about that incident to death! Get rid of him, please."

Xandra turned to leave the room, deliberately swishing the train of her Regency era dress. "Even if you earned my loyalty to do so, which you most decidedly have not," she emphasized as only a self-determined diva can, "I am unable

---

[179] Schist – A flaky metamorphic rock. "Schist," https://www.mindat.org/gm/48640

to do so. You are required to meet *her* and I *highly* recommend that you cooperate and be on your best behavior. She's waiting for you in the main common room."

Reese would swear he heard her muttering "cretin" as she left. "Oh, Xandra," he murmured as he headed out, "you say the sweetest things."

Reese sauntered into the central common room cloaked in the mantel of righteous indignation. He intended to spend the rest of his life never talking about that issue again.

Entering the room, he was met by a tall and statuesque woman.

"Keeper Reese, thank you for taking time out of your full schedule to meet with me."

Her jet-black hair was pulled back in a tight chignon and her ebony complexion was flawless. She spoke English with a heavy rounded accent…South African, he guessed.

"You've come a long way for nothin', I'm afraid. I've already had the debrief of the unfortunate inciden' and I'm done talkin' about it."

She smiled subtly. "Thank you for your candor, Reese, it's quite refreshing. May I call you Reese?" Not waiting for an answer, she continued. "First, let's back up, so I can introduce myself. I am Keeper Folade Xaba, a chief analyst with the Keeper European Legal Counsel, or KELC. Second, I think you are under the misimpression that I'm here in an advisory capacity. Let me assure you, I am not. Third, let me also impress upon you that I take my responsibilities *very* seriously. Anytime, and I do mean *anytime*, a Keeper or the rare untethered Exili[180] comes into contact with Commoner law enforcement in Europe, he or she must meet and debrief with KELC. I am sure you've been made aware of this."

Reese placed his hand on his hips and glared. "I've talked to many people about this already. I'm sure one of them was a member of your staff and they simply lost the paperwork. But you've come such a long way. So, let me offer you a coffee and some tucker before Xandra escorts you off campus."

Folade offered him a toothy smile. "How thoughtful of you, Reese. I already took the liberty of requesting coffee and…chocolate chip shortbread, if I'm not mistaken? That's your favorite biscuit, is it not? Keeper Sahila was so gracious to enlighten me."

Reese ran a frustrated hand through his hair, yanking briefly on the ends. "Sahila enlightened you? You know her?"

Folade sat down on the couch behind her, spine straight, and angled her legs to the side perfectly, in a manner every etiquette instructor in the world would applaud. Once comfortably settled, she opened her file folder. "Oh, we've been friends for a very long time. I'm not seeing the legendary Reese charm she promised, however; *what a thing to miss,*" she whispered.

Reese grumbled and threw himself into a chair, resigned to get the process over with as soon as possible.

"The staff at KELC and I appreciate your cooperation. I'll make this as painless as possible. I'm sure you appreciate the gravity of any situation involving Commoner law enforcement and Keeper Society members. In order to remain

---

[180] Exili – A Latin word meaning *adrift*. An Exili is an individual with abilities who has no community. They keep to themselves and don't fully understand who they are or what they can do. Exili can become either Keepers or Debilis, depending on their capacity for empathy and inner fortitude.

effective, we must vigilantly protect our silent existence and influence. And one of the many ways we accomplish that is by *thoroughly* examining and processing *ad nauseam* any possible cross contamination. Let's *not* force me into the role of the worst thorn in your heel that you can't find. And in the interest of full disclosure, I'm told I'm very good at it."

His only response was a grunt and the rhythmic tapping of a foot.

Folade decisively clicked the end of her pen. "Excellent. Shall we begin?"

CHAPTER 21 – Sc

## COLLEGE OF GEOEVOLUTION

No one was disappointed to learn their first full day of school would be largely spent indoors. Summer in southern Virginia was a hot, humid mosquito playground. Outside, it was strangely quiet, other than the rhythmic, symphonic music of crickets and cicadas; the thick humidity seemed to muffle any sound. Even the animals were trying to stay cool amongst the heavy green foliage.

Everyone slowly made their way to class for their introductory lesson with Keeper Dumisani. This first day of school was known as Elementum Matara (Elementary Purpose), a mixture of Latin and Hebrew—two languages inextricably linked through history and culture, mostly unhappily.

Although held in the basement, the classrooms were cool and well lit. In this main room, gentle LED lights lined the walls and ceiling and were covered by either semi-circle or full circle shades constructed with thin cross-sections of various stones. Each shade had two color hues with a clear crystal quartz top border. The stone panels were a vibrant juxtaposition of colors made up of carnelian, fluorite, sodalite[181] and smoky quartz.

All the stones helped to promote alertness, mental clarity, and concentration. The ceiling light covers were made of carnelian and smoky quartz. The carnelian was a shiny and vibrant red-orange. This stone helped with energy enhancement and confidence. It was paired with a smoky quartz in

---

[181] "Sodalite," https://www.mindat.org/gm/3701

varying shades of translucent brown, which assisted with concentration.

The wall shades showcased the fluorite and sodalite. Fluorite was a beautiful stone in various purple hues, which enhanced mental focus and was sometimes referred to as the 'genius stone'. Sodalite had a mottled dark blue, white, and light brown appearance and was often called the 'student's stone'; it heightened memory, focus, and organizational ability. The clear quartz border cap of each shade served to optimize and magnify the positive energy from each rock and harmonize their collective beneficial characteristics. A student would have to work hard to fall asleep or zone out in any of the classrooms.

"Welcome to Elementum Matara, your first official course day!" Dumisani looked up at the ceiling light covers, and with a flick of a wrist and a strong exhale, set them to gently spin. The carnelian and smoky quartz colors projected around the room, bathing the space in a soothing, yet vibrant energy. "Take a seat that you perceive will be most comfortable for you."

Salima perched on a stand to Dumisani's right and eyed the students as they funneled into the room. She seemed to pass judgment on each, as if verifying her master's choice in student selection.

Once they were all seated, the falcon seemed relaxed. "Mind Salima, by the way. I see your curiosity regarding her. Over time, she will become familiar with you and will be approachable. She is reserved, however, and if you attempt to pet her, she *will* bite. So, as lovely as she is, please admire her from afar. Phin, Keeper Fabek's dog, *is* friendly, as you all doubtless know, and you may pet him when he wanders into class from time to time."

Dumisani repeated the same gestures toward the shades and they slowly ceased their revolution. "Today is a momentous day indeed. We officially welcome you all to the College of GeoEvolution. Unbeknownst to you, since you arrived, we've been assessing your suitability, earnestness, loyalty, and honesty. These are all essential characteristics to our brethren. Before this day we needed to verify that you indeed belong here. Relax." He smiled. "You all passed."

He turned around, faced the gray slate board, and selected a piece of chalk. Today he sported a pair of khakis under his blue long-sleeved waist-length caftan. The same kufi hat remained.

He turned around and looked at them individually. "I will be one of your history professors and will teach geology as well. Right now, a very important history lesson. I'd like you to give me the names of secret societies, please. Whatever comes to mind; off the cuff is preferable."

He began writing every name that was called out to him. When the room fell silent, there was a familiar list on the board:

*Knights Templar*
*Freemasons*
*Order of Skull and Bones*
*Illuminati*

"Excellent. I am going to add the following."

*Rosicrucians*
*Knights of Pythias*
*Improved Benevolent and Protective Order of Elks*
*of the World*

## *Independent Order of Odd Fellows*

"There are more, but these will suffice. Some of them are still relevant to this day and all have certain goals and beliefs. Their ranks claim world leaders, well-known writers, and American founding fathers as members. And they all have one central characteristic in common." He paused for effect. "*All of these secret societies are known and largely understood; they are no longer secret.* Today, there exists only *one* secret order on Earth which remains hidden and has remained so for over two thousand years." He wrote on the board:

## *The Keepers of the Rock*

"And after three years of education, you will become a member for life. We serve to defend Earth and all of its resources. We protect it from destruction, neglect, and from evil forces bent on manipulating and abusing humanity and the world. Your very existence is for this purpose; your inherent abilities are meant for this honor and this life path."

KameKona raised his hand hesitantly. "Are we… Are we like superheroes?"

Dumisani laughed gently. "That's almost always the first question I get. There are two main principals that are crucial to remember. First, superheroes don't exist, and you do. They are the very creative and exciting invention of gifted storytellers and we are quite beholden to those brilliant minds.

Second, we are not here to serve humanity, as a superhero is supposed to do. We are here to serve the Earth and its resources. Humanity is a secondary beneficiary of our purpose and that's vitally important. But it is never our primary goal and will never be our purpose."

He held up his hands in supplication.

"I see some questions and some potential disagreement. I fully understand, but there are specific reasons for these very firm rules and we will discuss them with you at the proper time. We use our abilities in a myriad of ways all throughout the world. For example, we secretly infiltrate scientific research organizations and become employees there to assist with early warning detection systems for earthquake, volcanic, and tsunami activity.

"We *do* protect humanity, but only from supernatural forces intending to harm people and abuse Earth's bounty for their own gain; they have the same abilities, the Debilis. Yet they are soulless and selfish and are not entirely human. For this reason alone, we work in crime-fighting organizations, like the police, the FBI, and Interpol. At times, we act alone. We need to do this, because normal humans, Commoners, have no ability to effectively counteract these forces.

"We work in major financial institutions, such as the World Bank, and serve to follow and guide the world's use of and investment in Earth's resources. We become involved with government agencies in charge of developing mining regulations and insert ourselves into mining companies and determine if dangerous practices are caused by Debilis or corrupt human beings. We also follow gem and precious metal criminal activity and do what we can to prevent it. We are everywhere and have been for over two thousand years."

Stunned silence was Dumisani's typical response to this revelation and he was not disappointed. He took time to erase the board before turning back to his students.

"So, there are graduates from this school working all over the world and no one knows who they are or that they are part of this Order?" Aedan questioned.

"There are not so many of us as you may think, Scholar Aedan. There are seven of you in this year's class and none last year. The world is a big place and there are many, many important roles to fill. In addition to us, however, there are Guardians—human beings with no extraordinary abilities, but who are carefully selected to assist us with our endeavors. We cultivate and guide them. If they are deemed worthy, honest, and loyal, they become our trusted assistants and help us within organizations and other areas where we work.

"Our chefs, Ngai and Hattie, are Guardians. Quite a few employees at this college are Guardians and they literally will give their lives for our Order—it is their most sacred duty. These people are difficult to find, but after a thousand years, we're pretty good at vetting them. We owe them our deepest respect and loyalty in return for their service and sacrifice."

Dumisani drew five pieces of rock from inside the desk. Two were sedimentary: chert[182] and coal. The other three were metamorphic: schist, soapstone,[183] and a square base of marble[184]

He picked up the chert and eyed it critically. Next, he rested it on the marble base at an angle. When satisfied, he picked up a small chisel and brought it down upon the chert with a decided blow. The chert broke off in a clean straight line.

Dumisani repeated the motion three more times after repositioning the chert after each blow. The chert, often used by early man to make tools, was a shiny rock in various shades of brown. Dumisani held up the newly shaped chert, now a perfect cube.

---

[182] "Chert," https://www.mindat.org/gm/994

[183] "Soapstone," https://www.mindat.org/gm/9348

[184] "Marble," https://www.mindat.org/gm/9507

He eyed his charges. "Aedan, will you please assist me?"

Aedan extricated himself from his seat, eager to please. The others looked on, feeling either relief or mild envy at not having been selected first instead. After instruction from Dumisani, Aedan picked up the sample of coal. He held it between his two palms and, brow furrowing in concentration, squeezed it. Pieces of coal began to slough off onto the table. Eying Dumisani in concern, he asked, "Is it okay to let the pieces fall on the desk?"

Dumisani dismissed his apprehension with a wave of his hand.

Aedan shifted the coal in his palms to shape it. Tendrils of heat rose up from the coal and sweat gathered on Aedan's brow. When he was satisfied, he blew on the coal sample to cool it, and handed it to Dumisani. "Will this work, Keeper Dumisani?" The coal was now perfectly round in shape.

"Brilliantly executed, Scholar Aedan. I couldn't have done it better myself. Thank you." Dumisani offered Aedan a handkerchief that he drew from his trouser pocket and Aedan smiled gratefully as he wiped his brow.

The scent of roses meandered throughout the room, thanks to the rose water spray that Evren gave as gifts during the holidays. Dumisani placed the coal on the table next to the chert and blew on the desk at an angle, so the coal remnants conveniently dropped into a waiting trash bin below.

"Let's have Ming and KameKona assist next, please," Dumisani announced.

KameKona stood up. "Okay, glitter girl, let's do this!"

Ming rolled her eyes, laughed, and followed him to the front desk. After Dumisani relayed the directions, Ming handed KameKona the soapstone and raised an eyebrow.

"Am I correct in assuming you'd prefer this rock? Be honest—I don't mind."

KameKona clicked his tongue and grinned mischievously. "Works for me. Actually, I think it's for the best. I may shatter the schist."

Tessa groaned and laughed from her seat. "Kame, I don't know if you deserve a brownie or a wet noodle for that one."

"Honestly, if it's from a bowl of my mom's tonkotsu ramen, either one works," he replied.

He and Ming wielded their respective chisels and sculpted their rocks. Although it wasn't a contest between the two, KameKona finished first, as he worked with the easier medium.

Soapstone is a rock suited to sculpturing and is frequently chosen by artists. Ming followed close behind, but was working with the more challenging schist. This rock is softer and flakier and requires a gentler touch. Satisfied, Dumisani gestured for them to get back to their seats.

"I can tell from your quality work that you three will enjoy utilizing the equipment we have in our art room. Sculpting and creating art is a great way to relieve stress and relax; we highly encourage it. You all may visit our artist's wing as often as you like. The art our students have created over the centuries is beautifully extraordinary. But I digress."

When seated, the students noticed the four new fundamental shapes lining the front of the desk: a cube, sphere, pyramid, and rectangular prism. The entire process took Dumisani and his students only ten minutes to complete.

"Other than the information I imparted upon you earlier, this next lesson is by far the most important one you will *ever* learn here *or* in life. Who can tell me what is most salient about these four rocks?"

Hands went up and answers were given:

"They are four shapes."

"They are four types of rocks."

"They are varying colors."

"They all have Mohs hardness numbers."[185]

"They are relatively easy for us to manipulate and we need to respect the materials with which we work."

"I appreciate your responses, and they are all certainly true and correct," Dumisani offered. There is one answer that I'm looking for in particular, however. Take yourself back to your earliest school memories, to kindergarten or pre-school or indeed, even a *Mr. Rogers*[186] episode. For it is there that you learned this answer."

Élise raised her hand. "They are each different, in many ways."

He nodded. "Yes, that is precisely it. It's fundamentally simple. They are simply different, in a variety of ways." He turned and pulled the handle of one of the maps, a map of the current world. Dark purple and vibrant yellow stickers dotted the surface. "You seven represent six different countries from around the world. Including English, you collectively speak five languages. You are from different cultures, faiths, and have different skin, eye, and hair colors. If we also include our Keeper Professors," he said, pointing to the yellow stickers on the map, "we represent every continent on the globe, an additional seven countries from around the world, and six more languages.

---

[185] "Scratch Hardness." *Wikipedia*, Wikimedia Foundation, en.wikipedia.org/wiki/Scratch_ hardness.

[186] *Mr. Rogers' Neighborhood*, the television show developed for pre-school age kids, ran in the United States on public television from 1968-2001. It aired for over thirty-three years.

"The Keepers of the Rock have survived over two thousand years because of these very differences. We draw strength, wisdom, and endless energy from these variations. *This is significant.* I don't believe this will be unwelcome news to any of you, who have felt different and somewhat apart your whole life. There is no space here at the College of GeoEvolution or within the Keepers of the Rock for those who cannot embrace this fundamental tenet of our education and Order. We respect and learn from one another. You will soak up each other's cultures and cuisine while here. We will learn about each other's cultural holidays and faiths. Sedimentary and metamorphic rock are inherently formed by melding and bonding different rocks, minerals, and elemental chemicals together over time, so it is no surprise that this is the same for us. We are a whole made up of many different parts and the result is an unbreakable bond that can last thousands of years. Any questions?"

The dripping of a stalactite could be heard from the silence. Dumisani continued. "Before we break for lunch and your required self-defense and active instruction, I leave you with this: William Ross Wallace wrote a poem in 1865 entitled, 'What Rules the World.'[187] It was a poem about the importance of mothers and their influence on future generations.

"There is a famous immortalized line, 'For the hand that rocks the cradle is the hand that rules the world.' Wallace was a Guardian of our Order and wrote *the* original line of that poem solely for us. The altered one is famous in its own

---

[187] Wallace, William Ross. "The Hand That Rocks the Cradle Is the Hand That Rules the World." Edited by Kevin Watt. https://allpoetry.com/The-Hand-that-rocks-the-Cradle-Is-The-Hand-That-Rules-The-World

right. Our version is the hallmark of this Order, however, and is even more true. It is the reason why we can never cease our vigilant duty and the very reason our Order was created: 'For the hand that cradles the rock rules the world.'"

He walked over to Salima and gave her his arm. She perched comfortably as he turned back around and looked at his students, motioning them to follow.

## Chapter 22 – Ti

## College of GeoEvolution

After lunch, the little group walked along the campus cobblestone paths, past the Wellness Center, until they came to a large rectangular building similar to the main campus building design. The inside boasted beautiful, well-maintained, but weathered wooden floors and large picture windows; a few strategic skylights allowed even more light into the space. The room was filled with mats, ropes, ballet bars, and a multitude of other exercise equipment.

Three display cases existed along a shorter wall, one glass and two wooden. The first was filled with various swords, épées, and sabers: the weaponry of fencing. The other contained more dangerous-looking swords, Shaolin staffs, called "bo," and other staffs with menacing looking attachments. Above the cases, in large black script, was the phrase: WE SEND THE SOULS OF OUR ENEMIES TO HEAVEN.

Along another wall were pegs loaded with familiar fencing jackets and masks of all sizes. Although intriguing to the eye, the fencing and kung fu accoutrement were a brief distraction from the main event.

At the far end of the room a man and a woman actively battled with Shaolin bo. The quick-paced pivots, advances, and retreats were fascinating and beautiful to watch and the sound of the wooden staffs contacting echoed throughout the large space.

Equally interesting was the juxtaposition between the opponents. The man was tall and lean, almost statuesque in his graceful movements. In contrast, the woman was far shorter and almost petite in build. Although equally skilled, the woman made up for her size with swiftness and power.

Suddenly, the woman slid between the man's legs and quickly pivoted behind him. She popped him in the rear end with the bo, which sent him hurtling forward. He recovered, but by that time, she had started toward the gawking group, swirling her bo around her as she approached. She stopped, rested the weapon against one shoulder, brought her hands together, one fist meeting the other flat palm, and bent slightly at the waist.

"Welcome, new students. I am Shifu Ganzorig or Master Ganzorig, but I am simply referred to as Shifu Zoria. I will be your kung Fu instructor and one of your general physical fitness coaches."

Shifu Zoria sported black hair styled in a chin-length pageboy. She had a wide and open face with large meditative black eyes. She spoke English with a distinct accent, rolling her R's and giving emphasis to her consonants, a typical accent for someone from her native land.

"Although from Mongolia, I trained in China with the Shaolin monks in the Hunan Province for many years. Under my tutelage, you will gain a proficiency in kung fu and be able to protect yourself and your team against whatever you may face in the world. It is not our job or goal in our Order to seek violence or fighting. If you must face violence, however, we make sure you know how to end it. And I am not in this venture alone." She smiled as she turned to see her partner pull up alongside her.

"Greetings," he said with a quick bow, speaking with an amalgamated European accent...

"I see my partner has made your acquaintance. Allow me to do the same. I am Master Halbert Proulx, your fencing instructor and the other general fitness coach. I will teach you the art of swordsmanship. With our guidance, you will gain discipline, precision, and more elegance in your daily movements. And"—he gave a coy smile, his green eyes shining—"I assist with all school Shakespearian productions and work well with Madame Xandra."

Dismayed groans emanated from the students.

Master Proulx grinned, which empathized his dashing, pencil-thin blond mustache and goatee. He hailed from Bern, Switzerland, and was of Swiss and Italian extraction. "Your work may take you to many places around the world. We do not anticipate that you'll frequently meet with unsavory forces, unless you attract them like Keeper Reese," Master Proulx quipped sardonically. "But, as they say in Scouting, you need to be prepared, and you will receive that training here.

"In addition to the equipment in this room, through that door," he said, indicating to a spot at the end of the hallway, "is a gym with all manner of fitness machines for your use; it will come in handy, especially during the winter. We also have an indoor pool in another nearby building. There, you will also receive training from your Keeper professors to further hone your skills, should your abilities involve water displacement—a unique specialty."

"Since arriving, you've seen a great deal, and we imagine it's a bit overwhelming. So, you will be fitted for martial arts, fencing, and general physical fitness attire tomorrow and have your first lessons as well." She handed her wooden bo to Master Proulx and repeated her kung fu bow. "Come with me, I'll take you to our library, the next stop on your journey."

"Till tomorrow, giovani studenti,"[188] Master Proulx called out upon their departure.

The students were thankful for the shady canopy as they walked to the nearby library. Also designed by Sir Christopher Wren, it was stately and reverent, exact qualities one wanted in a library of a respected and historic college. Thankfully, it was cool inside and had the pleasant musty scent that old books often emanated. It was lit with the same ceiling and wall shades as the main classroom, creating a relaxing and harmonious environment.

Stained-glass windows, all the same size, covered three walls, and were topped with stone arch reliefs. The sun was currently uncooperative, muting the colored glass. When optimal, they were vibrant from crushed gems and followed the full spectrum of a rainbow. Ming envisioned the amount of crushed amethyst, jade, citrine, jet, garnet, blue sapphire, and other stones needed to produce such startling hues.

"Master Zoria, I see you are introducing the new students to our library."

A conservatively dressed woman approached the group with a subdued smile. Her all-black ensemble was sophisticated in its simplicity: various shades of black for her knit shirt, slacks, and ballerina flats. Her only homage to color was a violet beaded cherry blossom hair barrette securing long black hair to one side; it was the solitary clue to her Japanese ancestry.

Shifu Zoria smiled brightly. "Guardian Heikima Miyazaki, I leave our new students in your capable hands. I won't start exhausting them till tomorrow." She turned toward the group, gave a quick bow, and left.

---

[188] Giovani studenti – Italian for young students

"In a gesture of full disclosure, she means what she says. She and Master Proulx will have you sore for several days. As Master Zoria stated, I am Guardian Heikima Miyazaki, head librarian. We have an extensive library here and can assist you with any of your research needs. We also have a plethora of current fiction and non-fiction, as well as an enviable rare books collection." She noticed the students' preoccupation with the stained glass and large portrait above the fireplace.

Ming squinted. "I wish the lighting was better right now."

Heikima smiled. "If you stop by in the morning as the sun is rising, they are spectacular."

Tessa assessed the windows and glanced at the main desk. "I think I can satisfy your curiosity, Ming." She pointed to the desk and asked Heikima, "Do you mind?"

Granted permission, Tessa pulled her small black velvet bag from her front pocket. With practiced movements, she fished around and produced her handcrafted bi-concave shaped clear crystal. It loosely resembled a half-dollar-sized Smartie.[189]

Tessa approached the main desk and angled the green banker's lamp shade behind the bulb. Moving fluidly, she placed stacks of books in front of the lamp until satisfied with the height. Next, she put the freestanding crystal on top of the books in front of the bulb, set the angle to her satisfaction, and pulled the chain on the lamp. The light diverged through the crystal, in a wide array.

Light energy from the bulb passed through the crystal lens and shot toward the first glass window, illuminating the

---

[189] Smarties – The North American tangy fruit flavored treat made from calcium stearate; the American and Canadian candy (named Rockets in Canada) is almost guaranteed to be tossed annually into trick-or-treaters' Halloween baskets

jewel-toned colors. The first one depicted a lush tree covered with leaves in a rainbow spectrum.

"Whoa! That's lovely!" Aedan exclaimed.

Tessa changed the orientation of the lamp, book stack, and crystal and focused on the other two windows. The next one was a large rock in different shades of blue and gray. When looking carefully, one could see hidden images along the surface of the rock: a fissure in the rock, lava streaming from the side; an aggregate of purple amethyst; a deposit of iron ore; and a cracked-open clear crystal geode at the base.

The last window was the most striking. A beautiful woman stood before a large building wearing a white dress, a colorful hijab, and a Mona Lisa smile.

"Who is that?" Élise signed and asked.

"That, my young scholars, is Fatima al Fihri. The founder of what is arguably the oldest university in the world, located in Fez, Morocco. She opened the doors to Al-Qarawiyyin in 859 AD and established the oldest center for learning in the world. One of the earliest degrees they awarded was in the earth sciences, fittingly. She is also our oldest and most generous benefactor, although her largesse was not utilized until we began to build our school. We credit her with being the initial inspiration for our college. Keeper Dumisani is an adjunct professor there; her university continues to thrive today."

"Super cool," Tessa reflected. "Who are the people in the painting above the fireplace?"

"Ahh, one of my favorite questions. I'll give you a hint. It was painted in the 1800s by the famous British portrait painter, Thomas Lawrence, and it immortalizes an important historic event in 1816. It's titled *Birth of Genres*."

Everyone stared, fascinated by the four figures engaged in an animated discussion before a lit fireplace. The menacing shadows on their faces and clothes were masterfully rendered.

KameKona snapped his fingers. "Wait, that date is familiar to me! The Mount Tambora volcano erupted in Indonesia in 1815. It caused the infamous 'year without a summer' in 1816 and was one of the worst natural disasters in history. Over 100,000 people died, everyone in the Northern Hemisphere was cold, crops were destroyed, and people starved—scary times."

"Excellent, Scholar KameKona. Anyone care to add onto the volcanic dust trail KameKona was so kind to lay down?"

All eyes focused on the painting, hoping it would reveal a secret.

"It is the title, not the subjects that are particularly important here," Heikima added. "In fact, the subjects, although very famous, are neither heroes nor representations of altruistic human beings. They were actually deeply flawed, selfish, and complex individuals."

"Oh!" Ming proclaimed. "It's Mary Shelley! She created *Frankenstein* in 1816."

"Very good, Scholar Ming! Yes, indeed. The people portrayed in the painting are Mary Wollstonecraft,[190] Dr. John Polidori, Lord Byron, and Percy Shelley. One summer night during the year without a summer, in a house near Lake Geneva, Switzerland, Lord Byron suggested the party compete to see whom could write the spookiest ghost story. No doubt, the gloomy and cold atmosphere encouraged the guests, right? Mary Shelley created *Frankenstein* and Dr. John Polidori began a poem titled 'The Vampyre.' Mary Shelley is also credited with writing the first science fiction novel."

---

[190] Mary Wollstonecraft married Percy Shelley in 1816

"For us," Heikima said, smiling coyly, "this painting symbolizes the important link we have to the imaginary monsters of the world. This relationship was perfectly encapsulated during this terrifying event. In the past and today, we need our literary and filmographic monsters. When unusual events occur in the world, the Keepers of the Rock are more vulnerable to exposure. Commoners want an explanation for an extraordinary geocentric event. If it is caused by or further manipulated by Debilis, the true monsters in the world might become visible, as can we." She raised an eyebrow and glanced at her audience. "I'm sure you can understand how catastrophic that would be."

Heikima could see the wheels turning as her words were absorbed.

"Sooo are you saying that Keepers…*request* horror novels and movies when we need them?" Tú asked.

"Chosen Guardians within the literary world and later the film world became our allies. When necessary, a fabricated monster can do wonders. They become an instant explanation for what goes bump in the night. The author strikes the match and humanity lights the fire."

As hands shot up, Heikima added, "That's all I can say about that now." It was not her place to delve into the lore of those who pledged fidelity to the Keepers. Although Heikima longed to reveal the secret, there was a time and a place and the scholars were not ready. She led them toward the textbook section.

Next to each student's name was a stack of well-worn textbooks. Some contained the occasional underline or absentminded doodle. They were mainly written by Guardian authors unless supernatural events or explanations were not discussed. In those cases, books by Commoner authors were acceptable.

In addition, each student received a cloth bound kit embossed with their name, filled with rocks, minerals, and gem samples and a few select coins. Opening them was prohibited until the appropriate class; Heikima handed out leather satchels with embossed initials for their new loot. Afterwards, they were given time in their rooms to reorganize and further unpack until dinner.

As she walked them past the locked cabinet of rare books toward the exit, Tessa noticed the current graphic novel display. "*The Full Metal Alchemist!* I love that series!"

Heikima grinned. "You have great taste, Scholar Tessa. Feel free to check them out anytime you like."

## Chapter 23 – V

### College of GeoEvolution

Everyone needed time to unwind and contemplate the day's events and activities. It was thrilling to be surrounded by others who also experienced the world in relative obscurity and isolation. To be around adults who *understood* their experiences and *knew what to do* was a monumental relief. How does one live a unique existence without a roadmap and without a sense of purpose?

Tú pondered his new circumstance while creating a rare earth tower. Prokofiev's "Dance of the Knights" from the opera *Romeo and Juliet* played in the background on an old CD player left in his room. CD players and cassette tapes worked for Tú if he turned them off before changing the tapes or CD's. He learned the hard way that keeping the power on destroyed the magnetic mechanism inside.

Élise and the others stopped by to watch his impromptu performance art. He did his best thinking and relaxing while doodling with his rare earths. It was the one thing he felt confident about. He knew how the elements responded to him and to each other. For years, they were the only things that made any sense and gave him clarity. As they walked by his door and peeked in, he glanced up and smiled shyly.

The other boys stopped by and tried their hand at rare earth sculpture, but only Aedan was marginally effective. The other attempts were lumpy piles.

"We can touch these rare earths and be safe," Tú reflected. "But for Commoners, the mining process can be very dangerous, if it's not done carefully. It's really important to me that this valuable resource is mined humanely and safely without harming the environment. I hope I can make a difference; it can save a lot of lives."

After a while, everyone was starving and curious about the meal Tessa had chosen.

The cream cheese and cottage cheese mixture, instead of ricotta, gave the lasagna a richer taste. It was delicious with either sausage or spinach. Again, Sahila and Evren joined them for dinner and were accompanied by Jürgen and Alegria. If the gossip about the lasagna had not reached Jürgen, the delightful aroma certainly did! Evren and Sahila resumed their previous evening's discussion to those who didn't get a chance to participate earlier.

Tú, having had his confidence boosted by his impromptu "house party," felt emboldened to go first.

"I'm an only child and my parents had me later in life only after struggling for years; people who don't know my family think my parents are my grandparents; they're old enough. My mother's health isn't the best and when I was old enough, I wanted to help. I used to go to the park near my house and walk up to the top of the hill. I had space up there, and some freedom. Each time I went up there, small black rocks would roll toward me from nowhere. Even if I was on higher ground, the little rocks would roll up the hill to me. They would even burst out of the earth to get to me, like a…" Tú grappled to select the word he wanted. "Like a gopher. I would pick them up and they stuck together—they were magnetic.

"Eventually, I started making little animals with them; I didn't know what they were. One day, some men saw me on the hill; they were taking a break from work, I guess.

They saw my little rare earth collection, what I could do and got very excited. They explained that the pieces were valuable; the rocks were rare earths and the world wanted them badly for their tech: for cell phones, computers, and many other machines. They told me that they would pay me to collect them."

Tú was interrupted by an apologetic Ngai and Hattie, who delivered a wheeled table containing several types of ice cream as well as chocolate chip and sugar cookies. Since everyone had finished their dinner, however, dessert was a welcome treat. "Beg your pardon, Scholar Tú. But I believe ice cream sandwiches were requested."

Hattie put her arms around Jürgen and Alegria. "Storytelling is always better with ice cream."

"Scholar Tessa," Ngai preened, "if you want to have ice cream sandwiches, they must be top quality. I won't serve ice cream with guar gum, carrageenan, or any other thickener,[191] that's for mass-produced ice cream brands! We only make creamy organic ice cream."

"Hold that thought, Scholar Tú!" Jürgen launched from his chair toward the dessert table in a flash, an impressive feat considering his size. "Let's just get dessert! Letting this ice cream get warm would be an insult to Chef!"

Everyone took a moment to make an ice cream sandwich, some more impressive than others. Content, Jürgen motioned for Tú to continue.

Tú smiled shyly. "Compared to a rare earth mine, I collected only a small amount, which was safer. It wasn't enough

---

[191] Guar gum, carrageenan, locus bean gum, cellulose gum, and carob bean gum reduce ice crystal growth, thicken ice cream, and make it smoother; it was introduced in the 1950s in mass-produced ice cream

to alert buyers of a bigger opportunity. I didn't realize I was involved in the rare earths black market until I was much older. When I did finally understand, I didn't want to worry my parents. So, I told them the money came from a job in town, at a national geological park."

He looked in earnest at the adult leaders. "I want to be able to help. I want to help make it safer to mine rare earths. It's important to me. And now when my parents receive money for me being here, it's true where it's coming from."

Tú hung his head, feeling embarrassed, and pushed his bowl of ice cream away. He hadn't expected to share so much in such a public way. Somehow, he felt safe among this group and now they knew of his shame and dishonor. Maybe they would make him leave. If so, he deserved it for lying to his parents.

Sahila smiled warmly. "Thank you for opening up to us, Scholar Tú. That took great courage. Your parents are fortunate to have a son who loves them so much. I wish I had an opportunity to observe you on that hill making your little animals! Keeper Xandra loves Edgar; he's quite a capricious addition to our campus. Don't be so hard on yourself."

She glanced over at Ming expectantly. "I'm keen to learn more about your journey thus far, Scholar Ming."

Ming smiled demurely and bit her lip. She never enjoyed being the center of attention; her ability complemented her personality. In truth, she wanted to explore this issue at school. Was it a happy coincidence that her ability fit her personality or was her personality shaped from a tender age to *suit* her ability? She didn't really know.

To be empathetic and sense an individual's healing needs, she needed to pay close attention and be reflective. That didn't happen easily when one craved center stage; there was a difference between sympathy and empathy. And if she couldn't at some level absorb the actual emotions of another, she couldn't truly *feel* what they felt, and subsequently, know what they needed.

And Ming was uncomfortable with the idea of these Debilis, entities her grandmother never told her about. Could she learn to use her ability to cause harm, even if that meant preventing an evil being from harming an innocent and far more morally upstanding individual??

And was Ming expected to *decide* who was more worthy, as if their souls were being weighed on a moral scale? She hoped she could decide when the opportunity arose. She didn't even know *how* to do that. All of these thoughts and feelings flew through Ming's head in an instant while Sahila was waiting.

"I don't have a favorite stone that I prefer to use. I think it's because my grandmother taught me about many stones from a very young age, as soon as she recognized my ability. But if I grew up without a mentor…" She glanced at the others, feeling guilty. "I probably would have focused on only one. Perhaps I would have been clueless as to what to do at all."

She bit her lip again, thinking. "If I have to highlight just one, I would pick my citrine." She looked down and grasped the gem around her neck, rubbing it between her fingers. "It's a deep yellow color, see, and so pure, without any flaws. It helps my father with his…anxiety." She felt uncomfortable bringing up the subject, something so personal to her father. Yet, it was so integral to herself, so pivotal. She was paralyzed by indecision.

"Scholar Ming," Sahila interjected. "You are thinking so hard, I can see the wheel turning in your mind. Let's retreat to the common room, where we can all relax. Keeper Jürgen, an arrow, if you please!"

"My pleasure, Keeper Sahila!" Jürgen rose and ambled to the door leading to the main common room, his hands in his pockets. At the entrance, he pulled out two handfuls of rare earths and massaged them in both fists. When satisfied they were ready, he rapidly worked them together, forming a shape. "Ach, I like this one!" he chortled, as his right arm launched the object above his head. His left hand pointed to the ceiling, index finger wagging back and forth. "Follow me!" he bellowed. The sizeable silver arrow, shining from the reflective surrounding lights, followed Jürgen as he led the group away.

Comfortably settled and less anxious, Ming continued. "When my mom passed, my dad seemed so lost and anxious. Although my grandmother was there, his mother-in-law, I know he wanted to raise me as best he could, but he doubted himself. He really, really loved my mother.

"When I was little, my grandmother got me this citrine necklace for my birthday. When I wore it, my father seemed less anxious and more relaxed. Over time, I noticed a pattern when he seemed anxious to me. I would wear the necklace, give him a hug, and he was always much better… relaxed, even."

Ming laughed and remembered several times when the citrine had worked. She felt a pang of longing for home so sharply, she caught her breath. She looked back at the group, politely waiting for her to finish.

"I realized only a couple of years ago that my grandmother gave me that necklace on purpose! She knew about my ability and it was her way of getting me to understand my ability myself, by making that empathetic connection with my father.

"A hug and attention from me were always welcome, even when he wasn't anxious or sad. But there was usually an… undertone of preoccupation, without the citrine, I guess. I don't know; he just seemed better with it. My grandmother is so clever. My father never felt comfortable when she attempted to console him, no matter how hard she tried. So she gave me that job instead, my very first experience learning how to use my ability."

Sahila offered her an empathetic smile and thanked her for sharing.

"I like hearin' these stories," Jürgen said. "'Specially with such a wonderful meal! Young Scholar Tessa, you have great taste! We never eat so well as when our students are in residence!"

Thankfully, having spent more time with Jürgen, they had habituated to his fish odor. It also helped that when he was on campus, he ate much less fish. Enough to maintain a healthy diet, but not so much as to have it emanate from his pores. In addition, Chef Ngai and his wife Hattie made sure that flowers with a gentle pleasant perfume were always at the table, especially when Jürgen was in residence.

Evren instructed everyone to head to their rooms. Classwork officially began the next day.

C H A P T E R  **24** – **Cr**

## C OLLEGE OF G EO E VOLUTION

N ew satchels in hand, everyone filed into class the next morning after a modified continental breakfast. That morning, Ngai was overheard cursing loudly in Vietnamese when they arrived for the meal. Reese and Jürgen, having breakfasted earlier, had eaten more of the pain au chocolat[192] than was polite, and now Ngai had less to offer his students. It happened every couple of weeks and Ngai urged Hattie, who made the delightful French staple, to refuse the favorite treat to those "rude Neanderthals."

Having a soft spot for anyone who appreciated her baking, Hattie ignored him and put up with his outbursts. Thank goodness he was unaware that Jürgen often forgot the occasional pain au chocolat he smuggled into his jacket pocket, in case "he needed a piece."[193] If Jürgen didn't remember, one of the many visiting field mice certainly did.

In the end, the morning ended happily. Élise declared the pastry was excellent, since Hattie's version reminded her of the ones made by her favorite Parisian bakery. Although both pain au chocolat and the croissant were a staple everywhere in France and in many other countries, making them took great skill and technique. And like every corner of the globe, people had their favorite bakeries. Hattie was thrilled

---

192  Pain au chocolat – A croissant that includes a strip of chocolate inside

193  Piece – Scottish slang for snack

by the compliment and Ngai was subsequently mollified, the haggis in the bottom of the freezer was safe for another day.

Evren was waiting patiently in the classroom when his students arrived. They would begin with history that morning, one of their most important lessons. The large slate board was blank, but would soon be covered with a myriad of ideas and opinions.

"Tú, I want to thank you for your very heartfelt and honest contribution yesterday at dinner. Unbeknownst to you, it was the perfect segue into today's lesson. I want you all to take a moment and reflect on this question: Historically, what do you think happened to people with your abilities? Were their skills utilized during their lifetime, especially before the principles of scientific discovery were widely accepted?"

On the board, Evren created two columns and wrote *positive* and *negative*. "Let's begin with the positive possibilities, please." After a moment, hands began to shoot up.

Ming offered, "highly regarded healer," while Aedan supplied "sought-after blacksmith." After another pause, Élise suggested a "geographical forecaster" and "water dowser or diviner" and Demyan proposed a "gem and coin salesman" as well as a "criminal detective." In addition to these professions, KameKona advocated for "water purification expert." Tessa added "mineral and element prospector" needed for various professions.

"Excellent. I am certain that since the beginning of humanity, those with our abilities have performed this work as well as many other professions we haven't mentioned. And hopefully, many held these jobs for lifetimes without difficulty. Unfortunately, historically, that was not always the case." He pulled the handle of one of the large tubular canisters to reveal an enlarged painting. "Does anyone know where this is?"

The painting depicted a cobblestone street with businesses or houses crammed together wall to wall on both sides of the street. The houses were painted various colors and had slate roofs of different heights. It looked like an old European street. After no one answered correctly, Evren continued.

"This street is known as Golden Lane and it's in today's Czech Republic, also called Czechia, in Central Europe. In the late 1500s, Holy Roman Emperor Rudolf II ruled this territory. He was a big fan of alchemy, as was the case with many world rulers in the annals of history, such as Queen Elizabeth I. Everyone familiar with alchemy?" Evren was pleased to see that all seemed to have some knowledge of the "science."

"Many people in history believed it possible to turn more common elements into gold. The general idea was to use a 'philosopher's stone' or even create one by mixing and heating many different elements. After this stone was created, it was combined with metal and non-metal elements to try to create gold—*try* is the operative word here.

"This process, transmutation, was appealing to many in power, since having an unlimited supply of gold would seemingly keep both them and their country wealthy. The other important aspect of alchemy was the desire for immortality; it was another irresistible lure for a leader or wealthy individual at that time. The finding or the creating of the philosopher's stone was expected to assist with that goal as well. And history shows us that many throughout the ages tried."

Evren explained that Golden Lane was where Rudolf II housed all of his many alchemists and jewelers. Those who could not produce their promised alchemical gold, which was everyone, were either imprisoned for life or banished.

"So, who most likely claimed these absurd skills?"

The words "charlatans," "Debilis," and "swindlers" were thrown out.

"Yes! Largely these were convincing Commoner swindlers or Debilis preying on their employers' ignorance about the natural world and appealing to their greed and fascination with the unknown. When you combined these desperate charlatans with their manipulation of sometimes dangerous chemical elements, you got explosive results, often quite literally. Many a person blew themselves and others up in their lab on Golden Lane and elsewhere in the world, if they didn't first poison themselves over time by heating up very dangerous elements. Anyway"—he pulled on the brass handle and sent the picture back into its canister—"the history and science of alchemy will be discussed in another lesson. Let's continue. What negative mishaps befell some of our *altruistic* historic counterparts?"

To help them along, Evren began with "highly regarded healer." "If this healer used gems and minerals to practice her skill, as does our Scholar Ming, how might she be perceived by an average Commoner, ignorant of these abilities?"

"Oh, crap," Tessa said. "Ming might have been accused of practicing witchcraft!"

Ming looked at Tessa wide-eyed.

"Exactly!" Evren said enthusiastically. He continued to explain that, although one's goal was to help and heal, one might easily be misunderstood and feared. Many with this talent often were, if they weren't careful. And practicing their skill openly was very risky. "Only a few societies throughout history respected those with such talents, such as the Indigenous Americans, Indigenous Australians and various Asian cultures. So, being accused of witchcraft was frightening. What else happened?"

Aedan raised his hand. "Someone powerful who knew your ability would force you to work for them."

KameKona had an additional thought: "You would become a human guinea pig, studied and picked apart by scientists or someone powerful, like the evil villain in a James Bond movie!"

Demyan added one final example. "You are forced to travel with a circus in order to survive and are paraded around like an exotic freak."

Evren heard the laughter and smiled with his students, but soon sobered. "All excellent examples, and unfortunately, *all* valid and real." Everyone became solemn. "Since time began, those with our abilities were feared, abused, studied, and manipulated." Evren took a moment to glance at each of his students. "One of the worst disasters Keepers and Guardians experienced was not that long ago, unfortunately. And it is this relatively recent event, which resulted in one of our most tragic losses that reminds us why our concealment remains paramount; I will only touch on it briefly today, because it is an event we will study in great detail at a later time.

"During World War II, Dr. Josef Mengele, one of Adolf Hitler's henchmen, performed experiments on any Keeper he managed to capture. Hitler somehow learned about Keepers and Debilis and was fascinated by their supernatural abilities; he wanted Keepers and certainly Debilis working for him. Hitler thought they could keep him in power and increase the wealth of the Reich." He paused for a moment to allow the lesson to absorb. "What essentially has changed since those historic times, do you think?"

This statement was met with an uncomfortable silence.

Élise raised her hand. She signed and said, "Essentially *nothing* has changed, not really. Not yet, anyway. And we all know this already, subconsciously. It's why none of us, other than Ming, felt secure telling anyone about what we can do."

Aedan nodded his head. "If someone actually saw me creating a sculpture, they might think it was cool and novel, initially. But invariably, they'd want others to see. Those others might think it was cool or maybe unnatural and frightening. Either way, more would find out. Then someone eventually would tell the police, who would tell someone in the government. And from there, I'll either be a guinea pig or whisked away by some nefarious crime lord, if they thought I was valuable."

"Tú, thank goodness you didn't get kidnapped by some criminal!" Tessa exclaimed. Upon seeing Aedan's incredulous stare, she blushed, embarrassed. She added, "You too, Aedan. I mean, thank goodness you both are safe."

"Indeed," Evren quipped. "The most important lesson to take from this class today is obviously understanding why it is imperative to preserve our secrecy. Commoners, our term for those who have no abilities, are not ready for our kind, even in this modern age. I can comfortably say that Commoners are even *less* capable of understanding or accepting us today than they were over a century ago. The internet and social media are filled with disinformation that spreads faster than an invisible pathogen. People are flooded daily with visual and audible garbage and it's difficult to sort the truth from what's fabricated.

"In other ways, however, it's a golden time for us. With such a plethora of stimuli, hopefully rare glimpses of our existence are lost among the noise. One advantage in these modern times, I will acknowledge, is that the relationships with our Guardians is more effective than ever. They continue to be our emissaries into the Commoners' world and with their assistance, we effect change more than ever before, despite our constraints."

When Evren's class ended, everyone moved to their next lesson, inwardly focused, mainly realizing that they were just beginning to understand the strange world in which they found themselves. Evren's first history lesson was essential, but a bit alarming. He really was the best teacher for that session, being the lead ambassador for both Keepers and Guardians around the world. He was empathetic, patient, and delivered concerning information in the most appropriate, palatable manner.

The Keeper professors collectively learned this lesson when Evren had to leave for an emergency meeting in Europe one term and Reese taught the class in his stead. It took the better part of an hour to decompress their students.

Eyeing her dazed students after Evren's revelations, Alegria tried to be as enthusiastic as possible. This morning, her bountiful curly hair was swept into a jaunty pony tail and secured with a colorful scarf, emblematic of her bubbly personality. "Greetings, my young charges! Welcome to your first class in geology!"

"Come, take your seats and please open your geology books to the description of igneous, sedimentary, and metamorphic rocks—page 12, I believe…"

Their third-period course was Sahila's practicum on healing with gems and minerals. For this class, they finally got to open their personal kits; they were all excited to get started. Only Ming and Demyan seemed at home with the gem samples. The others were familiar, but not quite sure what to make of the specimens or the class itself. Sahila was dressed in a practical, but chic jumpsuit today and a jeweled barrette gathered her jet-black hair away from her face in a classic style.

Although some lessons were not geared specifically toward their unique skills, the students needed an understanding and appreciation for all abilities. In an emergency situation, they could harness a modicum of energy to be somewhat impactful with a different ability or be able to use their ingenuity to create an effective alternative until someone with mastery of the needed skill set arrived on scene. In graduate school, they would concentrate on their specific abilities and attend more concentrated practicum sessions.

Sahila instructed them to unlatch their kits.

"What is this, Keeper Sahila?" Tessa inquired. Inside each kit was a seal made from a mixture of lead and paraffin wax. It covered the entire opening of the kit. The wax was a pasty gray color with visible lead shavings embedded into it. A thin black thread was tied in a bow over the front of the wax seal.

"Untie the bow and gently pull the thread ends away from you. The thread will cut the seal and then you can lift it up. Just toss it into the hazardous recycling bin for purification when you are done." Sahila explained that the leaded wax was added after the kit was assembled for security. She pointed to a container of baby wipes used to clean off any residual paraffin left on the items or their hands.

"Inside your kit, you should find unloaded gemstones, minerals, and rocks. The samples were selected directly from the most plentiful sources around the world and were gently sculpted and polished specifically for your use. These are the most appropriate materials for new students to manipulate. An 'unloaded' sample is pure; it contains only the inherent energy typical of that rock or mineral. It has not been *loaded* with additional energy, either positive or negative—hence the term *unloaded.*

"We have a robust system of categorization when it comes to the energy intensity of rocks and minerals. You already understand that some are safe to hold and use, whereas others are incredibly dangerous and kept under lock and key." Sahila wiggled her fingers in a flourish and selected a piece of purple chalk, turning to the slate board. "Since this is your first lesson, we are focusing on the two essential categories.

"First, *unpolished stones* in their natural uncut state have the potential to be the most powerful, if they are further loaded with positive or negative energy. These are very difficult for beginners to sense and control. Why is that?"

Demyan raised his hand. "Is it because they haven't been cut or altered in any way?"

"Correct, Scholar Demyan. Good assumption! A completely unaltered rock hasn't been cut or polished. Anytime a rock or gem is faceted, it can lose some of its inherent strength, even if handled by an expert.

"So, when considering the negative loading potency of rocks and gems, the greatest threat lay within these uncut natural stones. Since they are unaltered, only the most seasoned Emogem and Resogem, has the ability and strength to infuse them with additional positive or negative energy. And only a Debilis will do so with the intent to harm. A few very dangerous unpolished and uncut stones exist around the world, but they are harder to discover and recover, since they inherently attract far less attention."

Ming raised her hand. "You mean they attract less attention, because they are not as beautiful and shiny?"

Sahila clicked her tongue. "Exactly. Humans and some animals the world over are attracted to polished and highly faceted gems over less visually appealing ones; we are not immune either, I have to admit."

Demyan mused, eyes wide, "It makes you wonder who is hoarding those less glamorous but seriously dangerous stones."

"Indeed. That's why we try so hard to get them out of circulation. Okay, the second level in the strength hierarchy are polished and expertly faceted stones, like the ones locked away in the safe room." Sahila wrote *highly faceted stones* on the board in green. "While certainly very beautiful and vastly preferred, as we discussed already, their altered state makes them more vulnerable and exploitable than the uncut, unpolished ones.

"The more a stone is cut and polished, the easier it is to load both positive and negative energy upon it; every additional facet can weaken the integrity of the stone. The lapidary[194]process might affect its durability and inherent stability. These rocks have the potential to become dangerous as their highly faceted designs expose them to the manipulations of even minimally skilled Debilis, who can take advantage of the stone's existing energy and further infuse it with more. But as dangerous as these stones may become, a skilled Debilis can wrought even more harm with an uncut stone, as its original integrity remains intact."

"I'm beginning to see how this can become a big problem," KameKona stated.

---

[194] Lapidary-the art of sculpting, cutting, and polishing rocks. A person with this skill is a 'lapidarist.'

"Unlike the few dangerous uncut and unpolished stones, the more compromised polished gems tend to have a following and be tracked by humans and Debilis alike throughout the ages. Much like a famous painting, these coveted prizes are desired for their beauty and allure. Occasionally, the unquenchable need for these gems makes them the most dangerous, if only for the perilous journey embarked upon to acquire them. A select few highly skilled Resogem experts dedicate their entire careers to hunting down and securing these specimens; it's not for the faint of heart!"

Tessa spread her hands wide in enthusiasm. "It's not my ability, but I have to say, that sounds like a really cool profession. Very adventurous! Like something you'd see in a spy show!"

Sahila continued. "Well, given these stone and mineral categorizations, you can see why we offer beginning students lightly faceted stones and minerals on which to practice, considering the potential for disaster!"

The students sat mesmerized by this first revealing glance into the strange and fascinating world they were destined to enter. Sahila wasn't yet finished, however.

"Let's take a journey into how the principles of energy-loaded stones also apply to works of art, shall we? I find this topic fascinating and we will only briefly touch on it now. But we want you to understand the far-reaching impact that loaded stones and minerals can have on the world.

"Historically, paint color was created by crushing stones and minerals into fine particles. These were mixed into the paint base, which often contained ingredients such as linseed oil, egg yolks or whites, conifer resin, lead compounds, and rosemary oil, among other materials. The vast majority of painters, of course—famous and not—were unaware if the minerals and stones used to make paint were 'enhanced' or loaded; they were ignorant as to the existence of the supernatural. And unbeknownst to these artists, throughout history, some of these artists *did* use positive or negative energy-infused gemstones in their pigments… and the results are legendary. Does anyone know the title of the most world-famous painting containing positively loaded pigments?"

Ming tentatively raised her hand, almost reverently. She seemed to be on the precipice of a great awareness, suddenly understanding something vitally important about the natural world. She all but whispered, "Are you referring to Leonardo da Vinci's *Mona Lisa?*"

Sahila placed her hands together and clapped once. "Excellent, Scholar Ming! You got it in one. After this lesson, you may choose a dinner to send through the pneumatic tubes."

Sahila walked to one of the brass canisters and pulled it down to reveal a large poster-like rendering of the painting. "Let's contemplate the *Mona Lisa* for a moment, shall we? This painting by da Vinci is just one among thousands hung in the Louvre in Paris. And it has captivated the minds of countless millions since it was completed around 1519. Her enigmatic smile perpetually mystifies. It's a unique and priceless painting, but many other works of art are equally incredible and beautiful."

Sahila gesticulated enthusiastically toward the painting with her hands. "Other than her smile, why does she continue to enthrall humanity through the ages? The answer is that Leonardo da Vinci was a Guardian and one of our most brilliant!" She waited a beat for that to sink in among her captive audience. "He was curious about the use of positively loaded stone pigments in his paint and was granted permission to try by the appropriate Keepers. The *Mona Lisa* was his experiment in satisfying this curiosity; he only used stones with the greatest positive energy to mix with his paints. And to this day, the energy signature from those stones remains as vital as ever." Sahila counted the number of open mouths staring at her, expressions either dumfounded or enlightened.

Aedan raised his hand. "Keeper Sahila, why does the energy from the stones not dissipate over time?"

Sahila smiled warmly. "That's a smart question, Scholar Aedan. "Every year, about ten million people visit the *Mona Lisa*. The vast majority of them are excited and in awe of both her and Leonardo himself. They are usually on vacation with family, friends, or are part of a tour group with like-minded individuals and are happy and filled with curiosity. All of this positivity further infuses the paint with beneficial energy; it is a synergistic relationship that keeps her vital and perennially relevant."

Élise raised her hand enthusiastically. "Keeper Sahila. This is incredible and eye-opening. But you mentioned that some works of art contain negatively loaded stones and minerals, yes?"

Sahila's eyes twinkled… "Indeed, I did! Unfortunately, throughout history and even today, we come in contact with paintings and works of art containing dangerous negatively loaded minerals and rocks. Debilis enjoy collecting and using them for their own gain."

Sahila talked about how Keeper and Debilis pigment specialists were very rare. To date, the Keepers of the Rock could count on only one hand the amount of expert pigment specialists existing within their ranks. The Debilis, thankfully, had only three that the Keepers knew of in their entire history, the most famous being the Cat Burglar of Brussels.

The exploits of this thief and the female Keeper pigment specialist who finally captured him were legendary in Keeper lore. This cat burglar had a heightened sensitivity to loaded paintings and made a business of stealing them for great gain and nefarious purposes. At the time, Commoners, although aware of the cat burglar, never managed to catch him. He seemingly disappeared one day and was presumed dead. Every Halloween, College of GeoEvolution students dressed up as the famous Keeper or the cat burglar.

"When he was finally caught," Sahila added, "only the neutral and positively loaded paintings and jewelry he stole were returned to Commoner individuals and museums; we kept the rest and started the rumor that the other paintings were destroyed. Most owners of such expensive works had them insured and that minimized the collective Keeper guilt and involvement. If a Commoner can recoup their loss through typical channels, we walk away."

"Do Keepers store dangerous paintings someplace?" Tessa inquired.

"Ah! You beat me to the punch! The answer to that, Scholar Tessa, is yes. We keep 'haunted' paintings on secured walls both here and at the Cambridge campus," she said, gesturing with air quotes. "The door is locked and none of you will be ready to enter until next year; you don't yet have the training or stamina."

KameKona gaped. "I'm sorry, I think I misheard you, Keeper Sahila. Did you say haunted paintings?"

"Don't fret, but where do you think stories of haunted castles and homes throughout the world stem from, other than from Guardian horror stories, I mean?"

"Seriously!" KameKona grasped the back of his head, no doubt looking for a ribbon. "Haunted houses exist and they stem from negatively loaded paintings and stones?"

Tessa screeched. "And Keepers encourage and commission terrifying stories and movies to cover it up? Mind blown!"

Sahila waved her arms in a calming gesture and giggled. "Seriously, relax, are baap re[195]! This happens every time; I should be used to it by now," Sahila exclaimed as she shook her head. "We'll always tell you the truth, remember? I will admit, these paintings are very dangerous, but mainly only to Commoners. The ones that are perilous became that way because of the residual evil energy existing in the pigment; it permeates the location where they are hung. Some of these paintings stay on the walls of homes or museums for generations and thereby 'haunt' the inhabitants. Most of them were created by Debilis. Historically, however, some of these paintings were created by mentally ill Commoner artists. If their symptoms caused great emotional and physical distress, the paint pigments could absorb some of the negative energy."

Sahila explained that Debilis painters influenced and gained commissions from disenfranchised Commoners, angry over their disinheritance or perhaps jealous of a sibling's happy marriage. Sometimes they were requested by an abusive spouse, seemingly doting, but keen on having the painting keep his or her betrothed in line with a menacing likeness. Commoners who were more happily situated in life tended to shy away from the unsettling disposition of these individuals. Discussing these works and how they came about was a master's degree class at Cambridge and was *always* full and in demand.

---

[195] Are baap re – Hindi for oh my, my father, or oh my God

"Okay, my charges," Sahila continued, "please make sure you can locate your deep yellow citrine, jade, and lapis lazuli;[196] they are yellow, deep green, and a mottled blue-gray-brown, respectively. Who can tell me how these stones can aid an individual?"

Although Ming was the obvious student to choose, Sahila was hoping that others had completed the required reading and were prepared.

KameKona eagerly raised his hand. "Keeper Sahila," he stated, "I believe that citrine helps control one's emotions and assists with relieving anxiety; it also detoxifies the body. Jade helps achieve internal peace and tranquility, can assist with healing the kidneys, improves the immune system, and fosters wisdom. And lapis lazuli…" KameKona paused here for a moment to remember. "Ah, it encourages relationship building and growing friendships. And also assists with building courage. Phew!"

"Excellent, Scholar KameKona, you've been completing your required reading."

Ming smiled encouragingly, clearly impressed. Sahila wandered over to a nearby fan and turned it on. "It seems to be getting a little warm in here, isn't it?"

Embedded in the fan blades were tiny chips of clear and frosted quartz as well as topaz, stones that aided in healing respiration. Everyone nodded and shifted around in their seats.

"Take note that at end of term, you will all be tested on the restorative characteristics of stones and minerals, so continue the assigned reading in between classes. In the second semester, we will focus on how negatively loaded stones and minerals can impact Commoners and Keepers

---

196 "Lapis Lazuli," https://www.mindat.org/gm/2330

alike and how to counteract the effects. Everyone, please select your lapis lazuli." Sahila had them hold it in the palm of their hand with their eyes closed for several minutes, so they could concentrate on its natural energy frequency and temperature. Sahila glanced around the room.

While teaching the class, she noticed the faint, but growing hum of an emotional cocktail consisting of dislike, heightened anxiety, and distrust. She began to wander the room as she continued.

"As with every object in nature, each lapis lazuli stone has a standard, recognizable, and constant vibration. Despite this universal truth, however, every stone, like a snowflake, is slightly unique. There may be minute inclusions of an additional mineral or other stone—a 'piggybacker,' we call it, another element or substance that gets incorporated into the larger whole. It won't alter the main fluctuation, but will add an additional residual sensation. It will be smaller, almost like a distant echo. You will learn to recognize these piggyback inclusions with practice. On the whole, they do not change the healing properties of the stone. If they do, the inclusions are more prominent and subsequently, your sample is not ideal; leave those stones for nature in their original habitat. They will benefit their nascent environment as the flora, fauna, and wildlife have a symbiotic relationship with it already."

Sahila next tasked Ming with passing around her own lapis lazuli to everyone in the class. They were to compare it with their own, to note that her sample was definitively warmer and more activated than theirs. This was Ming's primary ability and medium, so the distinction was expected. They were also to note if they felt any sensation after holding it for a while. The resounding answer was yes, they felt calmer and more congenial toward Sahila and their other classmates. There was a growing willingness to lower their guard and recognize the fraternity developing around them; they were actively forging an essential trust.

"I don't want to touch Ming's sample!" Demyan stood and shouted at Aedan when it was his turn. "It's dirty! Get your fat blond head out of my space, you moron!" He lunged toward the front of the room and grabbed the fan, still plugged into the wall. He faced them, clearly intending to throw it at the others. "As for you, Tessa, your awkward self-deprecating vibe is drowning me and your eagerness is sweaty and desperate!" He was breathing heavily and visibly angry, his face contorted with rage.

Sahila tapped KameKona's shoulder quickly and motioned for him to grab the fan. That done, she raced over to Demyan's desk, grabbed his personal kit, and ran back to him. She grasped her necklace and spun it rapidly, searching by feel for the stone teardrop she wanted. Yanking on the lapis lazuli pendant, she pulled it down by its individual chain from the main necklace and quickly warmed it in her hand as she faced Demyan.

"Scholar Demyan," she stated firmly, but with empathy exuding from within, "hand me your rock sample now, please. It's making you unhappy and that's an uncomfortable emotion. Let me have it, now."

She placed his kit under one arm and held out her empty palm. As he glanced at her, Demyan's anger visibly dissipated and his posture sagged with the emotional release. Glancing at Aedan, Sahila motioned for him to bring her Ming's lapis lazuli sample.

Demyan gently dropped his stone into Sahila's palm and took Ming's sample instead. Demyan sighed visibly and faced the group. He looked despondent.

"I'm so very sorry. I did not mean anything I said. All of a sudden, I was enraged. I felt that you all were out to harm me and hated me; I wasn't in control."

Sahila palmed his lapis lazuli and felt it for a few moments. Reflective, she opened his personal kit and lifted the citrine from its home, holding that stone as well.

"Scholar Demyan," Sahila stated kindly, but soberly. "Don't blame yourself. Somehow your citrine and lapis lazuli were negatively loaded. I'm not sure how that happened. It's unacceptable and we will get to the bottom of this immediately. I'll make sure you have another kit in hand by tomorrow—you mentioned that your wax seal came apart in two halves, correct? Whom else had that issue? Scholar Aedan, it was you, correct?"

At his nod, she had him bring his kit and Sahila examined every sample of both his and Demyan's. "Scholar Demyan, only your citrine and lapis lazuli are affected. Are you okay? Are you feeling better? Scholar Ming, take a moment and work with Scholar Demyan while I examine all of the other kits, please."

A thorough inspection of each kit revealed no other anomalies. After approving of Ming's amateur but positive healing effects, Sahila kept Demyan's kit and told the students to head to lunch. She needed to arrange an immediate emergency meeting with all Keeper teaching staff while the students ate before their afternoon classes began.

From her pocket Sahila removed a black velvet pouch. Inside was a faceted quartz crystal and a small brass hammer that comfortably fit in her palm. All Keepers, and most trusted Guardians, were issued and trained to use this standard communication equipment as well as become fluent in Lucidum code, their secret non-verbal language.

When it came to corresponding with each other, cell phones didn't work reliably. In addition, it was known that intercepting phone calls from both cell phone and landline conversations was accomplished fairly easily by those with the equipment, knowledge, and desire. The Keepers' communication system was similar to Morse code and was generally just as reliable.

Using the hammer, Sahila sent out a quick message to the other Keepers on campus for an emergency meeting. The message would be received by her peers' communication crystals and would vibrate with the exact same frequency, transmitting the message in code. Similar to Morse Code technicians, Keepers and Guardians memorized the code and could usually decipher it without taking pencil to paper.

To ensure the messages were understood clearly, it was imperative all crystals were faceted to the same size and degree and they originated from the same larger crystal. Minute distinctions or inclusions in different crystal samples might cause distortions. It worked very well throughout the college campus and beyond.

The communication system was so old, its provenance was lost to time. Dissertations by Keeper doctoral students were written and defended regarding the history of this secret cypher.

"I check those engrossing tomes out of the library when I have trouble sleeping!" Reese often quipped about them.

When it was necessary to reach Keepers and sanctioned Guardians further afield or in other countries, a similar but more involved network was used. Occasionally, a Guardian received a landline call. They were trained to converse in a unique coded language in these instances. Anyone listening on either end would be bored to tears and would disengage rather quickly.

To date, two fabled conversations between Keepers and Guardians were the stuff of urban Keeper legend. This never stopped students from perpetuating them, however. Keeper staff were consistently noncommittal when questioned as to their truth, which of course, further perpetuated the myth.

In the first discussion, a Guardian was drawn into a lengthy conversation about diaper blowouts. Apparently, the caller's healthy baby was producing copious amounts of poop that exceeded diaper capacity. In the second, the Guardian was asked about smelly cat food and which brand was sure to lure a certain recalcitrant cat out of a neighbor's tree.

Upon translation, baby poop and cat food were code for troublesome Debilis and the caller was informing the Guardian of the issue and asking advice on how best to proceed; the Guardians in both instances were experts in their respective fields.

Sahila met the necessary Keepers in the library while the students were at lunch. Included in the meeting were Xandra, Alesky, and Fabek, all who had responsibilities at the college year-round and were tasked with staying alert for any campus concerns. The two personal kits were open for inspection upon a wooden table while Sahila explained what transpired during the class.

"The stones were clearly negatively charged. Demyan will someday be a gifted Resogem, but he currently lacks discipline and the skills to make him impervious to negative energy. Right now, he resembles a sponge! He soaked up the heightened anxiety, anger, and fear almost instantly and began attacking the others. Had we not stopped him, he'd have thrown the fan at someone and then goodness knows what. He feels terribly guilty and responsible, but it wasn't his fault."

Nalin asked about how he was doing and if he needed additional therapy. Sahila responded that he was fine and that Ming helped with the recovery and did quite well.

"How could thi' hav' happened? Has it ever happened before?" Jürgen questioned.

"As far as I understand, it hasn't happened for well over two hundred years," Reese responded. "I communicated with Keeper Dumisani and explained the situation."

Concerned, Evren ruffled his hair. "It seems a deliberate attack. Occasionally, the wax comes apart in two pieces, but stones are never loaded negatively. No. He was given this box deliberately to elicit the reaction we saw."

"The question," pressed Alegria, "is why? What was to be gained by this invasive act? And who is responsible?"

Reese walked over to Heikima, the head librarian, and asked for a piece of butcher block paper. He spread it out on the table and began writing. He placed a circle around Demyan's name. After that, he drew a line radiating from his name and created branches from that line. "What's the *why*, right?"

Reese was the Keeper expert in black market trade and Debilis activity; his initial career made him an ideal candidate to patrol those worlds. He proceeded to list possible motives: *infiltrate the college, ascertain Demyan's strengths and weaknesses for potential abduction, cause Demyan's expulsion, attack reputation of the college, and end relationship with personal kit company (rival company?).*

"I don' really believe it's the last one, but you can neva be too sure when I comes to bushrangers,[197] ya know? If a rival company is desperate enough…" He added another line from Demyan's name and created branches as well and labeled it *Who?* "Okay, what are the possibilities?"

Alegria immediately mentioned "Debilis."

Jürgen added *disgruntled kit designer* and *rival kit company personnel.*

"I really doubt it's as pedestrian as a fight between rival companies. I'm more concerned that it's Debilis activity," Sahila interjected.

Evren added, "I want to know how this was accomplished in the first place. How does one tamper with a kit? We have proper surveillance throughout the entire process of the kits' design and delivery."

"Noted," Reese remarked. "I'll get in touch with our Guardian contact and look into where the breakdown occurred."

Nalin looked at the information in front of them. In Dumisani's absence, she was the next senior staff member in charge. "We've all sensed the heightened energy; Fabek certainly notices alterations to the land and crops. That we welcomed these many students this term and none the year before is a barometer of change.

"Dumisani will return soon and we will continue to pursue this threat. In the meantime, I want the campus on higher alert. Fabek, take your staff and thoroughly check the grounds every day; look for any aberration or peculiarity. Alesky, please verify the buildings are secure and that we've had no issues. Xandra, have your staff increase their school entrance perimeter searches and make sure the students feel

---

[197] Bushranger – Australian slang for outlaw

safe. Reese, do what you do best—look for whatever criminal element is responsible, please."

Although a cloud of confusion and anxiety hung over the students during lunch, they seemed to rebound quickly. They were safe and nothing bad had ultimately happened, as far as they could see, and the staff was clearly invested in their welfare.

As far as Demyan was concerned, if some entity intended him harm, he was safest at school. Most likely, their intentions were the same whether he was at home or here; he'd take his chances at school.

The rest of the day was fairly uneventful. Classes in chemistry, classic literature, and their first physical education class seemed routine. As was the case with most freshman classes at any institution, students began with introductory material and learned initial theories and formula before exploring the more interesting information. They were tasked with studying the elements of the periodic table by section in chemistry. In literature, they received their copies of *Beowulf*, one of the first literary monsters. They were disappointed to have a physical assessment in PE and were instructed in the safe use of all of the machines. Although they doubted that they would get to fling around a bo right away, hope sprung eternal.

A large common room sat at the end of the student dormitory hallway, especially popular since each student had their own small living space. The tiny student population size allowed individual quarters, but the school was also designed this way intentionally. Navigating through the teenage years was stressful enough without adding ever-increasing abilities into the mix.

Students might practice their ability in their own space, lest they inadvertently release energy when irritated, cranky, or overwhelmed. The common room was generally conflict free, although teenagers often practiced in there anyway. The space was large, so it was significantly less hazardous.

Plenty of books, puzzles, and games served to occupy and entertain students. The large fireplace was lit on cold evenings, covered by a mesh screen of platinum and iron to prevent potential mishaps.

After dinner, Élise changed into sweats and a sweater and was heading toward the common room. She enjoyed the camaraderie and respected the other students. They were a good group and she felt they were beginning to mesh, despite their different abilities and cultures. As she headed down the hall, she felt a faint tapping sensation.

*What was that?* she wondered. She turned in a slow circle, searching for the culprit. *Where are you?* She found the constant tapping difficult to pinpoint. Curious, she walked up and down the hall and stopped in front of each door.

She didn't sense movement from any room until she came to Tessa's. She could tell that Tessa was inside, but the vibration she noticed didn't match Tessa's movements. She knocked on the door.

Traditionally, when students were in their rooms, they often kept their doors open to welcome interaction and socialization. It made it easier to ask for homework assistance from one another as well as encourage study group sessions. Everyone wanted alone time at some point, however.

When they first moved in, everyone agreed to a specific response signal if there was a knock upon their door, in case it was Élise. So, they devised a quick knock code on their wooden desks. Élise noted the 'come in' knocking signal now and opened Tessa's door.

"Hey, do you hear a tapping sound in the hallway?" Élise said and signed. She pointed to the hallway. "I was just headed to the common room when I felt it."

Tessa shook her head and raised an eyebrow, intrigued. She followed Élise out into the hallway.

"You don't hear or sense that?" she signed quickly as she whispered. "I can't figure out where it's coming from, but it's a rhythmic tapping." She walked down the hall, trying to pinpoint the sensation. She slowly stopped and turned in a circle at the entrance to one of the stairwells and felt a distinct temperature difference. It was colder in this spot. "It's coming from right here. Look around. Do you feel cold air?"

Tessa peered into the space around her. "I don't know how you perceive anything," she said, mystified. "It looks completely normal here to me. I know your other senses are heightened. I don't feel or hear anything. It does feel a bit colder, however." The hair on Tessa's arms rose as she walked closer to the cold patch.

Élise continued her slow turn around the space and raised her hand in indication. "Do you see something there, Tessa?"

Tessa looked at her, confused. "Élise, I don't hear or see *anything*. What do you see?"

"It's a haze, like a cloud in the hallway—it's very faint and not a distinct shape. But it's moving around and the rhythmic tapping is following the haze."

Tessa motioned toward the common room. "Everyone else is in there. You stay here and I'll grab them. Are you okay?"

Élise smiled. "I'm not scared, actually. I don't feel anything negative. I'm just curious."

Élise had learned to be patient over the years. She was used to signing very slowly, since she spent the majority of her time among the "hearie."[198] It took significantly longer, but she knew it would pay off; she was appreciative of others trying to learn her language. She understood—in high school, she'd studied Spanish. Tessa gave her the thumbs up as she ran off to get the others.

Élise kept her attention on the mist in front of her. It continued to repeat the patterned tapping, consistent and unwavering. A moment later, as Tessa and the others arrived, Tessa filled everyone in as they quietly peered into the space.

Someone stated softly, "It's cooler here."

Ming whispered urgently, "I'll be right back." She ran to her door. After a few moments, she tapped Élise on her shoulder to get her attention.

"Élise, I don't hear or see anything, but let me know if anything changes, okay?" She opened her palms and revealed a large oval stone, too large to be made into comfortable jewelry. It was a gorgeous deep purple, with swirls of black and white inclusions and a pearl-like luster; it was utterly unique.

"That's charoite!"[199] Demyan whispered, excited.

"Yes," Ming responded. "It only comes from Russia, in Siberia. My father bought it for me on one of his trips. I've never actually used it."

Tessa leaned forward to get a closer look at the gorgeous stone. "Ming, that's stunning! If it only comes from Siberia, you must be loaded!"

KameKona swung his stunned gaze from the stone to Tessa and whispered loudly. "Tessa! You got foot-in-mouth

---

[198] Hearie – A term used by the Deaf community for those who can hear

[199] "Charoite," https://www.mindat.org/gm/972

syndrome? You have to think before you talk… I'm from a middle-class military family in Hawaii, but I still couldn't run my mouth like that, without inviting trouble. And believe it or not, you and I are a great deal alike right now, 'cause we're in unfamiliar territory. We barely understand this new world we've entered and we don't know what we're facing. Plus, really. That's just plain rude." He shook his head as he moved closer to the cold patch in the hallway.

Tessa flushed bright red, her fair complexion hiding none of her instantaneous anger and mortification. She didn't know which emotion to feed, so she quietly took a deep, cleansing breath, concentrating on the stress and anger reduction exercises Dya encouraged her to practice.

When she was younger, after a similar encounter, she usually wound up in the principal's office after mouthing off at the "offending attacker." In her soul, she knew her anger was largely directed toward herself. What was wrong with her? Why did she impulsively say exactly what she thought, as if no verbal filter existed in her mind?

She knew this was a fresh start for her and, for the first time in her life, she was surrounded by like-minded-students her age. If ever she was around those who understood her, it was now. Would she alienate this group as well? She bit her lip and licked her wounds, focusing on what was happening around her.

Ming, deciding her best option was to focus on the present and ignore the awkward exchange, walked closer to Élise.

"Please don't be afraid," she said to the space in front of her. "Do you need our help? Are you trying to communicate with us?" Ming rubbed the stone between her palms, warming it up. She held the rock with outstretched hands. The air became even colder and Élise's long blond hair blew around her, as if manipulated by a wind, but there were no air vents near them.

Ming felt the stone heat in her hands and it seemed to take on a brighter hue; it almost glowed. "Do you notice anything?" Ming said while looking at Élise.

"Yes!" Élise exclaimed and signed. "The fog is getting more concentrated and the tapping is happening faster!"

"I don't see anything!" Tú whispered. "Does anyone see or hear what Élise notices?"

Everyone shook their heads.

"Élise, you need to tell one of the professors," Aedan urged as he approached Élise. "Many people don't believe in ghosts or spirits, but in England, numerous places are supposedly haunted. Sometimes I've sensed something, but I've never actually seen anything. But just because I haven't, doesn't mean they don't exist."

Élise nodded in agreement and turned to the mist. "I know you are trying to communicate. I'm not walking away; we're going to get help to try to understand what you need. I won't forget."

Élise turned and walked with the others to the common room, looking behind her every few steps like everyone else. She rubbed her arms, trying to get warm. Despite her unique life experiences, she never encountered anything like this before. She knew she wasn't dreaming and didn't believe her mind was manufacturing the sensation because of stress or anxiety. The others had felt the cold too.

When they all funneled back into the common room, it was filled with a sense of excitement and trepidation. How did one explain the experience?

KameKona approached Tessa and gently pulled her arm to slow her progress. "Hey. I'm sorry I yelled at you like that. I didn't handle that well."

Tessa shook her head and looked down at the carpet. "Naw. It's okay. What I said was rude. I blurt things out sometimes without thinking. I don't know what's wrong with me. I need to figure it out. In the future, however, when I do it again, do you think you can pull me aside instead?"

KameKona nodded quietly. "Awright, but Tessa," he said as he gently clapped her on the back, "being impulsive like that, in our new environment, can get you or someone else killed. We don't really know what we're facing."

## CHAPTER 25 – Mn

### COLLEGE OF GEOEVOLUTION

Classes began the next day with a sense of anticipation. Thankfully, the students had kinesiology first thing that morning and everyone would spend most of the class moving around outside.

"Come in! Come in! Let's talk abou' harnessing and manipulating energy! We're focusing on rare earths and magnetic elements today. Other than rare earths, what elements are magnetic?"

Several hands shot up. Jürgen grinned at Aedan's eager expression. The boy was certainly invested.

"All right, Scholar Aedan. Give it a go."

"Other than rare earths," Aedan said, gesturing to Tú, "they are iron, nickel, and cobalt."

"Very good. Now, Scholar Tú and Scholar Aedan, you know the answers to the next question so I'm goin' to have the others respond. I'll need your input a bit later. What do you sense or feel when in the presence of iron, nickel, cobalt, rare earths, and steel alloys, which often contain various combinations of these and other elements?"

It was quiet as each student pondered the question. Did Tú and Aedan sense these elements in a manner similar to the way they sensed their own material? Did an identical patterned identification response work for them all?

"Is there a tingling sensation, almost like when you're walking through a spider web? Not in a gross or scary way; it's a vibrating *awareness*. That's the best way I can describe it," Tessa remarked. "For me, the feeling becomes more pronounced when I come across a powerful crystal or when I am getting closer to one that I sense."

"I like your description, Tessa," Ming added. "I do get that sensation, but I also feel different grades of heat energy, depending on the type of stone or rock. Each one has a different energy signature."

Tessa nodded in agreement. "I definitely feel the heat generation, but only after the crystal is in my hands."

Demyan raised his hand. "I don't think heat is the first sensation with magnetic rocks and rare earths. It takes intense heat energy to change a magnetic rock, but not a rare earth, correct? So, I think the first sensations will be the tingling and spider web feeling? For me, the first sensation *I* notice is a vibrating energy and I do feel differences in heat immediately, like Ming."

KameKona was visibly thinking and analyzing each contribution.

"Scholar KameKona, please enlighten us wi' your thoughts; I can see th' wheels a-turnin'."

"Okay," he responded. "I'm just playing with this in my head. When you accidentally bite your lip or the inside of your cheek, you taste blood. And even if it's just a little bit, you sense that iron, metallic taste in your mouth. That would definitely be a distinct sensation compared to what you all have mentioned. Me? I'm all about the heat. And instead of vibrations, I sense waves of heat; I think it might be a different feeling, based on what I'm hearing. It's almost like a real wave, from the ocean; it has an ebb and flow to it, just at a faster speed. Know what I'm saying?"

"Very well done, all of you. Scholar KameKona, that was a very perceptive comment. Boys? Want to enlighten the res' of the class?"

Tú smiled shyly. "I'm taking a photo in my mind. It's the first time I've ever felt others understand my experience and how I see the world. I'm really grateful. Kame, I do have that sensation sometimes. Some rare earths have iron inclusions, and when they do, I do have that sense and taste even. Otherwise, I feel what Tessa mentioned. It's difficult to describe, but I like your analogy, Tessa. I have a rippling sensation and the closer I get, the stronger it is."

Aedan raised his hand. "Yeah, good job, Kame. It's a weird characteristic, but one I often have. The rippling and pulsing sensation is accurate. It's almost like a heartbeat, as if the rock was alive somehow."

"Excellen'," Jürgen interjected. "We're going to head outside for the outdoor portion of our class in a moment. But we have one essential issue to discuss. How do we exist wit' all of these sensations and feelin's surrounding us in our everyday lives? You walk around campus an' are not inundated by all of them. Why is that? Does Aedan taste iron everywhere he goes? How can he enjoy his food? Why does Tú not have rare earths clinging to him every time he heads outside?"

Tessa was set to raise her hand and exclaim, "We handle it the same way we handle your fish odor; we got used to it!" But she controlled herself. She was trying to gain the upper hand on her impulsivity. She liked and respected Keeper Jürgen.

Instead, she said, "It's similar to breathing and blinking. Our autonomic nervous system handles that; we basically don't notice it. Take meditation, for example. For that, we need to focus on our breathing. So, unless we *need* to attune to our surroundings or come across a particularly important or unique sample within our abilities, we let our autonomic system handle it and tune it out. I think it's so we keep our senses sharp and not tire them out by always being vigilant."

Jürgen clapped his hands together. "Very good, Scholar Tessa! That's exac'ly correct. There is no need to sense every bi' of metal or rare earth, jus' as we are no' aware of every breath and blin'. It's our body workin' for us and keepin' us sharp. Our brains are taking in all of those stimuli and cataloging and assessing it, but we are no' aware of it. It will notify each one of us if there *is* somethin' we *do* have to attend to; our bodies are marvelous machines! Okay, outdoors we go!"

Once outside, Jürgen explained that magnetic iron, cobalt, and nickel samples as well as rare earths were scattered and hiding around the nearby campus green. The aim was for everyone, other than Aedan and Tú, to search for them first. Although they would never be as proficient as those two, in an emergency situation, they might have to utilize what skill they had.

Jürgen first gave a tutorial and Aedan and Tú demonstrated their techniques. Ming mimicked the particular hand gestures well, keeping her palms exposed to best harness any magnetic vibrations. At first, all she found were small gem inclusions that naturally occurred in the area.

When Tú aided her a bit more, she began to understand what she was looking for. "These vibration feelings are different than what I'm used to!"

When she really concentrated, after holding her hand over one spot for several minutes, she pulled a tiny old iron figure from the earth. "Yeah!" Ming said with fake enthusiasm. "I'm going to need a lot of practice."

Tessa and Élise began working a different area. Although Élise used the hand techniques that she'd been taught, her feet were far more sensitive. She kicked off her shoes and walked along the perimeter of the green, wiggling her toes in the grass. She forced herself to ignore the minute earth shifts beneath her feet miles beneath the surface. If she concentrated, she could even sense large earthworms slithering underground.

She giggled. "I remember fishing with my grandfather in upstate New York in the summer and digging up worms early in the morning; I always knew where the best ones were and Grandfather called me his 'good luck fishing charm.' He never knew about my ability, of course; I kinda felt I was cheating. I don't think he would've believed me if I told him anyway; he'd probably find me strange or weird," she said, sounding sad. She loved him and treasured those summer vacations in New York with her grandparents.

Élise switched her focus from earth and shifting crust to pulsing waves. "Okay. When I really pay attention, I can tell the difference!"

She bent down and pressed against the pulsing energy. She drew her hand up, wiggling her fingers, like a puppeteer manipulating a marionette. Slowly, bit by bit, a piece of something metal began to emerge from the soil. She released a pent-up breath as an old Indian head nickel appeared, along with several juicy little worms who came along for the ride.

Demyan and KameKona had similar levels of success. Tessa began in kind and used the proper hand gestures, keeping her palms open. The technique was not unlike her own, although she was searching for a different set of sensations. After a few minutes, however, she grew frustrated. She was used to acquiring what she sought much faster and with better accuracy. She reached into her pocket for her velvet pouch and drew out her multi-faceted crystal. While warming it in her palms, Tessa also angled it to capture the maximum amount of sunlight, imbuing the crystal with energy. Although it was already loaded with some energy from being in her pocket every day, she pushed more into it.

Task accomplished, a golden laser shot out from the crystal. She navigated it around the perimeter of the green and quickly glanced it off KameKona's and Élise's legs. Collective cries of "What was that?!" barely registered in her mind. She moved it along until she felt a change in the beam right in the middle of the green: the steady vibration changed to a pulsing sensation.

Tessa pocketed the crystal and ran to the spot. Using a circular motion as if opening a jar, she forced up her quarry: a beautiful chunk of cobalt, colored a mottled turquoise and brown. "Gotcha, sucker!" She grasped her prize and held it up.

"Well, Scholar Tessa, that was no' wha' I had in min', but far be it fo' me to fault you on yer technique. You found wha' you sought and in record time, too. Unorthodox manner, bu' there are a few Keepers I could name who tend to do the same."

Reese and Nalin burst onto the green. "Sorry to interrupt, but we have a situation!" Nalin exclaimed, breathless.

"Hol' yer horses, Keeper Nalin! What's wrong?"

"We have word of some imminent Debilis activity goin' down and we need to intervene now. It interferes with state and national Commoner interests," Reese said.

"Are we leaving our students on campus?" Jürgen questioned.

"Nah, I think we can bring 'em," Reese said. "Good experience and they may help run interference. We're headed to that specialized coin shop in Williamsburg. Fabek's getting the van."

Once loaded into the van, Reese stood in the aisle, hands resting on top of the bench seats, and faced their group. "Okay, here's the dealio. As you know, we are a college institution which follows worldwide instruction standards… yada yada. However, due to the nature of your abilities, future employment, and the unique upcoming challenges you will face, we also embrace hands on learning or 'on the job training' as you will," Reese gesticulated air quotes to emphasize his point. Nothin' replaces real world learnin.' So, we embrace the opportunities when they arise. We'll make sure you're safe…we won' risk your lives here for the sake of a lesson learned. Anyway, this here is a delicate situation. We are being deliberately provoked by certain Debilis forces. There is no other reason why this local coin shop would be targeted." He put his hands out in a placating gesture. "We'll keep you safe, no worries there."

Nalin continued. "About two hours from here, west of Richmond, is a town named Dillwyn. Anyone know why it's important? Don't stress if you don't know the answer; we don't expect you to."

"There are some important mines in Virginia, right?" asked Aedan.

"Excellent, Scholar Aedan, you are correct. Dillwyn is home to the world's largest Kyanite[200] mine. It's an incredibly important metamorphic rock—a silicate of aluminum. It's used in the production of high temperature cookware, spark plugs, specialized bricks and mortar, and kiln furniture, among other things. This mine is highly profitable and the company ships its product worldwide."

---

[200] "Kyanite," https://www.mindat.org/gm/2303

"What's kiln furniture?" Ming asked.

"When objects are fired at incredibly high temperatures in an industrial kiln, they must rest on an object that can withstand the heat—hence, kiln furniture."

Reese added, "Because this mine is so important to Virginia, the US, and the world, it's vulnerable to Debilis interference and that's what's happening here. And because Debilis are the culprits, we have to intervene."

"What does this have to do with a coin store?" Tú asked.

Nalin answered. "We've gotten word, through our Guardian contacts, that one of the senators of Virginia unknowingly hired two Debilis onto their staff. They have plans to infiltrate the office and manipulate the senator into changing important policies that will affect the whole state and the country as well."

"That doesn't sound dire," Tessa remarked sarcastically.

"There are recently acquired coins at this store which will greatly assist them with their goal; we've been looking for them for years. They are powerfully negatively loaded gold coins used to force compliance; Commoners have no ability to repel their affect."

Reese added, "We're racing to get them out of Debilis hands. If we don' get them now, it may be years before we find them again. The potential damage would be staggering. Specifically, the Debilis spearheadin' this venture wants the senator to greatly increase Kyanite production. Apparently, they have a financial stake in the mine. With those coins enhancing already dangerous Debilis abilities, the mining company leaders will be powerless to refuse."

Nalin massaged the crystal turtle on her necklace. "Mining employees could be killed if the strict safety protocols are ignored and the whole town will be at risk. Rate of production in a mine is highly regulated and monitored; thousands of lives in that town are in jeopardy if unsafe gases or other mining byproducts are not carefully managed."

"What do we do?" asked KameKona.

Jürgen stated, "I'm assuming we'll try to buy the coins first. Correct, Reese?"

"Of course, we always try to take the path of least resistance; we'll have to see who's there, however."

The van stopped across the street from the store.

"All right. We will all casually exit the bus and cross the street, as if we are on a routine field trip." Nalin ordered, "Follow our lead and stay close."

Reese and Jürgen led the way, with Nalin at the rear.

"What is that thing?" Ming wailed, pointing to the right side of the store.

"I see it!" Jürgen interjected. "Over cycled Debilis on the wall! I'm on it."

"They are already here!" Reese growled. "New game plan. Stick close!"

The students halted, eyes staring in horror. Skittering up the side of the store using its feet and hands was what appeared to be a part human, part praying mantis-like creature. It had the appearance of a bedraggled human in ill-fitted clothes, but moved its limbs in a halting and rocking manner, the way a praying mantis progressed;[201] it was altogether disconcerting and otherworldly creepy and was headed toward the roof.

Aedan barked, "Is it even human?"

"What is that awful smell?!"

"What the hell *is* that thing?"

---

201 "Mantis Walking." *YouTube*, WildlifeVideoSponsor, 29 Sept. 2012, www.youtube.com/watch?v=NXN_3fgYcjM.

"Stay near me," Nalin said. "Jürgen will get it. It's a Debilis on its last legs."

"Tú, combine your rare earths with mine," Jürgen ordered as he quickly removed the cache from his pockets. For such a large man, he moved with effortless grace when necessary. He bent near Tú and discussed their plan. Jürgen handed Tú his rare earths and Tú got to work grouping them together.

"Shield your eyes," Jürgen said, as he began sweeping his arms wildly from the ground up, palms wide, as if gathering items. Bits of rare earth ripped from the ground around him, swirling together in a mass as he gathered them. Pieces of dirt flew by as if they were encompassed in a small tornado.

"Now, Tú!"

The two used their combined rare earths together to form a large black birdcage, which Jürgen pushed toward Nalin.

"Nalin and Tessa!" he shouted. "I'll trap it when it comes down!"

Nalin pulled out a crystal and gestured to Tessa to follow her lead.

Tessa complied, hyper-focused. Using their crystals, she and Nalin created lasers, intense and painful to anyone who got in their path. They shot them toward the roof and Tessa knew she was correctly following directions, when she heard an unnatural screech.

The Debilis, trying to avoid the lasers, started to crawl back down the side of the building. Jürgen raced behind the rare earth birdcage and lifted it up on one side, trapping the creature. Jürgen and Tú gathered remaining rare earths to the birdcage base, essentially cementing it into the ground. The Debilis would not escape.

Reese shouted, "Keeper Security are on their way! And I am officially pissed off! I'm goin' in."

The students tentatively approached the defeated Debilis. "It smells so, so bad!" Tessa said, her face scrunched. The creature opened its toothless maw and hissed, backing up in its cage. It looked barely human. Its eyes were sunken into its face and its skin had a gray and yellow tinge, like sun-baked clay, cracked and leached of all moisture. Its nose was squat and unnatural, having lost its cartilage structure. The limbs were stick-like and it resembled a mantis or other insect from a nightmare.

"It's the sulfur," Nalin stated. "When a Debilis gets to this decrepit state, they positively ooze it. It's one of the reasons you rarely see them; they can't hide it."

"Commoners never see them?" Ming asked, her hand over her mouth.

"Rarely. They avoid public places and keep to sewers or storm drains, a forest, or sometimes the crawl spaces of houses, unless they are compelled by a more powerful Debilis to assist them; they bait these creatures with the promise of pain relief and nourishment. A Commoner would most likely perceive them as a homeless person in dire shape."

"How very sad," Tú said.

"Sad when they are in this pitiful state, but potentially deadly when stronger," Jürgen added, his face pinched. "Don't be fooled, however. Even now they can wreak havoc and are dangerous. A bite or scratch is hazardous and may cause necrosis,[202] like you see from a bite from a brown recluse.[203] You'll recover, but it's painful and it takes a while to heal;

---

[202] Necrosis – Death of skin tissue or organ cells

[203] Jacobs, Steve. "Brown Recluse Spiders: Eleven Species of Loxosceles Are Indigenous to the Continental United States, Four of Which Are Known to Be Harmful to Humans." https://extension.psu.edu/brown-recluse-spiders

you'll become intimately familiar with our leech family! What's keepin' Reese?"

Aedan, KameKona, and Demyan walked into the store with Reese. The store was very organized, with large cloth binders, presumably filled with coins, stored on tables with slanted tops. Posters of enlarged coins covered the walls. A man behind the counter was sweating and clearly anxious. Seeing Reese and the younger students, he angled his eyes to the left and toward his shoes.

"Well, Mr. Landers, looks like you've had a bit of trouble. Sorry about that. I'm here to collect a couple of items. You were notified I was coming?"

The man nodded subtly.

"Are you still in possession?"

He nodded again.

Nalin walked in and made eye contact with Reese. She gestured to the store's interior and walked further inside, searching.

Reese leaned over to the boys and whispered, "Do you both happen to have a nice sample of rock on you?"

They both nodded and pulled lava rock and some pieces of iron out of their pockets, respectively.

Reese nodded and they activated their mediums, heating them quickly in their hands. Reese pulled a large diamond out of his pocket, blew on it, and showed it to Demyan, whispering.

Suddenly, Aedan tossed his heated rocks over the front counter. They heard an angry shout and a man, teeth bared, jumped up, a sharp knife in hand. KameKona shifted to the side and lobbed his hot lava rock down the man's shirt. Instantly, his shirt caught fire and he popped over the counter, screaming as he raced outside.

"Incoming!" Reese shouted.

"On it!" responded Jürgen.

They all heard Nalin state calmly, "I wouldn't do that if I were you."

Another man raced around to the front counter, a red burn line along one arm, empty of a weapon. Reese tossed him the diamond, to the boys' surprise.

"This is certainly valuable!" Reese quipped. The man caught it and froze, mesmerized by the diamond's facets.

"Works most of the time, on weaker Debilis. He'll be stuck there for half an hour, enough time for Keeper Security to arrive. It's a negatively loaded diamond, with a mesmerizing overlay." Reese grinned. "Don't forget to take the advanced psychology class in hypnosis at Cambridge; it comes in handy."

When Reese and the others went outside, coins purchased and secure, Keeper Security had arrived.

"We've got them now, Keepers. And we apprehended the two staff members in DC. The senator's story is that they were homesick and hated DC, so they quit."

On the van ride home everyone was excited, but exhausted. "I think you are finished for the day," Nalin said. "Just settle in and get fed."

"What's going to happen to the Debilis?" Élise inquired.

"Keeper Security will try to rehabilitate the main two. If it works, they can be released in due time and resume normal lives. They are not too far gone," Nalin responded.

"What about the other one, the one in the cage? Demyan asked, tentative.

"He'll be euthanized, mate. It's the kindest thing to do. There isn't anything human left there to save, its brain activity is minimal, and its body is slowly shutting down. He's just suffering something awful."

Everyone was quiet the rest of the trip home.

## Chapter 26 – Fe

### College of GeoEvolution

Everyone was still digesting the events from yesterday, but they were eager to learn more. The cohort was excited for their heroes and villains history class to begin.

They had not discussed what Élise and the others experienced in the common room, and they were relieved to be able to share it with a teacher. Nalin Fink greeted them outside the classroom in a wheat-colored shift dress. Her long black hair was braided in the back and wound with a colorful woven cloth. Nalin's necklace included her ever-present turquoise turtle charm with its clear crystal eyes.

Once seated, she looked at them in an inquisitive manner. "Good morning. I can see by looking at you all that we are not going to make progress in our studies this morning until we discuss the duck in the room."

"Umm, Keeper Nalin, isn't the phrase usually the *elephant* in the room?" KameKona inquired.

Nalin grinned mischievously. "Yes. However, among my people, the Zuni, a duck symbolizes the spirit of those who have passed. I can tell from your collective expressions that you all experienced something within the supernatural realm. I sense confusion mixed with a bit of fear."

Élise proceeded to explain the situation she encountered before and the others interjected their own opinions.

"After class today, Keeper Alegria and I will meet you at the residence hall and we will see. I imagine, Scholar Élise, that the experience was a bit disconcerting. We will get to the bottom of it, one way or another.

"Almost every society and religious faith has beliefs or lore regarding the afterlife. The world is divided mainly into those who believe, those who don't, and those who are too afraid to entertain the issue. I would add another characteristic altogether: those who are receptive to inexplicable experiences and those who are not. An upper-level class in graduate school exists for those of you who are interested."

Nalin pulled on a brass canister cord and brought down a canvas painting. The painting depicted individual men and women, each contained within an identical painted rectangle frame with their name below.

"I'm sorry that Keeper Dumisani is not here to teach you today. If possible, he prefers to teach this important class; he was called away unexpectedly and will be back tomorrow.

"We've told you already that we serve as expert consultants to our Guardians and other Keepers around the world. These individuals conduct clandestine work within the Commoner world. And although you may think the word 'commoner' is derogatory, as how a lord referred to a serf in times long ago, it is not intended to be so. We refer to regular citizens as Commoners, to remind us that they are unaware of those with our abilities, both evil and good; they are purposely kept ignorant to the existence of supernatural forces. We already discussed the grave dangers that befall a world where the two realms merge."

She stepped alongside the canvas and held out her arm. "Are these individuals familiar?" She went to a portion of the slate board free from the canvas and raised a piece of chalk, poised to write.

Students raised their hands and began to call out names. *Attila the Hun, Vlad the Impaler, First Chinese Emperor Qin Shi Huangdi, Adolf Hitler.*

"Isn't it remarkable," Nalin remarked, "that although you come from different regions of the world, you can all readily identify some of the worst monsters to exist on Earth? Certainly, you've also learned of brave and extraordinary heroes as well. But we seem compelled as human beings to keep the worst of our kind in mind, lest we miss a new monster brewing in our midst."

Nalin pointed out some of the other names on the canvas: the infamous pirate *Ching Shih* and *Leopold II*, among others.

"In this world, some of these monsters are Commoners and some are Debilis. And in time, you will learn about them all. It is critical that you understand the difference between these two. *And that is because we only involve ourselves with Debilis monsters.* We are not sanctioned to use our abilities to combat the Commoner monster, as difficult as it is to restrain ourselves from doing so."

Tessa's eyebrows rose in alarm. "You mean, even if we *can* do something to prevent a disaster started by some sadistic human loser, we can't get involved?"

KameKona piggybacked onto her comment. "Why do the Avengers, Superman, and Batman get to assist and we don't?"

Nalin hooted. "What a fabulous world it would be, Scholar KameKona, if we had their assistance! Unfortunately, Captain America, the Hulk, Scarlet Witch, and the others don't exist; only we do. Keeper scholars throughout history continue to argue this point—and yes, that philosophical class is also available at Cambridge. Point of fact, Scholar Tessa: A very strong argument against this policy was made in the not-so-distant past and the rules were temporarily amended to meet the emergency situation. And we live with the result of that decision every day. Many of us are still proud of our involvement, but the price was devastating."

Nalin approached another blank portion of the slate board. She asked the class to engage in a hypothetical crisis: *A Commoner world leader misuses and hides millions of dollars from their country and jails or executes those who oppose him or her. What should the Keeper Society do?*

Ming's hand shot up. "Keepers and Guardians secretly use their abilities to replace the leader with a more ethical Commoner leader."

Aedan contributed, "Keepers and Guardians should find the money and return it to the people's government and then somehow embarrass the leader or punish them."

"I appreciate your well-meant ideas," Nalin said. "But let me throw in the proverbial monkey wrench. How do you choose a replacement leader, in Scholar Ming's situation? What right do Guardians and Keepers *have* to make such a decision for Commoners? By virtue of our specialized education and abilities, do we know better than them? Have we lived in their society enough to know what is best? Are we better, smarter, and wiser than they? What if whom we choose, through no fault of our own, becomes worse than their original leader? Shouldn't the people in that society decide what is best for themselves?

"Generally, history in the Commoner world demonstrates that when world leaders choose another country's leader, havoc, strife, and war eventually ensue. We'll examine numerous examples later on."

Nalin addressed Aedan's example in a similar fashion. "We'll examine the numerous world powers throughout history that have assumed control of another country, their leader thinking they know best—or believed they could better harness or exploit that land's resources. Consider how this very country was ruled by England and look how that turned out! We do not have the *right* to determine the fate of Commoners or their sovereignty. It is a distinct possibility that if we do, we make those problems worse."

Nalin wandered over to the painted pictures again and approached one in particular. "In the recent past, we ignored our sacred code and chose to get involved. It was an untenable situation and we felt that we *must* immerse ourselves."

She walked over to the painting of Adolf Hitler. "Hitler was a monster. Unfortunately for us, he was a *Commoner* monster. Had he been a Debilis, we could have done more, gotten involved without detection, eradicated him, and saved far more Commoner people. Instead, we still lost too many Commoners and lost many ourselves as well.

"Adolf Hitler was fascinated by the Occult, the supernatural. Because we felt the need to stop his murderous and diabolical plans, we enmeshed ourselves into the Reich and got too close. At some point, Hitler became aware of our existence, or gained awareness that some otherworldly force existed around him. With his manpower, he ferreted out our people, whose goal was to help the various resistance groups around the world. He wanted to manipulate and use our Keepers as a weapon toward his ultimate plans. He employed Josef Mengele, his evil and sadistic doctor, to figure out our Keepers' abilities. They were tortured and experimented upon.

"The majority of those captured sacrificed themselves to prevent the Nazis from learning about our collective abilities. That knowledge would be devastating in Hitler's hands. Who knows what he may have done had he succeeded?

"We lost over two hundred of our friends during World War II in our quest to help—over two hundred Keepers who were experts in their fields of study. We closed our college and university for three years, because we didn't have the personnel to properly operate them. We missed a generation of potential Keepers who didn't get the opportunity to learn about themselves and their abilities.

"It took years to search for them and when we did, only a handful were interested in becoming involved; they were attached to other schools or work and were otherwise invested. We were devastated and forgot our central goal, the reason we exist in the first place. *We are not on this Earth to assist humanity.* We exist to assist the Earth itself and protect humanity from Debilis involvement, because humanity, Commoners, are unaware that this supernatural evil exists. And they won't know how to combat it and will never have the proper tools to do so. *The most important lesson here is that we involved ourselves in the wrong way.* What was an alternative?"

She glanced around the semi-circle of students. Silence greeted her. No one wanted to suggest they knew better than hundreds of expert Keepers.

Tú tentatively raised his hand. "Should the Keepers have relied more upon the Guardians? I don't mean any disrespect."

"Exactly! Scholar Tú, thank you for taking the chance. We needed to work with our planted Guardians and offer our best advice and guidance. We needed to give them the tools to help the resistance and the Allied forces. It would have been a more strategic and impactful way to offer assistance. We are ultimately human as well, however, and were overwhelmed by the sheer horror of it all, the tremendous loss of innocent life from the Holocaust. We acted before we thought it through and we suffered the consequences."

Everyone was relieved to escape the essential, but maudlin class and head to physical education in hopes of burning off the tension. Thankfully, they were not treated to a repeat tutorial on exercise equipment. Instead, they learned the differences between the art of fencing and kung fu. The Keepers of the Rock did not seek out violence or glorify in it. But if a fight came to them and the opponent refused to choose reason, they were trained to win.

"Your Shaolin kung fu training focuses on disabling an opponent and protecting yourself," Shifu Zoria explained. "Learning how to properly stand, pivot, and kick are emphasized."

Fencing also stressed the importance of stance, but the dominant motions are in the arms and wrist with the use of the saber or épée. In addition to the fencing accouterments, the students would become familiar with the Shaolin bo and other weapons.

Once they became proficient using these tools, if desired, they could also learn to use swords. That is, if they believed their potential career necessitated it, they had a deep desire to learn—or as Xandra always held out hope, they became a famous Shakespearean actor.

Halbert walked over to the weapons case and looked inside in an exaggerated fashion. "There are many types of arms in these cases, but one major kind is missing. Any idea of what it is?" He stroked his mustache as he looked at everyone in anticipation.

Everyone stared back at him, gaping in surprise or visibly alarmed.

"It wasn't that tough a question and it's not as if I am going to punish you if you don't know the answer. Did Keeper Reese say something to the contrary? Petite hémorroïde!"[204]

Élise turned red and clapped a hand over her mouth, the only one to understand what Halbert said.

"There's—there's something hovering behind you!" Tessa shouted.

Halbert whipped his head back toward the glass case. Seeing what it was, he put his hands on his hips. "There is no need for you to be here! I have this class well under control!" His accent was more pronounced than usual when he spoke quickly.

"I'm sorry—what exactly are we looking at? That dude doesn't look well!" KameKona declared.

"He's not a dude," Élise added. "He's dead."

"So, he's a dead dude who isn't touching the ground?" Aedan inquired.

Ming flung out an arm. "Why is no one pointing out that this dead dude has a scary-looking sword in his hand? And that thing is real!"

The hovering figure with a menacing expression bore down on Halbert, sword whipping around. He wore period clothing from the nineteenth century and was hovering a few feet above the ground. Halbert raised his saber, preparing to fight.

He spat, "This is highly inappropriate! We spoke about this, many times!"

"I am not a dude! I am Master Eduardo Russo, your senior fencing instructor!"

---

[204] Petite hémorroïde – French for small hemorrhoid

Shifu Zoria jumped in front of the two posturing figures. "I assure you all is well. Master Russo has decided not to move on for reasons he won't disclose."

"I know why he won't depart this mortal coil!" Halbert shouted. "He's an unremittent control freak!"

"I am still the senior master instructor here. I am needed. Major threats are coming and you are not training these apprentices fast enough!"

Shifu Zoria motioned to Halbert that assistance was on the way.

"I assure you we have everything well in hand. By all accounts, you were a fantastic leader two hundred years ago—a legend, truth be told. But you are also very dead! You promised last time not to interrupt our classes!"

Master Russo floated forward, his sword thrusting at Halbert.

Sahila threw herself through the main door, breathless, and halted with a jolt in front of the dueling pair.

The students looked on in fascination, no longer alarmed. "Are we really seeing and hearing a ghost?" Demyan asked, shocked.

Sahila yanked two gems from her necklace and began heating them in her palms: moldavite[205] and labradorite.[206] Used together, they assisted with communing with spirits and calming them for more harmonious communication.

One could spend hours staring into either; they were both gorgeous stones. Labradorite was a pearlescent stone in mottled shades of blue, amber, and green. Moldavite was a translucent vibrant green; if dragons were real, surely one could envision their eggshells included a moldavite finish.

---

[205] "Moldavite," https://www.mindat.org/gm/10860

[206] "Labradorite," https://www.mindat.org/gm/2308

"Treacherous sorceress! Stay away from me!"

"Nah ah ah, Master Russo," Sahila replied, her voice as smooth as silk. "We had an understanding, did we not? We promised you that if you were needed, we would summon you." As she spoke, she slowly glided toward the ghost.

Unbeknownst to him, Shifu Zoria and Halbert were behind his back, slowly opening the glass case to extract a large and heavy sword, beautifully decorated with scroll etchings and a goose-egg-sized sapphire embedded in the silver hilt.

"I felt I was needed; I thought you summoned me," Master Russo stated in a petulant tone; he was clearly losing steam. He began to back away from Sahila.

"I can assure you that we did not. You remember the consequence of your little faux pas?"

Master Russo twisted around, clearly anxious.

Keeping to his back, Shifu Zoria and Halbert suddenly rushed Master Russo with the sword, the sapphire hilt angled forward just as Sahila tossed a large-faceted crystal into the ghost.

He screamed and left with an audible pop, leaving a lingering sulfuric vapor and his sword, which clattered harmlessly to the ground.

Sahila released an audible sigh. "That should trap him for a few more months, I believe. That's one determined Italian fencing master!

All the students looked to be in a trance, stunned by the activity.

"You have nothing to fear. If anything, you should feel even safer!" Halbert explained.

"Even our past instructors care so much, they linger in the 'in between' to teach in perpetuity."

"Boy," Shifu Zoria spoke in sotto voce. "That's one way to spin it."

Sahila addressed the students. "Master Russo was one of our finest fencing masters—two hundred years ago. He's feisty and a bit of a narcissist, so he thinks that no one can teach as well as him. I assure you that you are in the best of hands with Masters Zoria and Halbert."

"Where did he go?" Tú inquired.

"His soul is contained in the sapphire embedded in that sword. For the most part, he remains there, in stasis. It's a powerful sapphire, but he manages to squeak out once in a while, when he believes he's needed. I can assure you he's never injured any student—or Master Halbert.

"It's a sword from James VI of Scotland and it was given to him by a powerful Debilis. The Debilis approved of the king's desire to accuse and punish those he considered to be witches. Many of those accused were Keepers and Guardians, of course; you can imagine the Debilis's glee! We stole and repurposed it."

She smiled kindly and glanced at Halbert as she turned to leave. "Carry on, Master Halbert, carry on!"

Halbert cleared his throat and pulled his goatee. "As I was saying, there are many types of arms in these cases, but one major kind is missing. Any idea what it is?"

After a prolonged minute, Tessa raised her hand. "Umm, guns."

Halbert snapped his fingers and pointed at Tessa. "Précisément!" he exclaimed. "And why is that?"

Aedan's hand shot up. "Keepers and Debilis probably find guns unreliable."

Halbert gesticulated with his arm, indicating for Aedan to elaborate.

"Those of us with the ability to alter rock and metal can easily break a gun, either by heating the metal bullet casings or the gun mechanism itself. It can hurt the user or other people nearby and it's dangerous. Even if it's our own gun, it won't likely work well." Aedan's face colored and he looked at the ground. "My dad took me duck hunting twice. I broke his gun each time by melting some of the interior and locking it up. The damage wasn't obvious, so he just thought I wasn't technically inclined. I played that bit up and pretended I hated it."

Halbert nodded his head. "It's not as unusual as you think, Scholar Aedan. "That's why both Debilis and Keepers don't use them. As you know, the melting point of a sword or knife is far higher. It will take a great deal more concentration to damage one of them—not inconceivable, mind you, but only possible with the most skilled Ferro or Magro."[207]

He explained that carrying and using unreliable weaponry was dangerous and foolhardy as well as impractical. "The Keepers of the Rock have survived this long precisely because we adhere to such strict regulations. You may question or be confused by some of our tenets and rules, but they all exist for excellent reasons. That said, we welcome your doubts and criticisms; it is all part of the learning process here. Être parti!"

Élise began walking toward the door leading to the outside and everyone slowly followed suit, slightly befuddled. She laughed. "We were dismissed. He said, 'be gone!' I guess class was over."

---

[207] Magro – A Magro is particularly drawn to rare earths, even in the smallest of quantities. They collect them from the earth and can amass, compress, and shape them to their will; a Magro is able to work with other magnetic rocks and elements in the periodic table as well, but rare earths are their specialty.

Dr. Kelly was waiting off to the side of the building entrance and made eye contact with Tessa. She silently tilted her head, motioning for Tessa to approach her.

"Enjoyed your lesson with Keeper Halbert? Never mind—I guess that's a loaded question. You met our resident fencing ghost!" They talked a bit about the recent class and waited for everyone to pass out of earshot.

"Nurse Patel informed me you gave us permission to discuss your concern."

At Tessa's nod in agreement and slight flush of embarrassment, Dr. Kelly continued.

"First, I want you to understand that you have no reason to be embarrassed and every reason to be proud of yourself! Realizing you have an issue and wanting to understand and address it is the first critical step, and not often an easy one to take. After talking with Nurse Patel and observing you last week around campus, I believe you are dealing with a learning difference, and one that is not uncommon, at that."

They walked along the path toward the residence building and discussed the symptoms Tessa noted: distractibility, impulsivity, some anxiety, and occasionally "blanking out" on tests.

"And sometimes, I'll be concentrating on a project or homework and I won't notice anything going on around me, even if my name is called! I feel like I'm letting everyone down."

Dr. Kelly nodded. "The term for that is 'hyperfocusing' and again, it is not uncommon. I am fairly confident in my diagnosis, but we are going to have you come to the health office and take some testing batteries. I promise, it's not physically invasive; there are no needle sticks. You might even find them fun and interesting—there are puzzles to solve, equations to ponder, and all manner of other exercises that will help Nurse Patel and I verify what we think is happening. We have an adjunct Guardian psychologist from the College of William and Mary who specializes in these diagnoses who will visit our campus and administer them over several days during the next week; we don't want you to miss much class. If you were not a College of GeoEvolution student, I would send you over to the college to take many of these tests on their computer systems. We know how well that will turn out, however." She smiled warmly.

"As it stands, you will try one or two tests on their computer later in the week; ones that are not easily administered on paper. They are quick, which will hopefully minimize any interference from you. If it doesn't work, not to worry. Those two batteries are not crucial and are just two more data points.

"The therapist will ultimately make the diagnosis and at that point, we can talk about your options for treatment. Believe me, Tessa, there are many ways to help you gain impulse control, understand how you best absorb information, and ultimately, learn to master your learning difference. Okay? Think it over and come up with any questions you have. We'll meet tomorrow afternoon and talk it over before we take the next steps."

Tessa watched Dr. Kelly walk away and felt apprehensive, but also hopeful. Dr. Kelly and Nurse Patel understood and recognized her symptoms! The biggest emotion she felt was relief.

Dinner was a welcome event after the full day of classes and homework. Ngai served one of his favorite meals, a variety of salads featuring the vestiges of summer's bounty. He included his popular watermelon, mint, and feta cheese salad as well as the black bean, mango, and cilantro one. He also added a chicken salad with red grapes and walnuts and a tuna salad with crisp celery and curry. Lastly, he included a garden pea with basil made with homemade pesto and an enormous fruit salad.

Everyone was given a plate that resembled a four-leaf clover. It had four bowl-like sections, so everyone could sample several salads at once. Accompanying the salads was homemade cool lemonade and unsweetened tea infused with honey and lime.

He finished the meal with choices of either delectable brownies or strawberry rhubarb pie. All the teachers, save Keeper Dumisani were able to join the students for dinner. Evren looked over at the students and casually mentioned, "We have two students who have not had an opportunity to participate in our welcoming tradition. There is no pressure, but we didn't want you to feel left out, should you want to participate tonight."

He glanced at KameKona and Demyan with a kind smile and raised an eyebrow. KameKona glanced at Demyan, and seeing his eager nod, raised his hand casually in the air and said, "Nah, it's cool. I can go."

When encouraged by Evren, he began. "I've always had a thing, an affinity, with any type of lava. Even from my earliest memories, I noticed that it warmed quickly in my hands; I never thought it was unusual or weird, 'cause I'm native and I've lived in Hawaii all of my life.

"We call ourselves 'kama'aina'; it means 'child of the land.' I grew up with all the stories of my people. And we're very attached to and integrated with the land. We learn about the many spirits in Hawaii and their relationship with the islands and the people. So, to have a relationship with our rocks and land made sense to me; everyone who is kama'aina has this connection to some degree.

"At first, I didn't think my ability was somehow unique. I didn't honestly notice anything special until high school. That's when friends noticed that rocks I picked up were too hot for them to touch. They just thought the sun heated them and I had a higher tolerance for pain or that football had somehow lessened the sensitivity in my hands; it never occurred to them that I was the source of the heat and I never chose to tell anyone. It was probably for the reasons we talked about in class. I just had a sense that it wouldn't be a good idea.

"It was such a relief when you all found me; it suddenly all made sense and I didn't feel so alone anymore. I have a good group of friends and was liked in high school, but I still felt so apart and alone. I remember telling my dad how important it was for me to attend the college."

He looked at all of the Keepers. "Volcanic rock is central to Hawaii and is a life source for plants and animals. It's even used on the Big Island in constructing buildings. Volcanic eruptions are part of nature and continue to build up the islands and land masses in other parts of the world. It's problematic when they erupt though, because humans have always chosen to live near volcanoes."

He lifted his forearms in equal parts enthusiasm and frustration, forgetting his fork remained in one hand, and obliviously launched an errant wedge of pineapple into the air.

"Think of Mount Vesuvius and Pompeii. Over two thousand people died back in 79 AD! I know no one can ever stop volcanoes from erupting. But I can help improve early warning sensors and escape procedures, so as many people get away as possible. And I can encourage the respect and protection of volcanoes as well; we have to learn to live with them harmoniously." KameKona speared another wedge of pineapple from his plate and noticed he was missing one. "Sorry, I'm a bit passionate on the subject."

Alegria smiled enthusiastically. "Scholar KameKona, don't apologize! Certainly not when I am around. I understand you perfectly and can assure you that each of us here is equally passionate about our particular interest. Have I told you one of my favorite sayings?" She placed a bejeweled index finger on her chin, contemplative. "Ah—no, you have not had that class session yet. So here it is. In the immortal words of one of the most influential writers and poets, Maya Angelou: 'My mission in life is not merely to survive, but to thrive; and to do so with some passion, some compassion, some humor, and some style.'" She ran her fingers through her hair. "I'd like to think that I am well on my way to accomplishing that goal. And you all will be as well."

Sahila laughed and rolled her eyes toward the ceiling. "Keeper Alegria is our residential poet laureate. Her dedication to the craft knows no bounds. Scholar Demyan, we'd like to offer you a chance to participate, if you so wish."

Demyan blushed and looked down at his plate, conflicted. He was just about to grab a piece of pie; he'd never had strawberry rhubarb. "Thank you, Keeper Sahila. My uncle manages a prominent jewelry shop in Riga; it's been in the family for many generations and my father is a businessman who oversees the family holdings. We own several retail stores and the jewelry store is one of them.

"During the summers when I was little, I often spent time with my father visiting the various businesses; he told my mother he wanted me to get involved early on and learn how to follow in his footsteps. I loved visiting my uncle and aunt at the jewelry store the most, and they encouraged me—they let me look at all the loose gems, jewelry, and coins. I noticed almost immediately that when I came close to pieces and touched them, I felt an energy from them, like a strange vibration. When I really drew my attention to each one, I learned that I sensed its history, where it originated from and any trauma it was exposed to.

"I never told anyone about my intuition, but I'd ask my uncle and aunt about a certain piece and listen to what they knew. Sometimes, they had great detail and sometimes, none at all. But when they did, my own sense of the item was often validated.

"I hated going to business meetings with my father and as I got older, I think he sensed my disinterest as well, much to his disappointment. I finally was brave enough to ask if I could help my uncle at the store."

Demyan pulled on an ear, self-consciously. "Honestly, I think he was happy to let me go. I know my lack of enthusiasm was becoming obvious and I was an embarrassment to him." He blew a raspberry.[208] "I didn't care at all. I was thrilled to work at the store and my uncle and aunt were kind to me; they began to teach me the business. As I learned

---

[208] Blowing a raspberry – Releasing air through the lips, causing a vibrating sound

more, I figured out a way to use my abilities to help, without revealing my secret. Uncle taught me about reading people when they came in, especially to sell items. He said it was like playing poker, where people have…what do you call it here? 'Tells'?" When he saw several nods around the table, he continued. "So, I learned how to 'discover their tells,' as my uncle says. You know, if a customer appears guilty, angry, embarrassed, or happy, for example. Over the years, I think my uncle thought that I got really good at this skill. Really, I just started to rely more and more on my ability. I loved working there and if I told my uncle and aunt the truth, I'm not sure how they would react."

Demyan remembered feeling uncertain about talking to them. If they knew, would they find him odd? If his father found out, what would happen?

He was already displeased with Demyan; that was not hidden. And his father was not a very patient or demonstrative parent; he didn't think he'd exploit him, but would most likely further ignore him. He might also find his ability strange, however, and blame his uncle and aunt for influencing him.

Their relationship was strained anyway and this could really harm it further. He certainly didn't want his father and uncle's relationship to become strained either. No, he didn't want to be the cause of any rift and chances were, revealing his ability would cause any number of negative consequences; it simply wasn't worth the risk. He smiled and shrugged. "And for all that, I'm still not a very good poker player."

Alegria caught Demyan's attention and smiled warmly. "Thank you for sharing that with us. All of us here can understand your predicament, Demyan. Please always remember that you are never alone." She turned to address the other students. "Now, as we finish our dinner, what is this I hear about a potential ghost?"

Everyone waited while Élise recounted her experience. A few others threw in their ideas as well.

"Well, there is nothing to it, except to go and check. Keeper Nalin and I will meet you all in the residence hallway tonight, around eight o'clock this evening. Of course," she said with an exaggerated sigh, "hopefully we won't encounter the proverbial home appliance enigma: The appliance decides to work only when the technician arrives to fix it!"

Tessa stood in the residence hallway that night and surveyed her surroundings. It was hard to believe that she was here, enmeshed with other students like her, feeling for the first time in her life like she belonged somewhere, like she had a tribe. She knew she was rough around the edges and was known to be prickly, at least that was the word around her high school. She didn't care at the time. If people wanted to ignorantly embrace gossip, she didn't want to know them anyway.

That didn't mean that she wanted to be alone. It felt so good to finally be around others with whom she could be honest. Hopefully she'd be appreciated here, quirky and prickly nature notwithstanding.

Keepers Nalin and Alegria arrived right on time and met everyone in the hallway. Nalin ushered them into the common room. "We'll remain in here for a while. If there is a spirit around, it might not feel comfortable in a crowd."

After noticing Ming's apprehension, she added: "Regardless of what we discover, I'm confident there will be an explanation and we will figure it out." She opened the conversation up to questions about the campus or life at school in general while Élise took a look. She mentioned that they would visit Colonial Williamsburg that weekend for a fun and informative outing.

Élise rushed back from checking the hallway. She gestured to Alegria and Nalin. "It's in the hallway!" she spoke and signed.

Keeper Nalin gestured that everyone should follow quietly and placed a finger to her lips.

Tessa laughed inwardly as they followed two by two; it was an experience she'd never had before. She wondered what Dya would think about it.

Their teachers stopped as Élise halted in front of empty space. She turned around and faced them, her exhalations visible in the air; the temperature had definitely dropped a noticeable amount. She signed and spoke, "The cloudy mist is right behind me. Can you see it?"

Both of them shook their heads. "I'm sorry," Alegria stated. "We don't see or hear anything. Do you feel the vibrations you mentioned?"

Élise nodded and tried to describe what she felt. "They are in a repeating pattern, but I don't understand it. It's the same one I noticed yesterday. Sometimes it speeds up, as if whatever is creating it is frustrated."

Nalin explained that she wanted Élise to repeat the pattern, either using her hands or her feet, whichever was less distracting for her. Élise nodded and began to tap her feet, so she could complete the exercise while still communicating with her hands if she needed to, not unlike rubbing one's belly and tapping one's head at the same time.

She began a staccato tapping that included a sliding of one of her feet occasionally. Alegria interjected after Élise completed one cycle of the pattern.

"What does that sliding gesture represent?"

Élise signed and spoke. "One of the vibrations is elongated. Somehow it lasts longer than the other ones."

Nalin nodded her head. "I understand where you are going with this, Keeper Alegria. Do you think Élise is detecting Lucidum code?"

The students looked at her questioningly. Nalin turned to the group. "That is our primary method of communication. You are scheduled to learn it in a couple of months. It's not listed in the formal curriculum, because the lessons don't last a full semester. In light of this curiosity, I'll request that we begin that course imminently."

The teachers worked with Élise for another minute to see if they could gleam any discerning message from her foot work. Considering Élise didn't know their communication system, it was unlikely that she could interpret the vibrations, should they actually be some sort of correspondence.

Nalin motioned for them to return to the common room. She looked at Élise and the rest of their fledgling brood. "Despite the fact that Élise appears to be the only one among us who is aware of this entity, we didn't dismiss her out of hand. We didn't outright reject Élise or anyone else's observations because they are not experienced by us."

"We need to do what we can to understand it through her eyes. Although we live in a realm of reality separate from the Commoner, we still adhere to the scientific method; we develop a hypothesis and test it, as you all know. So that is what we will do. If we are dealing with a spiritual entity of some sort, I trust it will remain patient during this process."

Nalin spoke that last statement louder and looked around the room, as if communicating with their unknown specter. For all they knew, Élise was noticing a residual energy surge, either human or otherwise, who was unaware of even its own existence.

# Chapter 27 – Co

## College of GeoEvolution

Although never dull, the prospect of an upcoming day away from campus, was very welcome. Everyone was excited to wander through Colonial Williamsburg and experience life as a Colonial American in Virginia. Since their school was within minutes of the historical park and the College of William and Mary, they had multiple opportunities to visit, as well as intern at the historic monument during the summer.

Jürgen expounded about the peanut soup and "game pye" served at one of their period food restaurants. Before excited discussions ensued about their impending field trip, Xandra walked swiftly toward their impromptu gathering on the green. Today she wore an old-fashioned forest green "walking dress," complete with a beekeeper hat with veil perched at a jaunty angle on her head. She lifted the veil from her face as she approached and had a focused, disconcerting gaze.

"Greetings, Scholars," she exclaimed, rolling her R's. "I'm sorry to interrupt your afternoon sojourn, but duty calls. I need the services of Scholars Tú and Tessa right away."

Tú and Tessa looked questioningly at one another and stood up from the grass. "What the actual what?" Tessa whispered.

"At least once a semester, sometimes twice, we must rebuff the attentions of curious visitors and ensure they never return. This task falls to me and I often elicit the assistance of our students. Scholar Tú, for this subterfuge, I will require your substantial cache of rare earths. Please collect them quickly and meet us at the van. Scholar Tessa, follow me and take Edgar from Keeper Fabek; we are going to include him in the ruse. He's becoming quite useful. I will explain the situation as we are escorted by Fabek to the main entrance."

She turned on her booted heel and marched toward the waiting school van. Once the two returned and they were underway, Xandra continued.

"As I mentioned, it is not unusual for us to receive visits from prying eyes; almost all of them are vulgar adolescents who heard rumors about a haunted private school or residence. We keep to ourselves and mind our own business. However, that periodically creates an air of mystery and intrigue as to who we are and what we do here. It also doesn't help that 'The Farm," the CIA's training facility is a six-minute drive from here.[209] Our job is to quell the curiosity and keep these disturbances to a minimum."

Xandra instructed Fabek to park the van off to the side of the road behind a large tree. They proceeded down the remaining length of paved road toward the entrance gate. Her outfit was the same, but now she sported one large shiny black spider, a half dozen smaller ones pinned to the bodice of her dress, and another larger one affixed to the side of the beekeeper's hat.

They hugged the tree line out of sight per Xandra's instructions. From what they could see, there appeared to be three or four people outside the gate. Two were peeking through the bars of the wrought iron fence and another one, who resembled a bug hanging on a curtain, was trying to climb the gate. His hands and legs were wrapped around the gate bars and he seemed confused as to how to proceed.

---

[209] The CIA-The Central Intelligence Agency

Xandra approached and removed a large key from her pocket. She quickly fit the key into the lock and turned. The gates swung inward, carrying its human passenger as it opened. "May I help you?" Xandra said firmly, hands clasped.

All four in the group stared at her, some openmouthed. The lone female whispered, "What is she wearing? It's not even Halloween!"

Xandra turned her head to the side, signaling to Tessa and Tú. "I certainly hope you all do not attend any nearby learning academy, for your manners are atrocious. Once again, may I help you?"

The teen standing with the young woman let go of her hand and took a step forward. "We just wanted to take a look at this place. You have a nice…umm, garden, and we wanted to see it."

The teen on the gate managed to extricate himself and jumped to the ground. "Dude," he chastised his friend, "don't be a moron! Actually, the truth is, we heard this place was haunted and we want to check it out and, you know, make sure it's safe. Can people come in and look around? We won't touch anything."

Xandra smiled tightly and placed her hands by her side. "Unfortunately"—she spoke in her most dignified accent— "we are a private residence and do not accept visitors, as the sign clearly states. But I can assure you that we pose no threat to the area and never have."

The teen near the young woman stepped forward and scuffed his feet in the dirt. "Well, you know, we need to make sure the people and stuff in our neighborhood are safe, so we kinda insist." His eyes shifted over to the side, where Edgar hopped along at a quick clip toward Xandra.

Somehow, between the van and his current location, a leg had once again affixed to his head like a TV antenna. He picked up one of the small spiders that had fallen from Xandra's dress, tossed it into the air, and proceeded to swallow it whole. Xandra held out her arm and Edgar jumped and flew in a clumsy arc toward her shoulder and landed instead on the top of her hat. She eyed the youths outside the gate and the one within with bemusement.

"What do you mean by 'and stuff'?"

The teen near the young woman blinked and scratched his cheek. "Huh? I don't know what you mean."

Xandra smiled. "Well, wonderful! That makes two of us."

The teen within the gate opened his mouth and exclaimed, "You have a black bird with a TV antenna on your head!"

Edgar, hoping for a larger snack, began poking at the spider on Xandra's hat. Quite suddenly, it began to move, as did the spiders on her dress. The larger hat spider crawled down and all the others crawled up.

"How astute of you to notice. I marvel at your powers of deduction." The hat spider chose to cover one of Xandra's eyes while the shiny one on her bodice settled around her neck. All adolescent eyes looked on in horror. While Edgar began pecking at the hat netting, three small spiders scuttled toward Xandra's lips. She separated them, let them crawl inside, and smiled.

The young lady screamed and one teen leaned over and vomited into the dirt. The telltale sign of wetness showed on the pants of the group spokesman. If that wasn't obvious enough, the gathering puddle under his feet certainly was.

"Darling," Xandra addressed the young lady with slightly slurred speech as she worked her tongue around the rare earth spiders "I recommend that you develop better judgment regarding your dating partners. Escorting you to view potential hauntings and urinating on himself is quite disappointing; I think you can probably do better. Don't you?"

This statement likely fell on deaf ears as the entire party was scrambling away as fast as possible. Experience in these matters suggested that a subsequent visit was unlikely and all would remain quiet until another similar group made their own ill-advised attempt. Tessa and Tú were still laughing when Xandra returned to the van. They felt privileged for being chosen to support the ruse.

Xandra delicately removed the spiders from her mouth, dried them off, and slipped them into her pocket. "I'll clean your rare earths properly, Scholar Tú, before I return them to you. Scholar Tessa, please dislodge dear Edgar from my hat. I fear the curious beast is wreaking havoc with my netting. It's vintage and I'm quite fond of it."

Tessa assisted with extricating Edgar and Tú once again replaced Edgar's foot where it belonged. Tú asked if most uninvited guest removal was equally entertaining.

"Well, not always as amusing as that one, I'm afraid. It depends on my mood, the additional actors I can involve, and the props at my disposal. You both are very good at your craft. No one saw your laser, Scholar Tessa, and I barely felt it. I doubt dear Edgar or his companions would follow Tú's commands without the lure of the exciting shiny light."

Later, Tessa and Tú's enjoyed recounting their adventure to the others in the common room. Tessa pantomimed Xandra's responses as well as those of the impromptu visitors and Tú reanimated his spiders. Tessa was game, but stopped at putting any rare earth spiders into her mouth. Xandra, although still eccentric in their collective opinion, was elevated in esteem for her gutsy performance.

Afterward, Élise and Ming walked through the hallway, but Élise didn't sense the strange presence that night. She'd realized that it was intermittent, but even after Ming, Tessa, and Aedan tried speaking to whatever it was, there didn't appear to be a response.

"Don't worry, Élise," Ming stated as she patted Élise's shoulder, "after meeting a bona fide talking ghost, we all believe you!"

Tessa agreed. "Witnessing Master Russo was a game changer! We're going to solve this mystery with you."

They headed to bed, excited for their impending tour of Williamsburg the next day; a chance to get away and mingle with society at large was alluring.

Fabek was quiet on the drive to Colonial Williamsburg. Aedan realized he was disappointed to not hear any unusual poetry recitations; although he and the others thought Fabek perplexing and a little disturbing, there was something about him that stirred their curiosity and empathy. Fabek seemed deeply lost in his own thoughts, however, and they respected him enough to give him space.

Tessa realized that she was learning to be more accepting of others' idiosyncrasies and personalities. Her school was entirely comprised of unique individuals and she was firmly among them.

She had started a journal when she arrived at school and smiled as she remembered her recent entry: *Dya mentioned that I needed to be more trusting of others and accepting. She obviously knew that I'm where I need to be right now. Thank goodness I listened to her.*

Thinking of Dya's comforting presence resulted in an electric zing of longing through her nerves. *Dya feels more like a mom to me than my own. Should I feel guilty that I don't feel guilty?* She loved her mom and her whole family, of course, but the bond with Dya was profound. She cleared her head after they entered a private Colonial Williamsburg parking lot.

Aedan asked, "Keeper Jürgen is a big fan of this historic site. Is he joining us?"

Reese winked. "It's not recommended, considering his current perspiration issue. Drawing attention to our group isn't a good idea. Not to worry, however! Keeper Alegria will bring him back his favorite tucker. That's mainly why he comes anywa', right?"

Everyone followed Reese and Alegria to a main historic thoroughfare, the Duke of Gloucester Street. KameKona whispered, "It's so weird to be walking among Commoners right now! Less than a month ago, we didn't know the difference."

Ming nodded. "I know. And to realize that we and only a few others know the truth about the world is surreal."

Alegria must have sensed their change in temperament as the realization began to sink in. "You all are doing well; it will take a bit of time to adjust."

Reese had a more practical response and simply said, "Keep it together and stay calm."

They first wandered into the apothecary. The room was small and the walls were covered in wooden shelving filled with a multitude of glassware and pottery in unusual shapes and sizes. They looked around while Alegria spoke with the colonial pharmacist behind the counter and motioned to her group.

When the last members of a group tour left, Alegria closed the door behind them and locked it. She turned toward the students and introduced the apothecary as Mary Smythe.

"Welcome, new students! Let me show you what we do here." Mary discussed common remedies used during early 1700s Colonial America.

"I don't know about you, but I'm so glad we live in a far more modern time, especially when it comes to tooth extraction!" Tessa exclaimed.

Mary nodded. "Agreed. But some treatment methods are relatively timeless."

Mary reached behind the counter and retrieved a small pottery jug with a burlap cloth lid secured by string. She placed it on the counter and removed the lid. Inside, leeches swam around in liquid or attached themselves to the inside walls of the jug.

Tú's eyebrows reached his hairline. "They don't look like the leeches at school."

Alegria nodded at him. "An astute observation, Scholar Tú. Mary is not only an employee at Colonial Williamsburg, but she is one of our invaluable Guardians, unbeknownst to the staff here. Guardian Mary is a pharmacist who is able to assist local Keepers. We have a select few who live in this area, particularly since our school is here, and we have specific needs. When a Keeper is in need of certain treatments, Guardian Mary often assists if our local Guardian doctor isn't available."

Guardian Mary pointed to one of the leeches currently attempting to wiggle over the rim of the jug. "These leeches are in need of cleansing." She lifted the leech with a finger and placed it into the palm of her hand. Ming tugged nervously at the end of her hair and looked askance at the leech.

"Don't worry!" Mary said enthusiastically. "This little guy is completely full of blood and won't need to eat for weeks!"

Aedan and KameKona shuffled their feet uncomfortably. Mary snorted and continued. "All of these leeches have ingested lead or other elements that needed to be purged from a couple of Keepers. They had a run in with a Debilis a few miles from the school. Don't worry, the Keepers are fine. The Debilis, not so much. Anyway, they'll be as good as new in a couple of months, but I don't have the environment to purify them. I understand they will accompany you all back to college, yes?"

Alegria proceeded to open the shoulder bag she was carrying and placed the jug in a specific compartment designed to protect various random items she might collect throughout the day. While she was doing this, Mary placed a smaller gray and decidedly heavier container on the counter with a gentle *thunk*. This one was covered with a silver screw top.

"This is the container I communicated with you about earlier."

Alegria screwed off the lid and took a brief peak, Reese spying over her shoulder. "Oh, you very brave little soldiers, well done!"

At the curious looks from her students, Alegria explained, "There is a Commoner law office in Newport News, a city near Williamsburg. They took a case defending the owners of a jewelry business who were being sued by an investment firm that was accusing them of fraud. Unbeknownst to the lawyers and the business, the investment firm is owned by Debilis. They wanted to shut down the jewelry business, so they could set up their own operation there, a black-market center in Hampton Roads, the name of this region of Virginia. The jewelry business is historic and successful, so it was seen as a threat. Quite simply, the Debilis began poisoning the law firm with radon gas. Anyone know what that is?"

KameKona waved his arms enthusiastically. "Wait! Wait! Before we get to that, I'm just soaking this in. So, these Debilis, evil mutant human creatures, really mess with and attack Commoners anywhere? And we have to stop them, 'cause regular law enforcement won't know what to do and may make it worse?"

Reese clapped once. "You got it in one, Scholar KameKona! Bravo!"

"Now back to radon gas, people!" Alegria took control once more.

Élise raised her hand immediately. "Radon is a noble gas on the periodic table. It was discovered in 1900 by Friedrich Ernst Dorn and is radioactive. It's found in the ground naturally and, in large amounts, can cause cancer and other serious illnesses. Many people have radon detectors in their home, just to make sure their levels are safe." She squinted as she thought. "The largest levels in the United States are found in Alaska and the lowest levels are in Louisiana. Hawaii has nearly zero amounts of radon."

"Wonderfully done!" Alegria exclaimed.

"Winner, winner, chicken dinner, I think," Reese added. Pick your tucker for tomorrow when we get back, ya?"

Alegria continued. "Anyway, to make a long story short, a Debilis Volco drew large amounts of the radon underground and concentrated it under the law offices, in hopes of causing havoc for the legal team. Our local Keepers and Guardians became aware and took action. Our very own Keeper Xandra stole the show, I'm told?"

She glanced at Mary Smythe for confirmation. "Yes! She and Keeper Alegria played the parts of highly regarded alternative medicine doctors and convinced the entire legal team to subject themselves to the leech treatments of Nurse Practitioner Hestia Patel! They turned it into an employee wellness retreat. And as of yet, no staff member tested positive for radon poisoning."

Mary added, "Due to the fact that Debilis caused the poisoning, Keepers need to try to remedy the situation. Obviously, most medical personnel would eschew the use of leeches, but they neither have our specially treated leeches nor our particular understanding of this intense level of poison extraction."

Mary patted the gray container in front of her. "Anyway, these little guys are heroes and are radioactive. That's why they are inside a lead case. They can live in there without additional air for about ten hours, Keeper Alegria."

Alegria grinned and added them to her bag. When she did so, all students backed away a few steps.

"What happened to the employees at the law firm?" Tessa questioned.

"Ah. Yes, well they've moved their offices to a safe building and their existing office is being treated. That largely involved removing the contaminated soil under the building. It's a very costly and a messy business, unfortunately. They did manage to throw out the Debilis's case, however, so the jewelry business can live on. And the Debilis fled, I was told, unfortunately."

After they left the apothecary, a nice lunch was had by all at Chowning's Tavern after they walked the historic town: savory helpings of Welsh rarebit and shepherd's pie washed down with apple cider.

"I love wandering around here!" Aedan flung his arms around. "I love immersing myself in an accurate historical experience!"

Alegria placed the shepherd's pie and Welsh rarebit for Jürgen and Fabek into her increasingly full bag and Reese complained about attracting "critters" on their way back.

The group slowly meandered after lunch toward the gardens near the Governor's Palace. Reese quickened his pace at the rear and pitched his voice toward Alegria. "We're being followed. Head toward the beech arbor."

Alegria nodded and headed toward the arbor made from American beech trees. It was a narrow path with trees framing either side of the walkway. Each one curved like a hook at the top, creating a canopy of green along the walkway. It was a peaceful part of the garden that felt secluded and protected.

Alegria slowed her pace, so she and Reese effectively shielded the students between them. He moved to the side and pretended to look at something in his hand, effectively clearing the way for the oncoming individuals.

Two people—a man and a woman, ostensibly a cozy couple with arms linked—just wandering through Colonial Williamsburg on the weekend. When they got within passing distance, the woman suddenly leaned toward Demyan and tried to put something in his jacket pocket.

"No ya' don', you dero! Reese swung the woman away and blocked her from Demyan. The two tried to run off, pushing past their group. Alegria quickly passed her bag to Ming, the closest student, and faced the fleeing couple.

She placed her feet firmly on the ground a foot apart and pulled her hands into fists at her sides, Alegria's eyes firmly on her quarry. Her curly hair rose in individual strands around her, as if she was attracting static electricity. In front of her, the two perpetrators wobbled as the ground underneath their feet began to buckle and shake.

They threw out their hands as they fell toward the ground. Alegria exhaled a long and cleansing breath as her hair returned to normal. Reese raced past her to the couple and pretended to help them to their feet, but forced an item into their palms instead.

While they examined the items, Reese acted. On the middle finger of one hand was a simple wide platinum ring the students had noticed and dismissed, since it appeared unremarkable. Reese used his thumb to rotate the ring around his finger. On the other side was a channel setting[210] of small rectangular stones inset into the band. Each were a vibrant orange with pink undertones, a very rare type of sapphire called a padparadscha[211] found mainly in Sri Lanka and Madagascar. He grabbed the man's palm with his left hand and with his right, pressed the plain band portion of the ring into the man's palm. The man visibly startled and winced and suddenly relaxed, opening his mouth as if in a stupor, his attention riveted on Reese. He quickly repeated the process with the woman.

Having their complete attention, he took another item from his pocket and rotated it over his fingers, back and forth. It looked as if it was a coin.

All the while Reese spoke to the couple. When finished, he had them both empty the contents from their pockets.

Reese verified their possessions himself and was apparently satisfied. Neither foe carried a purse or bag. Reese reached

---

[210] Channel setting-a ring setting where stones are set between metal channels or walls. The stone is flush with the metal setting.

[211] "Padparadscha," https://www.mindat.org/gm/39947

into his back pocket, took out his wallet, and handed over a wad of bills. He tipped his right fingers to his temple in an unofficial salute, and turned around to walk back to the party.

As he strode over, the couple turned and headed away as well, walking toward the exit. Questioning glances greeted Reese upon his return. Knowing what most fascinated them, he showed them the ring on his finger.

"I find the very rare and precious padparadscha stone to be quite helpful. It's useful for seeking clarity abou' human nature, showing someone the truth about their goals, and the shallowness and danger that exists in their relationships."

He used his thumb to push down on the small stone closest to his index finger." On the other side"—he swung the ring around again, so the plain platinum band was visible—"you can see the needle of chrysoprase."[212]

The sharp needle-like stone was a vibrant green, and stuck out from the platinum base. He pushed on the same rectangular stone and the needle disappeared into the band. He repeated the gesture and it reappeared. "It belongs to the chalcedony family. When injected into the bloodstream, a small amount of the powdered stone enters into the body. It fosters relaxation, peace, and acts like a tranquilizer in an agitated Debilis. Combining the padparadscha and the coin flipping by someone well-trained creates a hypnotic state."

Alegria raised an eyebrow. "Do I dare ask what you suggested to them?"

Aedan raised his hand, alarmed. "Wait please. Were those two Debilis? Did we just actually come in contact with two more seemingly normal human Debilis?"

Reese smiled ruefully. "Actually, yes. Those were two healthy Debilis."

---

[212] "Chrysoprase," https://www.mindat.org/gm/952

Ming looked perplexed. "But they looked like regular people, like Commoners."

Alegria held out a hand and took the bag back from Ming. "Don't worry. You will have enough training by the time you graduate to be able to tell the difference almost immediately. Now, Keeper Reese, don't keep us in suspense."

He ruffled his hair with a palm. "I told them it was clear they were not fulfilling their true purpose. They have a desperate and deep desire to open a fried chicken restaurant in Uruguay. The gentleman has relatives there who miss him. They also need to explore the strong vibe between them they have neglected; there exists a lasting love that can't be denied.

"I gave them money and told them to pick up a pumpkin spice latte at the nearest Starbucks, 'cause 'tis the season, and afterward, hitch a bus to begin their journey toward South America. They will purchase new clothes and sundries from the nearest store, never look back, and will always keep the coins that I gave them. They will always associate them with their new mission and completely forget whom they used to work for and their previous purpose. They will also permanently forget that Keepers, Guardians, and most importantly, Debilis, exist, and live as Commoners for ever and ever, amen. I wish them godspeed, a successful fried chicken business, and a couple of Commoner brats in their future.

"We have a couple of Guardians who will meet them in a few hours at the bus station to give them a new credit card and ID. It will be pre-loaded with enough money to get them to their new destination and a bit of seed money to get them started in their new pursuit. They handed me their ID information before I left them as well as their Lucidium-like communication devices. They shouldn't be able to be traced."

Alegria held up her hand. "We know you have lots of unanswered questions and we promise to get to them. Right now, however, we've had an eventful day and we need to get back home."

Reese began walking toward the bus and Fabek. Relieved to think about something mundane and comforting, Élise decided she wanted coq au vin and gratin Dauphinois, both traditional and hearty dishes: the chicken stew in a rich and flavorful sauce and a potato and cheese casserole.

Reese circled back to the issue at hand. "Most importantly, we need to find out why the Debilis find you so fascinating, mate." He glanced at Demyan. "You're a hot commodity." He looked at Alegria. "And Keeper Jürgen better be properly grateful for that tucker! It told you it would attract vermin!"

CHAPTER 28 – Ni

COLLEGE OF GEOEVOLUTION

# MID-OCTOBER

There was a collective sigh of relief when the prickling heat gave way to cool and crisp fall weather, complete with the sound of colorful dry leaves crunching underfoot.

Everyone became familiar with the consistent pace of classwork and activities. They developed a muscle memory for the elements on the periodic table as well as the fundamental structures and composition of the earth.

The excitement in the air was palpable when Shifu Zoria announced that everyone was ready to begin working with the wooden bo. They spent weeks practicing exercises and stances in preparation for the advanced training.

In the evenings, Élise and the others frequently peered into the dorm hallway, hoping to make sense of the presence Élise perceived there. "Although it's intermittent, it's clear that something is trying to make itself known," Élise stated enthusiastically.

"I know," Ming agreed. "The rhythmic tapping always has a similar pattern, but it can subtly change and come at different times during the day."

"And as I said before," Tessa interjected, "after our other Debilis and ghost experience, we know this is something significant. And from your descriptions, Élise, I doubt it's a residual haunting!"

Élise, Ming, and Tessa found a few books in the library on ghosts and hauntings and poured through them. Heikima allowed them to access some of the texts from the locked cabinet, home to the rare and oldest books in the library.

When reading these fragile books, they had to wash their hands in the library bathroom beforehand and not touch their face, lest they leave oils on the pages. Heikima had thin cotton gloves available, but only for the old books that contained green ink pigments such as Paris green or Scheele's green.

Everyone was a bit freaked when she told them: "All of these contain the element arsenic and can inadvertently poison you. The use of the element was meant to protect the book from pests or insects. The arsenic laden green paint was a cheaper ink available at the time and made the book less expensive for buyers. During the Victorian era, the ink was often selected because the hue, Scheele's green, named for its creator, was a popular vibrant shade of green at the time."

These special texts were normally only accessible in their second year of college, but Heikima made an exception for the specific volumes they requested.

"Listen to this," KameKona read one afternoon, when he and the others joined the existing study group. "For believers, a residual haunting is usually the result of personal trauma. A person or animal experienced a traumatic event and upon their passing, continued to revisit that event, but not as a conscious spirit."

Tú asked, "So it is more like a movie clip stuck on a loop?"

"Yeah," KameKona continued. "It says that the soul of the person no longer remains, but the event creates a strong residual energy manifestation that repeats endlessly—unless somehow the energy could be dispersed or recycled into the atmosphere."

Élise believed there was more to what she was sensing. "When the presence is there, I always feel both desperation and hope, as if I'm absorbing the emotions of whomever is trying to communicate with us."

Élise and the others began their lessons on the Keeper communication system, but they only had rudimentary knowledge at this point. She couldn't quite interpret what she experienced.

"We'll figure it out," Alegria assured them. "We're just as curious as you."

Evren *did* also notice the pattern, but at present, it was very faint and he couldn't make it out. "I feel vindicated, so that's something," Élise stated, relieved. "It isn't all in my head."

The general consensus was that she needed to understand the communication system more fully.

Shortly after returning from Colonial Williamsburg, another library meeting was arranged with Keeper faculty to discuss the Debilis incident. Motivations for targeting Demyan were analyzed.

"Do we believe this collective activity is the beginning of what Fabek predicted?" Dumisani suggested.

"We investigated Demyan's individual kit," Reese explained. "We discovered that it was switched after it was picked up by the package truck. The driver was a legitimate Commoner employee who completed the majority of his delivery route that day—except for the last thirty minutes."

"Wha' happened?" Jürgen inquired.

"Guardian intelligence reported that his phone app revealed an unusual delay between his last customer and his return to the delivery depot hub. Research into his route that day showed no significant traffic delays or unusual stops. The van idled for thirty minutes in a residential neighborhood, however, and the driver reported he didn't remember stopping there."

"That doesn't sound good," Alegria commented between sips of herbal tea.

"No, and it gets worse," Reese said. "He started scratching his neck for several hours after the incident and an employee at the depot noticed an irritated area and a small pinprick red mark, like a bee sting. Concerned about keeping his job and wanting to prove he was not negligent, the employee consented to a doctor visit and a subsequent blood test that same evening. The analysis revealed a trace amount of propofol in his system."

"That's an anesthetic medication, right?" Nalin interjected.

Reese nodded. "It's often referred to as 'milk of amnesia,' and can leave the body quickly, making it a popular Debilis tool for temporary control of their targets. In addition to its active ingredients, the liquid drug includes soybean oil, egg phospholipids, and glycerin. It's usually tolerated well by most people, even people allergic to soybean oil or eggs. But small reactions can sometimes occur—and lucky for the delivery driver, he had a minor allergic rash due to the soybean oil, hence scratching the injection site at the back of his neck. Without this proof, being fired from his job was a distinct possibility."

Sahila shook her head. "That poor man."

"Our senior security officials discussed measures to increase campus safety and local Guardians were notified of the incident and tasked with increasing vigilance around Williamsburg and beyond," Reese confirmed.

"Presumably," Evren noted, "a Debilis approached the driver and distracted him, so that he or she could inject the drug into him. Then he was most likely ordered to handover the package, given a replacement, and the driver would have no memory of the encounter."

"Yes," Reese affirmed. "In addition, my Guardian and Keeper staff couldn't locate the object the woman tried to place in Demyan's pocket at Colonial Williamsburg; I think that insane Debilis swallowed it! I would have made her chuck[213] it, but we didn't have the time."

During class today, the students were beginning a week-long learning unit, a hybrid class incorporating geology, kinesiology, and history. Upon entering the classroom, the desks were set against a wall and in their place stood four tables pushed together in the center of the room. The chairs were set around the table configuration in the familiar semi-circle.

Upon the tables were wooden boxes each filled with numerous square compartments. Nestled in each was either a precious or semi-precious stone or a valuable elemental rock, such as gold, silver, platinum, or copper. The beautiful samples glinted from the lights of the ceiling and wall sconces.

---

[213] Chuck – Australian slang for vomit or throw-up

Sahila welcomed them in a silk emerald blouse and flowing black crepe pants. Her black hair was set in a chignon at the nape of her neck and held together with a comb studded with vibrant purple stones.

Ever-present was her signature necklace with various pendants. The one prominently displayed today was a stunning Botswana Agate,[214] a stone with smaller concentric ovals of various hues—this one in shades of purple... From their classwork, they knew the stone enhanced the wearer's internal fortitude and mental and emotional strength. It also assisted with deflecting negative energy and emotions.

"Join me for my favorite study unit; I look forward to it every semester during the first-year!" Sahila beckoned them to sit in the chairs as she walked over to the wooden boxes of stones. "You are all aware, no doubt, that thousands of stores and boutiques all over the world sell stones such as these for their healing benefits. The vast majority of these businesses are owned by Commoners who are firm believers in the properties of these stones and gems. This is a fascinating phenomenon, considering that only a very small group of us in the world are enhanced with the ability to truly harness the healing properties of these stones to any significant effect."

"That's pretty amazing, considering Commoners don't have the knowledge we do." Ming stated enthusiastically.

"Exactly so. One of the mysteries of life, I believe."

"Anyway, there *are* some Commoners who are more attuned than others to perceive and utilize this healing energy. Although they possess just a small fraction of our own capability, they are no less important. It is because of them that these businesses exist and flourish at all. What I find even more fascinating, however, is that Commoners

---

[214] "Botswana Agate," https://www.mindat.org/gm/7592

have believed in the restorative characteristics of these stones since the beginning of humanity; they *sense* what we fully realize and harness whatever small healing properties are available to them.

"And," she snapped her fingers, excited—"science has yet to prove the healing efficacy of these elements and rocks. That may seem implausible, but it is simply because scientists have not found or developed the proper equipment needed to examine, test samples, and determine their effects on subjects; their current tools are not yet sensitive enough. Take note, we are not talking about the ingestion of certain elements. Humanity has consumed elements orally forever—look at the ingredients in a basic multivitamin!

Tessa twirled a lock of hair and raised an eyebrow. "Are there Keeper and Guardian scientists at research universities assisting Commoner scientists with developing more precise testing techniques?"

"Indeed! In locations where Commoners study alternative medicine. Hopefully, in due time, the health benefits of these elements and gems will be realized, just as the health benefits derived from many plants are used in medications today.

"Now, for fun, let's discuss the historic beliefs about some of the most marvelous creations on Earth!" Sahila began to pick up individual stones and elements. She cradled a vibrant faceted amethyst. "Amethysts were thought by Leonardo Da Vinci to help control evil thoughts and sharpen one's intelligence and they were believed to make one savvy in the business world. Buddhists believed they enhanced meditative states. In the Middle Ages, priests believed they helped maintain celibacy."

"Wait!" Aedan held up his palms. "The great Leonardo Da Vinci believed in the power of gems and stones as well?"

Sahila pointed her index fingers outward as she shimmied in place. "You will be surprised who believed in their efficacy!" Next, she grabbed a piece of Rhodonite,[215] a startling reddish pink stone. "Rhodonite was first discovered in the Ural Mountains of Russia and was embraced by the Russian Court. It was called the 'singer's stone' and was believed to assist singers with maintaining a healthy throat."

She replaced the Rhodonite and selected the hematite[216] sample. "Hematite has a long-storied history. The dark silvery magnetic rock was used by the Ancient Egyptians to ward off evil spirits and the warriors of ancient Rome and Greece kept hematite on them in battle, because they believed that it would protect them from being wounded and would cause their enemies to be injured instead."

"Well, that was generous of them!" KameKona snorted.

"Wasn't it just?" Sahila smirked.

Élise stood and pointed to a vibrant green stone. "What's that vibrant green one, Keeper Sahila?" she signed and asked.

"The peridot?"[217] Sahila selected a rough specimen of peridot, a clear green stone and held it up. "In ancient Rome and in the Middle Ages," she stated, "peridot was thought to help relieve depression. Both the Ancient Egyptians and Aztecs thought that peridot helped *cleanse the heart*. Now, let's process that for a moment. Think about the great geographic and time line differences between those two cultures! I find it fascinating that two, very distinct groups developed similar beliefs about this stone."

Aedan scratched his chin. "Maybe a Keeper in each location spilled the beans to an important individual or healer?"

---

215 "Rhodonite," https://www.mindat.org/gm/3407

216 "Hematite," https://www.mindat.org/gm/1856

217 "Peridot," https://www.mindat.org/gm/7710

"Perhaps," Sahila reflected. "If so, it's been lost to the ages."

She replaced the peridot and selected a bloodstone,[218] a form of chalcedony. It was a beautiful deep green stone with small red splotches, mottled with cream and orange patches.

"Pliny the Elder, the Ancient Roman naturalist and philosopher," Sahila began, "believed that magicians used bloodstones to help them with invisibility. He is credited, by the way, with the modern concept of the encyclopedia. Unfortunately, he perished off the Coast of Stabiae, not far from Pompeii, shortly after Mount Vesuvius erupted."

"That super sucks!" Tessa blurted before smacking a hand over her mouth. "Sorry! But what a bummer. He was an important person, right?"

"Yes!" Sahila agreed. "Your comment was fine, Scholar Tessa. He left many writings behind and was very impactful to the Ancient Romans. A bit too inquisitive, perhaps—it was reported that he either had an intellectual curiosity about the eruption or that he was nearby to help rescue a friend; his true intention is no longer known I'm afraid. And yes, that little historic tidbit has nothing to do with our lesson, but I love sprinkling those esoteric historic 'gems' around when apropos."

Sahila was going to continue, but noticed that her students were all still dutifully writing in their notebooks. They were all expert at this task, since no one used a computer.

"The ancient Romans also believed bloodstone helped stop bleeding and the ancient Greeks thought that having a bloodstone on one's person helped ward off being bitten by a venomous snake!"

Tú smacked the table, incredulous. "Seriously? That one seems anecdotal and really hard to prove. If you carry a

---

[218] "Bloodstone," https://www.mindat.org/gm/7616

bloodstone and are careful in general, you don't get bitten by a snake!"

"If that's the case," Demyan began, twirling his pencil expertly, "why didn't they do that in Australia? Don't they have some of the most poisonous snakes in the world?"

"Yes!" Élise shouted, excited. "I studied this once. They have over twenty species of very poisonous snakes! Researchers have determined it has something to do with the continental drift."

Sahila twirled a finger in the air. "I am sensing the formulation of a research paper. You two should discuss that."

"Oof. Sorry! You two stepped into that one," Tessa snorted. "But I think it would be really cool!"

Sahila grinned. "Moving on. In India, they too believed that bloodstone helped to stop bleeding and they would place a bloodstone on a wound after dunking it in cold water. What is interesting about that belief is that bloodstone contains iron oxide, which is an astringent."

Sahila walked back to the box and switched the bloodstone for iolite,[219] a lustrous beautiful blue-violet stone. "Although it looks similar to amethyst, it belongs in another family.

"It was called the Viking Compass Stone, because the Vikings were known to use thin pieces of iolite to aide them with sun navigation at sea, especially when it was cloudy or misty. It was thought to act as a visual filter and help reduce glare."

Lastly, she wiggled her fingers over the boxes, as if contemplating which chocolate to select, and picked up an opal. The one she held was perfectly round and milky white and it glittered with luminescent shades of orange, purple, and green.

---

[219] "Iolite," https://www.mindat.org/gm/5119

"Opals have a fascinating societal history. In the interest of time, I will stick with the anthropological highlights. In the Middle Ages, people believed opals assisted with good eyesight and blond-haired women would wear opal necklaces, because they thought opals would preserve their hair color. There were no bottles of hair color around at that time, am I right? Anyway…" She rolled her eyes at her lame joke. "These are just some of the healing properties Commoners attributed to gems and stones throughout the ages. And as with any historic healing tool, we will learn which are accurate and which are old wives' tales. I *will* share that the link between bloodstone and venomous snakes is 'fake news'" she stage whispered while using her fingers to signal air quotes.

Ming raised her hand. "Thank you, Keeper Sahila for the amazing lecture." She paused. "Do you think it's possible that these beliefs began because a Keeper used a stone to help heal someone in various instances throughout history?"

Sahila smiled. "That's an insightful question, Scholar Ming. I think it's certainly possible that many of these Commoner remedies developed after either receiving or witnessing Emogem healing. That said, we must remember that our code of honor and loyalty to our Society is sacred. If an Emogem had no other remedy at their disposal to assist a Commoner, they might have utilized our methods, but also had to be careful not to reveal their knowledge or skill."

Aedan waved a hand. "Did they somehow cover up their abilities?"

"That's a great question, Scholar Aedan. Hiding the techniques and adding unnecessary steps or ingredients to mask the true method was likely employed. Remember, until Commoners are able to scientifically prove and validate our knowledge for themselves, we can never reveal what we know.

We discussed the great damage and chaos that would cause. That's the very reason why we have quite a few Keepers and Guardians embedded within science, education, medicine, and finance enterprises around the world. If we can gently guide humanity in the right direction, over time, they can make significant advances. Historically, however, it's always been dangerous for us to reveal our true selves, even when people around the world chose to believe interesting theories and remedies based on superstition or other unusual sources." Sahila walked over to the pneumatic tube attached to the wall in the room's front corner. "We always appreciate questions and analysis. So, Scholar Ming, what is your request for dinner tomorrow night?"

Sahila removed a blank slip of paper from a small box near the pneumatic tube and handed it to her. Ming looked around the room and at her classmates and finally looked down at the paper.

"My country, Singapore, is known for delicious traditional dishes. Two immediately come to mind that I think everyone should like." She wrote down her choices and handed the slip back to Sahila.

At her raised eyebrow, Ming offered, "I chose Laksa and Hokkien Mee. Laksa is a noodle dish with a protein, vegetables, and herbs in either a curry or a gravy. Hokkien Mee is a seafood dish with shrimp or squid, egg, bean sprouts, spices, and noodles; they are both delicious and can be made vegetarian or without seafood, if anyone has an allergy?"

Sahila took the slip over to the pneumatic tube system and opened its door. She took the tube out of its casing and placed the paper inside. When Sahila replaced the tube back into the casing, she pressed a button and everyone heard the *whoosh* as the meal request made its way to Chef's kitchen.

"They both sound delicious and there are no shellfish allergies on campus this term; all staff are made aware of significant allergies. Thank you, Scholar Ming. We're all looking forward to tastes from your home tomorrow. Now, we're going to begin the kinesiology portion of the class." Sahila looked directly at her students. "It is not lost on me that only one of you is an Emogem." She gracefully gestured to Ming. "Scholar Demyan is a Resogem, which is certainly closely related, but still a very different skill. Throughout your two years here, you will all become familiar with the abilities that exist. It's very important you have a concrete under-standing of your compatriots' expertise for several reasons."

She explained that, first, in crisis situations, different abilities could work harmoniously when facing multiple threats. It paid to practice together in preparation for any eventuality.

Second, many Debilis, she noted, are sycophants and blindly follow their leaders. They are not keenly aware of the kinesiology of the Keepers. Confusing the enemy using the skill set of another's ability, in addition to one's own, can come in handy.

Lastly, Keepers are obviously most adept and proficient with their own innate ability. Despite this, however, a skilled Keeper will be receptive, to some degree, to the abilities of their comrades. They will learn to understand and absorb some of each other's skills. A Keeper will never master them, nor necessarily become proficient, but they will be able to assist a compatriot with their ability, should it be necessary, or to successfully manage a small task.

Sahila looked over the wooden boxes and selected three stones after a quick perusal. "Okay, I am going to have us work with the three stones that I also first learned to master.

Before we begin, it is important to remember that these stones are *positively loaded or charged.* They are utilized in healing and have been for many years. Your personal kits contain some of the same stones, but are *unloaded,* so you all should be able to tell the difference, especially Scholars Ming and Demyan. It's also important to note that all stones can be loaded with negative energy and subsequently become harmful and dangerous.

"That said, all rocks and gems are not alike. Those most utilized in healing are naturally more resistant to deliberate or even accidental negative energy absorption. Others, however, are not and these tend to become the most dangerous."

Élise started scribbling so vigorously in her notebook, she tore the page clear across. "Umm, Keeper Sahila? Will this information become common knowledge to us? Will those of us who usually don't work with stones learn this and not accidentally hurt ourselves or others if we can't tell the difference between a safe and unsafe stone?"

Sahila orchestrated perfect jazz hands. "Yes, yes! Of course. I'm sorry if that didn't come across. Also, you will be tested on it frequently, till you each have it down."

Collective groans reverberated throughout the room.

Sahila held up a small light pink rock. It was a milky, subtle pink with white lines running throughout. She held it up with a question in her gaze, challenging her students.

Tessa raised her hand. "It looks to me like rose quartz."

Sahila smiled. "Yes, Scholar Tessa, it is indeed, good job. What do you know about rose quartz?"

Tessa blew her hair out of her face and bit her lip. "What I know about rose quartz may not be the information you're looking for. It's regular quartz with small amounts of manganese, titanium,[220] or iron. It still vibrates consistently, but with a different signature than clear quartz. It's not the type of quartz I'd usually pick when making a laser, because it's more sensitive to the sun and the inclusions might throw off my trajectory."

Sahila responded with a finger wag in Tessa's direction. "Scholar Tessa just illustrated my previous point perfectly!" Sahila elongated the P sound with elegance.

"You ask an *Ingenio* about their crystal knowledge and you get information about optimal laser quality or vibration reliability! Thank you. That's essential information, Scholar Tessa, and we'll discuss those in detail in our unit that combines geology and chemistry, with a physics component. This unit, taught by Keeper Nalin, is fascinating! I always see lots of smoke, flame, and colorful lasers in the lab and around campus during that class. For now, what do we know about rose quartz in terms of its healing properties?"

Ming quirked an eyebrow at Tessa, seeking acquiescence. Tessa gave her a thumbs up and drummed her fingers on her desk absentmindedly. Sahila, seeing this exchange, gestured for Ming to continue.

"I believe rose quartz is used to help bolster self-confidence, creativity, unconditional love, forgiveness, and self-esteem." Ming pulled at the cuff of her thin sweater. "It's probably the crystal that I used the most among my friends when they asked me for help."

Sahila clicked her tongue approvingly and added, "Rose quartz can soothe a broken heart and balance emotions if one feels out of sorts." She moved toward the rear of the class and gestured for the others to follow her. When they were far enough away from the other rock samples, Sahila

---

[220] "Titanium," https://www.mindat.org/gm/7339

opened her palm and held the rose crystal between her left thumb and index finger.

"You can see that this crystal is dusty rose in color with white occlusion lines. This sample contains manganese deposits. Manganese is needed by the body to heal bones, wounds, and assist with both carbohydrate and amino acid metabolism.

"I'm going to activate this crystal now and I want to get your impressions afterward. Pay careful attention to my actions. Every one of my gestures is purposeful and targeted toward maximizing the benefits of this crystal's healing properties. Master healers also have their own signature motions, but these don't undermine the basic necessary kinesiology."

Sahila placed herself in the middle of the group. She first held the crystal in a palm and began massaging it. After thirty seconds of this, she cradled it toward her heart, closed her eyes, and blew softly upon it. The stone deepened in color and took on a slight sheen from the heightened energy.

"Now, walk by me in single file and place your hand briefly on the crystal to get a sense of how it activates." Sahila kept her eyes closed.

"Oh wow!" Élise whispered. "I can feel its constant vibration. That's amazing!"

"How weird! When I touch other rose quartz samples containing manganese, it's not as warm as this, but the vibration is the same," Tessa added.

"I've never even touched rose quartz." Aedan looked at the boys.

The rest of the students walked by and followed suit.

"It's also best to clear your mind as much as you can of other thoughts and stimuli. There are times when your safety or the safety of others will prevent that ideal condition.

The more practice you have, however, the sooner this step is achieved subconsciously. It is imperative that your mind center on the thoughts that will help optimize this stone's healing potential. I'm focusing on kindness and empathy. Each of you is a special gift to our society and has different skills that are important and necessary." She opened her eyes and looked around.

KameKona had a smile on his face. "I'm exactly where I'm supposed to be and I feel less stressed."

Tú was next to KameKona and he appeared to be napping while standing.

KameKona wagged an index finger toward Tú. "Dude took relaxation to a whole new level," he chuckled.

Aedan took a cleansing breath. "I feel relaxed and content, like when we were in the salt cave."

Out of the corner of her eye, Sahila saw a few tears streaming down Élise's cheeks. "I've never felt like I was completely where I belonged. Even at home, I felt like the odd one out. It's different here."

The others expressed similar thoughts and feelings as Sahila walked the quartz back to the boxes.

"Before we move on to the next sample, we need to address an important issue. An Emogem is someone with the ability to heal people and animals utilizing natural elements, rocks, and crystals. It is our natural inclination and inherent gift. Scholar Ming, you can see, will be a skillful and gifted healer."

Ming shot a glance at Sahila. "Thank you! I really hope so!"

Sahila patted her shoulder. "Despite this, sometimes Emogems are called upon to use their ability contrary to their instincts and purpose. In order to protect others from harm or stop an enemy from inflicting pain we must go on the offensive. We do not appear threatening. In fact, we are often thought to be the least dangerous of the Keepers, and maintaining that illusion works to our advantage. When necessary, we can harness the energy from a healing stone to cause intense feelings of despair, worthlessness, fear, and pain.

"We can tap into the insecurities of Debilis and enhance those unpleasant thoughts and emotions instantaneously or manipulate an enemy to turn on their leader and attack their own partners or even themselves. For the truly accomplished Emogem Keeper, this will be intensely distasteful, but absolutely necessary. I can see the fear in your eyes, young Scholar Ming, and I empathize with you."

"That isn't like me at all! How will I learn to be able to do that if it's against my nature?"

"Not to worry! You will become an expert at it. Perhaps one of the most skilled. A proficient Emogem can enjoy an entire career as a healer, filled with removing pain and never inflicting it, but a *Principal* Emogem Keeper will never have that luxury; we are charged with a larger responsibility. If you have the aptitude, artistry, and courage to become a Principal Keeper, you may be called upon to save the life of a fellow Keeper or Guardian using those skills. Within the next three years, we will learn where your destiny lies. Now, let's move on, shall we?"

The hearty beef and vegetable stews served with warm crusty bread were well appreciated at lunch and the fresh apple cobbler with fragrant vanilla and lavender ice cream was a welcome treat.

Everyone was adjusting to the shorter days and need for warm coats and umbrellas for chilling rain. After class that afternoon, Élise, Evren, and Nalin dedicated another hour working on interpreting potential phrases emanating from the spectral presence, while the others looked on from the common room.

Nalin felt the prickle of goosebumps when they deciphered what they thought were the phrases "…still here" and "…bracelet prevented."

Evren, eyes closed and fingers clasped together, took a deep breath in relief. "I find hope in our small progress. Scholar Élise, you should be proud of your efforts here; this is a novel experience for me, and Keeper Nalin as well."

Everyone settled down to a quiet evening studying for their economics test. The focus was the history of Debilis activity on the European economy from the Middle Ages to the 1800s. Some studied near the fireplace and others chose their own rooms with their doors open.

The melodious tones of Yo-Yo Ma playing Bach's "Suite in Cello #1 in G Minor" drifted from Tú's room and created a soothing atmosphere. Tessa took surreptitious glances at a catnapping Aedan in between bouts of studying. KameKona and Élise quizzed each other in a corner.

Ming lifted her head when she noticed a flickering yellowish-white light outside the common room windows. Seconds later, she and the others heard intermittent shouts as the unexpected light grew in intensity. They ran to the windows and looked outside at the developing scene below.

Pockets of flame sporadically erupted from the cobblestone sidewalk, like cloudy geysers of yellow-white lava. Tú ran to the group as KameKona and Tessa headed toward the exit, determined to understand the situation.

Before they got to the stairs, Jürgen reached the top, breathing heavily, and holding his arms to the side, blocking anyone's egress. His signature pescatarian cologne had significantly diminished the more time he spent away from his other duty station on the Navarino Islands. Unfortunately, he was now exuding a new, noxious sulfurous odor.

"You can' go outside jus' now, Scholars, it isna' safe."

Aedan, who woke up during the commotion, questioned, "What's happening, Keeper Jürgen?"

Looking stern, Jürgen gestured for them to head back to the common room, despite the shouts outside becoming louder and more insistent.

Xandra could clearly be heard below, her voice piercing and furious. "How *dare* they enter our sanctuary! This is inexcusable! Where on Earth is Keeper Alesky?"

Jürgen ruffled his hair and sat down on a chair. "We've had some kin' of breach in security by Debilis. It's been deal' wi' already, so don' mind that. Keepers Reese and Alegria ran them off campus; they won' ever bother wi' us again."

At the students' look of alarm, Jürgen held up his hands, fending off the concern. "They didn' kill them, mind you; we only do that as a last resort, part of the code and all. I believe they were directed to make a life in Key West, Florida, openin' a ol' timey photo company. You kno', the kin' where you dress up in ol' fashioned clothes and look silly. Anyway, the threat is gone, but it's no' safe outside righ' now."

Curious, KameKona craned his neck to get a better look out the window. "Why isn't it safe?"

"Well, wha' you see outside is our early warning system for th' grounds. There is a percentage of zinc mixed in wit' the grout in the' walkway. Every two years or when necessary, it's replaced. Almost all Debilis contain substantial amounts of sulfur. If they somehow make their way onto th' campus grounds, th' sulfur in their bodies is shed through their pores an' their higher heat signature ignites th' zinc."

Ming's eyes looked concerned. "That does sound dangerous!"

"Not to worry! When this happens, it causes th' grouting mixture to spontaneously combust into yellow-white flames. Especially at night. It lights up aroun' us and lets us know we've got some beasties on th' grounds. If th' light doesn' alert us, th' smell certainly does! No' worry, thou, it hasn' happened in many years and' it's under control."

Tú spoke up. "Keeper Jürgen, if the threat is gone, why is it dangerous for us to go outside?"

Jürgen stood up and pulled on his jacket. "Th' zinc and sulfur chemical mixture creates zinc sulfide, which is hazardous. It can result in metal fume fever, which causes flu-like symptoms or worse, and can make it difficul' to breathe, causes dizziness, and nausea. It can also irritate your skin. It's nasty and you'll be in the treatmen' room wi' Nurse Hestia and Dr. Slaine for a week if your exposure is great. Welders can sometimes get it if they aren't careful. It's nighttime anyway, so no reason for you to come outside just now. Staff is makin' sure nothin' was taken and we'll let you know. Keeper Xandra will come up shortly and remain in the common room for several hours if you have concerns."

Tessa spoke up. "Keeper Jürgen, you said that *most* Debilis contain extreme amounts of sulfur. What about the ones that don't contain sulfur and what stops Commoners from storming the college campus?"

Jürgen pulled on his beard and smiled. "You don' miss a thing, do you, Scholar Tessa. I doubt mos' of you do. Newer Debilis never attempt a campus visit; they don't have th' experience or th' ability. As for Commoners, our other security protocols would readily catch them, but there's no motivation for them to attempt it, other than th' occasional pedestrian nosiness or a foolish dare."

CHAPTER 29 – Cu

COLLEGE OF GEOEVOLUTION

# LATE OCTOBER

The next morning, everyone was filled with excess palpable energy. Xandra already warned Shifu Zoria and Master Proulx to prepare a particularly exhaustive exercise session for the day.

The logical first step before breakfast was examining the walkway grout. Other than seeing some zinc residue on the cobblestone path, nothing seemed amiss.

Dumisani, recently returned from his required travel, anticipated their curiosity and concern and patiently waited for each student to assemble near the walkway; he knew each couldn't resist the lure to investigate.

"Good morning, my young scholars." He wore gray wool slacks, a midnight blue cashmere sweater, and a kufi hat. Black gloves were his only concession to the cold weather. "I assume you might have some more questions," he addressed the group. "Though I know that Keeper Jürgen explained what happened last night."

Aedan eagerly raised his hand. "Keeper Dumisani, I want to understand the mechanics of the controlled explosions."

Dumisani grinned, appreciating Aedan's enthusiasm. "Of course! I expected as much." He pointed down to the walkway grouting. "If you look carefully, you will see small metal canisters sitting flush with the grouting." He waited for each student to find a place along the walkway. The canisters were difficult to see if one didn't look for them. They were embedded in the grouting at even intervals and were perhaps five millimeters in diameter.

"These canisters are made of titanium. They are corrosive resistant, which means their shape can withstand our rain and snow. They are also incredibly strong and resilient. Titanium will expand and contract with the weather, but the grouting surrounding each one acts as a buffer, and largely absorbs the energy from those processes, which helps retain their shape. Inside each titanium canister is compacted zinc powder. Should a seasoned Debilis manage to get onto our campus, the heightened amount of sulfur in their bodies, combined with their higher body temperature, reacts with the zinc, creating zinc sulfide.

"This combination is volatile and creates yellowish-white flame, which acts as an early warning mechanism, especially at night. Although we hear grumbling from students regarding our relentless teaching and testing of the periodic table and the chemistry of such, this is one of the reasons why it is imperative you learn and intuitively understand these elements."

"I think we all just about have it memorized," Tessa exclaimed, defending her brethren.

Dumisani raised his palms in a calming gesture regarding his statement. "Of course, I am not referring to this elite class! I have it on good authority that you all *never* complain. Anyway, we can't work with what we don't comprehend or respect; to do so is foolish and reprehensible." He looked over at Aedan and asked, "Speaking of titanium, Scholar Aedan, what other ways is it utilized by humans?"

Aedan, hands in pockets to warm them from the cold, nodded his head, thinking.

"Titanium is used to make quite a lot of stuff, actually. First, it's becoming the metal of choice for replacing body parts, like hips, knees, fingers, heart valves, and joints. Also, it's used in tennis rackets, goalie masks, bicycle frames, scissors, surgical tools, and jewelry. It's in cell phones, equipment for the military, and it's what makes white paint white, when it's mixed with oxygen and becomes titanium dioxide. That's just to name a few."

"Great job, Scholar Aedan. It's an essential substance for Commoners in this modern world, that's for sure. Let's walk to breakfast. It never ceases to amaze me how the Earth continues to provide what humans and animals need to survive and thrive. It's all the more reason why our mission is so critical; we need to ensure that the relationship remains symbiotic."

Breakfast was a hearty protein and fruit offering. Gone were bready carbs or potatoes that morning. When Jürgen politely complained to Chef Ngai about missing his daily toast, Chef politely explained with restrained patience that "his students" were excitable already and didn't need extra carbs and sugar to cause pandemonium and poor results on their upcoming exam. If Jürgen remained agreeable until dinner, Hattie would offer Singapore Pandan dinner rolls with Ming's choice meal.

As Ngai expected, this seemed to mollify Jürgen. The meal was filled with further explanations about the previous evening's activity.

"Nothing was taken or disturbed, especially from what we ingloriously call the rock room." At one end of the table, in sotto voce, Nalin recounted the evening's adventures she'd had with Élise and Evren.

Alegria dropped her fork in surprise. "Oh, my goodness! Could it be Ariane?"

Dumisani placed his hand soothingly on hers and said calmly, "We won't discard any possibility, Keeper Alegria. I have contacted Keeper Diamond Lee and asked her to assist us with this matter when she can get time away."

Aside from the present conversation, the only sounds were the gentle clattering of utensils and china. Every student focused on eating and made a great effort to not appear eavesdropping, to varying degrees of success. Once Tessa heard her mentor's name, however, she gave up trying. "Dya Lee is coming?"

All eyes suddenly met hers and she colored.

"Umm, sorry. Just kinda slipped out."

Dumisani smiled. "Your dedication to your mentor is commendable. There are several locations where we relax our formality. Mealtimes are meant to be enjoyed in a calming environment; it's better for the digestion and socialization. Keeper Diamond is one of our most talented Emogems and is an expert in paranormal activities. We'll see if she can help shed light on our potential intelligent presence. Do not distress, Scholar Tessa. I will make sure you are notified when she arrives, if she doesn't contact you first."

Reese clapped to get everyone's attention. "Remember to study for your upcoming exam and focus! We hope to be impressed with your academic acumen and prove that I'm the best teacher on campus!" He stood up, nodded at Dumisani and the others, and headed out to prep for the exam.

Two hours later, Reese finished collecting the exams and watched his students stretch and commiserate. He knew it was a reasonable test, but in fairness to them, it was a lot of information to grasp.

His earlier conversation with Dumisani and Sahila came to mind. While it was true that nothing had been removed or altered during last night's invasion, the students were not told the complete story. They would learn the rest that afternoon, after classes. He needed to head over to the library and discuss the situation with Heikima.

Nalin reached into her peasant skirt pocket and rubbed the shell of her carved turtle totem. She needed a surge in patience. Teaching elemental chemistry to a group of exhausted but fidgety college students would try anyone's patience. She felt empathy for them, but still had to get through the lesson and assign the homework. It was a relief to them all, she thought, that class was *finally* over; it had been a long day.

She cleared her throat and looked toward her students. "We have a change in the afternoon schedule today. We are going to head over to the library now. I know you all need to do research for your term paper on the complete history of your individual ability and we thought this was a good time to find resources. Follow me."

Nalin internally winced. She could practically feel the eye rolling and definitely heard the knuckles cracking. This was truly the *last* activity her students needed today and she knew they questioned her sanity, but "needs must when the devil drives"—or in this case, the Debilis.

Tessa took a slow, deep breath as she left Keeper Nalin's class with the others. *That box breathing technique Nurse Hestia taught me really did reduce my anxiety before the exam in Keeper Reese's class!* Although it took a while for her to get the hang of it, practicing frequently *was* making a difference. The breathing, mixed with positive affirmations about her testing ability and academic competence, calmed her; she didn't blank out during the exam and forget what she knew.

Tessa grinned as she realized the changes in her behavior. *It's such a revelation to know I have a learning difference! It explains so much about my academic struggles and impulsive proclivity—my loose verbal filter.*

Learning how to master these issues gave her a sense of control over her life, and her self-confidence was slowly growing. After an extensive and comprehensive battery of testing, she learned she had ADHD–Inattentive Type. The College of William and Mary psychologist who administered some of the testing explained it to her.

"It's not uncommon for students with your diagnosis to be overlooked by teachers, parents, and other adults who interact with them. You are not hyperactive and don't often disrupt the class or activity; students with your type are more apt to start daydreaming if they aren't engaged. Unfortunately," she explained, "a teacher might think a student with ADHD doesn't care or isn't that bright."

Tessa realized that she didn't disengage from *any* class at the College of GeoEvolution. Every class to her was fascinating, but she definitely remembered mentally checking out in high school, frequently.

"Students with ADHD are usually keenly intelligent and are capable of accomplishing their goals. They often hyper-focused on a task that intrigues them and this characteristic can actually be positive and serve the student well, when employed appropriately at the optimal time." She finished by letting her know that many brilliant and successful people throughout history who made monumental contributions to humanity had learning differences. "You need to learn to master your ADHD and not let it master you, and we'll help you with that."

So, she now took a small dose of medication each morning and paired that with new organization skills that helped her with what was termed "executive functioning skills." Those two components, the breathing exercises, and the mental affirmations were helping her immensely. She was slowly learning to become the best version of herself.

The unusual energy in the library was immediately palpable. Although she felt distinctly uneasy, Heikima welcomed her students with her usual greeting and told herself that Xandra would applaud her performance. It needn't have mattered, however. Not one minute after their arrival, Scholars Ming and Demyan were commiserating, sensing something was amiss.

Reese emerged from the center of the room. "Scholars Ming and Demyan, I notice you two are toey. What's wrong?"

Demyan looked at Ming and Reese. "Keeper Reese, something's different. There's an unnatural energy here."

Ming stood alongside Demyan. "There's a negative presence here I haven't felt before."

The others circled around the trio.

Tessa piped in. "Something feels off." She pushed up her sleeve and lifted her arm. "It's literally hair raising."

KameKona nodded. "I feel it too. I don't recognize it, because it isn't tied to my ability, but I sense some alternate force of some kind—and it isn't good."

The others nodded in agreement.

Keeper Reese nodded. "Good. You're all out of the top drawer.[221] I'll admit, we were not completely forthcoming yesterday about what happened. Nothin' was taken, that's true. But it seems our uninvited guests left us a little gift. We're not quite certain of their motives at the moment, but we'll figure it out. Rather than ferret it out ourselves, however, we thought it a great learnin' experience for you all to manage."

Sahila entered the library and headed toward them. "Is everyone up to speed?" she inquired.

At Reese's acknowledgement, Sahila nodded. "Okay. We'd like Scholars Ming and Demyan to take the lead."

Demyan shot a glance at Ming. "You ready for this?"

"I hope so!" She nervously played with the gems on her necklace. "I think this energy aligns better with your experience, but Sahila *did* say I needed to become good at this."

Sahila continued. "Everyone else, take the opportunity to get a sense of the threat. Feel its energy signature and even if it doesn't resonate with your ability, be aware of how you perceive its existence. This is a unique opportunity in

---

[221] Out of the top drawer – Australian slang for top quality

this familiar insular space to become attuned to how each of you individually respond cognitively and emotionally to this type of negative presence."

They walked through the library alert—listening, feeling, and looking around, unsure of what they might find. Demyan and Ming followed an identical path alongside one another. They did this unconsciously, whether it was for camaraderie or the instinctive awareness that an existing trail from their quarry remained. For the two of them, there was a keen feeling of enmity and the tendrils of a vague lingering heat signature. Both intuitively had their arms up and their palms facing outward, fingers splayed apart, almost like antennae, sensing the environment. This kinesthetic lesson had yet to be taught, but to a Keeper, it was largely instinctive, perhaps even genetically programmed into their DNA.

Angry thoughts began invading Demyan's mind and swirled around in a frenetic pace: *This is my kingdom! It is my divine right to rule. I am no cuckold! Damn any fool who disobeys me!*

Demyan stopped and closed his eyes, trying to calm his mind and shield it from the menacing thoughts as Keeper Sahila had taught him. He felt slightly queasy. Ming placed a hand on his shoulder, squeezing gently in support. She was affected as well, but had a stronger inherent ability to protect herself.

The others noticed the malevolent presence as well as it permeated the library, but were spared the assaulting thoughts. To Sahila and Reese's trained eyes, Ming and Demyan wandered through various aisles in a seemingly random pattern, following what seemed like the frenetic pace of an anxious Debilis.

They both finally stopped in the fictional section about literary monsters. Heikima's respect for the Dewey decimal system notwithstanding, these stories were conveniently shelved together, rather than just by author.

Sitting on top of a popular novel about zombies sat a perfectly oval translucent stone, the color of a vibrant plum and the size of a large lima bean. Demyan was hesitant to touch it, considering his recent issues with negatively loaded stones. But he wanted to protect Ming, not knowing how she would be affected by such a toxic rock.

Her eyes were glued to the stone, seemingly innocuous, as it rested on the book. "It's beautiful," she whispered, "but I know it has evil energy."

Demyan pulled the cuff of his sweater, so it stretched over his right palm. He gingerly plucked the stone off its perch, but held it away from him as if it was radioactive.

Ming, hesitant to yell in a library, stated in a large whisper, "Demyan has it," as they rushed back to the front where everyone gathered.

Sahila had set up a small blue velvet cushion and a leaded glass lid beside it. "Place it here, Scholar Demyan, quickly."

Once the stone was on the cushion, Reese placed the crystal lid atop it, halting any further energy transfer. Sahila immediately placed peridot and obsidian stones in Demyan's right palm, cradled his hand, and began a healing cleanse. She had previously activated the stones in anticipation of the impending need.

"Peridot helps to counteract negative emotions while obsidian heals the skeletal structure, veins, and muscles; it is also effective in helping to ground and calm an individual," Sahila explained. "In addition, it encourages serenity and helps alleviate negativity."

"Let's have a look, shall we?" Reese inquired.

"That stone looks familiar to me!" Sahila announced as she peered closely inside the glass.

"It should, actually, Sahila, because it's quite legendary." Reese approached Heikima and quietly made a request. She rushed off and shortly returned with a book.

She flipped through till she found the appropriate page. "Is this what you wanted, Reese?"

He bent down to look at the page and tapped it with an index finger. "Thank you. Bingo!" He turned the text around so everyone could glance at it. "There you go. Look familiar?"

Sahila and the others peered closely at the book and the rock sample. "Oh my. Yes, I think you're right," she said, amazed. "We'll have to test it to be sure, however."

Tú gently touched the page. "It's an elaborate crown; that's a lot of jewels."

The picture depicted an ornate gold crown adorned with pearls, sapphires, emeralds, diamonds, and rubies in a simple, but elegant pattern.

"This was believed to be the crown of King Henry VII of England," Sahila began. "When he passed on, his son Henry VIII took ownership. And there is *indeed* a great deal of jewels, Scholar Tú: 344 to be exact, as well as five little sculptures. As I am sure you all know, Henry the VIII had six wives." She looked out at her group.

Élise raised her hand and waited for a nod. "I always remember it as divorced, beheaded, died, divorced, beheaded, survived."

Sahila laughed. "Yes, that's an easy way to remember both the order and the unfortunate fates of his wives!"

Reese continued. "King Henry VIII was an intense ruler, and he was plagued by numerous health issues later in life, including gout, leg ulcers, a leg injury that never healed, and potentially Type II diabetes, among other possible problems. These issues, coupled with running a country in a dynamic world, and difficulty siring a vibrant male heir, made for a very cranky, paranoid, and unpredictable king. Every time he wore that crown and divorced, beheaded, or buried a wife, he further negatively loaded those stones with his pernicious thoughts."

Sahila took up the reins again. "Fast forward five rulers and we arrive at Charles I. This was the time of Oliver Cromwell and the English Civil War. Cromwell and his supporters had Charles I executed in 1649 and almost all of the crown jewels, including Henry VIII's crown, were melted down and sold off. The jewels in the crown, all 344 of them, were sold off in packets."

Reese pointed to the ruby under the leaded glass. "Our belief is that some of these stones and pearls were acquired by new owners who added many years of positive energy to them, thus healing the negatively loaded ones. We hoped this was the case for many of them. We know, unfortunately, that some found their way into the hands of equally unhappy and unsavory new owners, who served only to render them even more dangerous. There's been random reports of sightings over the centuries and we've managed to acquire two and get them out of circulation. They are in our legendary rock room." He peered down at the stone again. "I believe that we are looking at our third, a ruby from King Henry VII's crown. It's incredibly toxic."

Sahila raised her hand to add one point. "Before we remove this specimen to the rock room, I want to point out the obvious, the question none of you are asking, but are all thinking: The image in the book is a color photograph, which, of course, seems impossible, I know. It exists because Harry Collins, Queen Elizabeth II's jeweler, was part of a team that recreated the crown and completed it in 2012. It's housed in Hampton Court Palace and is open to the public for viewing.[222]

"When the crown was originally designed, meticulous records were kept regarding the type and number of jewels included and what the crown looked like. And if that wasn't enough, Charles I posed for a portrait by Daniel Mytens[223] in 1631, standing proudly next to the crown. I find it particularly macabre and believe it foreshadows his violent demise.

"It serves to further reinforce the fact that these stones are dangerous and need to be removed from society; that portrait of Charles I is hanging in the National Portrait Gallery in London."

Demyan and Ming sat with the Keepers in the dining hall and drank soothing cups of tea, discussing the latest event. Demyan and Ming were asked if there was anyone at home with whom they had a complicated past. Anyone with an axe to grind? Other than Demyan's cantankerous relationship with his father, neither could think of one.

Dumisani dismissed the two back to the residence hall.

"The central question, of course, is why a stone was placed in the library," Nalin pondered. "I wonder if the Debilis are testing our students and if so, why? This has never happened before."

---

222 Historic Royal Palaces. "Henry's Crown." https://www.hrp.org.uk/hampton-court-palace/whats-on/henrys-crown

223 Daniel Mytens, painter. "Portrait of King Charles I." 1631.

Evren nodded. "Whomever did this is taunting us and are sophisticated. It's very nearly impossible to get on campus; it was clearly well-planned."

Reese mentioned that he would check with local Keepers and see if they noticed any unusual occurrences or recent local Debilis criminal activity.

Dumisani looked around the group. "It is clear that we are seeing a disturbing pattern of escalating infiltration. The goal seems to be to harass our students or to antagonize us. The most pressing question is why? I would like each of you to check with your contacts and develop an analysis of intent: What is the purpose of the Debilis incursions and whom do you suspect is leading this endeavor?

"In the meantime, Sahila and Reese, thoroughly analyze that stone and get it secured in the rock room. Reese, check and see if any of your contacts have interacted with that stone and know some of its providence. We'll reconvene again in three days to review."

CHAPTER 30 – **Zn**

COLLEGE OF GEOEVOLUTION

# LATE OCTOBER

Venturing toward the rear perimeter of campus in late October to harvest walnut trees was a College of GeoEvolution tradition going back centuries. Choosing Halloween itself began around the mid-1800s. The students enjoyed the unusual activity as much as the potential scare factor.

Walking among the stately trees with their large gnarly trunks in the fall's waning daylight was a creepy experience. The students needed poles to shake the branches and dislodge the walnuts; collecting them from the ground was the easiest and safest way to gather the harvest. One of the Keepers, usually Reese or Alegria, read an Edgar Allan Poe story to heighten the experience.

Before leaving, however, they had several hours of instruction and the students needed to get through their heroes and villains class first. Evren whistled a jaunty tune as he waited for them to arrive; he loved this unit and it was always enthusiastically received by his students. The entire month, the students kept Heikima busy checking out the various horror, thriller, and mystery books from their library.

Evren clapped his hands loudly, bringing the class to attention.

"Okay. Let's get through this alchemist Debilis unit in one piece, shall we? We are talking about Ramon Llull, who arrived in England during the fourteenth century, claiming to be the famous Spanish Franciscan friar of the same name. He was actually a scheming Ferro Debilis with dreams of hoodwinking King Edward III, widely known for his obsession with alchemy."

KameKona clicked his tongue and shook his head. "Man, there sure were a lot of bad Debilis running around manipulating rulers throughout history!"

"Don't forget, Kame, we witnessed a Debilis group trying that a few weeks ago," Ming added.

"Yeah—that's true, that's true! Boy, things haven't really changed much, have they?"

Tessa blew a raspberry. "These Debilis really suck!"

Evren shook his head, smiling. "Thank you all for the entertaining running commentary. You are not wrong. Anyway, the real Franciscan friar died two years after King Edward III was born."

Aedan waved his arm enthusiastically. "Modern communications were centuries away! It was virtually impossible for those in England to verify that charlatan's story. How would they know?"

"Exactly so, Scholar Aedan. It was easy to commit that fraud. Llull knew that King Edward III wanted money to fund his desired war with France, so he tricked him with a flashy demonstration using his Ferro ability."

"That he could transmute something into gold!" Tú shouted, getting into the story.

"Precisely. You all are catching on! Llull declared that he could transmute lead, tin, and mercury into gold. Enthusiastic to join the club of rulers who were investing in the alchemical science, Edward III eagerly set Llull up with a lab of his own."

Tessa threw her hands up, excited. "But we know that's impossible! How did he do it?"

Evren barked in laughter. He loved their enthusiasm! "Our Keeper history tells us that Llull had a complicit partner working inside the kingdom who stole large amounts of gold coin from Edward III. In addition, he had a loyal network of well-paid pickpockets who pilfered from the nearby nobles and the church. This booty was secretly passed off to Llull, who melted the gold down and made new coin, claiming it was created from the lead, tin, and mercury alchemical processes."

Élise smacked her table loudly. "How cunning! I hate to praise an evil Debilis, but that was really clever!"

"Nah, you're right, Élise. Dude was a slick one," KameKona agreed.

Evren continued. "King Edward III was thrilled and paid Llull handsomely for his incredible skill. That was when our Keeper brethren stepped in, before Llull broadened his network and either took further advantage of the king or traveled to dupe another sovereign.

"Our record tells us that Keepers tried to convince him to stop and when that failed, they used our trademark hypnotism-based tactic. Unfortunately, Llull was an accomplished Ferro Debilis and a sociopath. He made it clear that he had no intention of curtailing his scheme. In a fit of anger at being cornered, he started a fire in the nearby inn where the Keepers were staying and killed the innkeeper and two other guests."

"Okay. Never mind. That guy was a tool!" Élise signed and stated.

"The local Keeper Council determined he was too dangerous to Commoners and Keepers alike, and he was quietly taken by Keepers from the kingdom lab. After a Keeper trial, he was executed in 1374."

Aedan raised his hand. "How do Keepers determine when it's necessary to execute a Debilis?"

Evren, hands in pants pockets, turned to face Aedan and nodded. "A crucial question, Scholar Aedan. And I promise that we will discuss that at length in our ethics course. For now, I will say this: Killing an evil entity is always a last resort. No matter how justified, *ending a life leaves a bruise on your soul you will always carry.* You need to be certain before you take such an action. Now, Scholar KameKona, lead us through our next example from yesterday's required reading."

KameKona leafed through his textbook and rhythmically jiggled a leg.

"Um. We read about John Dee and Edward Kelley from England.[224] Oh, and the story of these two cats begins in 1570. Kelley, who got in trouble for faking land deals, bought a piece of paper and some mysterious powder from an innkeeper. The innkeeper told him it was an alchemical formula he stole from the grave of a church official. Kelley believed it was directions for transmuting elements into gold and he convinced John Dee to work with him.

"John Dee was a famous scientist and philosopher who was favored by Queen Elizabeth I. Kelley, the *Ferro* Debilis

---

[224] Harkness, Deborah E. *John Dee's Conversations with Angels: Cabala, Alchemy, and the End of Nature.* Cambridge University Press, 2006.

in this dude duo, performed a fake transmutation in front of John Dee and turned lead into gold."

KameKona stopped and put his palms out to halt his explanation. "I just need to add that this was really crappy. John Dee was a respected Commoner at the time. I mean, the world was his oyster! He had the attention and appreciation of Queen Elizabeth I, who was an intimidating monarch. And this con artist Debilis led him down the garden path, convinced Dee to participate in his scheme, and ruined his life!"

Evren smiled. "Thanks for the accurate colorful commentary, Scholar KameKona. And you are spot on. Understanding the toxic impact Debilis have on the natural world and humanity is vitally important. It's one of the central tenants of our society. Please continue."

KameKona got comfortable in his chair and began again. "Anyway, Dee and Kelley wrote about their success and got the attention of a Polish noble named Prince Albertus Alasco, who was visiting the court of Queen Elizabeth I. At his invitation, Dee and Kelley traveled in 1583 to Alasco's castle in Cracow, Poland, with their families."

"Wait a minute!" Ming interrupted KameKona. "I'm sorry, Kame, but these men brought their families with them on their crime spree?"

Tessa stopped twirling her pencil—a habit she cultivated to help keep her mind on task. "It's a rotten thing to do, but his family, at least his wife, probably knew too, right? They were in on it?"

"Oh yeah," Ming conceded. "That's possible."

KameKona nodded in agreement. "Kelley continued his machinations and manipulated Dee into thinking they were transmuting various metal elements into gold, without success. Prince Alasco paid them a great deal of money for this

Debilis subterfuge until 1585, when he finally figured out he was being swindled. He made them pack up and leave."

"Pack up and leave?" Aedan barked, incredulous. "They were lucky they and their families weren't killed!"

"I'm not bloodthirsty, you know, but that's a bit anticlimactic, Kame!" Élise laughed.

"Sorry, I'm just reporting the facts! Anyway, their entourage wandered around for a few years, peddling their nonsense, until 1589, when Dee evidently got some sense and packed up and went home. Queen Elizabeth took pity on him and gave him a license to practice alchemy, but he never regained his previous fame and fortune. Commoners burned down his famous library and lab because they thought he was involved with the devil. And when Queen Elizabeth I died in 1603, her successor James I did not renew his patronage. So, he died poor with a diminished reputation in either 1608 or 1609."

"There's a life lesson for you," Tú pronounced. "Don't practice crappy science!"

"My thoughts exactly, Tú. Kelley seemingly just disappeared. One account was that he fell out of a window in 1597, but Commoners don't know for sure."

Keeper Evren smiled brightly and clapped once. "Excellent job, Scholar KameKona. That was an insightful synopsis and you truly captured the emotional and financial damage that a Debilis can deliver upon a Commoner. In truth, with Dee and Kelley's frequent moves, it took longer to find them. When our Keepers arrived in Bohemia in 1589, they easily convinced John Dee to return home to England and provided an escort for him and his family. They did not encourage him to give up his desire to better understand alchemy, however."

Eyebrows drawn in confusion, Aedan asked, "Seriously? Why not? He was a criminal!"

"I understand your incredulity, Scholar Aedan. But the Commoners' interest in alchemy was a forerunner to advances in chemistry and helped foster the creation of the scientific method, developed by another alchemic enthusiast, Sir Francis Bacon, in 1621."

"Oh wow, that *is* cool!" Tessa interjected.

"Indeed. Kelley was another story altogether, however. He agreed to leave Bohemia and begin a new career that year. He started his journey toward Western Europe, but the call of his former life proved too strong and he set up shop again near another wealthy noble in the Swiss Cantons to begin anew."

"Dude was a menace to *both* Commoners and Keepers. Maybe another sociopath?" Aedan queried.

"Perhaps. Regardless," Evren continued, "before he could approach any wealthy alchemical supporters, he was arrested by Keeper Security and taken on the arduous journey to the Scottish Highlands, specifically to the European Debilis prison west of Thurso. He did try to escape en route, and somewhere in France he climbed out of an inn window using bed sheets and fell to his ignominious death."

"Well, you can't say it was not deserved!" Élise exclaimed.

"I don't know, Élise, you might be a tiny bit bloodthirsty!" Ming threw her hand up, defensive at Élise's surprised expression. "Don't misunderstand! you're usually so composed and calm; it's reassuring to also see your fiery nature. Still waters can run deep."

"Okay, let's move on." Evren tossed his book on the table. "Scholar Élise, please introduce our last alchemic Debilis for the class, please?"

Élise nodded and turned the page to the correct entry. "I'm going to talk about Johann Friedrich Böttger. He first made a name for himself in 1701 in Germany when he was just a young man—what we now call a teenager. He was a pharmacy assistant and his employer asked him to transmute silver into gold in front of some wealthy observers. Using a kind of alchemical mixture, he was able to accomplish it, or at least the observers thought so. His impossible experiment got the attention of Frederick I of Prussia, whom Böttger had the right to fear.

"When alchemists failed to deliver his promised gold, he was known to execute them. So, Böttger fled to Saxony and wound up getting stuck working for Augustus the Strong of Saxony, otherwise known as Frederick Augustus II of Poland."

Aedan knocked on his book. "When reading this portion, it was obvious this was not going to end well."

Élise smirked. "Frederick had a hanging scaffold decorated in shiny tinsel on public display as a reminder to those who worked for him what their fate was if they failed to deliver. He toiled for eighteen years, never delivering and forever promising."

"Okay, you made this ruler seem incredibly threatening, but he worked there for eighteen years! Frederick actually seemed a bit lenient!" Ming suggested.

"You'll see! Böttger was always nervous and could not escape Augustus II. What really saved him, however, was King Augustus II's other passion, *porcelain*. Being a great admirer of Asian porcelain, he demanded in 1706 that Böttger try to learn how to make it. He succeeded and the king opened a factory making porcelain in 1710.

"In 1713, however, the king once again demanded that Böttger make gold for him. Somehow, he was able to generate a small amount of it mixing copper and lead with some kind of substance, probably gold itself! It kept him from being hanged, but he died in 1719, probably from poisoning himself working with mercury and other toxic elements."

Evren signed "Thank you" to Élise and told her she did a great job. "So, in this case, we have one of our most successful Debilis conversions and in actuality, one of our spies."

KameKona slapped his forehead. "This Keeper history is so cool! We had spies?"

"It's difficult to accomplish, but Böttger is a good example. He thought he could utilize his abilities and follow in the footsteps of other Debilis who made a great living fleecing Commoners. Instead, he found the reverse: a Commoner king who made it impossible for him to escape, literally. Obsessive royalty and nobles had enough money for security to constantly watch their alchemists day and night."

"That's pretty scary," Ming interjected.

"Local Keepers had a few opportunities to talk with Böttger, but he initially refused any assistance. In the end, Keeper Security encouraged Böttger to promote the idea of a porcelain factory, changing King Augustus II's obsessive focus to one that was actionable.

"Böttger, although a Debilis, was still a bright scientist and was desperate enough to try to change his boss's demands. He was successful and made his king very rich from his sale of porcelain. You may have heard of it? It's called Dresden porcelain, and is still valued today."

"That's a great success story," Aedan said.

Evren agreed. "Böttger continued his relationship with his Keeper contacts and passed on intelligence he heard about other Debilis alchemists who were trying to take advantage of Commoners or who were also caught in King Augustus

II's alchemic web." Keeper Evren closed his staff textbook and placed it inside his satchel. "And now, I believe we are done for the day! Please drop your essays on the desk as you leave and make sure you are bundled up before you enjoy Keeper Fabek's hay ride to the walnut grove. Be careful! As Shakespeare wrote: 'Hell is empty and all the devils are here.'"

Thankfully, the forecast called for clear skies that afternoon. It was a brisk fifty degrees Fahrenheit as Fabek and Blue Peter led the students to the black walnut groves. A large wicker basket in the wagon contained pairs of sturdy gloves and heavily padded newsboy caps.

Phin sat in the wagon enjoying the adoration of his young fans. Although he stayed by Fabek's side most of the day, he was allowed to roam the campus freely. He had a familiar schedule for himself, which included daily visits to Chef, Heikima, and the residence hall. If someone heard him tap on the wooden door with his paw, he would be allowed to wander into the common room or each dorm room to greet the students.

In honor of the holiday, Tessa belted out the song "Love Potion Number 9" by The Searchers[225]. Aedan followed along with a ditty about Guy Fawkes: "Remember, remember, the fifth of November, gunpowder, treason, and plot...we see no reason why gunpowder treason should ever be forgot."

The students were relaxed and excited to get an afternoon off for scheduled fun. Once they arrived, Fabek explained

---

[225] Love Potion #9" released in 1959 by The Clovers (Capitol Records).

how to harvest the walnuts, which were largely still attached to the tree branches.

"The gloves are needed to avoid staining your fingers with juglone, a chemical excreted by the trees to prevent other plants from taking root in the area. Walnut trees are selfish and isolating, wanting the water and soil for themselves. They are beautiful, but haunting."

The tall trees created a lush canopy above, but also blocked out much of the sun below. Even in the fall, while most leaves had yellowed and fallen, enough stubbornly clung to the dark brown branches, asserting their commanding presence in the forest.

Fabek passed around impressive wooden poles that were at least twelve feet long.

"You need to gently whack the branches to dislodge the walnuts," Fabek explained, oblivious to the hijinks going on behind him.

"Oy! This isn't kung fu class! Knock it off!" Reese bellowed as the kids began fighting each other with the poles.

Fabek spun around, bemused, and shook his head after they stopped and resumed his lecture. "Each nut is protected by a husk and hard outer covering, insulating the healthy goodness inside. The newsboy caps are necessary to protect your heads."

Alegria was tempted to ask if they had the latest edition, hot off the presses! But she didn't want to disrespect Fabek.

"The last items for the task are those nut gathering baskets. They are the metal oval cages attached to the long handles over there. They roll on the ground, trapping the nuts inside."

Fabek and his crew had spent two days raking up the deluge of leaves to make the harvesting easier and more entertaining. True to Keeper expectation, the students reverted to the mentality of kindergarteners and all clamored to gently knock tree branches, avoid getting hit by falling projectiles, and run the nut cage around, vying to be the champion forager.

Reese mentioned that the two students who collected the most walnuts could choose meals in the near future. Cher Ami Deux rested warmly in her traveling case, ready to take the menu choices back to chef.

While their charges let off steam, Reese and Alegria took turns reading Edgar Allen Poe's "The Telltale Heart" with much enthusiasm, doing their best to channel the spirit of the holiday. When they finished and their energy was spent, they rode back in the wagon fortified with mugs of hot chocolate and spiced apple cider doughnuts.

This was Chef's yearly concession to his rule about snacking just before dinner. In truth, he was the one who started the tradition. Several years back, Xandra had chastised Chef about the indulgence and was soundly rebuked. No one contradicted Chef Ngai, and that was that. Xandra needed to stay in her lane and so would he.

Aedan and KameKona, extremely competitive and eager to select meals, both earned the title of "champion forager." Aedan requested mushroom, leek, and stilton cheese soup and a Yorkshire pudding. KameKona missed his mom's fresh poké bowls and requested a fill your own poké bowl meal, with ahi tuna and salmon with rice, along with his mom's non-traditional additions. To make it more fun, his mom included a variety of additions, such as edamame, fried onion, small fish eggs (tobiko), fresh sushi ginger, wasabi, lettuce, avocado, black sesame seeds, and ponzu or soy sauce.

KameKona serenaded the group on the way back with his rendition of Bobby Pickett's "Monster Mash"[226] as best as he could remember it, since his sisters were always making up their own lyrics.

The next morning, just as the sun rose, everyone woke up to Demyan's mad pacing and scrambling. He was slamming drawers and doors, racing up and down the hall, and creating a horrible racket in the common room. After a flurry of grooming and dressing, everyone left their rooms one by one, wondering what was bothering Demyan.

Tú reached him first and called out, just as Demyan launched another pillow into the air.

"Demyan, what is the matter?"

Demyan dragged his hands down his pale face, clearly distressed. "My uncle's watch is missing and I can't find it anywhere!"

Tessa jogged up to meet them. "You mean the Vostok watch your uncle gave you?"

Demyan pulled on his hair. "Yes, I had it on yesterday and when I woke up it was gone! He gave it to me when I left for school. He trusted me to take care of it! I have to find it."

KameKona joined the group. "Hey, man, we'll find it. Do you remember when you last saw it?"

Demyan looked up at KameKona and brightened. "Wait! Yes! It was at the grove. I remember because I saw it glow in the dark as I smacked the walnut tree branches." He grabbed his left wrist and looked past his fellow students,

---

[226] "Monster Mash" released in 1962 by Bobby Pickett and the Crypt-Kickers (Garpax Records).

remembering. While the others joined in, Demyan smacked his forehead. "It must have fallen off somehow at the grove! I have to go and get it right away!"

Élise placed a gentle hand on his shoulder and steered his eyes and attention to her. "Demyan, you can't just leave right now. You can't miss breakfast and class."

Ming added, "We're also not supposed to head to that area without staff, remember? They made that clear."

Demyan rubbed his naked wrist. "There were so many squirrels around there yesterday! I can't wait till someone is free later on. One of them might run off with it!"

Aedan rubbed his chin. "I don't think squirrels like shiny objects."

Demyan looked at everyone imploringly. "I can't take a chance! I need to find it!"

Tessa held her hand up. "Guys, could we go with him right after classes? We'll have plenty of daylight. We can also see if one of the Keeper staff can go with us. Ming, Tú, and Élise, you were planning on returning to the library to do more research, right?"

At their affirmation, she continued. "The rest of us can go with Demyan and we can ask Keeper Fabek to take us. That way we can check the wagon bed and see if your watch fell off there, right?"

They went to breakfast, Demyan much calmer with a plan and camaraderie. Tessa offered to find Keeper Fabek before lunch to make their request. They all managed, minus a slightly distracted Demyan, to focus on their class discussions and fencing lessons. By the time they were finished for the day, Demyan was almost vibrating in his seat from the unreleased tension.

Just as promised, Fabek, Phin, Blue Peter, and the wagon were standing at the ready. On the journey toward the walnut grove, the group scoured the bed to no avail, reinforcing Keeper Fabek's claim that no watch was left in the wagon. He was unusually silent during the ride, seemingly lost in his own thoughts again.

Other than the occasional chirping of birds or the scurry of confident squirrels, it seemed unusually quiet. Only the crunching of dried leaves and the snapping of fallen tree limbs penetrated the crisp and gray ambiance.

The group agreed to fan out and take sections of the grove, walking around their given tree perimeters. Although the watch had lost its initial bright sheen, it would still hopefully catch the light of the waning sun.

Aedan led the search, hopeful he would find the watch for Demyan. The Vostok was primarily made of stainless steel and as he began the search along his grid, he sensed the hum of the metal almost immediately. The cold magnified its signature pulse, making it seem tinny, not unlike the metal hasp for a flag, hitting its pole in a stiff breeze.

He reminded himself to keep his body temperature regulated, so he wouldn't damage the watch once he found it. He tasted the requisite iron tang in his mouth and wondered, as he worked, what history was buried deep within the earth. He made a mental note to ask if he could dedicate some time to ferreting out these objects. His keen interest in and respect for history seemed a natural pairing, considering his ability. He hoped, that since education was the primary focus of their college, his request would be enthusiastically granted.

Instinct had Aedan wandering into the far end of Tessa's search area. He felt a surge in energy intensity as his fingertips began to tingle with pinpricks of jolting heat. He looked down and saw the telltale silver metal of a band.

Tessa stopped to watch his process in fascination. She was making her way to the same area, albeit at a slower pace. Once he moved some leaves and verified that his quarry was Demyan's watch, he called out. "I've got it, Demyan!"

He looked up, expecting to see Demyan's eager face. Instead, he met with the confused stares of his fellow searchers.

KameKona looked at Tessa. "Where's Demyan? Wasn't he next to you, Tessa?"

She swiveled her head around and searched the forest. "Yes. I saw him just a couple of minutes ago. Come to think of it, where is Keeper Fabek and Phin?"

They all left their specific grids and journeyed further afield, peering in between the branches and trunks of the walnut trees. KameKona shouted out, "Keeper Fabek!" and raced to the edge of the grove.

They found him on the ground, blinking dazedly and rubbing his head. Tessa went behind him and peered between his fingers.

"He's bleeding. It looks like he was hit on the back of his head."

Aedan looked into Keeper Fabek's eyes. "Keeper Fabek, sir. Do you know what happened?"

Keeper Fabek made eye contact with him. "To push is to shove, to shove is to push." He grabbed Aedan's arm and shook it. "Can't let the guard notice. Quota not met. We must keep going."

Aedan glanced at the others. "I think he's confused. We shouldn't move him in case he has a head injury."

KameKona glanced around. "We still need to find Demyan and Phin."

Tessa jumped back up. "KameKona, let's look around for them while Aedan watches Keeper Fabek. After that, one of us must head back and get help."

The two split up and circled the walnut grove.

Tessa cried out. "Phin is over here!" She bent down to look at him lying on the ground as if taking a nap. What appeared to be the remains of a tasty snack fanned out around Phin's muzzle. Tessa bent down and sniffed the food and Phin's mouth.

"Guys, I think he was poisoned! I smell something sickly sweet and he's sleeping deeply." She stood up, her eyes wide in alarm. "This was planned. Whomever did this was waiting for an opportunity and we just gave it to them!"

KameKona rushed over and confirmed Tessa's observation. "Look, Demyan's gone. I think he was taken. Are either of you familiar with horses?"

Aedan stood up. "Yes, I grew up near my gran's horses."

KameKona nodded. "Okay. Aedan, why don't you ride Blue Peter back to campus and find staff to get up here. Tessa and I will watch Keeper Fabek and Phin. We also need either Dr. Kelley or Nurse Hestia."

Aedan nodded and hurried off, while Tessa and KameKona picked up Phin and brought him over to Keeper Fabek and laid him by his side.

"It will give Keeper Fabek comfort," Tessa stated sadly. Keeper Fabek mumbled incoherently and patted his dog.

Ming caressed the binding of the original text in her hand. She loved the feel of an ancient book. To have access to the first edition was amazing; she still couldn't believe they were allowed to actually touch these rare books, albeit under careful supervision.

She was thrilled she could reference them when writing her ability paper. Although engrossed in her work, she heard the gentle movements of both Tú and Élise as they researched their own sources.

Suddenly, Élise stood up and ran to the library entrance and threw open the door. Her abrupt movement alerted the others and they rose in curiosity, Heikima included. They saw Aedan jump from the box seat of the wagon and run toward the Wellness Center.

Heikima bolted out the door and called out to Aedan. "Scholar Aedan, what's happened? What do you need?"

Aedan turned around abruptly. "The walnut groves! Keeper Fabek is injured and Demyan is missing!"

Heikima's hands covered her mouth in shock. "I'll get the other Keepers. You stay on course, Scholar Aedan!" She turned back around to her three charges, ready to relay the information.

Ming, anticipating her next steps, jumped in. "We'll close up here, Keeper Heikima, don't worry."

Heikima nodded and ran off.

Ming turned and looked at Tú and Élise. "What happened? Since Aedan was with them, I figured they'd find the watch easily."

Élise wrinkled her brow. "I'm not sure. They even had Keeper Fabek and Phin with them. They followed the rules."

Tú ruffled his hair. "Let's quickly tidy up here and see how we can help."

All three jumped to it and got busy putting away materials. Ming headed toward the rare book cabinet to return the volume Keeper Heikima had loaned her. She took a second to marvel that it was unlocked.

Heikima, although welcoming and encouraging to her students, was proprietary over the rare volume cabinet. She kept those books under lock and key and they were only perused on site and under her constant supervision. Ming respected the rules, but couldn't resist the pull of curiosity, just for a moment.

She ran her fingers along the spines and quickly read their titles. There were incredibly valuable first printings of works such as Shakespeare's plays and *The Origin of Species* by Charles Darwin. She pulled a copy of *A Midsummer Night's Dream* and turned the first page. There appeared to be an inscription, which Ming quickly read. She cocked an eyebrow and shrugged, and quickly replaced it.

"Ming, are you ready to go?" Tú questioned.

"I'm just coming." She rose from her knees and was about to close and lock the cabinet when she noticed something. She pulled another volume off the shelf and looked at it more closely. She glanced at the first couple of pages. Some vague and ephemeral thought was swirling around her mind, niggling at her. She put that book away and took out another one right next to it and another. Again, she flipped through the first two pages as the thought began to take form. She put those two back and rapidly took out the next two and repeated the same action.

She inhaled sharply and looked into the heart of the library without focusing. "Oh, my—"

"Ming!" shouted Élise. "We have to go!"

Ming raced to return the last two books, locked the cabinet, and ran over to Heikima's desk. She placed the key under her tea cup, a cobalt blue ceramic mug that read *My other cup is a tankard of mead* in gold medieval-style lettering, and ran out of the library, thoughts turning to Demyan and the crisis at hand.

Alegria stayed with Tú, Élise, and Ming at the Wellness Center, while Aedan and the others sped as fast as they could in the wagon back to the walnut grove. Dr. Kelley and Nurse Hestia drove ahead in the school's ambulance truck.

At Alegria's urging, they gave her an accounting of what prompted the return to the grove. Tú mentioned Demyan's distress and his determination to find the watch. Élise discussed the plan of who would accompany Demyan and the necessity of taking a Keeper with them, aware they were not allowed to go by themselves.

Alegria listened intently, until she shoved a hand in the pocket of her pants. "Excuse me, my apologies." She quickly pulled out the black velvet pouch and upended the contents into her left palm. The faceted crystal and brass hammer rested in her open hand. She stared at the crystal and absorbed its vibrations, concentrating. She nodded in agreement.

"Dr. Kelley and Nurse Hestia are on their way back here with Keeper Fabek and Phin." She put up her right palm, halting any interruption. "Fabek is stable and was apparently jumped—this is coming from Reese. You all stay here with me and observe Dr. Kelley and Nurse Hestia, okay? We'll get more information when they return."

She took the little hammer and began to send her response by striking the crystal gently several times with precise taps in a halting fashion, some close together and others a little further apart. Élise's face lit up as she realized that she could follow some of Alegria's response.

Both Tú and Ming had a similar reaction, albeit a bit slower than Élise's.

"Roger that—taking the— I lost the rest," Élise stated.

Alegria replaced the two items in the pouch and re-pocketed them. "Excellent. You are all making good progress. I communicated that we were at the 'brew house.' It's Keeper Reese's name for the Wellness Center, since Nurse Hestia is always 'cooking up' her remedies—yes, I know." She shook her head, chagrined. "We ought not to encourage him. Anyway, let's go and see how Keeper Fabek and Phin are doing."

In the heart of the walnut grove, a similar conversation among the Keepers and other scholars was transpiring. Tessa was shedding frustrated tears and wiping them away haphazardly with a sleeve.

She wailed, "We followed the rules! How could this happen? It's broad daylight! We just wanted to help him!"

Sahila ran a calming hand down Tessa's hair.

"We understand you all just wanted to help him and we're going to find him. Listen." She lifted Tessa's chin up with her hand to make eye contact. "We'll go over every step of what happened, I promise. Right now, however, let's take a deep breath, clear our heads, and look around us. We need to find any clues, any evidence, that can help us find Demyan faster and catch the people who took him. Okay?"

Tessa sniffed and wiped her nose on her other sleeve. "Okay," she said dispassionately.

Reese put his hands together. "Thank you, Scholars, for bein' so forthcoming. We're lookin' for any item that seems unnatural in this space. No object is too small: hair strands, unusual rocks or metal, paper, the leftover snacks fed to Phin, anythin' at all, right? I've got evidence bags for whatever you find; just shout out, okay?" Everyone nodded soberly. "Go to it."

Tessa, Aedan, and KameKona started from Demyan's search area and radiated outward. Everyone else went to the perimeter of the grove and worked inward. The ominous sounds of leaves crunching and sticks cracking were amplified in the otherwise silent wood. The invading humans halted any hidden wildlife activity and created an atmosphere of desperate foreboding; time was critical and every minute lost drifted them further from the recovery of a precious life.

Everyone focused on their particular area; they scattered fallen leaves with precise fingers or the end of a tree limb, like primates searching for concealed grubs, and ran their eyes down tree trunks looking for a careless trace of traumatic residue.

Tessa quieted her mind and filtered out extraneous forest noise. Her favorite crystal lens was in her right hand, between her thumb and forefinger. Similar to an owl hunting for prey, Tessa kept a laser-like gaze on the ground, searching for any unusual light emanating from the forest floor.

The lens in her hand was as much for comfort as well as a tool. She hoped it would help detect anything unusual or foreign beneath her feet. Her left hand was parallel to the forest floor, sensing any residual heat signature from a quartz crystal. Instinctively, she undulated her fingers, like the antennae of a caterpillar carefully navigating its way across an unknown surface.

The intensive energy search was all encompassing; she was never so glad for her ADHD than she was at this moment. Her keen ability to hyperfocus, excluding all else, was now an essential skill. Her surprised exclamation radiated throughout the grove. She quickly, but expertly, cleared away partially eaten acorns and other detritus and honed in upon her find.

She didn't dare touch it with her fingers. Reese and Sahila, nearby, rushed over but gave her a wide berth lest they disturb the clearing. They peered down at the tiny clear quartz crystal the size of a seed bead, dotted with minuscule particles of earth.

"Scholar Tessa, you brilliant gem!" Sahila whispered in admiration.

Reese bent closer and handed Tessa a small plastic bag. "Ripper, Scholar Tessa! Hold up."[227] He pulled a rectangular leather case from the inside pocket of his jacket and tugged on the zipper.

Tessa's eyes widened in surprise. "Is that a—"

He selected a pair of tweezers from his set of lockpicking tools and handed them to her before she could reply.

"A jack of many trades needs a multitude of tools," he quipped. Despite their rush, he felt a pressured obligation to seize the teachable moment. He exhaled a relieved sigh. "Now, I can also agitate the crystal and draw it to me, right? But we can't do that in this situation. It's an important skill, but that technique can remove possible evidence. Understand, Scholar Tessa?"

She nodded at his explanation and he gestured for her to proceed. Tessa very carefully picked up the tiny crystal with the tweezers and placed it in the bag. She impulsively wanted to examine it, but knew they needed to wait till they returned to campus proper.

Reese took the proffered bag and looked at Sahila and the others. "I think we've done a pretty thorough search. We need to head back and get this under a microscope, yeah?"

Although the chemistry lab had excellent microscopes, Dr. Kelley had both a stereo and a compound microscope.

---

227 Ripper – Australian slang for great

The stereo used lower magnification and clearly showed a 3-D image; it was frequently utilized by forensic crime laboratories.

By the time Reese and his protégé arrived at the Wellness Center, Fabek and Phin were resting and recovering. As Tessa had surmised, Keeper Fabek was attacked from behind and unfortunately, never saw his assailants.

After examining the contents of Phin's stomach, Dr. Kelley and Nurse Hestia found that his meaty snack was coated with a canine anesthetic. They suggested the obvious conclusion: Phin was given the food prior to Fabek's attack, rendering him too sleepy to come to his master's aid.

Relieved that both were out of danger, attention now turned to locating Demyan. Acting as Reese's assistant, Tessa carefully removed the crystal with the tweezers and placed it on a thin clear glass plate. Evren and Alegria stood with the students and observed.

Both Reese and Sahila, as well as Tessa, took turns observing the crystal with their naked eye. Aside from almost microscopic bits of dirt, there appeared to be tiny amounts of a yellowish substance on the crystal as well. Placing it under the microscope didn't immediately clarify what it was.

After a minute of reflection, a theory began forming in Tessa's mind. As if she needed the bolster in confidence and support, her fingers grasped the ring Keeper Dya gave her and twisted it as her thoughts crystallized. "I think I know what it is!"

Reese and Sahila looked at her inquisitively, encouraging her to continue.

"It's earwax! I thought of it because my mom once had to take my brother to a specialist to remove a tiny piece of paper he had shoved into his ear canal while at school.

They also found a tiny pebble that he'd apparently put in there as well."

Dr. Kelley and Nurse Hestia took turns peering into the microscope lens to verify her hypothesis. Dr. Kelley grabbed a small cotton swab, gently ran it along the crystal, and placed it on a thin glass microscope slide. She inserted that under the microscope for her and Nurse Hestia to examine. "It most definitely is earwax. Excellent powers of observation, Scholar Tessa!"

Sahila and Reese glanced at each other, as if sifting through one another's memories and knowledge. Sahila's hands covered her mouth in horror as the realization hit her.

"Of course! It all makes sense! I can't believe we didn't discover it earlier."

Reese glared at her, impatiently waiting for her explanation.

"Whoever took Demyan had placed this crystal and another one just like it into his other ear canal before he even arrived on campus! It was the only way they could track his whereabouts without our knowledge! No wonder he reacted the way he did to the gems in the rock room and to the loaded stones placed in his personal kit!"

Reese snapped his fingers as it all came together. "As well as in the library! It explains his unusual sensitivity to the effects of those stones. The crystals in his ears amplified their signature frequency and made him more vulnerable to their toxic negative emotions. The poor kid's been compromised since he arrived here! And it explains why we experienced the issues with the personal kits, the incident at Colonial Williamsburg, and the gem left in the library."

Reese slammed his hands on the counter in anger. Although normally congenial and approachable, he now exuded the animosity and malevolence he encountered routinely outside the safety of the college walls.

"The bastards were testing him! They wanted to see his capabilities and they didn't mind hurting him in the process! He's lucky his ear drums weren't ruptured! We'd never know until he went to Nurse Hestia and Dr. Kelley in intense pain. Or he might have dropped out of school, thinking he couldn't handle the intensity of our program!"

Sahila nodded unhappily. "The possibility exists that they were testing us as well."

Reese ran a hand through his hair. "Yes, that thought occurred to me as well. We have them now, however!" he growled as he looked around the room. "Even without the crystal, we would find him. But with it, we'll find him much, much sooner!" He looked at his charges and pointed to the crystal. "Scholar Tessa did a great job locating this one—a real needle in a haystack, honestly. We didn't find another one, however, and we were thorough. So that means the other one is likely still in his other ear canal and we can track him that way." He wandered over to Dr. Kelley and asked her to place the crystal back into the evidence bag. "We'll use the Debilis's own tactic to get Demyan back!" he all but roared.

"Let's head over to the residence hall and get these heroes settled before we organize a search party." At the students' concerned looks, Sahila added, I'll explain later."

Dumisani and Sahila sat with the students by the common room fire while Nalin clarified.

"We'll be able to locate Scholar Demyan fairly quickly using the crystal Scholar Tessa found. Assuming that the other crystal remains on Scholar Demyan's person, what do we know about the other crystal?"

Aedan raised his hand. "It's most likely the same size and shape as the one Tessa found and has a nearly exact frequency."

Nalin nodded her head. "Exactly. And why can we make that assumption?"

Each student looked around, expecting one of them had the answer.

"It's okay. It may not be obvious, especially because we haven't studied that in anatomy and physiology yet. Our ears are used for hearing, obviously, and the cochlea is responsible for that. But maintaining balance is the other responsibility of the ear and that's handled by the vestibular system. It's why pressure when diving or altitude when hiking is important to consider.

"Human beings, which encompasses Commoners as well as us, are affected by balance issues. If the crystals were different sizes or types, Scholar Demyan would likely be experiencing vertigo, headaches, nausea, or some other problem related to balance and we know that he was not suffering from any of those symptoms. Before we disperse, so our staff can plan Scholar Demyan's retrieval, are there any questions?"

Tessa raised her hand tentatively. "Have you seen this tactic used before by Debilis?"

Nalin raised an eyebrow. "That's an excellent question, Scholar Tessa. I believe the answer is yes, but Reese would know for sure. I'll find out for you. We have seen many unusual tactics over the centuries and we always manage to best our antagonists; we will find him," she stated confidently.

Chapter 31 – Ga

Unknown Location

# EARLY NOVEMBER

Rua-Jian Chu walked into the clean, nondescript, fairly isolated rented farmhouse with a satisfied smile. They were surprisingly ahead of schedule and this pleased him immensely. After all, it was best practice to under-promise and over-deliver to impress your client. This was, of course, in reference to his sanctioned projects around the globe. His staff were not aware that this current enterprise was his pet project and enlightening them was unnecessary.

His operatives were largely competent, with a few under-performers in the mix. As with natural selection, these individuals were quickly sloughed off, having hoisted themselves on their own petards,[228] and left to fend for themselves.

Rua-Jian walked into the living room of the house and was greeted almost instantly. Two of his most proficient staff approached him and bowed.

"Master Rua-Jian Chu, good morning to you sir."

---

[228] Petard – French word for breaking wind or blowing something up; therefore, hoisting oneself on one's own petard suggests someone does themselves in with a poor decision. It was used by Shakespeare in *Hamlet*, Act 3, Scene 4

Rua-Jian nodded his head and inquired, "And how is our young guest faring today?"

Larisa, the more nurturing of the four people involved, gestured for him to follow her to an upstairs bedroom. "He is still wary and only responding with one-word answers. I have no doubt this will change with time as we continue to work with him, however. As I told you before, I know his family, and his father is stoic and aloof. His mother is loving, but is deferential to her husband. Young Demyan is used to this dynamic and tends to turn inward when stressed; he is protecting himself, naturally, but I am not concerned."

Halldar, Rua-Jian's chief Debilis gem hunter, approached and waited to be acknowledged.

"Master Rua-Jian Chu, shall I begin his conversion education? From my observations and from our GeoEvolution clandestine analysis, young Demyan is capable of becoming a skilled gem hunter, a Resogem."

Halldar pulled out a rectangular box lined with lead from his pants pocket. Inside were two large gems, an emerald and a sapphire. "The ruby was less potent than these and he found it quickly; he's very receptive and I can begin immediately."

Rua-Jian Chu's looked inside the box and fingered the stones briefly and closed the lid. "Halldar, I appreciate your enthusiasm, but I will remind you that we are dealing with a young and impressionable mind. Much as I value your expertise, you must realize that even a short amount of time spent with these emotive stones will overwhelm and short circuit his mind. And I was clear with you about this earlier. Turning this boy into another gem hunter is a poor use of a valuable resource. I want to insert a loyal agent—an inside man, so to speak—who can become my eyes and ears into the most selective and unique institution in humanity's history. When that task is accomplished, and after a period of study, I can decide whether to destroy the college and its sister institution in Cambridge or restructure it to my purposes. I will take my time with this process. Do I make myself clear?"

Halldar bent low again and acquiesced. Larisa walked Rua-Jian up the stairs and to the door.

"He's in here, Master Rua-Jian Chu, sir."

Rua-Jian knocked on the door and waited for an answer. When none arrived, he knocked again and opened the door. He quietly entered and noticed Demyan sitting on a braided rug on the floor, his knees brought up to his chest and his head down.

"Oh, young Demyan, come now! I have it on good authority that the chairs are very comfortable in here! I arranged for them myself." Rua-Jian sat in the chair next to the desk and placed his hands on his knees. "I hope the food and accommodations are to your liking, Demyan. We have gone to great lengths to make your stay here quite pleasant. You will even see a stack of books on the bookshelf for you to enjoy.

"My name is Master Rua-Jian Chu and I have brought you here because you are a bright and unique student. Your parents are concerned that your education is not progressing at the pace that it should. And your uncle and aunt are eager to work with you in the future and want to make sure that you become an expert in your field."

Rua-Jian looked to Larisa and motioned for her to enter the room. He placed a hand in his pocket and brought out a small silver coin. It danced across each finger below his knuckles before he flipped it over toward Demyan. The coin landed exactly on Demyan's left knee.

Distracted from his purposeful ambivalence, Demyan saw the coin and was drawn to it despite himself.

"It's fascinating, isn't it? It's a coin from Alexander the Great's reign, minted in 324 BC, and made from the finest Persian silver. It's a gift for you. I imagine that your uncle will appreciate it when you show it to him."

Demyan reluctantly looked up at his sudden benefactor and found Rua-Jian sitting, relaxed, with his hands linked together and resting over his crossed legs. On one finger was a ring with a large square stone; it was sea green with white stripes and small patches of light brown. Demyan recognized it as amazonite and grew alarmed. He turned away, but not before Rua-Jian shifted the stone subtly on his finger, making it look more vibrant in the afternoon sunlight.

"Demyan, I know that you are pleased to be here. And you will be eager to begin your studies tomorrow. We value your loyalty to your family and are impressed with your growing ability. Your school is withholding valuable information that will keep you safe and will make you far more powerful than you ever thought possible."

Demyan glanced sharply at Rua-Jian with obvious skepticism.

"I know you are eager to have your freedom when you are older, to be released from your father's demands and expectations." Rua-Jian wiggled the ring again, although Demyan didn't see it. "I'll be back tomorrow. Enjoy your dinner; I understand that it's pizza night and I'm rather jealous."

Rua-Jian left Demyan alone and headed back downstairs.

"I expect you will work with him per my instructions, Larisa."

She executed a stiff bow and queried, "Sir, shall I remove the other quartz from his ear canal?"

He waved dismissively. "No. I don't want to cause him any unnecessary discomfort at the moment; it's of no consequence that it remains. And Halldar, we need to maximize the impact of the two crown gemstones. I want you to arrange a private sale in Brazil and Australia, one stone in each country. They have some of the largest mining holdings worldwide. Ensure the buyer has great influence within the highest echelons of their governments; no one lower than their leader's senior most trusted political staff. Don't squander the opportunity. Reese Rolding is currently preoccupied and won't have time to task his close associates with anticipating any unusual impending sales. I expect nothing less than perfection, understood? The price is negotiable. It's more important they are placed into impressionable hands. Is that clear?"

Rua-Jian walked out of the house after Halldar promised to comply.

CHAPTER 32 – Ge

COLLEGE OF GEOEVOLUTION

# EARLY NOVEMBER

The staff meeting in the dining hall was tense. Chef provided excellent cabernet sauvignon and mead from Williamsburg for those in need of a bit more than coffee or tea. Not only was it necessary to formulate a grand plan, but it was also imperative to understand what had recently transpired.

Dumisani held up his hands in a calming gesture. "We have two main goals at the moment, that is certain. I, for one, believe that Fabek's prognostication was correct. At our schools, we've been spared this type of interest and infiltration for decades. Yet recently, four attempts were made to harass our school and scholars in some fashion. And unfortunately, the last attempt was *temporarily* successful and it appears that some or all of these events have centered around young Scholar Demyan.

"So, that is where I want to begin tonight, before we plan our immediate rescue. As an aside, I already contacted Demyan's parents and have sent a Guardian emissary; they are understandably upset and frightened. I am certain that if we don't rescue Scholar Demyan in the next few days, they will involve Commoner law enforcement. I don't have to remind you that this action will only serve to jeopardize the lives of both Scholar Demyan and any Commoners involved."

Sahila stood up to address the group. "Reese and I are in agreement. Scholar Demyan has the potential to become an exceptional Resogem. His natural aptitude is higher than any student we've seen here in a long while. What Reese and I thought was sensitivity or youthful inexperience in Demyan might actually be the result of the crystal ear spyware. We'll make sure to further study that when we bring him home.

"The mystery we have before us, however, is *why* some intelligent force has an interest in our particular budding Resogem. At this point in his education and ability, he's no more promising than the handful of our other students or adult Resogems in the world." She sat with a tight smile, her anxiety readily evident on her face and in her gestures. "I'll let Reese take it from here."

Reese stood up and ruffled his hair, venting frustration. "First and foremost, I checked with my Keeper and Guardian contacts, including those within Interpol, the CIA, and a multitude of domestic law enforcement agencies. From the few who responded thus far, I verified my understandin' that there is a history of quartz crystal spyware and tracking.

"Intelligent Debilis cartels occasionally use it to infiltrate Commoner businesses, political groups, or government offices. When employed, they can be very dangerous. Individuals can be closely tracked and if the crystal is negatively loaded, it can induce severe mental illness. We've seen that historically in a few world leaders throughout history."

Nalin tugged on her turtle necklace, anxious. "To my knowledge, this approach isn't utilized frequently; it's difficult to employ, even under the most optimal circumstances."

Reese continued. "You are correct, Nalin. It doesn't immediately come to mind, because it's rarely used. Our Order doesn't need it, since our network is vast and reliable, and we frown upon such exploitative practices. Employing obtrusive methods on a frequen' basis over time will fracture our sacred code and makes us weak. The better alternative is to keep our network loyal, flexible, and resilient, and for us to stay vigilant. Debilis don't usually employ it because they are not that cunning, nor very organized. Which leads us to Fabek's belief…" He gestured to Sahila and Evren. "We believe Demyan's kidnapping is part of a larger, organized plan of attack. As talented as he may become, there are a lot of easier ways for a Debilis crime organization to acquire a competent Resogem."

He tapped his knuckles on the table and sat down. Evren gave Reese a brief smile as he took his turn at center stage.

"I never like to be the bearer of unpleasant news, but I'm deeply concerned, as is Jürgen, that we are potentially seeing the resurrection of an enemy we thought permanently vanquished long ago. We know that it's been a Debilis goal to destroy not only our college and university, but to eradicate our very Order, much like what was done to the Knights Templar in the 1400s by King Philip the IV of France. Our continual growth and resilience remain the biggest threat to Debilis efforts to gain any permanent traction in this modern world. Only a capable Debilis leader can mount this kind of offensive. Jürgen and I have no solid evidence to substantiate this claim, but with Reese, we are mounting a comprehensive investigation."

The reactions around the table ranged from incredulity to horror.

"Jürgen," Alegria lamented, "can this be a real possibility?"

He looked at her sorrowfully. "I'm afrai' so, pet. We'll get through, bes' we can."

She cleared her throat and stood. "I don't think it's out of the realm of possibility that Demyan was taken solely for his innate abilities, but also for the purpose of espionage. Perhaps whomever is responsible is training him to become his agent. We've heard rumors for years about Debilis trying to infiltrate our Order and education system."

Sahila stood so quickly her chair toppled over. "If that happened and we didn't initially realize it, think how many centuries of our secret and proprietary knowledge would be stolen? Not to mention an innocent child would be sacrificed and likely turned into a Debilis!"

Evren wiped his forehead, intense concern displayed on his face. "Think how a 'turned' Demyan could sabotage our relationships with our other students and fill them with lies; he might manipulate them to leave the college—or worse."

"We trust our students. What if they began attacking us or stealing from the secure gem room, offering those dangerous items to Debilis?" Alegria rubbed a hand over her heart. "I feel sick."

"Worse come to worst, if they overpowered us and took control, they might use our communication systems to send out contrary or dangerous orders," Reese offered.

Dumisani cradled his chin between a thumb and index finger and released a deep sigh. He took a moment to compose himself, nodding.

"Thank you all for your candor and well-justified concerns. I want you to update your Keeper and Guardian contacts and have them intensify their search for any unusual activity. When we do find Scholar Demyan, we need to keep in mind the trauma he has likely experienced; coerced hypnosis to become an operative is possible." Dumisani released another pent-up sigh and glanced at the ceiling, before looking at Reese. "Reese, although I'd like you at the forefront of this overall investigation, I imagine I can't tear you away from rescuing Demyan; am I correct in that assumption?"

Reese placed his fists to his forehead and leaned back. "With all due respect, Dumisani, I'll not leave till we get him back."

Dumisani steepled his fingers on the desk and treated each Keeper to a penetrating glance. "All right. What is the plan?"

# CHAPTER 33 – As

## COLLEGE OF GEOEVOLUTION

The convertible and two nondescript sedans drove slowly down the country road. The hazard lights blinking on the convertible lent credibility to its meandering pace; passing drivers were forgiving as thoughts of a flat tire drifted through their minds. Salima, Dumisani's falcon, followed the caravan flying discreetly along the nearby tree canopy.

Nalin sat in the front passenger seat in the convertible, her hair pulled tightly into a thick side braid since the car roof was retracted. To any onlooker, she appeared to be taking a nap in the morning sun while Dumisani drove.

In her dominant open palm, however, sat a small, thimble-sized silver bowl with a flat bottom. It was unadorned, bare of any decorations or etchings. Placed inside the bowl was the quartz crystal found by Tessa. About every thousand feet, Nalin tapped the bowl with an equally tiny silver tuning fork and listened with a deep concentration.

The technique was ancient and simple, but took decades of training for even a Keeper of Nalin's exceptional ability to master. Each time she used the fork, Nalin was listening for a reciprocal ping from the crystal, which was amplified by the silver bowl. In addition, she attended to the amount of time that passed between using the fork and when—and if—she received a responding sound.

The process was similar to active sonar used in military ships or submarines, albeit sparingly, when searching for other vessels. A military submarine used the system judiciously, since it would also alert others in the area to their own location. Similarly, Nalin felt for any vibration response from the crystal that hopefully remained in Demyan's ear canal. Though the two stimuli were distinct, one a vibration and the other a sound, understanding the relationship between the two was complicated and challenging.

This crystal connection resembled their personal communication devices. Of all elemental metals on the periodic table, silver conducted energy the most effectively. Copper came in a close second and thus was frequently used in electrical wiring by Keepers and Commoners alike.

The process was slow and inexact and the caravan made several false turns before Nalin became confident in the legitimate quartz connection—the pings and vibrations now followed one another very closely; it was a relief to all Keepers when their assumption was verified that Demyan was fairly close.

The cabs of all three vehicles remained quiet as team members were either helping track Demyan or mentally preparing themselves for certain battle, one in which failure wasn't an option. Each brought their particular expertise, their ability, honed like an intimidating weapon. Only Reese brought additional hardware, his collection of Ninja shuriken, commonly known as throwing stars.

Traditional Japanese shuriken were designed to distract and wound an opponent, not kill them. It was the perfect weapon for Reese; a well-thrown shuriken surprised his quarry and gave him precious seconds, allowing him to disarm and subdue his opponent.

Reese's shuriken were specially designed for him: the four-sided pinwheel shape was forged from tempered steel and each blade was edged with copper. When painfully removed from the targeted Debilis appendage, small amounts of copper remained in their bloodstream, increasing their body's conductivity. This made them vulnerable by hampering their movements and poisoning them internally. The vulnerability increased the potency of a Keeper's targeted assault. When working on a team, this tactical advantage helped everyone.

Reese's use of shuriken was judicious, however. In many countries and in some US states, shuriken were prohibited and with good reason. Reese only took them when he expected encounters with nefarious and proficient Debilis.

Before they left, Dumisani reminded them of their sacred code. The taking of even a Debilis life came with consequences for the victor; there was always a mark left on the soul that needed addressing, lest it fester and grow, like damage to an apple's flesh. Ending the life of a Debilis while rescuing Scholar Demyan was allowed, but each Keeper understood and accepted the repercussions.

When the vibrations and audible pings became almost constant, Nalin gestured to Dumisani that Scholar Demyan's prison was a house on the left.

"I'm going to bypass the house and turn left at the next intersection. We'll park on the nearby Farm Road, near the copse of trees," he whispered. "And approach on foot."

When parked, they headed toward the house in groups of two and advanced from different directions at varying paces, trying to remain as inconspicuous as possible. This would prove difficult, however, as the house was located in a farming community, where few groupings of trees remained. Adding to the complexity, the crops were already harvested and the ground was fallow, making a stealthy approach tricky. Salima swooped down and landed gracefully on Dumisani's shoulder.

While walking to the house, Sahila selected the two stones she wanted and began warming them, ensuring the energy between the two flowed freely. She and Dumisani reached the house first and as Sahila climbed the stairs, Dumisani hugged the side of the porch, just out of view.

She took a deep breath and knocked on the front door, confident the jade and rhodonite stones between her fingers were positively loaded and ready. After a full minute, the door was opened by a tall gentleman sporting a scowl. He was dressed in worn jeans and an old sweater—clothing expected of a farmer on a winter work day. Sahila smiled warmly and made direct eye contact.

"Good day to you, sir. I need you to release the young man imprisoned in your house. You will feel a great sense of relief and know it is what's best for the child. This work isn't fulfilling and you have a dream you are not pursuing, am I correct?"

Sahila channeled all her energy into manipulating the thoughts of the Debilis. He looked at her with a perplexed expression, but was visibly fighting the onslaught. He began sweating profusely and blinking rapidly. Suddenly, his eyes rolled back into his head as he teetered back and forth on his feet.

Sahila scowled in concentration. "You have an emptiness inside you and are desperate to fill it with a purpose. You can free the child and free yourself; you can take my car."

The man walked fully onto the porch and rubbed his hands together rhythmically, as if in a trance.

The front door remained open and a second man rushed through. He elbowed his disoriented compatriot to the side, knocking him off the porch, and impaling him onto a thorny rose bush. "You won't fool me, vile witch!"

He flicked his wrist and sent a copper chain toward Sahila's neck. But before it reached her, a hand shot out and a visible wave of intense heat zapped into the chain and it radiated toward its owner. He screamed as the chain burned him, the copper cauterizing his palm.

"Much obliged!" Sahila grunted as she pivoted out of the way.

"Think nothing of it," Dumisani breathed as he flicked his wrist, directing the copper wire to snake and tighten around the man's ankles.

"He's going to be tied up for the foreseeable future!" Dumisani yanked a titanium rope from his coat pocket and tossed it onto the man's chest.

"Do you see any other immediate threats?" Sahila growled while looking around.

"Not at the moment!"

Dumisani's left palm faced the man and with fingers splayed like a starfish, he forced energy toward the titanium rope and concentrated on its transfer. It uncoiled and wrapped around the man's waist and a nearby sturdy pillar.

"Make it impossible for them to free that monster!" Sahila seethed, her normally tamed hair wild like Medusa's.

Dumisani whipped around to Sahila, hearing her uncharacteristic outrage.

"Trust me, there is no chance of that happening!" Dumisani grunted.

Squinting his eyes with a pinpointed focus, and circling his index finger in the air, he tied a constrictor knot and stuffed a handkerchief in the Debilis's mouth. Satisfied it was secure, Dumisani and Sahila glanced at the befuddled man who was enmeshed in the rose bush. He whimpered in pain.

"I won't sacrifice any energy to even care a bit," Sahila snarled.

Hearing a noise, they plastered themselves against either side of the front door, waiting for other Debilis to emerge.

Evren and Jürgen paused briefly to watch the revolting tableau on the porch.

"That's rather disturbing, even for Salima." Evren cringed.

Dumisani raised an eyebrow and risked a quick glance. True to his word, the imprisoned man had no chance of rescue. Salima had perched on his chest, glaring at her captive. When the Debilis groaned again, she pecked at his nose, drawing blood. When satisfied he would cause no further trouble, she proceeded to disembowel the dead mouse she had recently caught.

Dumisani jerked his head toward the house before Evren and Jürgen ran off. "I detect four more heat signatures inside; I'll send a quick message to alert the others."

As he and Jürgen raced to the back of the house, Evren shot out four fingers.

"There are three cars and a Ducati motorcycle parked at the back of the house."

Running as stealthily as possible, they rounded behind the vehicles and stopped about fifty feet away.

"Are you ready, Jürgen?"

"That's our young charge in there, Evren. 'Course I am!"

Splaying his feet wide for stability, Evren held out his hands parallel to the ground, each finger and palm sensing the earth, like finely tuned seismometers.

Although Evren could feel the vibrations of the earth with his shoes on without any enhancement, the soles of his shoes incorporated a dense mixture of silver, copper, and gold particles, which allowed his feet to detect any ground vibrations and amplify them even faster. Every pair he owned was specially made for him in Istanbul by Guardian cobblers.

Staring at the ground, Evren concentrated on the information his fingers and feet relayed to him…He sensed the faults in the earth below the surface—where the earth was less stable due to decades of crop rotation cycles, the location of rabbit and groundhog family burrows, and to his surprise, even the burial ground of several Indigenous Americans one hundred feet to the right, either Powhatan, Monacan, or Cherokee. These, thank goodness, were safely clear of the cement parking area.

Quick assessment complete, the energy from his hands and feet also sensed the vibrancy of the earth and its subtle tremors. He focused on the ground upon which the three cars rested and began to heighten its energy, targeting the weak dirt underneath and the small fissure created by nature thousands of years ago.

Interrupted, Evren jerked his head toward the house as he heard the sound of glass breaking. From the second-story window, he watched a sharp metal object hurtle toward him. He lunged just in time to avoid what he realized was an antique fireplace poker. It penetrated the back windshield of the first vehicle on the left and shattered it.

"Watch out!" Jürgen shouted, as another Debilis ran out the back door, this one sporting multiple throwing daggers, his arms wrapped in leather cuffs.

The Debilis shouted, "I knew I smelled something foul!" He flexed his fingers as he prepared himself for battle. He glanced at both men and lurched to attack Jürgen.

Evren doubled his efforts, a decision he never took lightly. He took great pride in his work and stressed the importance of precision and deliberation with his Techto[229] scholars. In rare instances when he purposely *caused* earthquakes, the safety of Commoners and their property was paramount.

He agitated the ground under the cars, targeting the portion of the fault just under the parking lot.

"No! Oww!"

Surprised by the earthquake, the Debilis near Jürgen screamed, his hand and knee slamming to the ground as the earth shook violently. A sink hole opened up close to the cars and they teetered near the gaping hole.

"Well done!" Jürgen bellowed over the cacophony.

Evren nodded sharply. "Let's remain focused, Jürgen!"

"Like two old English Yew trees in a turbulent storm!"

While Evren continued his task, Jürgen began drawing bits of earth from the new crevasse. His hands worked at lightning speed. To those passing by, he seemed to be pulling an invisible rope. His face looked fierce as he amassed rare earths, backhanding unwanted clumps away.

Between their efforts, a large cloud of dust formed, stinging their eyes as they worked. Jürgen, his particular rare earths collected, quickly built the prison around his foe. It was built so quickly, that between the dust and the gathered rare earths, the Debilis had little avenue for flight.

Desperate, the imprisoned Debilis threw three of his daggers; two missed Jürgen's head, but one embedded into his back.

---

[229] Techto – A Techto's inherent ability is sensing the vibrations and shifting of the earth to the depths of its internal crust. A Techto can sense when an earthquake is imminent from thousands of miles away, much faster than an expert Commoner can detect. If necessary, a Keeper can manipulate the earth to cause an earthquake of some magnitude, through harnessing the natural existing fault lines below the surface

"Ya feckless diddy,[230] that hurt! Now I'm really angry!" Jürgen snarled, his face red.

The dagger, slowed by his thick leather jacket, proved a minor nuisance—nothing a couple of stitches wouldn't fix. Jürgen sent up a prayer of thanks that the weapon wasn't dipped in poison; he well knew the telltale sensations.

"Beautifully rendered, Jürgen!" Evren smirked.

Jürgen took a deep breath as the jail was complete. It totally encompassed the prisoner, and despite being literally thrown together in haste, it would hold all but the most skilled Debilis.

Jürgen began to sweat as he further bonded the rare earth atoms together. Upon close examination, the individual elements navigated up and down the cairn like ants building a matte silver pyramid. The pieces found locations where they created their strongest bonds.

"There's little room for you to sit, let alone stand. Pity that!" Jürgen taunted.

The Debilis's remaining metal daggers flew to the magnetized walls of his cell and stuck fast.

Jürgen pivoted when he heard the loud wrenching and snapping of metal and the popping of inflated rubber. The three teetering vehicles folded onto themselves as they fell into the large jagged hole, their axles broken and most of the tires flat.

Only the Ducati remained, flung onto its side and hopelessly scratched. The shiny model was an elegant machine and the owner, who clearly appreciated expensive toys, would be most displeased.

"Ach, that's a right shame, that!"

---

[230] Diddy – Scottish slang for idiot

"It's a beautiful machine, I'll give you that, Jürgen!" Evren agreed.

Dumisani and Alegria bolted to the back of the house and glanced at the broken panes of the second-story window and the copper drainpipe that ran up the corner.

Alegria's brows furrowed. "What an alarming mess!"

Dumisani quickly updated everyone.

"At the moment, no one else has emerged out the front door. Nalin verified there are now three left inside: Scholar Damien and two remaining Debilis."

He motioned to Alegria and Evren and spoke sotto voce. "Grab hold of the copper drainpipe."

While they kept it secure, Dumisani and Jürgen quickly gathered rare earths, small bits of lingering steel, and other metals. When satisfied, they began layering it onto the drainpipe, creating a stronger alloy.

"Make it incredibly durable, Jürgen. The best you've got!" Dumisani commanded.

Waves of heat radiated from their hands and the drainpipe heated up immediately, but not enough to become a liquid metal mess. The pipe more resembled a sunken mast covered in barnacles.

"It won't garner modern sculpture praise," Alegria quipped, "but it can be scaled quickly by someone sure footed."

Dumisani, his arms held above his head, focused on the middle of the copper pipe and bent it toward the left window.

Slightly winded, Dumisani looked at Alegria sharply.

"All joking aside, my dear Alegria. Be careful climbing that pipe ladder, you understand?"

She patted three of Reese's shuriken that were snugly inserted inside a pouch attached to her belt.

Alegria offered her kinsmen a tight smile. "I promise I will. I'm always careful."

She began to climb the heated structure, Evren following closely behind. Once at the top, she whisper-hissed, "Close your eyes!"

Protected by her winter pea coat, Alegria knocked out the remaining glass with a few elbow jabs, and mindfully climbed inside. She hurried to the center of the room while looking around and waited for Evren to join her.

All was still.

Evren gestured that he would check the other spaces. His furtive search into a bathroom and closet revealed no other signs of life. Alegria took a deep breath as she reached the door, which provided access to the rest of the house.

*You ready?* she mouthed.

Speed was essential, but Alegria took a moment to analyze the knob using sight and sensation. Her hand hovering around the knob revealed no traps or hazards and her visual scan corroborated this conclusion.

*Okay. Let's go,* she communicated with her eyes and a flick of her head, and slowly opened the door.

Alegria looked above the door jam and around the hallway before she stepped out. She had a memory flash of newly graduated scholars attempting the tired prank of a bucket filled with unsavory liquid hung precariously over a door jam. In this case, if tried, the contents would undoubtedly be deadly.

She shook off the passing thought. Somewhere in this house were two more Debilis and a frightened Demyan. Evren jutted his chin to the right, indicating his intention to head in that direction. Alegria blew him a silent kiss and turned left.

The house was eerily quiet. Like the lingering scent of faded potpourri, the house retained the layered signatures of life, both present and long gone. People who were largely content with their labors and families lived here for decades. She felt the spirit of peace and love that permeated the house, like the first notes detected in a fine wine.

*Superimposed onto that*, she thought, *is the current sensation of malevolence and decay; I don't like it.*

It crawled slowly up her spine and she could almost hear the sounds of a waterphone[231] in the background. After thoroughly checking another bedroom on her left, she reached a third room at the end of the hall, the door slightly ajar.

In her right palm, she cradled a couple of her favorite activated obsidian rocks from Chile's Laguna del Maule volcanic region. From experience, she knew they were incredibly hot and malleable, although not quite at the magna stage. Even at this temperature, however, they were a formidable weapon.

She eased open the door with her left hand and looked around. Standing behind the couch to the left side of the room was a Debilis and Scholar Demyan. The Debilis stood directly next to him, holding his arm in a vise grip. Attached to her back was a sheathed katana sword, the hilt displayed over one shoulder.

She bared her teeth and hissed, "You needn't have come, Keeper Witch. The boy is in good hands."

Alegria calmly stated, "I doubt his frantic parents would agree with you. Release him unharmed to me, right now."

The Debilis replied coaxingly, "Demyan wants to remain with us, don't you?"

---

231  Le Marquand-Brown, Abigail. "10 Facts about the Waterphone." https://blog.oup.com/2017/08/10-fac ts-waterphone/

Demyan nodded subtly, but Alegria saw the abject terror in his eyes. "Yes, mistress. You are teaching me the valuable skills I am not learning at their worthless school."

Alegria looked piercingly into Demyan's eyes and made sure he connected with her freely and without influence. She released a quiet sigh of relief; they had arrived in time.

After regarding Alegria a moment, he conveyed her meaning and nodded almost imperceptibly. "I will not ask again. You must release him without harm immediately."

She felt Evren close by, just outside the room. The Debilis gripped Demyan's arm more tightly and in a blur of motion, drew her katana. Yet before she even had time to threaten Demyan with it, Alegria whipped an obsidian rock at the Debilis, hitting the hand wielding the weapon.

Demyan wrenched himself away from her, lobbed himself over the couch, and rolled toward the front of the room. While Alegria threw the second rock at the Debilis's neck, Evren grabbed Demyan and guided him out of the room.

"Well done, Scholar Demyan," Evren whispered.

"If I had the opportunity, I would have *burned* you at the stake!" the Debilis screamed as she cradled her hand toward her chest. Large red burns began to form and acrid smoke rose from the injuries; the smell of sulfur and rotting flesh permeated the room.

Alegria could hear Demyan gag as he was led down the hallway toward the stairs. She grabbed her titanium and lead cuffs and forced the Debilis's arms behind her back, handcuffing her expertly and securely.

She grabbed a hunk of the Debilis's hair, wrenched back her head, and spat, her teeth bared. "I would have liked to see you *try!* Do you *really* think I've forgotten all your transgressions? It's finally caught up to you, vile piece of putrid garbage! Your cycling days are *over!*"

Alegria searched the Debilis for more weapons, grabbed the katana, and left the room, heading toward the stairs. She had to get to Evren and Scholar Demyan in case they encountered the last Debilis.

"Ugh!" Alegria yelled. "I can still smell that vile harpy in my nose!"

The quick descent down the stairs was free of any obstacles. She left through the front door and met with Evren, Scholar Demyan, and half of the team.

"Nalin, Jürgen, and Sahila are at the back of the house," Reese barked. "The last Debilis hasn't emerged, so it must still be inside."

Alegria's eyes widened. "Evren and I thoroughly checked the upstairs. There is no attic or crawl space up there. I'll go back in and look." She turned to re-enter the house.

Reese grabbed her hand and halted her progress. "No. You've done amazing, love. I'll get the dero."

He raised his hand in a jaunty salute and entered the house, a shuriken at the ready. He immediately sensed the same oppressive spirit Alegria and Evren felt—a strong Debilis presence permeated the house. *This house isn't empty.* Reese slowly walked around the living room and entered the kitchen through an old-fashioned swing door. Those rooms were empty, save a neglected coffee cup or two.

"I should have flippin' known!" Reese grumbled.

He sighed in resignation as he headed into the dining room—the faint hint of familiarity became more pronounced as he moved forward. When he entered the room, he understood why.

The Debilis sat in a chair at the table, relaxed, hands around a steaming cup of tea.

"Somehow, I am not surprised you are the one to greet me," Rua-Jian Chu stated calmly. "I did tell you we would meet again at some point. It pains me greatly that it's under these circumstances. You never should have left, you know. I thought you would someday become my chief mercenary, not choose the path of the misguided Pollyannas," he sneered.

Reese's nostrils flared, smelling something distasteful. "I should have known it was you all along. To sit here quietly drinking tea while you try to brainwash another innocent recruit? That takes a special type of psycho."

Rua-Jian Chu raised an eyebrow and placed his palms flat on the table. "You were never innocent, Reese Rolding. I only offered you a home and a chance to purposefully channel your inherent skills. You instead chose to waste your life and have it end here, fighting me. Don't forget when I found you, that you were Exili."

"Stand up, you unrepentant psychopath. I have a traumatized child outside who needs attention." He leaned in and purposefully taunted him, because even in a dire situation, it was Reese's nature to push his luck. "I left because I knew you were doomed to be a complete failure, today being a perfect example."

Rua-Jian Chu stood with dignity, gently pushed in his chair, and sneered.

"I was actually enjoying my tea when you and your miscreants arrived. It's an interesting blend I found in your Colonial Williamsburg; I was pleasantly surprised for such a provincial town. Can you detect the scent of apricot and ginger? I've been waltzing all around you. Where was the legendary security I heard so much about?"

Reese held up one of his shuriken and wiggled it for emphasis. "Let's get on with it, old man. I only smell old rot an' dog farts."

Rua-Jian Chu audibly sighed as he grabbed the Himogatana stiletto off a nearby chair.

"I could never teach you proper manners, Reese. Some things never change."

Rua-Jian Chu stepped away from the table and approached him. When clear of the table, Reese pitched a shuriken at the hand holding the stiletto. Rua-Jian Chu was faster, however, and anticipated the maneuver. The stiletto caught the throwing star and he launched it into a nearby wall.

In a blur, Reese lunged forward, dropped to his knees, and rammed his shoulder into Rua-Jian's gut, just as he raised the stiletto. Before it connected, Reese wrapped his arms around Rua-Jian tightly and tossed him over his head in a classic wrestling move. Rua-Jian Chu was tall and imposing, but Reese was solid. Rua-Jian slammed onto the dining room table and flipped onto the floor, landing with an audible thud onto his stomach.

Although winded, Rua-Jian growled, "You think your so clever, boy, don't you!"

Reese drove his knee into Rua-Jian's back, making him wheeze.

Rua-Jian somehow managed to leer. "I see you have kept in shape," he said, his voice muffled by the dining room rug.

Reese anchored Rua-Jian's left arm and reached for his cuffs. Rua-Jian Chu's other arm was stuck under his body. Reese ignored his verbal jibe and concentrated. *Always be hypervigilant around this devil.*

He was set to cuff Rua-Jian's left arm when he felt a searing pain on his back. He arched for just a second to reach behind and feel the wound. His hand came back bloody, but no weapon was embedded.

Rua-Jian took that opportunity to bash his head into Reese's jaw and throw him off balance. He grabbed the stiletto, the culprit that created Reese's second injury, and escaped out a nearby door.

"Slimy piece of rodent dung." Reese growled.

Reese raced after him. The front door remained open.

Dumisani, Evren, and Sahila looked at him in alarm. Reese wiped the sweat from his forehead and sniffed.

"You didn't see him exit the door?"

Evren quickly shook his head. "No!"

Reese jerked his head in acknowledgement, blond hair flopping into his piercing blue eyes.

"Keep a look out. I almost had him! I'm going around to the back. Be careful, he's got a stiletto!"

Dumisani glanced at Evren and Sahila. "I'm going to look inside the house, in case he managed to evade Reese."

Multitasking, they nodded as they kept eyes on Scholar Demyan and their four prisoners, all cuffed, subdued, and brought to the front of the house.

Reese met with Nalin, Jürgen, and Alegria at the back.

"Has the last Debilis made an appearance?" Nalin asked.

"He got away from me, dammit!" Reese cursed.

Alegria looked on him in alarm. "Reese, you're bleeding!"

He smirked. "Just a flesh wound, darlin'." She rolled her eyes as he turned and headed toward the altered drainpipe. "Be prepared, in case he exits near you; he's armed with a stiletto."

Jürgen jolted toward the back door. "I'm goin' inside."

He stepped over the cache of Debilis weapons, purposely kept apart from the prisoners. Reese gracefully shimmied up the drainpipe and into the window.

He carefully surveyed the bedroom and found it empty. He reached for the door to the hallway, but stopped short, as he took a moment to chastise himself.

*Rua-Jian thrives on verbally sparring with those he intends to manipulate or conquer.*

Reese released a deep breath and centered himself.

*Be calm, cool, and collected, man.*

As he finished a thorough and uneventful search of all upstairs spaces, something Rua-Jian said came back to him. *He mentioned how he enjoyed the apricot and ginger tea he brewed in the kitchen.*

"Son of a schist!"

A memory of one of Rua-Jian's tactics slammed into him. Reaching the stairs, he grabbed a throwing star for protection and slid down the banister. After a 360-degree turn around the room, Reese encountered Dumisani.

"He's not upstairs, but I think he's employing xenon gas! He's done it before."

Dumisani threw his head back, horrified. When oxygen is liquified, xenon gas, an element, can be separated from the oxygen. *It's odorless, colorless, and tasteless and can cause dizziness, vomiting, confusion, and other dangerous side effects, including death,* Dumisani thought, furious.[232]

Using a sarcastic tone Reese whispered, "he's not using it to make a laser or a photography bulb, I can tell you that! I think he's pumping it through the house to confuse us,

---

[232] Xenon gas is illegal in sports, as it's used to enhance red blood cells and give an athlete an advantage over others.

to help mask his location! If I'm right, we're going to need some help to rapidly counteract it!"

Reese raced out the front door and checked on Demyan. "Are you all right, young Scholar Demyan?"

Demyan nodded and Evren looked down at the young student. "He's coping remarkably well."

Suddenly, they heard a muffled shout from the rear. Reese took a cleansing breath, readying himself to lend assistance, and smiled at Demyan as he jogged around the house, heading toward the shout.

Alegria's eyes rounded with horror and she opened her mouth to shout a warning. Much later, when she had time to reflect, she was appalled by her instant clinical reaction to the situation. Her fencing instructor's lecture came to mind.

*A katana makes what the Japanese call "tachikaze" or "sword wind," if the blade precisely follows its target trajectory—its path to properly cut its intended object. It makes a whistling sound that is sudden and sharp. When this occurs, the edge line or "hasuji" is correct. Will the intended recipient of the swing know of their impending fate? Sadly, they are often not able to confirm.*

Nurse Hestia explained it was a psychological protective mechanism, but it did little to relieve her torment.

It happened so quickly. Alegria's scream pierced the air. "Reese! Move!"

"What's wrong?" he yelled, pivoting to lend support, however it was needed. He watched, confused as Alegria and Nalin raced toward him.

From the corner of his eye, he saw the long, shiny elegant blade of a katana sword rush toward his neck.

*Schist, but I love my family.* He didn't feel a thing.

Alegria caught him as he fell and cradled him, wailing. The others reacted to the scream and ran to assist; it was all Evren could do to press Scholar Demyan's face toward his chest, averting his eyes.

"What a coward!" Alegria screamed. "He attacked Reese from behind!"

Jürgen and Nalin saw Rua-Jian Chu racing down the street.

"He's running away!" Jürgen shouted. He and Nalin ran after him.

Salima launched herself from Dumisani's shoulder and soared after them in hot pursuit. A minute later, her indignant shriek pierced the silence.

"No!" Nalin's distant yell rang out right before a heavy, dull *thump* was heard.

After what seemed like forever, Evren, his hands shaking, sent a message to Keeper Security alerting them that transportation was needed for potentially five criminals, if they intercepted the last Debilis. From Evren's brief glance, he believed the fleeing figure to be the legendary Rua-Jian Chu. Everyone sat silently, trying to process what just happened.

Jürgen and Nalin returned, solemn. Jürgen all but whispered, exhausted and subdued, "He managed to elude us; I can't believe we couldn't stop him."

Nalin gently cradled a bleeding Salima and approached Dumisani, tears flowing down her cheeks. "She's alive, but the despicable man threw his stiletto at her."

Conscious of their vulnerable ward, Evren and Nalin loaded up Scholar Demyan and headed back to school with the wounded Salima. The others sat around Reese and waited for security to take away the prisoners.

After a thorough interrogation, they would prepare the Debilis for the arduous journey to the Keeper prison on

Baffin Island, in Canada's Nunavut Province. If they could fully rehabilitate, they might become loyal Guardians. If not, a variety of other less pleasant fates awaited them.

An hour passed before security arrived.

"Jürgen," Dumisani quietly stated. "Let's search the house and find any remaining incriminating items."

Although it was soaked, Sahila continued to wipe her tears with Evren's handkerchief.

Dumisani looked at the sky, imploringly.

"I can't believe this happened; I just can't believe this happened."

They all knew returning tomorrow to cleanse the house and the grounds would be Nalin's job. She would pay particular attention to the Indigenous American burial ground, making sure it remained at peace.

Thinking about that, Jürgen added quietly, "I'll come back tomorrow with Nalin. She shouldn't come here herself."

Alegria was oblivious to the conversation around her as tears painted her face.

"You always had to have the last word, didn't you?" she whispered. "You always needed to step over the line." She brushed his hair from his forehead. "Your hair is such a mess."

In shock, Alegria didn't register the blood that soaked her clothes. His crystalline blue eyes, now vacant, only registered surprise.

Sitting now with Alegria, Sahila noticed this, bereft, and thought it apropos. Just as he was in life, he was never terribly stressed about anything.

Keeper Security arrived and loaded up the prisoners quickly and relatively quietly. The Debilis looked around for their leader and were surprised they were abandoned. It was a shock, apparently, that their venture had failed. It was an unexpected outcome.

"It was all arranged. We were told it would be easy."

"We were to be rewarded for our loyalty! Where is he?"

Dumisani stood in front of them, arms crossed. "You were part of an evil plan and we would never have allowed it to succeed. We are wounded, but we will never be vanquished."

He addressed Keeper Security. "Get them out of our presence. I want a full debrief after their questioning."

A member of security offered a large bag surreptitiously to Jürgen with words of support and Sahila took a walk to retrieve the second vehicle and parked it near the house.

Subconsciously, Alegria noticed Dumisani and Jürgen opening a bag and fiddling with it. To distract herself from the noise, she quietly sang a Scottish sea shanty to Reese that she knew he loved. Sahila hugged her and joined in the bawdy song, silently crying.

Jürgen approached Alegria. "My dearest heart, it's time to head back."

Alegria acknowledged him and nodded. She bent down, softly kissed Reese's lips, and closed his eyes.

Jürgen reverently took Reese's head from Alegria and added it to the bag.

CHAPTER 34 – Se

COLLEGE OF GEOEVOLUTION

The remaining caravan drove back slowly to the college in silence. Although Keepers were always prepared for the worst, to some extent, in their subconscious, the reality was a horrific shock. Various degrees of despair, anger, and disbelief cycled through each mind. Thick and expanding individual emotions left no room for conversation.

When they returned, Dumisani insisted on carrying Reese to the Wellness Center and Jürgen accompanied him. They brought him through the back entrance to avoid upsetting Demyan. There was a side room attached to the Wellness Center for a purpose such as this. Although rarely used in this capacity, the school's storied existence necessitated protocols for nearly every possibility. Since the cause of Reese's demise was not under question, an autopsy wasn't necessary.

In an adjacent room, Demyan was resting after a thorough physical exam. The remaining crystal was removed from his ear and reunited with the one Tessa located at the walnut grove. After a complete assessment, the pair would be incorporated into their physics; kinesiology; and human anatomy and physiology classes. "Your body is recovering quickly, Demyan," Dr. Kelly gently offered. She and Nurse Hestia agreed they would begin assessing him for emotional and psychological trauma the next day. Although he was spared the visual loss of his professor, he was still aware of his death. It would take time for everyone to come to terms with that horror.

"The specially trained Keeper Security group began the prisoners' interrogation process yesterday," Evren told his compatriots at the subdued staff debrief in their common room. Mentioning this was meant as a consolation of sorts, the first steps toward some measure of justice.

"Are you referring to the vermin responsible for our tragedy, Evren? Let's dispense with the official terminology! They don't deserve it." Sahila snapped.

Evren winced. "The Debilis prisoners are being held offsite at our isolated property nearby. You know you all are welcome to speak to any of them if you need closure, have specific questions, or need issues addressed."

Sahila's hands covered her mouth, mortified by her outburst. "Evren, I am so sorry; you are just doing your job and civility is helping us keep it together."

Evren placed a supporting hand on Sahila's shoulder and squeezed. "Don't apologize, Sahila, we are all still in shock and will be grieving for some time."

Dumisani and Sahila didn't look forward to updating their restless scholars in the residential wing. They were greeted by an overwhelming bouquet of teen anxiety, fear, and excitement. Sitting in the common room, Dumisani raised his hands to calm the group.

"Demyan is safe and resting in the Wellness Center. I anticipate he will be back here in a day or so. You will see him when he returns to the residence hall, where he will remain for the rest of the week. After that, I will be escorting him home for the time being. His parents, justifiably, want him back with them."

The relief in the room was palpable. To know that a member of their unusual little family was safe was significant. They trusted their college professors and administration. The rescue, for the most part, reinforced that their faith was well placed. Though shocked by the recent events, there was no going back to life before their arrival. Their new knowledge of the world could not be forgotten, so staying put was the safest bet.

"During the rescue, however," he continued, "we engaged a dangerous Debilis, one we thought already eradicated. I am sorry to report that we lost Keeper Reese in the process."

He was met with disbelief and confusion.

"What are you telling us, Keeper Dumisani?" Tessa stated, her brows furrowed in concern.

KameKona looked at Dumisani with alarm. "What exactly do you mean by lost?"

Sahila placed a hand on Dumisani's shoulder. "Our effort to soften the news isn't making it easier, is it?" she all but whispered. She was met with fearful glances and unshed tears. "I'm sorry to say that Keeper Reese was killed this afternoon during the rescue attempt. He fought very bravely against a formidable enemy, one we rarely encounter."

Stunned silence greeted them. It was torture watching the pain and incredulity on their faces. They prepared themselves for the onslaught of reactions and tears and it was not long in coming.

They relayed the plans the Debilis had for Demyan and how he was rescued before any long-lasting damage was done. All but one Debilis was captured and Keeper Security had begun a search for the one who killed Reese.

Dumisani stood, hands linked together. "We will have a funeral for Keeper Reese in two days and afterward we will resume our normal class schedule."

Sahila stayed for another hour to talk with the students as a group and individually.

"The entire staff is available to you at any time if you need support and the Wellness Center is also preparing grief counseling." It was tremendously difficult for her to leave them.

The meeting in the dining room was subdued and miserable. Chef offered tea and chocolate chip shortbread, Reese's favorite dessert.

Alegria could barely contain herself. "I thought that vile Debilis was killed years ago! We're sure he was the one behind this exercise in stupidity?"

Evren wiped his hand down his face. "I heard Reese say that it was his nemesis."

Jürgen chuffed. "That's Shakespearian irony if I've ever heard it. If Reese were here, he'd be piss'd tha' it was he who got one over him. And it only happen' because tha' Debilis was a coward and couldn't face him."

Dumisani slowly drew his arms out, as if his span could somehow contain the enormity of what had occurred. "How exactly did it happen?"

Nalin sighed and offered an explanation. "We were guarding all the weapons at the back of the house and Reese ran around to warn us of the last Debilis, who turned out to be…Rua-Jian. Not two seconds later, he launched himself out the second-story window and seized the katana sword. I grabbed a stiletto and Sahila threw a shuriken at his leg; there was no time to try anything else. We both wounded him…but not enough to stop him." She paused to sigh. "And you know the rest."

Dumisani rested his steepled fingers on his forehead for a moment. "I know you don't want to name him, but Rua-Jian Chu is no ordinary Debilis, a fact we all know. It is going to take far more than our previous efforts to eliminate him permanently. Yes—I said it. I have no qualms about ridding the Earth of this vengeful and sadistic menace. We will learn what we can from security before his lackeys are transferred to Baffin Island."

Jürgen pulled on his beard and cleared his throat. "Although it will take effort and time before Rua-Jian Chu can develop and implement another plan, we will keep our security tight. I jus' hope I can perform the job with half his flair."

"We know you will do a stellar job, Jürgen; we have every faith, Evren offered."

Nalin, anxious, subconsciously pulled on the end of her braid, unwound it, and re-braided it. "I don't like mentioning, it, but we'll need to divide up Reese's classes."

They all knew that none of them could teach them with his measure of swagger and humor.

"Such is the brilliant life of a former Exili," Alegria sniffed. "I miss that egotistical moron already."

CHAPTER 35 – Br

## COLLEGE OF GEOEVOLUTION

Alegria noticed everyone wandering around campus was understandably morose; they grieved quietly and politely, not wanting to disturb others.

While planning Reese's funeral with her fellow Keepers, Alegria tearfully whispered, "as difficult as it is, you know I believe in ripping off the bandage to get the mourning process started. It's as much for our young charges as it is for us."

Dumisani vividly remembered the 'onboarding' conversation they had when Reese formally joined the Order; typically lasting an hour, theirs was over within fifteen minutes.

*"If one of us needs to go six feet unda', then obviously we've got bigga' issues to deal with. Say a few words, play 'The Parting Glass,'*[233] *and let me start pushing up daisies. Oh, and bury me with my hat. That's it. What's next?"*

He smiled wistfully. "I will follow your instructions to the letter, Reese, but I can't speak for your brethren Keepers."

Dumisani knew Reese wouldn't completely get his wish. Alegria and he were forever quibbling with each other like ornery siblings.

---

[233] The Parting Glass is a well-known Scottish and Irish folk song. Many artists have covered it.

The funeral was short and sweet, just as Reese had willed when he became a Keeper. Alegria read a poem and sang Queen's "Who Wants to Live Forever."[234]

Sahila instantly began to cry and sobbed, "You total cow."

"You know Alegria would never let you have the last word, dear friend." Dumisani released a nondescript noise, hovering between a sigh and a sob.

The song, poignant and lyrical, was apropos, and Alegria's voice easily cut through the frigid air.

Afterward, everyone funneled out of the clearing and walked toward the dining hall for the reception. The graveyard was a campus attraction the students had yet to see; it wasn't included on the normal welcome tour. For those interested in history, it was a captivating study of legendary Keepers and dedicated Guardians who had no family to bury them. It was as far as the walnut grove, but tucked away in an area further west.

For Reese's ceremony, the students were escorted to their seat and afterward, quietly guided away again, without time to wander and reflect. Ming was wearing her best hat, a black felt number she believed appropriate.

As they began the long walk to the dining hall, a sudden breeze blew it from her head. "No, no, no, no!" Ming wailed. She sprinted after the errant hat, which smacked various gravestones on its journey, a prisoner to the capricious wind.

Tessa noticed her plight and raced to assist her.

---

[234] "Who wants To Live Forever" released in 1986 by Queen (EMI Records).

"If ever a hat needed a strap! That thing yearns to be a frisbee! Set it free!" Tessa giggled, forgetting for one blissful second the purpose for the day.

"Ladies, what's the situation?" Evren asked. "Let's not be late to the reception, today of all days—Chef Ngai will never forgive you!"

Ming pantomimed her hat taking flight and running after it.

"Ming! Come on! This is not charades! Evren seems stressed."

"I know, I'm trying!" Embarrassed, Ming knelt down and crawled, navigating around various headstones to quickly nab the hat before it blew away again.

Tessa approached from the other direction, preventing the hat from enjoying a longer adventure.

"I've got you!" Ming growled. "What a troublemaker you are! You were so *not* worth the price!"

Prize in hand, Ming glanced at the gravestones. Tessa walked up, resting her head on Ming's shoulder.

"Ming?" Tessa whispered, tentatively. "Are you looking at some of these?"

Ming nodded distractedly. "Yeah— I know." She raised her eyebrows. "But I'm not really sure what I'm seeing."

"Woah! I know; I don't understand it either—but, boy, am I curious."

Evren walked to the edge of the sidewalk. "You rescued your lovely fashion accessory, Scholar Ming? Reese would have been flattered!"

The pair turned and nodded. "Sorry for delaying us, Keeper Evren."

He smiled. "No problem. Shall we go?"

They followed him to catch up with the group. Ming was grateful to Evren. Even on a day like today, when he had lost one of his closest friends, he went out of his way to make *her* feel better.

Tessa bumped her shoulder with her own as they walked purposefully. "We are where we're supposed to be, Ming. We'll make Keeper Reese proud."

CHAPTER 36 – **Kr**

COLLEGE OF GEOEVOLUTION

# LATE NOVEMBER

As promised, classes resumed two days after Reese's funeral and most were grateful for the distraction. The day before American Thanksgiving, Tessa was relieved to hear that Dya Lee was finally visiting campus and was expected that afternoon. She was thrilled to learn Dya had accepted the invitation to reminisce and enjoy the holiday with former professors and current students; since their Thanksgiving break was only a few days, everyone stayed on campus.

Despite being inattentive all day, she managed to stay alert during her Economics and English classes. In English, there was more incentive, since they were studying Oscar Wilde's creepy book, *The Portrait of Dorian Gray*. By late afternoon, however, Tessa was walking briskly around campus, burning off nervous energy, at loose ends.

*It's freezing, but better this than irritating the snot out of everyone else right now! At least I know I'm not fit for company; self-awareness is a good thing. I'm making progress! Oh my gosh! Where is she?*

When Tessa spotted Dya standing in front of the residence hall, she tore down the path and launched herself into her arms. Dya braced herself and hugged her fiercely.

"Tessabear, honey! You've had a rough month."

Tessa, feeling overwhelmed with grief and relief, sobbed in Dya's arms. If she tried to talk, she would really lose it. She could only nod vigorously and bury her head more into Dya's shoulder. After a minute of calming, deep breaths, she finally felt composed enough to speak.

"If I could choose a person, just one person in the whole world to be with right now, it would be you—it would always be you."

"I hear you, Tessabear, I hear you," Dya cooed as she rubbed Tessa's back and snuggled her in closer.

After another moment, Tessa extricated herself and wiped her eyes on her shirt sleeve.

Dya chuffed. "Some things never change, I'm relieved to see!"

Tessa smirked. "I'm supposed to bring you to dinner, but I wanna show you my room first. I'm curious to know which one you had when you were here. By the way, did that girl Henrietta introduce herself to you last summer?"

Dya beamed. "You're a good egg, Tessabear. She did actually, and she's lovely. She'll never replace you, of course, but she stops by for tea and shortbread once a month and we talk thrifting."

When they discovered Dya's long-ago assigned room was on the opposite side of the hallway from hers and down the hall, Tessa was affronted.

"I'm so disappointed!" Tessa lamented.

"I can't believe it's empty and being used as a catch-all for everyone's crap!"

The room was littered with random items, such as large neglected stuffed animals and skateboards that didn't work well on cobblestone paths. A basketball hoop was hooked over the door for impromptu games when the weather was inhospitable; circular dirt marks on the wall validated its popularity.

Dya watched Tessa peruse the room like a budding detective.

"Are you examining every corner and wall of my old room, looking for graffiti or some sign I was once there?" Dya teased.

Tessa rolled her eyes. "Of course I am! But I know I won't find anything. You wouldn't dare stoop to deface the hallowed rooms of the *College of GeoEvolution*," Tessa quipped.

"Well, let's go, my dear; I'm hungry and am nostalgic for Ngai and Hattie's cooking It's been a while!"

At dinner, Dya greeted everyone warmly and with the proper reverence befitting the occasion. But her eyes sparkled upon approaching Sahila.

"I approve of the updated look! You need to stop by my store for some appropriate bling. I'll hook you up."

Sahila kissed both of her cheeks and gave her a quick snuggle.

"Give me some time and I promise to do that. When we know it's safe, I'll bring Nalin and Alegria; we'll make a girls' weekend of it. We're so glad you could come and lend your expertise to better understand our resident spiritual presence. We'll head there after dinner—Ngai made his famous hearty stew with crusty rustic bread!"

"Oh, good! I'm famished!"

The excitement and anticipation heading back to the residence hall after dinner was subdued, but still palpable. Élise and the others headed into the common room and waited for Dya, Dumisani, Nalin, and Sahila. It seemed to take forever for them to arrive. Dya walked with Élise into the hallway and waited.

"I don't sense anything at the moment," Élise signed and said. She dropped her shoulders, clearly disappointed.

Dya squeezed her shoulder. "That's all right, hon. Sometimes spirits, if they are cognizant, remove themselves from a particular location—usually out of frustration, boredom, or another reason personal to them. Let's see if we can have this one honor us with a visit."

Dya closed her eyes and took deep, cleansing breaths. From her purse, she removed a purple velvet pouch and pulled out what looked to be a clear quartz prism—except that it had incongruous facets at each end; it was beautiful in its clarity and simplicity.

One end had a seven-sided facet while the other end had only three. She faced the students and explained. "This is a channeling quartz crystal. I've had this one for many years and we are familiar and well-attuned to one another. And before you ask, no, it doesn't summon spirits. What it does do, however, is help facilitate my ability to clear my head and be receptive to whatever might be around me. If your resident spirit is nearby, it may notice that I am willing to communicate and have a peaceful and responsive energy. We shall see."

Dya let the crystal rest in the open palm of her left hand, barely cupped, but enough so it didn't topple onto the floor.

She placed her other hand underneath and closed her eyes. Her daily meditation practice made relaxing among an expectant crowd feasible.

After a minute, the energy in the area altered distinctly and the temperature dropped by several degrees; the hair on Dya's arms and those around her rose. Dya opened her eyes and looked around the room.

Élise signed and whispered, "It's here! I can sense it!"

A pale green mist hovered several feet in front of Dya.

"Oh, sugar-honey-iced-tea! I actually see it!" Tessa blurted, her hands cupping her mouth in shock. The other students were similarly astonished.

"Good for you!" Dya addressed the misty presence. "That's very impressive. It takes a great deal of energy to manifest that way." She placed the crystal back into the bag, slipped it into her purse, and looked at Élise. "Do you think this is the same entity who has tried to engage with you?"

Élise, amazed to have visual validation, nodded several times. After a second, she shook her head, as if clearing her mind from a fog. "Yes—yes, it's the same! I can't believe everyone can see something now!"

Dya lightly squeezed Élise's shoulder. "It's wonderful and quite remarkable that you are receptive to her. She's clearly been trying to communicate for quite a while!" Dya stepped closer. "She is definitely trying to communicate by Lucidium. It's faint, but I recognize some of the words—"

Dya was able to focus for one more minute before the apparition vanished and she beamed at Élise. "You did an incredible job, Scholar Élise! There is indeed a presence. It's a woman and she communicated that her name is Ariane."

Dya turned to the other students. "It was incredibly thoughtful of you to support Élise and believe her, even when you couldn't feel or sense what she could. I'm heartened. She has good, trusted friends in you all; that takes maturity and respect."

Looking at the Keeper professors, Dya stated, "I'll fill you in on my specific impressions. I was only able to glean a bit more than you all did. But I do know someone who can help, someone far more attuned than I am."

"One more thing," Dya said to everyone. "The famous astronomer Carl Sagan wrote in his book, *The Demon Haunted World*, that the 'absence of evidence is not evidence of absence.' The experience you just witnessed is my and Scholar Élise's ability to sense a particular energy. As you know, matter is neither created or destroyed. Science doesn't yet have the tools to verify what we are able to sense; it's outside the realm of what is considered rational and verifiable. Hopefully someday it will be.

"In the meantime, support your friends, but retain a healthy level of skepticism. After all, one of our main goals and responsibilities is to bring humanity forward in its understanding of the natural world, through the scientific method and rational thought. It's the only way we can ultimately save Earth."

The Keepers met in Dumisani's office. Dya didn't have much more to offer, but verified a vital tidbit.

"The presence communicated her name is Ariane and that she is looking for her bracelet. Is this the same Ariane, do you suppose, who was a Keeper professor?" Dya inquired.

"Oh, sweet rose quartz!" Sahila cried, placing her hands over her heart. "If this entity is looking for her bracelet," she said, frowning, "I believe it is our Ariane; I can scarce believe it."

"My word! If it's indeed her, I can't even *contemplate* what that sweet soul is going through! It must be abject torture. You realize she is trying to do more than communicate, right?"

Nalin nodded gravely and whispered reverently, "She is probably trying to cycle."

Dya pursed her lips in thought. "I recommend you immediately contact my best friend, Aramantha Dane. You will recognize her, Dumisani, from the annual Well Earth Summit; she's on the board. She will be able to assist you and Ariane as well; she's incredibly gifted."

Dumisani stood and thanked Dya. "We are ever grateful for your expertise, Keeper Dya, and even more thankful you brought us Scholar Tessa; she's going to be a magnificent Ingenio[235] someday. We'll address this issue right after Thanksgiving. We've got a busy day tomorrow."

---

[235] Ingenio – Ingenios have the ability to harness the intrinsic structure and vibration energy of crystals. Essentially engineers, they understand the scientific properties of a crystal and can manipulate it to become a tool, such as a laser or a communication device; Ingenio Keepers can assist scientists in discovering more effective ways to positively use crystals.

## CHAPTER 37 – Rb

### COLLEGE OF GEOEVOLUTION

As far back as anyone could remember, Thanksgiving at the College of GeoEvolution was a holiday involving "all hands-on deck." Chef and Hattie insisted that all students, as well as Keeper professors, assist with the cooking and preparation.

"I will not let my charges graduate from our college without knowing how to properly feed themselves!" Hattie had insisted years ago. "Thanksgiving is the perfect meal where they can all learn to cook or keep their culinary skills from rusting."

Despite Reese's absence, everyone managed to enjoy the meal and roasted him as often as they could.

"I can't believe I am saying this," Nalin whispered, "but I miss Reese's annual wishbone theatrics."

Jürgen rolled his eyes. "I swear, he cared more abou' that contest than all the bloody food! It was absolute madness!"

"Well, goddess knows, at least he kept the contest fair!" Sahila interjected.

"I even miss him launching peas with his spoon at the loser," Alegria sniffed. "Speaking of which, we need to continue that tradition. Who is picking up the reins?"

At the other end of the table, the students were avidly listening to every word of the exchange. Apparently, since there was only one wishbone per turkey, Hattie had all Thanksgiving participants select numbers from a bowl. When one turkey was served, the guest who picked the lowest and highest number got to compete. Each held one side of the wishbone and pulled. Whomever retained the largest part of the bone got to make a wish. Since there were two turkeys, the two lowest and highest numbers got to compete.

KameKona rubbed his hands together vigorously. "This sounds like fun! My parents always let my sisters compete for the wishbone, since they were younger. At least I now have a chance! And we have more than one turkey!"

Aedan elbowed him. "Your odds have never been better, mate! By the way," he whispered to him, sotto voce, "what am I supposed to do with that pink cranberry stuff? I've never done a Thanksgiving."

Tessa listened to the conversation, but since Dya was leaving the next day, she wanted to be in her presence for as long as she could. That didn't stop her errant thought, however.

*Any time peas are being launched, that's where I want to be!*

Quickly learning how to master her impulsivity, Tessa wisely kept silent and didn't share the desire with Dya.

*Better for her to leave with a higher impression of me, than not.*

The day after Thanksgiving, preparations began for winter finals. Every class had a mixture of paper tests, oral exams, and practical demonstrations. The week before exams was grueling and many hours were spent sitting by the fire in the common room studying and drinking tea, hot cocoa, or spiced cider. Healthy snacks and plenty of baked goods were available as well, to ease the stress level.

"I don't care what Xandra says, Ngai, I am not spoiling our children! They need a little something to look forward to as they stuff all that information into their heads!"

Chef Ngai took pity and brought sandwiches and his famous extra chocolaty caramel brownies to keep them fortified and caffeinated.

"Maybe we should have mid-semester finals?" Tessa groaned as she licked her fingers of the caramel goodness.

"What? You better keep that insane thought in your head!" KameKona shot back.

"I don't know, Kame." Élise teased as she poked him. "Chef Ngai's brownies are killer. I'm siding with Tessa on this one!"

"Oy! Trying to *actually* study here!" Aedan shouted. "Pipe down! But toss me a few brownies first, Tú, would ya?"

When exams were finished, everyone on campus needed a well-earned break. Before they left, they played frisbee in the unexpected snow and had snowball fights.

"You, Demyan, and I have never been so popular in our lives!" Tessa elbowed Élise. "We have the most experience crafting snowballs."

"You have to be on opposite teams, Tessa, to make it fair!" KameKona shouted, laughing.

"Sorry I'm no help, guys!" Élise pouted. "I was never allowed to be in a snowball fight! It wasn't 'proper behavior befitting a lady'!"

When cold and tired, they wandered inside in search of a warm drink. After shedding their boots and winter wear by the door, they walked quietly on stocking feet toward the dining room. Suddenly Aedan blocked them with an arm near the threshold to the main common room. A finger to his mouth told them to be quiet. They were close enough to hear fairly well, since the main common room had an echo effect, but were still out of sight.

The Keepers were drinking hot chocolate in front of a roaring fire, enjoying a quiet moment without the students.

"Do you think—is there a chance for Reese?" Sahila asked.

Alegria deeply exhaled. "I don't know. I've thought about it a thousand times and I'm of two minds. He's stubborn enough to manage it, but he's also reckless enough to botch it."

Evren barked a laugh. "I don't think I could have summed it up any better, Alegria."

"We know the answer to this, my Keeper brethren," Dumisani stated solemnly. "We just never know and it's not for us to decide."

"Ah yes!" Jürgen growled. "Tha' ol' gem! 'It's above our pay grade,' he said. "Well, whomever that or they may be, they betta be wise enough to make it happen! That man waits for no one! He'd make the verra devil beg for rescue!"

Amongst the students, eyebrows met and jaws dropped.

"What is that about?" Tessa whispered.

KameKona grabbed arms and pulled them out of the way.

"I have no idea!" Élise frantically said and signed.

"I want to ask, but it isn't the right time, I don't think," Aedan offered.

"We're getting ready to leave for break," Tú agreed. "Let's all think about it alone during our time away."

"Let it simmer and percolate, you mean?" Ming suggested.

"Yeah," KameKona whispered. "I'm down for that."

Since cost of travel was never an issue, traveling home for the month of December was feasible. Many international students in other schools around the world did not go home during any school breaks, as the cost was prohibitive and the break wasn't long enough to justify the long hours of travel and jet lag. Since the students at the College of GeoEvolution had internships during the summer, sending the students home in December was beneficial for their emotional and physical health.

"I never worry when they go home," Dumisani responded when once questioned about the wisdom of the tradition. "We have an excellent track record. We're doing something right, because they always come back!"

"Students heading home and seeing family and friends is restful and relaxing," Keeper Nalin added to the conversation with the head of security a few years ago. "But it's hardly worrisome. We frequently discuss the importance of secrecy and the trust we place with them. The students almost never discussed their abilities before entering the college and they are even less likely to do so now. Nowadays, they feel like part of a close-knit family that they would never want to betray; they all understand the serious consequences."

Wiping his forehead with a handkerchief as the last group left for the airport with Xandra and Fabek, Dumisani confided in Jürgen and Evren.

"I'm sad to say I'm relieved no one asked me that question this year; I would have answered less flippantly."

Jürgen grabbed hold of Dumisani's shoulders and shook lightly. "Brother Reese none withstandin', all is well with young Scholar Demyan! We got him back. We did right!"

"And it bears remembering," Evren added, eyebrows furrowed, "we weren't the ones who perpetrated the appalling scheme."

"We will find that wretched cockroach, from whatever rock he's hidin' under!"

Although the students went home, the Keeper professors chose to stay on campus and spend the holidays together this year. Between losing Reese and the potential communication with Keeper Ariane, it seemed particularly apropos that December. Although they relaxed together, they still had lots of work to do.

January felt like a fresh start, a reset from trauma and sadness upon returning to school. For some—like Ming, KameKona, Aedan, and Tú—coming home was joyous and relaxing. A time to enjoy family whether in a quiet or boisterous environment. It was a refreshing return to living with their Commoner families and appreciating the anonymity and temporary ignorance of the unnatural evils that existed in the world.

For others, like Tessa, Élise, and Demyan, being home was both restful and unpleasant. Familiar lectures and disappointments were meted out randomly like holiday treats.

A bittersweet awareness grew within them that schoolmates and college professors, a seemingly random group of individuals brought together by circumstance, were rapidly becoming family. They could identify with the famous line: "the blood of the covenant is thicker than the water of the womb."[236]

For the latter group, returning back to school was a relief and they relished beginning another semester with even more enthusiasm than their classmates. The pleasant surprise was seeing Demyan back at school. He was hugged and harassed until he explained how his parents allowed him to return.

"My parents understood, once I was back for a while, that if I was wanted for my expert knowledge of gems and coins, I could be kidnapped anywhere. My uncle defended the college and told my father I was lucky I was taken while at school! He told them that Keepers Dumisani and Reese were professionals and rescued me much faster than Interpol or the FBI could, had I been taken anywhere else. If my uncle only knew how true that was. Once they really got that, they let me go back. I didn't want to go to a school they picked for me or worse, begin working for my father."

He looked down at his feet after mentioning Reese.

"I feel very guilty about Keeper Reese—he died rescuing me. My uncle's watch was important to me, but it wasn't worth anyone's life."

KameKona punched his shoulder. "Hey man, it wasn't your fault. It was premeditated and they were gonna try at some point."

Tú jumped in as well. "And we followed the campus rules, Demyan, remember? You didn't do anything wrong."

Ming was reflective. "I hope it doesn't happen again, but this is what we are training for. Depending on what we

---

[236] By Heinrich der Glïchezäre from his medieval epic German poem, "Reinhart Fuchs (Reynard the Fox)." Avery, Anne Louise. *A Fox for All Seasons.* Bodleian Library, 2021.

choose to do in our careers, and maybe no matter what, we will need to protect and defend others."

Tessa agreed and added, "It's part of the code. And Keeper Reese was one of the best. He always ran toward danger. It's humbling to think any one of our professors would guard us with their lives. I'm not even sure if my own family would do that for me. I *hope* they would, but I don't instinctively *know* they would, you know?"

To lighten the mood, Aedan gave Demyan a head noogie. "I know! Keeper Reese loved chocolate chip shortbread and rich hot cocoa, right?"

Élise smiled. "Yes! And not 'crappy watery cocoa,'" she said, attempting a 'Reese-like' phrase.

Aedan laughed and continued. "Let's go ask Guardian Hattie if we can make the shortbread with her and we'll have cookies and cocoa in his honor. It's not a Viking send-off in a flaming ship, but I think he'd like it."

## Chapter 38 – Sr

### College of GeoEvolution

February and March found the students busy with their studies alongside experiencing Xandra's enthusiasm for her annual Shakespearian play. Although they didn't perform until mid-April, they began in earnest in February.

True to her promise, she insisted on Shakespeare's "The Taming of the Shrew," albeit with a more egalitarian ending. She offered the male lead Petrucio to KameKona, whom she believed embraced the comedic aspect of the role exceptionally well. KameKona's partner in sarcasm and agitation was Tessa, who played Katherine.

One afternoon, after suiting up for a dress rehearsal, KameKona asked, "I enjoy verbally sparring with you, Tessa. Don't get me wrong, but other than our professors, who exactly is our audience?"

Scrunching up her nose, Tessa whispered, lest their director hear her, "Beats me! I just want to do what the eccentric lady says! And it's kinda fun, watching us perform in roles different from our personalities."

Aedan was the one brave enough one afternoon to pose this question to the great lady herself. She seemed surprised by the query.

"My dear! My productions are legendary among the local Keeper and Guardian community! We entertain a full house both nights and during our Sunday matinee. We've even had Keepers travel from other states to see us!"

Although some of KameKona and Tessa's classmates were more reserved and would prefer working behind the curtain, the rule was that all students *must* act. Xandra frequently stated emphatically, "Your very *life* may someday depend upon your ability to play a role!"

KameKona welcomed the distraction as they all mourned Keeper Reese. In addition to practicing for the play, he was thrilled to begin the geological unit on volcanology. They learned about volcanoes before, of course, but each ability received a week dedicated to its study.

"It's really interesting, learning about our abilities this way!" Tú explained when they began the volcanology unit.

Every class they took during that unit, whether economics, chemistry, or paranormal studies, focused on an aspect of volcanology from that subject's perspective.

"It's sick that my classmates are going to learn about *my* ability!" KameKona enthusiastically shared. He knew his fellow compatriots felt the same way. To have other classmates better appreciate his interaction with and impact on the natural world diminished the loneliness, the feeling that no one else understood how it felt to be him.

He walked into the classroom and found samples of volcanic rock on the lab tables around the room's perimeter. Alegria greeted them as they entered. "Welcome! Have a seat, so we can begin. You will see different types of volcanic rock from many different countries. Believe it or not, there are numerous active volcanoes around the world. The samples I have here today are from twelve different countries: the Democratic Republic of the Congo, Guatemala, Columbia, El Salvador, Ecuador, Iceland, Indonesia, Italy, Japan, the Philippines, Mexico, and the United States. Scholar KameKona, how many volcanoes are there in the United States?"

KameKona scratched the back of his head, thinking. "Umm. I dunno—maybe about fifty?"

Alegria's laugh sounded more like a snort. "That's a good guess, but no! There are 169 volcanoes considered active."

"Seriously? How did I not know that?" he questioned, incredulous.

She offered him a crooked smile. "And you don't have to worry, Scholar KameKona. The samples we have from Hawaii were given to us freely by a well-known native cultural leader many years ago, with the understanding that they are for educational purposes only." She looked at her other students as she added, "It is illegal to remove volcanic rock from any of the Hawaiian Islands. I can assure you, however, we treat all of our rocks and gems here with respect."

She walked over to one of the counters and picked up a beautiful sample of obsidian, a smooth and shiny piece of black volcanic rock or "glass" created from cooled magma.

"Even in our time, with numerous technological break-throughs, there is still no coordinated international system for volcano watches or warnings. There are two reasons for this: First, there is no 'volcanic eruption signature,' if you will," she stated with air quotes. "Each volcanic eruption is unique. Even the same volcano can erupt differently over time. Second, countries vary in their ability to monitor vol-canic activity depending on the number of volcanoes they have and the funding they can allocate toward such systems."

"I guess I never really thought about that," Aedan stated, sounding surprised. "It never occurred to me that it differed by country."

"We aim to please." Alegria grinned. At least, when talking about her favorite subject—geology, her personality was beginning to emerge again, little by little. Although all of the Keepers were grieving, Alegria managed to be more effusive than the others; although not easy, she knew it was what Reese would have wanted. "Right now, the one similar type of worldwide system comes from airplane pilots, believe it or not. As they fly over a volcano, they report any activity and ash emissions they see and these warnings are color coded, depending on the level of severity."

"Oh wait!" KameKona exclaimed. "I read about this. The system is monitored by the International Civil Aviation Organization."

"Excellent, Scholar KameKona, you know more than you thought you did. In addition, several international organizations assist with the goal of better understanding and improving volcano warning and watch systems. The biggest are the World Organization of Volcano Observatories, run by the Earth Observatory in Singapore. In the United States, we have the National Volcano Early Warning System."

Ming became slightly animated when she heard Alegria mention EOS. "I remember going to EOS on a school field trip! It was *really* interesting."

Alegria smiled at Ming's subdued enthusiasm; no one was quite ready to allow happiness, however fleeting, back into their lives.

"Anyway," Alegria sighed, "despite these organizations and collective research, it still doesn't closely approach your level of awareness, Scholar KameKona, and mine, regarding impending volcanic eruptions. We're highly attuned to this type of event and we are inherently connected to this Earth creation."

KameKona nodded in agreement. "Even when I was a toddler, I always felt it—it's a deep rumbling. I can hear and even smell the sulfurous vapor well before an eruption.

My parents teased me when I scrunched up my nose for 'no reason,' as far as they could tell. They would say, 'Kame, what's that phantom odor you're smelling?' and my dad would sing that Lynyrd Skynyrd song 'That Smell' every time I did that."[237] KameKona smiled briefly at the memory. "When I was old enough to realize they couldn't sense it and other people around us couldn't either, I stopped visibly reacting—didn't want to draw attention to myself. And then there's holding lava rocks and being able to heat them myself. I learned *real* quick not to make that obvious, especially with two nosy younger sisters." He looked over at Aedan and gestured with his chin. "I'm guessing you know what I'm talking about."

Aedan nodded then shook his head. "You don't know the half of it."

Alegria added, "your description is perfect, Scholar KameKona. You and I can feel and hear the rumblings of an impending eruption and even sense the gas movements underground, if we're close enough. They are less synchronous than earthquake vibrations, Scholar Élise, but I know you can tell the difference. Keepers with your abilities often work together, as earthquakes quite often precede volcanic eruptions and can often happen at the same time."

Alegria walked over to the counter where the sample display began, still holding the shiny obsidian in her hands. Its glossy patina was even brighter and visible heat waves emanated from its surface.

Tú raised his hand and waved it to get Alegria's attention. She noticed his gesture and arched an eyebrow in anticipation.

---

[237] "That Smell" released in 1977 by Lynyrd Skynyrd (MCA Records).

"Keeper Alegria, what happened with Mount Vesuvius? Were there no Keepers? And if there were, why couldn't they prevent so many people from being killed?"

"Wonderful question, Scholar Tú." She gestured to the pneumatic tube system in the corner. "Make sure you choose a meal for tomorrow after class, okay?" Tú nodded and she continued. "Our historical record shows that we did have a Keeper living in Pompeii before the eruption. And that Keeper did continually warn those in positions of influence and government about the impending eruption of Vesuvius. However, the people of Pompeii were used to Vesuvius having small and seemingly inconsequential eruptions, so most of the populace didn't take the warnings seriously. Also, they had great respect for science in Ancient Rome, as did the ancient Greeks. So, I imagine they asked, 'Where is the proof?' And what could our Keeper say?

"Now, let's add another complex layer to this dynamic culture. Although they embraced scientific thought, ancient Romans took omens and superstitions seriously as well; they had a plethora of philosophers, oracles, and fortune tellers. So, if ancient romans were willing to believe utterances from these groups, you would think they would take the advice of a seemingly reasonable Keeper. Some of these eccentric thinkers were revered and compelling and others were considered charlatans and dismissed as crazy. Based on the results, it appears as if our embedded kinsman was not convincing enough. We were not there, however, so it's not really appropriate to judge—look at what that Keeper was up against."

"People never really change, do they?" Ming stated cryptically.

"What do you mean?" Élise asked.

"Well, this sounds really familiar, right? It doesn't matter which century, does it? From the very beginning, our kind—those with abilities—never fit in or were trusted at face value."

"At least, in these modern times," Alegria countered, "a Keeper forecasting a volcanic eruption can point to the latest research and diagnostic tools and likely encourage action that way. Back then, not so much. As tragic as Pompeii was, I'd like to point out that tens of thousands of residents *did* survive and relocate to neighboring cities."

Alegria motioned for her cohort to approach the sample table. She pointed out the different types of volcanic rock and encouraged them to be held and examined. "Scholar KameKona, what elements are contained in volcanic rock?"

He pinched his ear in thought. "From what I know, there are quite a few: aluminum, calcium, iron, magnesium, oxygen, potassium, phosphorus, silicon, sodium, titanium, and some other elements in smaller amounts."

Alegria smiled wanly. "Winner, winner, chicken dinner," she all but whispered. "Fantastic. Make sure you select a meal as well, okay?"

The students began examining the volcanic rock types. In an earlier lesson, Alegria explained how volcanic rocks were divided into two types: intrusive rocks and extrusive rocks. The intrusive volcanic rock or *plutonic* rock never reaches the surface and cools slowly. Extrusive volcanic rock is exposed to the surface and thus cools faster. These rock types varied greatly from each other in color, texture, weight, and other characteristics.

The samples were divided on the countertops and further categorized by the amount of silica or silicon dioxide they contained, one of the myriad of ways to differentiate volcanic rock. Alegria reminded them that silica was quartz and was, in essence, sand, when shaped into tiny round pieces over millennia from weathering.

Alegria added, "Believe it or not, silica is a valuable trace mineral in human and animal connective tissue, like cartilage. It's a component in bones, teeth, tendons, hair, and blood vessels. Paradoxically"—she narrowed her eyes—"it's potentially hazardous to the lungs if large quantities are inhaled. Miners who work with silica need to protect themselves, as do people who work to cut and shape countertops and other slabs made of the material."

The students all held the samples after KameKona did, marveling at how quickly the rocks heated after he handled them.

"If I wanted to, I could fry an egg on this peridotite[238] right now!" Tessa exclaimed.

"The temperature of the lava rocks is similar to the temperature of the rocks Aedan manipulates, the sedimentary and metamorphic ones," Ming noted.

"I noticed that," Aedan remarked, frowning. "But when I heat the *volcanic* rocks samples, I can't get them to the same effective temperatures that Kame can."

"True enough," Alegria stated. "A significant and astute observation, Scholar Aedan! It's critical to be aware of your ability limitations. In your case, Scholar Aedan, what's happening?"

"I believe I'm actually heating the iron, titanium, and other elements within the volcanic sample. They, in turn, heat the larger surrounding material, but at a much lower temperature."

---

[238] "Peridotite," https://www.mindat.org/gm/48407: an igneous rock ranging in color from deep gray to translucent green; it is comprised mainly of olivine

"Yeah, but Aedan, man, I have the same issue. If I'm only working with the rock your ability is attuned to, the sedimentary and metamorphic, I'm not going to be as successful either."

Everyone continued to work with the samples, getting a feel for the igneous material. Aedan tried to turn some of the rock samples lying around into a fish sculpture, similar to those he made at home, but was unsuccessful.

"That 'waste rock' you are trying to manipulate is a bit of a misnomer," Alegria quipped. "I call any rock samples I am willing to sacrifice for the edification of my pupils by that name. Actual waste rock is the seemingly worthless rock left over in a mine after the valued rock product is excavated. What happens to it?"

"Oh!" Tú raised his arm quickly to answer. "I know the answer!"

The granite sample flew from his hand and headed toward one of the light shades. KameKona took a flying leap and launched himself into the path of the soaring projectile. As if intercepting a touchdown worthy pass, he caught the sample and rolled as he hit the ground, skidding to a halt at Alegria's feet.

Tessa grinned. "Nice!"

Smirking, Alegria noted, "Apparently, you can take the player out of football, but not football out of the player— nicely executed. You've gone several notches higher in Keeper Xandra's estimation for saving that light shade; Keeper Reese would have loved that," she mused, "but would have preferred you had missed."

Tú apologized profusely and banged his head on the desk.

"Happens to the best of us!" Élise kindly offered. "What's the answer?"

"Oh. Right. Waste rock is often used to line embankments for roads, dams, or railroads."

"Correct. When we truly appreciate Earth and its resources, we try to repurpose everything; ideally, there is a use for everything somewhere in this wide world."

"Keeper Alegria," Aedan called, sounding disappointed as he tossed his sample down. "If KameKona wasn't with me and this is all I had at my disposal, I could, what—chuck a sample at a Debilis and hope to incapacitate him?"

Alegria raised an eyebrow, knowing from where his self-deprecation rose. "Don't become frustrated, Scholar Aedan. You can never discount the well-timed rock throw. You need just remember the story of David and Goliath. An accomplished Keeper excels at their abilities, but in an emergency, uses what they have available to them."

A minute after this exchange, the smell of rotten eggs permeated the room.

"Okay," Alegria announced. "Scholar KameKona, are you holding the scoria[239] sample?"

KameKona, embarrassed, held up the rock sample. It was dark gray in color and covered in small holes of different sizes. "Hey, I'm sorry. The other samples didn't release any smell."

Alegria walked over, removed the sample, and returned it to the table. "I must apologize, Scholar KameKona. Forgive me this teachable moment; I expected that to happen at some point today." She addressed the class. "You are smelling hydrogen sulfide. It has that telltale unpleasant rotten egg smell." She wrinkled her nose in distaste. "What's more off-putting is that it's the same gas you smell in a sewer or a swamp, anywhere there is decaying material or human or animal waste.

---

239 "Scoria," https://www.mindat.org/gm/48578

"We studied this earlier. When a volcano erupts, it releases large amounts of hydrogen sulfide, hydrogen halides, carbon, sulfur, and carbon dioxides. All of these are hazardous to animals and humans. The collection of them, when released during a volcanic eruption, is deadly. If a Commoner is anywhere near a volcanic eruption and the ash or lava doesn't kill them, the noxious gas clouds will—both from the heat of the vapors as well as the toxic gases. That's another reason why it's so important for Commoners to heed volcanic watches and warnings and leave when told."

She walked over to KameKona and placed the rock in his palm again.

"Keep your palm open and you won't activate it as easily. As a Volco, Scholar KameKona, you can use this porous volcanic rock to your advantage when defending against a Debilis. If you are not surrounded by Commoners, a small release of the gases trapped in that porous rock can disarm and confuse a Debilis, even render them unconscious for a while."

Alegria had them sit down as she wrapped up the lab. "So, Scholar KameKona, please remind your classmates as to how a Volco can use their abilities in defense against a Debilis."

KameKona pulled on his ear again in thought and looked at his classmates. "So…a Volco can heat any volcanic rock, extrusive or intrusive, and if we can launch it to within a foot of a Debilis, the heatwaves from the rock alone can cause them second-degree burns or light clothing on fire.

"If I am near an erupting volcano, I can harness small amounts of lava and direct it toward my foe. I can use this to surround them in order to protect nearby Commoners, as long as they remain unaware that I am the one redirecting that flow. I can also essentially imprison a Debilis until I can get them restrained for removal. I just learned that the porous volcanic rock, like scoria, can release noxious gases that I can use to temporarily incapacitate a Debilis."

He smiled and raised his eyebrows. "That's actually pretty cool. And, if all else fails, I guess, I can just heat up a volcanic rock or even pick up one of Aedan's rocks and chuck it at my foe using my awesome football prowess," he said in a joking manner.

"Quite. Well done, Scholar KameKona." Alegria held up another obsidian rock, this one much smaller than the original sample. "We'll keep working on your skills."

She held the rock in one palm tightly and massaged it with her fingers while she related the homework assignment. Just as she finished, she opened her palm slowly and allowed bright lava to flow viscously from her fingers onto the table below, made of dull tungsten[240]. The lava slid across the width of the table and settled into the grooved wells surrounding every edge, leaving no mark in its wake. This was one of Alegria's favorite visuals. She blew on her hands and the vapor from her breath cooled her fingers.

"Remember, tungsten has a higher melting point than lava."

---

[240] "Tungsten," https://www.mindat.org/gm/7982

## Chapter 39 – Y

## College of GeoEvolution

April was an exciting time at the college, because the students learned about internship opportunities for the summer. They were encouraged to return home for three weeks when school ended to spend time with family and friends. After that, they were sent to their chosen internship locations. Sometimes these placements were in their home country, but oftentimes they weren't. And if the internship *was* in their native country, they never stayed at their family residence. This offered too many complications and chances for unwelcome Commoner and Keeper cross-pollinations.

Instead, students stayed in an appropriate Keeper or Guardian host home. In most cases, host families were familiar with the process and had housed many students over the years. Dumisani enjoyed discussing the program with the first years, who generally only knew rudimentary information and whatever rumors circulated throughout the campus.

The little cohort wandered into their ethics class, one of the classes Dumisani taught if he was in residence. They were laughing and joking with one another as they entered. He was relieved to see that small amounts of joy had slowly migrated back into their lives.

When they settled, Ming raised her hand tentatively.

He raised his chin and eyebrows and smiled. "Yes, Scholar Ming. You have a question or comment?"

Ming smiled nervously. "Thank you, Keeper Dumisani. When you told us that we could ask you a question at any time, does that include questions not related to the class material?"

He nodded. "Absolutely. I want you to feel comfortable asking me any question at any time."

Ming smoothed her hair behind her ears and glanced at Tessa, who nodded encouragingly. "Umm. Okay, thank you. Tessa…Tessa and I noticed something perplexing at the cemetery during the funeral. We've been wondering about it ever since, and we can't figure it out. And in addition, I was in the library when we learned about Demyan's kidnapping and I noticed something unusual there too. I hope it's okay for me to ask about them?"

Dumisani walked in front of his desk and leaned against it, his hands gently clasped together. "We have no secrets here at the College of GeoEvolution. Sometimes, however, we wait for optimal moments to explore certain concepts and ideas. I believe we have reached one of them now. What is it you wish to understand?"

Ming looked at Tessa for support. "At the cemetery, we noticed some of the writing on the gravestones that was…confusing."

"For instance," Tessa continued, "one gravestone had several names upon it, like a vertical list. The first name was *Sahila F.* with a numeral II after it. The next name below it was *Sahila H.*, with a numeral III beside it. I don't remember the initials after that, but the first name was always *Sahila*, and the initials continued all the way up to IX."

Ming continued. "And when we heard about Demyan, I was working on research at the library. Keeper Heikima ran out to help and I had to put the rare reference book back myself. I know the books are valuable and we need her assistance to study them. She always takes them out of the special cabinet and puts them back by herself. I wasn't trying to pry, and I was rushing to put the book away anyway, but I noticed something interesting."

Seeing she needed reassurance, Dumisani encouraged her to continue.

"There was one particular book, *The Principles of Ethics*." Ming picked up the book of the same title on her desk and held it aloft. "It seemed to be this very same book, published by Cambridge University Press in various editions over time. The first one was published in 1586. And there are five more editions, including the one that we have now."

She paused to pull on the ends of her hair. "What is unusual is that the first name of the author each time is your name, sir: Dumisani. The only part that changes is the last name. The initial last name was Professor Dumisani Oead. The next last name is Pead, then Reade, then Sead, then Teade, until this volume, by Professor Dumisani Vead. The editions are published between ninety and one hundred years apart, all by Cambridge University Press. Keeper Dumisani, I mean no disrespect, but what does this mean?"

Dumisani freed his hands and stood slowly.

"I appreciate your astute and well-thought-out observations. Both times, circumstances afforded you the opportunity to be keenly perceptive. You all continue to mature mentally and emotionally and we're impressed with your collective progress. And despite it being a trying year, you all rose to the occasion. I will answer your questions, I promise, but today isn't that day.

"Instead, I want to be forthcoming about your futures. I'll be perfectly frank: We did not anticipate this level of

Debilis activity quite so soon. We sensed rumblings, but we thought we had more time. And all our reliable sources reported that Rua-Jian Chu was eliminated years ago. His ability to remain incognito all this time is rather alarming. It isn't in his character to be subtle or hide under rocks; there's no room for his ego.

"Now that we know he still walks among us and managed to kill one of our Keepers, we need to be extra vigilant and eradicate him from this Earth. He threatens our existence and the safety of Earth itself.

"You need to be prepared. Fall term, we will increase the intensity of your training and will remove the curtain entirely. There will be no mysteries and you will know everything we know—you are ready to learn all truths."

# END OF BOOK ONE

# ACKNOWLEDGMENTS

This first novel ultimately took almost fifteen years to write, if I take into account all of the research, character, and plot development. During that time, my husband and I were also raising our kiddos. They are not so little now! There are so many people who supported me along this journey and I want to express my gratitude and love.

I want to thank my children. Bradley, Ethan, Kate, and Grace, you never failed to encourage me when the nagging doubts surfaced; you lent me the strength to banish them. Also, thank you for the delicious dinners when I didn't have the time to cook! It was actually all a ruse to make sure you left the nest with the skills to properly feed yourselves!

To my sister and brother, and close friends who believed I could do it, your support meant everything! Amy and Kristie: Thank you for being my beta readers and keeping me company on this journey! Your suggestions and recommendations were invaluable!

Damonza Studio, thank you for partnering with me to create a fantastic cover! Your team did an outstanding job and I appreciate your patience as we refined every detail together.

To Kristen Hamilton of Kristen Corrects: My *smartest* decision by far was choosing you as my editor. You are worth your weight in gold, platinum, tungsten, red beryl, and every other valuable element and gem! You taught me so much and helped craft this novel into the best version of itself. I am eternally grateful for your patience, guidance, and expertise.

To Veronica Yager of Journey Bound Publishing: Thank you for formatting Keepers of the Rock with its unique Augie footnotes! Your advice on the best way to showcase Augie was invaluable. I'm grateful to you and your team for all of their myriad efforts.

# SCHOOL OF GEOEVOLUTION
## STAFF DIRECTORY

| Keeper Name | Country | Position | Ability |
| --- | --- | --- | --- |
| Nalin Fink | USA | Teacher | Ingenio |
| Shifu Ganzorig (Zoria) | Mongolia | King Fu Master/ Fitness Coach | Techto |
| Alegria Hinine | Chile | Teacher | Volco |
| Heikima Miyazaki | Japan | Head Librarian | Emogem |
| Master Halbert Proulx | Switzerland | Fencing Instructor/ Fitness Coach | Ferro |
| Reese Rolding | Australia | Teacher | Resogem |
| Fabek Sobalt | Poland | Keeper Agriculturist, Driver | Ferro |
| Jürgen Tilver | Navarino Islands, Scotland | Teacher | Magro |
| Alesky Petarov Todorov | Bulgaria | Groundsman | Ferro |
| Xandra Topper | England | Headmistress | Emogem |
| Sahila Yold | India | Teacher | Emogem |
| Evren Zin | Turkey | Teacher | Techto |
| Dumisani Vead | Morocco | Teacher, School Director | Ferro |

| Guardian Name | Country | Position | Ability |
| --- | --- | --- | --- |
| Dr. Slaine Kelly | Ireland | School Physician | None |
| Ngai Nguyen | Vietnam | Head Chef | None |
| Hattie Nguyen | Sweden | Head Pastry Chef | None |
| Hestia Patel, NP | India | Nurse Practitioner | None |

# SCHOOL OF GEOEVOLUTION
## STUDENT DIRECTORY

| Keeper Name | Country | Position | Ability |
|---|---|---|---|
| Tú Chen | China | Scholar | Magro |
| Aedan Colston | England | Scholar | Ferro |
| Élise Peters-Comtois | France | Scholar | Techto |
| Tessa Horton | USA | Scholar | Ingenio |
| Demyan Ivanova | Latvia | Scholar | Resogem |
| KameKona Johnson | USA | Scholar | Volco |
| Ming Sen | Singapore | Scholar | Emogem |

# TERM GLOSSARY

| Term | Definition |
|---|---|
| Commoner | A regular human being, unaware that individuals with special abilities exist. They may sense underlying evil, but don't comprehend it. |
| Debilis | Latin for *weak* or *feeble*. Debilis are human beings who have the same abilities as Keepers, but choose to use them for their own gain and become criminals. They are soulless humans who lack empathy. The more a Debilis uses their ability to hurt others, the more they lose parts of their soul. Eventually they become unrecognizable as human beings. Keepers call them "decayed ones," because they develop a rather pungent odor as they degrade themselves. Their humanity seeps out of them and they begin to literally rot. Similar to the word "sheep," the word Debilis is both singular and plural. |
| Emogem | An individual with an inherent ability to harness the energy and properties of precious and semi-precious stones, crystals, and certain elements from the periodic table. Keepers with this gift use it to heal. Although not preferable, an Emogem Keeper can manipulate the emotions of others, if necessary, for the greater good. When needed, this skill is used primarily as a defensive measure to disarm a Debilis who is threatening or hurting others. Emogem Keepers can guide Commoners toward developments in the field of alternative medicine. An Emogem Debilis is dangerous to the Commoner population, as they use their ability manipulate others for their own gain. |

| | |
|---|---|
| Exili | A Latin word meaning *adrift*. An Exili is an individual with abilities who has no community. They keep to themselves and don't fully understand who they are or what they can do. Few Exili can exist in the world without guidance and support. Without it, most become mentally and/or physically ill and are dysfunctional. Exili can become either Keepers or Debilis, depending on their capacity for empathy and inner fortitude. |
| Ferro | Those with this ability are particularly sensitive to iron, phosphorus, and other metals. They can easily manipulate many rocks and various elements in the periodic table, but excel at controlling samples with any concentration of iron or phosphorus. The hallmark of this ability centers around heat manipulation. Although a Ferro works with magnetic materials, their strength does not transfer as easily to rare earths. Ferro Keepers can guide Commoners toward improving mining and engineering standards and developing better sustainable methods. |
| Guardian | A Guardian is a regular human being who is aware that individuals with special abilities exist. They are trusted people who are tasked with assisting Keepers wherever they are needed in the world. Guardians are aware that otherworldly evil exists, but do not possess any abilities to directly disarm or attack a Debilis. |
| Ingenio | An individual with this ability harnesses the vibration energy of crystals. They are essentially engineers and comprehend the chemical and physical properties of a crystal. They turn crystals into tools, such as a laser or a communication device. Ingenio Keepers can guide Commoners toward discovering more effective ways to positively utilize crystals in scientific, medical, and engineering endeavors. |

| | |
|---|---|
| Keepers | A Keeper is a human being with an innate ability tied to the Earth. They are committed to Earth's care and its sustainability. They protect it from ignorant Commoners and evil Debilis. They are also charged with guiding Commoners, with help from Guardians, to better understand their impact on the Earth and learn to become better stewards. |
| Magro | A Magro is particularly drawn to rare earths, even in the smallest of quantities. They collect them from the Earth and can amass, compress, and shape them to their will. A Magro is able to work with other magnetic rocks and elements in the periodic table as well, but they especially excel with rare earths. Magro Keepers can guide Commoners toward improving rare earth mining and engineering standards and developing better sustainable methods. |
| Resogem | An individual who is highly attuned to the negative energy stored in precious and semi-precious stones, crystals, and certain elements of the periodic table. Keepers are often tasked with removing these dangerous items from circulation, keeping them away from Debilis and Commoners. Those with this ability often familiarize themselves with the criminal underworld, both human and otherworldly, and are skilled with harnessing this negative energy to disarm those who intend harm to others. Their skills do not involve having the ability to utilize stones to heal. Debilis who are Resogems are particularly dangerous because they purposefully use this skill to harm and manipulate others for their own gain. |

| | |
|---|---|
| Techto | A Techto's inherent ability is sensing the vibrations and shifting of the earth, to the deepest internal crust. A Techto can sense when an earthquake or tsunami is imminent from thousands of miles away, much faster than an expert Commoner or their latest technology can detect. If necessary, a Keeper can manipulate the earth to cause an earthquake of some magnitude, through harnessing the natural existing fault lines below the surface. When a Debilis chooses to create havoc, it is for their own purpose, with the intention of causing damage. Techto Keepers can guide Commoners towards more sensitive and faster earthquake alert systems. |
| Volco | An individual who is highly attuned to volcanoes and their activity. A Volco can sense volcanic activity far sooner than expert Commoner volcanologists or their latest technologies can detect. They have the ability to harness energy from a volcano and manipulate igneous rock and lava streams through heat manipulation. No Volco is strong enough to cause a volcano to erupt. Volco Keepers can guide Commoners towards more sensitive and faster alert systems. |

# INDEX OF MINERALS AND ROCKS

## (Health Properties Attributed to them)

For millennia, humanity has believed and continues to believe that minerals and rocks contain health properties and assist with the improvement and enhancement of various parts of the body and mind. Many rocks and minerals are also mined for various uses.

**Aventurine** – Boosts confidence in social groups, encouraging open communication. Some believe it also reduces tension and migraine headaches. Others believe it stimulates good luck and prosperity.

**Amazonite** – Relaxes the mind and dissipates anger. Thought to enhance trust. Some believe it helps heal the nervous system and fortifies the heart.

**Amber** – Helps filter negative emotions from the body.

**Aquamarine** – Calms anxiety and the nerves.

**Bloodstone** – Pliny the Elder, the Ancient Roman naturalist and philosopher, believed that magicians used bloodstones to help them with invisibility. The ancient Romans also believed bloodstone helped stop bleeding and the ancient Greeks thought that having a bloodstone on one's person helped ward off being bitten by a venomous snake. In India, they too believed that bloodstone helped stop bleeding and would place a bloodstone on a wound after dunking it in cold water. Bloodstone contains iron oxide, an astringent. Today, many believe bloodstone assists with wisdom, courage, and spirituality.

**Blue Azurite** – Stimulates clear thinking and promotes good oxygen circulation. Some believe it assists with cognitive disorders.

**Blue Lace Agate** – Helps relieve stress and depression and eases trouble with communicating. It's also believed to assist with mending bone fractures and strains. Some think it alleviates problems with the lymph and endocrine systems.

**Blue Topaz** – Enhances the awareness of fruitful financial ventures and improves personal wisdom. It can also assist with emotional stability.

**Botswana Agate** – Enhances wearer's internal fortitude in addition to providing mental and emotional strength.

**Carnelian** – The ancient Romans used it in jewelry for signet rings and as a seal on documents; the stone didn't stick to wax. Many believe it helps strengthen confidence, courage, and energy.

**Charoite** – Thought to help with understanding the spiritual realm and harnessing ethereal vibrations. Charoite encourages positive emotions over negative ones. It is often referred to as the transformation stone; it fosters positive self-esteem.

**Chert** – A sedimentary rock comprised mainly of silica. It is frequently mined for use in fieldstone, gravel, and the top surface for roads. Chert weathers well over time in this capacity. In ancient times, it was used to make tools and arrowheads, because it was easy to create sharp edges.

**Citrine** – Helps amplify cheerfulness and clear thought. It is also thought to aid in detoxification of the liver, spleen, kidneys (the whole urinary tract), and intestines. Some believe it assists with food allergies and helps with mood stabilization through reducing anxiety and depression.

**Coal** – A metamorphic rock used historically for heating homes and businesses. The use of this element is decreasing rapidly as it pollutes the air and releases dangerous amounts of carbon dioxide, mercury, methane gas, nitrogen oxide, and sulfur dioxide into the air.

**Cobalt** – Cobalt has many uses. It helps tint paints and varnishes and assists with the process of paint drying. It is utilized in air bags and combined in metal alloys for the aircraft and chemical industries; it is also used in creating magnets.

**Diamond** – Used in science in both the medical and manufacturing industries. It's also thought to assist with respiration and detoxification and to cleanse the body of mental dismay and fear. Historically, many believed it protected the wearer from the effects of poison.

**Emerald** – Considered the "stone pf prosperity." Many believe it assists with liveliness in spirit and an appreciation for life.

**Fluorite** – Improves mental focus and is referred to as the "genius stone."

**Hematite** – The dark silvery magnetic rock was used by the Ancient Egyptians to ward off evil spirits; the warriors of ancient Rome and Greece kept hematite on them in battle because they believed that it would protect them from being wounded and would cause their enemies to be wounded instead.

**Garnet** – Utilized in solid-state lasers for medical treatments, like eye surgery and precise metal cutting, among many other uses. Some believe that garnets enhance romance and intimacy. Others believe in its ability to improve self-esteem and willpower. Cultural lore suggests that placing a garnet under one's pillow wards off nightmares and helps one travel safely. Further still, the stone is thought to assist with detoxification of blood and other fluids and help with gallstones and kidney function.

**Iolite** – Referred to as the Viking Compass Stone because Vikings were known to use thin pieces of iolite to aid them with sun navigation at sea, especially when it was cloudy or misty. It was thought to act as a visual filter and help reduce glare. It is believed to assist with guiding the wearer home, aid in spirituality, and act as a conduit between the living and the dead.

**Jade** – Many societies believe jade helps in the healing of the kidneys and the immune system; others believe that it also assists with achieving internal peace, tranquility, and encourages wisdom.

**Jet** – Relieves depression, scary thoughts, and anxiety.

**Labradorite** – Assists with communing with spirits and calming them for more harmonious communication. It is also thought to enhance dreams and strengthens self-awareness.

**Lapis Lazuli** – Encourages relationship building, growing friendships, and building courage.

**Malachite** – Assists in eye health and helps regulate blood glucose levels.

**Marble** – A metamorphic rock. It is one of the most effective and appreciated mediums for sculptors. It is also used as a building material and can help reduce the acidity in soil. Crushed up, it is utilized as a whitening pigment in paper and paint. When turned into a powder, it is incorporated into veterinarian medications for its calcium component.

**Moldavite** – Assists with communing with spirits and calming them for more harmonious communication and is thought to help with fertility.

**Obsidian** – Heals the skeletal structure, veins, and muscles, and is effective in helping ground and calm an individual. In addition, it encourages serenity and helps alleviate negativity.

**Opal** – In the Middle Ages, people believed opals assisted with good eyesight. Blond-haired women would wear opal necklaces because they thought opals would preserve their hair color. Many believe the opal assists with addiction, hope, and truth.

**Quartz crystal** – Has a multitude of uses within science and the medical and manufacturing industries. Quartz is a critical material in our watches, cell phones, televisions, landline telephone systems, and radios. Quartz is piezoelectric, which means it vibrates at a constant frequency and produces an electric charge when put under pressure. It can be manufactured in a lab. Even that crystal, however, is made from quartz fragments or silica. Quartz is also used in water purification and GPS. In healing, it is believed to optimize and magnify the positive energy of other stones and assists with keeping the mind balanced.

**Peridot** – In ancient Rome and in the Middle Ages, peridot was thought to help relieve depression. Both the Ancient Egyptians and Aztecs thought that peridot helped cleanse the heart. It is believed to assist with counteracting negative emotions. In addition, it encourages serenity and helps alleviate negativity.

**Red Beryl** – Believed to help with metabolism, stomach, and heart issues. Others believe it helps with memory, self-confidence, and motivation.

**Red Jasper** – Assists with balancing emotions and aids in relaxation and healing, among other properties.

**Rhodonite** – It was called the "singer's stone" and was believed to assist singers with maintaining a healthy throat.

**Rose Quartz** – Used to help bolster self-confidence, creativity, unconditional love, forgiveness, and self-esteem. It is said that rose quartz can soothe a broken heart and balance emotions if one feels out of sorts.

**Ruby** – Assists with blood circulation, vitality, and eyesight.

**Sapphire** – Priests from ancient times believed sapphires could predict the future. It is thought to assist with communication and insight as well as bolstering happiness.

**Padparadscha Sapphire** – Useful for seeking clarity about human nature, showing someone the truth about their goals and the shallowness and danger that exists in their relationships.

**Schist** – A metamorphic rock. Generally, it is not useful for building, paving, or sculpting, as it tends to break and flake in sheets. It is effective as a roofing material or in gardening and landscaping.

**Scoria** – An igneous rock used in gas grills, landscaping, and water drainage.

**Soapstone** – A metamorphic rock often used as a medium for sculptors.

**Smoky Quartz** – Believed to promote alertness, mental clarity, and concentration.

**Sodalite** – Is often called the "student's stone"; it heightens memory, focus, and organizational ability.

**Topaz** – Aids in healing respiration. Others believe it assists with helping control addictions and insomnia.

**Black Tourmaline** – Thought to help repair inflammation and arthritis. Also thought to assist with the nervous and circulatory systems and reduce negative thoughts.

**Green Tourmaline** – Helps to dispel negative thoughts. Believed to assist with digestion, the immune, nervous, and circulatory systems. It also soothes frayed nerves and calms weary travelers.

**Turquoise** – Considered the friendship stone. Many also believe it helps foster open communication and forgiveness.

# INDEX OF MINERALS AND ELEMENTS

## Practical Uses

For millennia, humanity has mined and continues to mine many rocks and minerals for various everyday practical uses.

**Aluminum** – An important mineral. It is utilized in the production of refrigerators and cars. Pots and pans and silverware are made with it and we wrap leftover food in it. It's also used in the production of high temperature cookware, spark plugs, specialized bricks and mortar, and kiln furniture, among other items.

**Calcium** – One of the vital metal elements inside our body. It is essential for the strength of bones, teeth, and tissue structure. It is also important for our muscles, joints, and nerves.

**Cobalt** – One of the trace elements essential to the human body. It is essential for red blood cell production and assists with the nervous system. It's an important component of Vitamin B-12. Cobalt has many uses as well. It helps tint paints and varnishes and assists with the process of paint drying. It is utilized in air bags and combined in metal alloys for the aircraft and chemical industries; it is also used in creating magnets.

**Copper** – Copper has many uses and is one of the vital metal elements inside our body. It bolsters immunity, assists with digestion, is important in the circulatory and nervous systems, and decreases inflammation. It is utilized in purifying drinking water and plumbing, since it doesn't absorb substances as easily and doesn't corrode underground. Early thermostats used copper to help heat and cool homes. Also, copper conducts very well and is frequently used in electrical wiring.

**Dysprosium** – A rare earth utilized in building electric vehicles; it's in great demand.

**Erbium** – A rare earth used for making pink glass. It also assists with pulses of light in fiber optic cables, dental surgery, and treating the skin.

**Fluoride-**The main mineral compound in fluorite. It's commonly used to prevent dental decay and is included in toothpaste, mouth rinses, and often added to community water systems. Fluorite is also utilized in the making of glass, ceramics, and enamel. In addition, fluorite is employed in the refining of lead and antimony.

**Helium** – One of the most plentiful noble gases in the universe. It is utilized for balloons, air conditioning, and to cool off magnets in MRI machines, to name a few uses. It is not limitless on Earth. It's a component of natural gas and is a byproduct of decaying rocks—people can't make it! And because it is so light, once released, it disappears forever from our reach into the greater atmosphere.

**Iron** – One of the oldest metals used by humanity to design almost any tool or object. It is one of the vital metal elements inside our body. It is important for the immune and circulatory systems, gastroenterological maintenance, the regulation of body temperature, and energy.

**Kyanite** – A metamorphic mineral. It's used in the production of high temperature cookware, spark plugs, specialized bricks and mortar, and kiln furniture, among other uses.

**Lead** – Used to make batteries, bullets, glass, ceramics, and protective coverings when getting an x-ray. In the past, it was utilized to make pencils, an unhealthy and dangerous makeup for the face, and paint.

**Magnesium** – One of the trace elements essential to the human body. It is vital for the circulatory and nervous systems and digestion; it is involved in our sleep system too. Magnesium is imperative in the production of hundreds of enzymes. In addition, it is used in laptops, power tools, car seats, mobile phones, and many other essential objects.

**Molybdenum** – One of the trace elements essential to the human body. Molybdenum helps keep toxins from building up in the body and breaks down sulfites. In plants, molybdenum is an ingredient in two enzymes that assists with the conversion of nitrate to nitrite and then ammonia; it technically helps with amino acid production, necessary for plants. We really are what we eat, in the truest sense.

**Neodymium** – A rare earth used in cell phones for the vibrating function and in industrial turbines and drills.

**Nickel** – One of the trace elements essential to the human body. It primarily assists with iron absorption. It's also thought to be involved in bone strengthening and may play a small role in maintaining the body in other ways. It is used frequently in coin making and when part of an alloy, is also utilized within the construction and rocket industries, such as in turbine production.

**Phosphorus** – One of the vital metal elements inside our body, important for the health and storage of cells, teeth, and bones, in addition to other essential systems in the body. Phosphorus is inside dishwasher cleaning tablets and is used for rust removal. It is also utilized in animal feed and matches.

**Platinum** – An element used primarily in jewelry. It is very strong and resistant to corrosion. It is also used in the car and manufacturing industries.

**Potassium** – One of the trace elements essential to the human, plant, and animal body. It helps regulate fluid balance in all three. It can reduce high blood pressure in humans and assists in the circulation of carbohydrates and nutrients in plant life.

**Radon** – A colorless, odorless, and tasteless noble gas. It is also radioactive and dangerous. Despite that, in small doses it is sometimes utilized in treating tumors via radiotherapy.

**Sodium** – One of the vital metal elements inside our body. It can help eliminate toxins from the lungs and skin. People with bronchitis, allergies, asthma, colds, rosacea, psoriasis, and other conditions can attain many benefits from simply sitting in a salt cave periodically. It has antibacterial and anti-inflammatory properties. It is also used in glass and soap manufacturing. In ancient Rome, it was so valuable a substance that soldiers were even paid with it. "Sal" is Roman for salt. The French word "solde" means pay or salary. It is how the phrase "worth his salt" came into being.

**Scoria** – An igneous rock used in gas grills, landscaping, and assists with water drainage.

**Silicon** – One of the trace elements essential to the human body. It is important in bones, connective tissues, joints, and tendons. It is also used in a multitude of objects, including cookware, lubricants, adhesives, baby bottles, and medical tubing.

**Silver** – Conducts energy the most effectively and is utilized in batteries and mirrors. It is also used in solar panels and water purification.

**Sulfur** – One of the trace elements essential to the human body. It is very important for cell structure and protects cells from harm and spurious changes, which leads to illness. It is imperative for DNA development and repair. It also assists the body with digestion and plays a part in the integrity of tendons, ligaments, and the skin.

**Titanium** – Becoming the metal of choice for replacing body parts, like hips, knees, fingers, heart valves, and joints. It's also used in tennis rackets, goalie masks, bicycle frames, scissors, surgical tools, and jewelry. It's in cell phones, equipment for the military, and it's what makes white paint white, when it's mixed with oxygen and becomes titanium dioxide. It is also corrosive resistant and can withstand intense temperature fluctuations. It is also an incredibly strong and resilient element.

**Tungsten** – Has the highest melting point of all metals and is corrosion resistant. It is used to make cutting tools, electrodes, and is utilized in light bulb filament, among other objects.

**Xenon Gas** – Utilized in keeping food preparation safe by eradicating bacteria and is helpful in high-speed flash photography.

**Zinc** – One of the trace elements essential to the human body. Zinc resides in cells and assists with maintaining the immune system to help fight off viruses and bacteria. It's so important, it also assists with the manufacture of proteins and DNA in the body. In plants, zinc assists in the development of chlorophyll and helps in the formation of some proteins. It also can assist plants with resisting frost damage. When zinc is added to sulfide, it becomes phosphorescent and glows in the dark. This has many useful applications.

## SONGS IN KOTR BOOK ONE IN ORDER

"Sixty Minute Man" released in 1951 by Billy Ward and the Dominoes (Federal Records).

"Another One Bites the Dust" released in 1980 by Queen on their 'The Game' album (Musicland, Munich).

Prokofiev's "Dance of the Knights" from the opera *Romeo and Juliet*.

"Love Potion #9" released in 1959 by The Clovers (Capitol Records).

"Monster Mash" released in 1962 by Bobby Pickett and the Crypt-Kickers (Garpax Records).

"The Parting Glass"-a traditional folklore ballad in Scotland and Ireland.

"Who wants To Live Forever" released in 1986 by Queen (EMI Records).

"That Smell" released in 1977 by Lynyrd Skynyrd (MCA Records).

# ABOUT THE AUTHOR

E.K. Wise's endless curiosity about cultural history and geology developed in her youth after living abroad and traveling internationally. She is enticed by multicultural cuisine and will sample almost any food once. When not creating stories, she's likely wrangling teenagers, sweating on her stationary bike, reading, or studying cool rocks and minerals. Wise passionately advocates for learning evaluation, as she and three of her four kiddos (and maybe the dog) have ADHD. She earned degrees in psychology and clinical social work and lives with her family in Southern California.